W9-BZF-524

WINGS *of* GOLD

BOOK IV
TOP GUN

T. E. CRUISE

POPULAR LIBRARY

An Imprint of Warner Books, Inc.

A Warner Communications Company

POPULAR LIBRARY EDITION

Popular Library books are published by
Warner Books, Inc.
666 Fifth Avenue
New York, N.Y. 10103

A Warner Communications Company

Printed in the United States of America

First Printing: February, 1990

10 9 8 7 6 5 4 3 2 1

BOOK I:
1973–1975

CEASE-FIRE SIGNED
U.S. Agrees to Stop Fighting in Vietnam
Washington Star Reporter

U.S. PUTS SKYLAB IN ORBIT
First U.S. Space Station Begins Extended Mission
Boston Times

YOM KIPPUR ATTACK TAKES ISRAEL BY SURPRISE
Arabs Initiate Oil Embargo Against "Israel's Friends"
Cold War Heats Up as President Nixon and Soviets Trade
Charges of Interference in Mideast
New York Gazette

NIXON RESIGNS PRESIDENCY
President Forced Out by Watergate Scandal
Ford Takes Oath Of Office
Baltimore Globe

SAIGON SURRENDERS TO REDS
Vietcong Flag Flies Over South Viet Capital
San Francisco Post

CAMBODIA FALLS TO COMMUNISTS
Red Victory Ends Five-Year Civil War
Detroit Bulletin-Journal

AMERICAN SHIP SEIZED IN GULF OF SIAM
MAYAGUEZ Fired Upon and Boarded by Cambodians
Los Angeles Tribune

CHAPTER 1

(One)

Gold Aviation and Transport
Conference Center
Burbank, California
12 March, 1973

The executives and guests gathered at the conference center grew quiet as Don Harrison, the chairman of the board and president of Gold Aviation and Transport, entered the plush screening room. As Harrison slipped into his gray suede arm-chair, he gave the signal for the film to roll. The recessed lighting dimmed, the speakers built into the theater walls coughed and crackled. The rough cut of the industrial film, commissioned for the upcoming stockholders' meeting, began to roll.

Harrison watched as the screen faded to black. On the sound track there came the shrill scream of a jet engine, segueing to a trumpets' swell. The black screen was slashed with a diagonal beam of white light that dramatically lit the ghostly gray needle nose of a jet fighter within a darkened hangar.

The film's narrator, a famous actor who'd made his reputation doing biblical pictures, began his spiel:

"Since 1927, when Herman Gold sold his first airplane design to the government from out of a Santa Monica waterfront loft, Gold Aviation and Transport has been on the cutting edge of aviation technology . . ."

Spliced in was some splotched, amber-tinted footage of the single-engine, open-cockpit, G-1 Yellowjacket mail transport warming up on the tarmac. Waving to the camera were the ground crew in overalls, and a grinning pilot bundled up in sheepskin and a soft leather helmet. The pilot's white silk scarf flapped in the wind as he climbed into the pilot's seat, and then there was a shot of the stilt-winged, duralumin Yellowjacket taking off, soaring away into that long-ago sky.

The film cut to black-and-white footage of an airport, circa the 1940s.

"It was the GAT Monarch GC-2 and 3 series of commercial airliners that first brought safe, comfortable air travel to the public," the narrator continued, while the screen showed footage of nattily dressed passengers enjoying themselves within a prop-driven GC-3's pressurized cabin.

"The GC series of piston-powered airliners has since evolved into the GC 900 series of jetliners that have become the industry's standard for excellence—"

In rapid succession, from top to bottom, the screen was filled with drawings and specs for the GC-909, GAT's first jetliner; the smaller 909a, designed for short, domestic hops; and the stretched, intercontinental version, the 909i.

"And here is GAT's latest commercial transport, the incredible GC-999 jumbo jet liner, first flown in 1970. The GC-999 can seat 490 passengers and carry them over 7,000 miles at a cruising speed of 590 miles per hour. But GAT's unbroken string in the commercial transport industry is only half the company's success story—"

The film cut back to the darkened hangar that began the promo, and several more narrow-focus overhead spotlights flared to life. Now, in addition to that mysterious jet fighter's needle nose, the fighter's teardrop canopy and vertical tail were illuminated. The tail was painted a ghostly gray except for two diagonal slashes of turquoise and scarlet: GAT's signature colors.

Harrison smiled as the screening room erupted in excited murmurings and applause. The idea had been his to reveal GAT's newest experimental fighter, the GXF-66 Stiletto, in the manner of a stripper teasingly peeling off one article of clothing at a time. Marketing had become Harrison's responsibility—or, more to the point, his burden—since his father-in-law, Herman Gold, had relinquished control of GAT to him, back in 1967.

"GAT is much more than commercial avation," The narrator was thundering. *"For GAT has never flinched from going to war!—"*

Suddenly, Harrison and the rest of the audience were treated to a skillfully edited World War II gun-camera montage of American fighters shooting down German and Japanese airplanes, followed by an extended, color film sequence of a USAF GAT F-90 BroadSword jet fighter pursuing a fleeing, gunmetal-gray MiG wearing North Korean markings on its snout and tail.

"In both theaters of the Second World War, the GAT BearClaw fighter and BuzzSaw attack bomber helped our flyboys take command of the skies," the voice-over continued. *"While in Korea it was the GAT BroadSword that allowed our pilots to reign supreme over MiG Alley—"*

On the screen, the swept-wing F-90 began to pelt the MiG with 50mm slugs. The 50mm tracers looked like orange streaks of lightning as the MiG vanished in a cloud of oily black smoke.

"Due to the BroadSword's fabulous success over Korea, hundreds were sold to our NATO allies. Today, BroadSwords have been supplanted by higher-performance aircraft in the service of most major powers, but BroadSword fighter squadrons still patrol the skies on behalf of smaller air forces, and it is the BroadSword that is still the backbone of America's own Air Defense National Guard."

On-screen, the BroadSword pilot wearing his helmet with lowered visor and oxygen mask saluted from within his teardrop canopy before putting his warbird into a victory roll. As the BroadSword dropped away, the scene shifted to a contemporary, bird's-eye view of the sprawling Gold Aviation and Transport office headquarters and factory complex, situated on hundreds of acres in Burbank.

"It was here in California that the BroadSword was designed and built," the narrator intoned. *"Today, GAT is a vast manufacturing metropolis employing thousands of American workers who continue to turn out fighters, bombers and transport craft for the military and international commercial aviation markets."*

The scene returned to that darkened hangar. The music built as the hangar was suddenly awash in light. The sleek GXF-66 Stiletto jet fighter—forty-seven feet long, with a thirty-one-foot wing span—stood revealed in her extraordinary grace. She looked like a monstrous predatory insect on her spindly tricycle landing gear, her bubble of a teardrop canopy rising up like a cyclopean compound eye. The fighter's engine air inlet gaped beneath her needle nose like the yawning maw of a shark. She was painted entirely in a ghostly gray, devoid of bright color except for GAT's trademark gaudy slashes on her tail.

"Here to tell you about the Stiletto, the latest example of GAT fighter technology, is the company's founder, Herman Gold."

Don Harrison Watched as up on the screen his seventy-seven-year-old father-in-law stepped out from around the tail end of the fighter into a pool of light. The sequence had been shot a little over a year ago, just after Herman had recovered to the best of his ability from his second heart attack. Unfortunately, Herman looked like a shell of his former self. His lined face was drawn, his bald scalp was mottled with liver spots, and the reddish-gray fringe of hair around his ears, and his closely trimmed beard, looked dry and listless. His shoulders were stooped and his charcoal, double-breasted suit looked too big on him, but Herman's voice was clear and firm, and his pale blue eyes sparkled with youthful excitement as he spoke:

"Two years ago, when we first conceptualized the Gold Experimental Fighter, or GXF-66, we intended a multirole, air-combat, lightweight craft. A plane that incorporated state-of-the-art fly-by-wire computer-augmented controls, but also harkened back to the BroadSword in its dynamic sim-

plicity. I'm here to tell you, the stockholders—and the world—that we've achieved our goal."

The screen began to cut back and forth from Herman to animated visual aids as he spoke.

"The GXF-66 is wrapped around a single Rogers and Simpson augmented turbofan engine rated at 23,000 pounds of thrust. The GXF-66 has a service ceiling of over 50,000 feet, a tactical radius of 340 miles, and a ferry range of 2500 miles. She utilizes the latest in Hotas, or 'hands on throttle and stick,' technology: the pilot, in the manner of a skilled typist or pianist, will be able to operate his combat avionics, fly the plane, and fire his weapons without having to look at what his hands are doing. The GXF-66's armament includes a 20MM cannon, and she can accept all versions of the short-range Sidewinder and long-range Sparrow air-to-air missiles. In addition, the GXF-66 is designed to use the French Magic and Israeli Shafrir AAMs. The Stiletto can also be utilized in the short-range ground-attack mode, carrying beneath her wings up to 15,000 pounds of ordnance—"

Herman paused. Don Harrison thought the old man's smile was grand to see.

"But the GXF-66 was BORN *to dogfight,"* Herman firmly declared. *"She was born to* own *the sky!"*

Don Harrison felt chills; at that moment, he could glimpse within that frail old man the World War I ace who'd downed twenty Allied airplanes while flying with Von Richthofen, the Red Baron.

Herman continued: *"When we designed the GXF-66, we intended that form should follow function."*

Herman Gold then stepped aside, out of the light and into the darkness, so that only his voice could be heard as the music built and the camera moved to lovingly caress the jet fighter's lithe form.

"When we designed this fighter, we intended that she embody the timeless, elegant, lethal simplicity of her weapon namesake: 'Stiletto'!"

There came a cymbal crash like a peal of thunder, while thanks to the filmmaker's magic the fighter seemed to whirl like some caged animal, so that her needle nose thrust out at the audience.

The screen went white. There was more applause as the lights came up in the screening room. Don Harrison glanced across the aisle to where his brother-in-law, Herman's son, Steve Gold, was sitting slumped in his chair.

Steve was an Air Force colonel in his late forties, but he looked much younger. He was tall and lean, with thinning, light-blond hair worn moderately short, and squint lines etched vertically on either side of his nose and around his brown eyes, thanks to the long hours spent scanning the sky from various fighter cockpits during his thirty years in the Air Force. Steve was an ace several times over, a Medal of Honor winner with fourteen confirmed Japanese kills during World War II, and six MiGs accounted for during the Korean conflict. Steve had also flown combat missions in Vietnam. Harrison happened to know that his brother-in-law had "unofficially" bagged a MiG while flying incognito with the Israeli Air Force during the 1967 Six-Day War, but that episode was part of Steve's adventures while serving as an Air Force/CIA liaison. Understandably, Steve didn't talk about that part of his career too much. Currently, he was assigned to the Los Angeles Air Force Station at El Segundo, where he acted as a liaison between the military and the aerospace industry.

"That's all the film we have so far," Harrison confided to Steve as the others began filing out of the screening room. "That GXF in the hangar was just a mock-up. Later on, we'll put in shots of the prototype in flight, once we've finished building her, and we'll be adding in sections on GAT Aerospace and our participation in the Skytrain European consortium."

"You don't have much time before the stockholders' meeting in June," Steve pointed out. He took a scarlet package of Pall Malls from out of the pocket of his sky-blue Air Force uniform jacket and lit up a cigarette.

"I know, but we'll make it." Harrison smiled. "One thing we're used to around here is deadlines."

Steve nodded, looking pale as he exhaled cigarette smoke. "Damn, I wish that you'd warned me Pop was going to be in it."

"Yes, I suppose I should have." Harrison nodded, thinking that he had all along intended for Steve to be shocked by the sight of his father up on the screen, hoping the experience would soften up Steve for the proposal Harrison intended to make. "Now that I think about it, I see that it was thoughtless of me to surprise you like that. . . ."

Steve seemed to wave the matter aside. "Pop looked terrible, didn't he?"

"I didn't think so," Harrison fibbed to comfort his brother-in-law. "Actually, I thought the camera captured something of Herman's inner vitality."

"Yeah, I know what you mean." Steve smiled fondly. "Nothing Pop liked to talk about better than fighter planes."

"Anyway, there was no choice in the matter," Harrison continued. "Herman insisted upon being in the film."

Steve nodded. "Almost like Pop knew he was about to die."

(Two)

GAT Executive Offices/Administration Complex

Colonel Steve Gold murmured, "Every time I walk in here, I still expect to see him sitting behind this desk."

They'd left the conference center, traveling via electric golf cart along the half-mile of roadway beneath the California sun to the executive office complex, and were now entering Pop's huge office.

No, strike that, Steve Gold thought. It was Don's office now, as it had been unofficially since Pop had retired, and officially since Herman Gold had passed away in his sleep, succumbing to his third heart attack, a little over six months ago.

"You know, I appreciate the way you've left things here just the way they were when the office belonged to Pop," Steve Gold said, looking around at the wall-to-wall, moss-green carpeting, and the sofa and armchair groupings upholstered in supple burgundy leather. Custom-built display cases loaded with mementos highlighting Pop's decades in the aviation business lined the oak-paneled walls beneath ornately framed oil-painting landscapes and commissioned oil portraits of successful GAT airplanes in flight. In one corner, a glass case held scale models of every airplane designed and built by Gold Aviation and Transport.

"Hey, I kept things the way they were for myself." Don smiled ruefully as he ushered Gold to an armchair and then took his place behind the big marble-topped desk. "Keeping it all like it always was comforts me. It makes me think that maybe Herman's spirit is still around to help me guide the company."

The bank of telephone lights on Don's desk was flashing like small-arms fire. Don pressed a button on his intercom, said, "Hold all calls," and the lights quieted down.

"The only change is that now you're totally in charge," Gold said.

"Yep." Don leaned back in his thronelike leather chair. "Is that a problem for you?"

"I'm not sure," Gold admitted, eyeing his brother-in-law. Don was fifty, tall and broad-shouldered, with baby-fine blond hair that he wore combed back from his high domed forehead, and wide-spaced hazel eyes that missed nothing from behind the lenses of his gold-rimmed spectacles. In days past, Don had been an academic type who favored beards and baggy tweeds, but since taking over the company Don had cleaned up his act: his custom-tailored navy-blue double-breasted suit, pale-blue shirt, gold cuff links, and maroon silk tie radiated authority and power.

"You know," Harrison was saying, "there have been times since Herman died when I've been working here all alone late at night and I thought I heard his voice calling me. . . ."

"Mom says the same thing," Steve said, shaking his head. "I tried to talk her into putting the Bel-Air estate up for sale and moving into an apartment. I told her it's no good rattling around all alone in that big old house with nothing but the servants and her memories to keep her company."

"Erica will never sell that place," Don declared. "For the same reason, I haven't changed the office decor. Neither of us wants to bid Herman farewell."

Steve sighed. "You know, I promised Pop that he'd see me make General. . . ."

"You can still keep that promise," Don began.

"Maybe, but the notion has kind of paled since Pop died," Gold mused, remembering the conversations he'd had with his invalid father in the garden at the house in Bel-Air. "Pop always wanted it for me more than I ever wanted it for myself. As far as I'm concerned, being a general just means a bigger paperwork headache. And generals don't get to fly their own planes, which is pretty much the only reason I'm still in the Air Force."

"You can be a general and fly all the airplanes you want," Don said. "Right here at GAT."

"Huh?"

"Steve." Don leaned forward, planting his elbows on his desk. "Your father had always wanted you to come into the business, right?"

"Well, sure . . ."

Don nodded. "Well, now's the time. I need you. These past six months since he died have been hell. I can't run this company all by myself."

"Of course you can't, Don. Nobody can!" Gold comforted. "But you're not alone. You've got yourself a goddamned office building full of executives and managers."

"I need more than a bunch of yes-men following me around like baby ducklings in a row." Don scowled. "I need *you*. Just like your father needed *me* after he lost Teddy Quinn."

Gold busied himself lighting a Pall Mall in order to buy time to think. Teddy Quinn had been with Pop since the beginning, even before there was a Gold Aviation, when Pop was running a fledgling mail and freight air-transport company operating between Los Angeles and San Francisco. For over thirty years, Teddy had been Pop's chief designer, his sounding board for new ideas, and his best friend, until Teddy passed away in 1951. Pop, emotionally distraught over losing Teddy, had tried to go it alone, but even then GAT was too much to handle for just one pair of hands, no matter how capable. Without a copilot, GAT was suffering a severe downturn in productivity, never mind the fact that the company's heart and soul, its Research and Design Department, was drifting leaderless. When Pop was finally able to bring himself to begin his search for Teddy's replacement, it didn't take him long to realize that if he wanted the best there was only one choice: Donald Harrison, in those days aviation's boy wonder. In 1951, Don agreed to leave his position in charge of R & D at Amalgamated-Landis, another of the giant concerns that made up California's aviation industry, to join the GAT team. Don came aboard as chief engineer in charge of aviation research and development, but it wasn't long before he was Pop's right-hand man.

"It's as important to me as I'm sure it is to you that we keep family control of this business," Don was saying. "Someday I intend to bring my own son Andrew into GAT."

Gold had to grin. "I know Andy is precocious, but I very much doubt that the world is ready for a sixteen-year-old aviation-industry executive."

"I *did* say someday," Don reiterated, smiling.

"Well, you have another son."

"I *have* thought about Robbie. . . ."

Gold waited expectantly. Robert Blaize Greene, thirty, was Don's stepson, Steve Gold's sister's son by her first marriage to World War II RAF fighter ace Blaize Greene, who was killed in action. Robbie was a Vietnam veteran, an Air Force captain, and recipient of the Distinguished Flying Cross and the Silver Star. Steve Gold had always been extremely close to his nephew, but the bonds of affection between them had been further strengthened in 1965, when Robbie had risked his own neck on Gold's behalf by flying Rescue Combat Air Patrol when Gold had been shot down over North Vietnam.

"Well?" Gold asked. "Have you made this offer to Robbie?"

Don frowned. "You know as well as I do that there'd be no point to that," he said impatiently. "Robbie and I have never truly gotten along. . . . I don't know, I guess the kid blames me for taking his father's place in his mother's heart, or some such tomfoolery."

Don was blushing. Gold, feeling awkward, and sorry that he'd brought up the subject, said, "You know that's one point over which Robbie and I part company. As far as I'm concerned, you've always done your level best to be a good father to that kid."

"Thanks," Don said, almost gruffly. "Anyway, Robbie's got a fine career still ahead of him in the Air Force. There'll be time enough for him to come into the business once he's established a reputation and some clout in the industry." He winked. "Like his uncle Steve."

"I admit I'm getting a little antsy in the Air Force," Gold began. "There's no wars to fight. . . ."

"What the hell," Don said pointedly. "Face facts, Steve. You're too old to fight 'em even if there were some wars around."

Gold wistfully chuckled. "I can't argue that. But I guess I've had my share of furballs."

"That you have," Don remarked, smiling. "But you've got an even bigger challenge than any war waiting for you right here at GAT, if you're willing to take it on. I need you to help me overcome the Defense Department's resistance to the GXF-66 Stiletto."

"You're kidding!" Gold said, shocked. "Are you telling me the brass doesn't want that fighter? She looks like a beauty to me."

"She is a beauty, Steve," Don declared adamantly. "Unfortunately, the DOD's procurement teams can't objectively evaluate her. Their vision is too clouded by bad memories concerning the F-110."

"Goddamn . . . ," Gold cursed. Back in the late 1960s, Pop had harbored high hopes for the twin-seat, F-110 fighter bomber he'd dubbed the Super BroadSword, but the over-engineered airplane loaded with the latest in black-box technology had turned out to be a gremlin-plagued disappointment, and the Air Force canceled its contract after receiving just a few units. "Sometimes I think that damned airplane killed Pop," Gold said bitterly.

"I hear you." Don looked somber. "Herman had suffered setbacks before and had always been able to overcome them, but not the Super BroadSword. Your father just never seemed to be able to bounce back from that failure." Don brightened. "Until R and D came up with the prototype design for the Stiletto. Herman really perked up when he saw those specs. I think your father wanted the Stiletto to be his swan song, Steve. I think he wanted his last airplane to be a fighter pilot's kind of war bird: a fighter to follow in the tradition of the original BroadSword. . . ." Don paused. "Hell, a fighter to follow in the tradition of Herman's Fokker Dr. 1, the triplane he flew when he was serving with the Red Baron."

Gold nodded. "But you're saying that you can't get the brass interested in the Stiletto?" It was a sobering thought. Unlike many engineer types who couldn't get beyond their narrow specialties, Don had business savvy, the ability to comprehend the big picture. If Don couldn't sell the Stiletto, something was seriously wrong.

"I've got to be honest with you." Don shrugged. "The military aviation division of this company lost a good deal of its luster due to the Super BroadSword mess. Then came Herman's retirement, and then his death. I'm doing all I can, but I've made my mark in the commercial aviation side of the business. Those military procurement types don't hear me, but they'd listen to *you*. You've got a fighter pilot's reputation, and the contacts in the military to get the Stiletto a fair shake."

Gold stood up and went to the wall of windows behind Don's desk. The office was located on the executive/administration building's top floor, and had a view of the company's airfields filled with rows of finished GC-9 series jetliners awaiting delivery to their respective airlines.

Pop sure would have liked to see those fields filled up with fighters, Gold thought. He turned away from the windows. "I'd like to help, but I really don't know how it would work out between us. There's no denying that we've had our ups and downs through the years."

Don swiveled around in his chair. "I hope you don't think I still harbor a grudge concerning you and Linda?"

I don't know. Do you? Gold thought, going back in his mind to how the long-simmering feud between them had begun on that fateful summer morning back in 1952, when Steve, home on leave, had run into an old flame, a pretty little brunette of a newspaper reporter by the name of Linda Forrester, sunning her bikinied curves on the beach at Malibu. The two had gone directly from that beach to Linda's bed, which was where Don had found them when he'd come calling later that day. It was only after the fact—way too late to make amends—that Steve had found out that Linda was Don's fiancée.

"Steve, I got over that incident concerning Linda twenty years ago, the day I fell in love with your sister," Don assured. "As a matter of fact, I ran into Linda just last month at a commercial-aviation conference in Chicago." He paused. "Did you know she quit her television correspondent's job on the network to write full-time? That she's working on a book about the airline industry?"

"Yeah, I heard," Gold muttered, wondering why it still bothered him to talk about Linda. They'd gone together for a while after she'd broken up with Don, but eventually things became strained: Linda wanted to settle down and raise a family. Gold was wedded to the Air Force. It was all in the past. . . .

"Anyway, when I saw Linda, it was just like seeing an old acquaintance," Don continued. "Nothing more, nothing less, and that's the truth."

"I'm glad to hear it," Gold said wryly. "I'd hate to think you're two-timing my sister."

Don laughed. "If I feel anything toward you concerning Linda, it's gratitude. If it hadn't been for you, I wouldn't have married the *real* girl of my dreams: your sister, Susan."

"It's not just that," Gold murmured, growing serious. "There're other differences between us."

"Sure there are," Don agreed. "But on the whole, I'd say that we've become more friends than enemies . . . ?"

"That's an accurate assessment." Gold nodded. "But—"

"But nothing," Don cut him off. "Look, I didn't want to get into this, but I see it's necessary, so let's call a spade a spade. The truth is you've never been able to come to terms with your own anger and resentment concerning your father's affection toward me."

Gold flinched. It was true that Pop quickly came to rely on Don as a sounding board as well as a creative source, much as he had relied on Teddy. Thinking about it now, Gold could feel the old emotions he'd struggled to keep tamped down rising up in him, filling him with bitter rage. *It's yesterday's news,* he told himself, trying to rein in his temper. *Water under the bridge.* He told Don, "I don't want to talk about this."

"Come on, dammit!" Don said roughly. "You brought this crap up, not me. So now the least you can do is be man enough to admit that you're jealous of my relationship with Herman. You always have been!"

"You egghead son of a bitch!" Gold exploded. "How do

you *expect* me to feel? *You* were the son my father always wanted, not *me!*'' He stopped, taken aback by the way Don was smiling at him. "What's so fucking funny?"

"Nothing, everything." Don's amused expression turned wistful. "I guess it's funny how reality plays tricks on us. If only you could have heard the way your father talked about you. If only you could have realized how proud he was of his son, the fighter ace."

Gold found his anger had vanished, leaving him hollow and hurting inside. "I tried as hard as I could to be who he wanted me to be," he said softly. "And I think that toward the end we both realized how much we loved each other. . . ." He had to pause, his throat grown tight. "But I was never able to fulfill his expectations."

"Fulfill them now," Don said urgently. "Your father wanted the Stiletto to redeem GAT's reputation for building fighters. Help me make his last wish a reality."

Gold turned back to the windows, gazing out past the jetliner fleet glinting in the sun, to the immutable, tawny California hills beyond the high, barbed-wire fence. The offer was tempting, no doubt about it. He and Pop had unfinished business; this might be the way to make peace between them.

"Don," Gold began. "I don't think I could take orders from you."

"I'm not asking you to." Don got up out of his chair to come stand behind Gold. "We each have our areas of expertise. I know how to design and build airplanes. From all your years spent working for General Simon in Air Force Procurement, I believe you know how to market them."

"A team, huh?" Steve mused. "Kind of like a pair of fighters flying a swallowtail pattern, watching each other's backs?"

Don nodded. "You understand the term 'synergy'?"

"The whole adding up to more than the sum of its parts?"

"Close enough," Don responded. "What I'm suggesting to you is a synergistic partnership. We can work out the financial details and who gets what title later. The bottom line is that I'm hoping that us two working together can approximate more than the sum of our parts: in other words, one Herman Gold."

"Not a chance," Gold said. "When they made my father, they broke the mold."

"I think so too," Don replied warmly. "But with Herman gone, we're the best that GAT has got." Don paused, looking hopeful.

"So what do you say? It sure would make a dynamite splash at the stockholders' meeting this summer if I could announce that you're coming aboard."

"This summer," Steve said doubtfully. "That's not much time."

Don answered, "We've got no time to waste if we want to keep your father's dream alive."

Gold turned to see Don Harrison holding out his hand to him. "Can I have a big office like this?" Gold joked.

"Bigger!" Don promised.

"A pretty secretary?"

"We'll raid Hollywood."

"Ah well, then, what the hell," Gold said, shaking hands with his brother-in-law. "I'm tired of wearing Air Force blue."

Don laughed happily. "Welcome, partner. I've got a very good tailor I can recommend to you."

CHAPTER 2

(One)

In the skies over Germany, near Sembach Air Base
14 June, 1973

United States Air Force Captain Robert Blaize Greene banked his F-12B Sun-Wolf through the woolly cloud bank, breaking through into an extended vista of sky so blue it hurt his eyes. Greene was on routine combat air patrol above the green and brown checkerboard landscape of the Rheinland-Pfalz farmland region of Germany, near the French Border. His Sun-Wolf, the latest variant of the venerable workhorse air-superiority fighter of the Vietnam War, was part of the armada of American combat aircraft assigned to NATO's offensive and defensive air operations over central Europe. The F-12B was a huge, wide-bodied rear-fuselage warbird, with dual, square, engine-air intakes, sharply tapered wings, and twin, wide-spaced, vertical tail fins. She was powered by a pair of brutish, augmented turbofans capable, during optimum conditions, of moving the Sun-Wolf at Mach 2.5, more than two and a half times the speed of sound.

A voice crackled in Captain Greene's helmet. "Lonestar, this is Mother Hen. Do you read? Over." It was the familiar voice of Air Force Lieutenant Buzz Blaisdale, a fellow pilot and close friend who today was acting as Greene's air controller.

Greene pressed the radio call button on his throttle. "Mother Hen, this is Lonestar." Greene's mustache tickled beneath the close-fitting rubber oxygen mask, and there was a slight echo of his own words in his radio earphones as he spoke. "Am cruising in my patrol sector at 25,000 feet." He glanced at his airspeed indicator. "Speed 475 knots. Nothing to report." He twisted his head, taking advantage of the excellent visibility afforded by the Sun-Wolf's teardrop canopy to study the sky, and then sharply dipped his wings to view the cloud-swept, variegated terrain streaking by below. "Doesn't seem to be anything but cows, and guys in lederhosen around here, or maybe a blond milk mädchen in leather shorts. I should be so lucky. . . ."

"Listen up, Lonestar." Mother Hen sounded concerned. "AWAC has just picked up multiple bogies traveling low toward your sector at a head-on intercept with you. . . ."

"Mama Bird." Greene chuckled. "You sure your Air-born Warning and Control System boys haven't locked onto a wolf pack of Porsches truckin' down the autobahn or something?"

"Negative."

"Come on, Birdy," Greene teased. "It's happened before, and you know it."

"Repeat, negative. These are bona fides, Lonestar."

"IFF/NIS status?" Greene asked, becoming all business now.

"Working."

Greene waited for the Identification Friend or Foe and NATO Identification System linkups of black boxes to go through their electronic challenges and counterchallenges with the unknown airplanes' transponders in order to identify the bogies as either NATO good guys or Warsaw Pact undesirables.

"Mama Bird, just in case, how 'bout some backup?"

"Negative, Lonestar. We got bogies popping up in all sectors. Looks like World War Three from where I'm sitting."

"Uh-huh. How's that IFF evaluation coming along?"

"Just in, Lonestar. You got trouble, all right. Definitely bad guys. Forward Radar Air Patrol identifies them as a trio of Fishbed-Js."

"Fabbbulous," Greene said sarcastically, although he knew it could have been much worse, considering that it was going to be three against one. A Fishbed-J was just a later variant of the rather outdated MiG-21, which Greene had dealt with over Vietnam. These Fishbeds carried a 23MM cannon pack and—hopefully—nothing more lethal than a pair of short-range, heat-seeking Atoll missiles, the Soviet version of the Sidewinder.

Greene's Sun-Wolf was armed with a 20MM cannon mounted in the right wing root, a pair of Sparrow medium-range, radar-guided AAMs nestled under the fuselage chin, and a quartet of short-range, heat-seeking Sidewinders riding the outerwing pylons.

"Lonestar. Your bogies are still coming at you head-on. "Estimate intercept in . . ." There was a pause. ". . . one minute."

"Roger, Mother Hen," Greene muttered. He glanced at his rectangular, glowing green radar display mounted high on the Sun-Wolf's instrument panel, to the left of the Heads Up Display control board. "I've got them on my scope now. Three bogies, flying low but climbing. You copy?"

"Affirmative, Lonestar. Time to slip a round under the hammer."

"Arming weapons systems," Greene replied, flipping the toggle switch in the upper right-hand corner of the armament control panel. "Master arm on." He set his HUD display to short-range AA missile mode. HUD superimposed on his windshield a bright-green computer-generated graphic that displayed vital information—airspeed, altitude, flight-path ladder, etcetera—and aided in target acquisition.

"Lonestar, we've got those bogies coming at you now from less than twenty miles! Do you read?"

"Roger, Mother Hen," Greene drawled absently, his attention focused on the HUD view through his canopy, although he also regularly scanned the Sun-Wolf's thirty-four dials and eighty-five control inputs. The F-12's control panel was ghost gray with matte-black insets. The dials and controls themselves were white on black, here and there interspersed with garish yellow-and-black bumblebee-striped emergency controls. There were still more batteries of switches, buttons, and knobs bristling the control consoles on both sides of Greene's tan and gray chair.

"Lonestar, you are cleared to lock on and use your medium-range Sparrows!"

"Negative."

Mother Hen sounded appalled. "But the book says your only chance in a situation like this is to score a couple of long-range kills, before the Fishbeds are close enough to use their Atolls!"

"Negative," Greene repeated. "The book don't fly warbirds. People do."

"But the computer gives you only a thirty-three-percent probability of survival in a knife fight—"

"A one out of three chance is better than the alternative," Greene lightly responded. "You know as well as I do that a SARH utilization would be suicidal in a situation like this."

The medium-range Sparrow AA missile used a Semi-Active Radar Homing system that required the fighter pilot to continually illuminate the target with his nose radar during the missile's duration of flight. This was realistic in a one-on-one confrontation when the pilot could lock onto his adversary's tail, but self-defeating when flying head-on at multiple targets. "Mother Hen, you know that to guide home a SARH I've got to keep flying straight at those bogies. By the time the Sparrow hits, I'll be close enough for the bogies to let loose with their heat-seeking Atolls. I'll score a kill, but so will they, on me."

"Goddammit, Lonestar! You're diverging from the program!"

Greene smiled. "Hey, Mama Bird, this is war, ain't it? There's no rules in war. Just like Sinatra, I've got to do it my way."

"Lonestar—"

Greene mashed his radio transmit button. "No more time to chat, cowboy. I've got tallyho."

The three MiG-21s were almost invisible specks in the sky arranged at one-, twelve-, and eleven-o'clock level. Greene knew his F-12, which dwarfed the MiGs, probably looked as big as a locomotive barreling at them. That was too bad: in a dogfight, small was beautiful. As Greene closed, he saw the MiGs execute a three-way defensive split, their tail pipes glowing as they went to afterburn. The MiGs were trying to surround him in the hope that one of them could lock onto his tail pipes and let loose a heat-seeker.

Greene smiled. Small may be beautiful, but *speed* was king, and *visibility* was everything! The F-12 had almost twice the speed of the Fishbed, and its teardrop canopy had excellent rearward sightlines. The MiG-21s were notorious for their lack of view astern.

Also, when the MiGs decided to dogfight instead of maintaining their three-on-one, head-butt game of chicken, the bogies handed Greene a tactical advantage. Greene could snap off his shots, because he had a sky full of targets. The MiGs would have to be careful—a heat-seeker will drill any tail pipe—lest they shoot down their own comrades. Greene would keep his speed high, using his warbird to execute slashing attacks, like an eagle plucking pigeons one by one out of the sky.

Greene cobbed his own throttles, going to afterburn, watching the world leap toward him as the Sun-Wolf's twin turbojets spat fire thanks to the rings of nozzles that sprayed fuel into the engines' already superheated exhaust gases. The extra fuel, igniting, added thrust.

The horizon in front of Greene tilted crazily as he used the Sun-Wolf's superior speed to run a wide half-circle around the MiGs. Greene prepared a Sidewinder as he rolled in behind and on top of one of the enemy planes. He was a little over two miles away when he lined up the fly-size speck of MiG in his HUD display. He waited until he heard the warbling tone that told him his target was acquired, and then fired off the heat-seeker. The Sidewinder dropped down from the Sun-Wolf's wing pylon and then sprinted forward on its thrashing tail of fire. Greene watched the Sidewinder dwindle in size until it was only a glowing speck chasing after the distant MiG.

Any time now, Greene thought.

"Bingo!" he cried out as the enemy warbird erupted into an orange fireball. The Sidewinder had found the MiG's tail pipe. "Mother Hen, I've got a kill—"

Greene paused abruptly, realizing that in his excitement he had committed a cardinal error: The beauty of the Sidewinder was that it was a "set it and forget it" type weapon; once it launched, it guided itself to its prey. But Greene had been so engrossed in waiting and watching for his kill that he had neglected to keep his eye on the other two MiGs—

Which were now coming around on his tail. He could expect a heat-seeker up his ass at any moment. Wouldn't *that* be cause for a bad day. . . .

Greene threw his F-12 into a gut-wrenching break to starboard, a hard turn in the direction of the attack intended to generate maxium angle-off to spoil the enemies' aim. As long as Greene could stay on the outer boundaries of the lead MiG's missile-launching envelope, he felt reasonably confident he could rely on the Sun-Wolf's superior defensive capabilities to get him out of a jam.

Greene resumed his radio transmission to ground control. "Mother Hen, I've got a kill."

"Roger, Lonestar," Buzz replied. "Congrats, but what's your situation?"

"Two bandits on my tail," Greene murmured, jinking the F-12 for all she was worth to try and throw off his pursuers. It wasn't working. In order to line up his first kill, Greene had let his speed drop off. That was another bad mistake, which made two in a row. If he managed to get out of this with his skin intact, he would have his airplane's superior performance to thank for it.

But even a dream machine like the Sun-Wolf answered to the laws of physics. The Sun-Wolf had more brute power than the MiGs, but it took a while for that power to translate into sufficient energy to get the big airplane moving. Meanwhile, at medium speeds, the nimble little Russian fighters were more agile. Initially Greene had been an eagle preying on pigeons, but now he was a bull being tormented by a pair of hounds. There was no way the Sun-Wolf was going to outdance the MiGs in a close-in knife fight.

"So the hell with it," Greene murmured. He quit jinking, went to full 'burn, and climbed, subjecting his bird's structural frame to maximum G-stress in order to gain altitude. His pursuers dropped back, but Greene knew that he was now perched dead-solid perfect within the lead Fishbed's missile envelope.

At 40,000 feet, with his fighter's nose pointed toward the sky, Greene looked back in time to see the lead MiG fire off an Atoll heat-seeker. Greene thanked the Lord that his Sun-Wolf carried state-of-the-art countermeasure gear as he waited for the Atoll to sufficiently close, and then fired off an IRCM infared countermeasure flare. The 40MM expendable was propelled away from the chaff/flare/jammer dispenser mounted on the Sun-Wolf's stern, between her two afterburner nozzles. The IRCM ignited, burning bright, creating a heat source stronger than that of the aircraft for about three seconds. Greene, meanwhile, put the Sun-Wolf into a spiral dive.

And prayed.

The ploy worked! The Atoll shifted its lock-on to the flare, chasing it instead of the Sun-Wolf as Greene continued his steep, turning dive. The MiGs, meanwhile, followed his spiral. Greene waited until he was sure his pursuers had committed themselves to the chase, and then eased off on his throttles. As he'd hoped, the MiG drivers realized too late what he was up to and overshot him, coming around past and above him. The horizon whirled like a pinwheel as Greene executed a hard rolling reversal and pull-up, putting him behind and beneath his attackers at a range of less than a mile. The MiGs were flying in staggered lead and wing positions. Greene pushed the Sun-Wolf for all she was worth, further closing the gap. Greene was close enough to see the blood-red, white-outlined five-pointed stars on the MiGs' dirty-gray aluminum wings and rear quarter fuselages when he locked onto the closest bogey and fired off a Sidewinder.

The heat-seeker dropped away from the Sun-Wolf's wing and then arced up on its cone of exhaust, flying a beeline toward the MiG's tail pipe. At this point-blank range, there was no time for the Russian pilot to execute evasive maneuvers, and the Fishbed-J—the Soviets' plain-vanilla version of a fighter—didn't carry a flare dispenser. The Sidewinder found the MiG and blew it away. What remained of the tarnished silver airplane went cartwheeling across the blue sky trailing thick, black smoke, throwing off bits of flaming wreckage.

"Mother Hen, Lonestar," Greene radioed. "I've got kill number two."

He eyed the last MiG, which had broken off the engagement and was hightailing it out of the sector. Greene knew he could chase it with a medium-range, radar-guided Sparrow, but that would have been about as viscerally satisfying as mailing an enemy a letter bomb. So much of air combat today was accomplished by fucking remote control, when your enemy was nothing more than a blip on your radar screen, or a fucking black-and-white picture on a five-inch television set mounted on your instrument panel.

That was the way of the world, Greene guessed. He certainly realized there was nothing he could do about it, but when he had a choice he would opt for the close-in kill. He was one sky warrior who happened to believe that there was no point in spilling another's blood unless you could smell it, unless you could *feel* the *heat*.

Greene again went to afterburn. The MiG had no chance in an out-and-out horse race with the Sun-Wolf: the enemy plane loomed in Greene's windshield HUD display like a bird caught in a camera's telescopic zoom lens.

Greene throttled back so as not to overshoot the MiG as he entered into a gentle turn. He was now about 2,000 feet astern of his prey. He'd already shifted his HUD display to gun air-air mode, and armed his M61 cannon. The vertical-scale airspeed indicator on the left side of the HUD display told Greene his present speed: 525 knots. The readout just above the indicator scale told Greene he was pulling 1.5G. The HUD's right-side altitude vertical scale read 22,235 feet. The computer-generated round aiming reticle in the center of the display indicated that he was closing on his target.

The MiG tried to use its superior radius of turn to break away, but the Sun-Wolf's superior speed translated to a superior *rate* of turn: the Sun-Wolf wasn't as nimble, but a tight turn wasn't essential just now because there was nobody chasing Greene, and because there was plenty of sky. The Sun-Wolf could cover a larger section of sky while making its wider turn faster than the MiG could cover a smaller section of sky while making its tight turn. This allowed Greene to hold his position relative to the MiG: the Sun-Wolf's nose stayed angled at the enemy.

Greene, peering through the HUD display, boxed the MiG in the small green square just to the right of the aiming reticle, letting his lead computing optical sight radar-track the MiG. Once he had the HUD's round pipper corralling the MiG, he squeezed the gun trigger on his control stick. The M61 snarled like a buzz saw, its six revolving barrels spitting 20MM rounds at the rate of 100 per second. The orange tracers raised sparks off the MiG, which began jinking in agony as Greene stayed locked on his quarry. The Sun-Wolf's gun magazine held 900 rounds, which translated into nine seconds of firing time. The ammo remaining was indicated by the fast-dwindling counter display in the lower left-hand corner of the HUD as Greene walked his rounds up the MiG's spine, hosing the canopy, obliterating it in smoking shards of twinkling Plexiglass.

The MiG dropped away, spinning out of control. Greene followed it down, watching as it plummeted to earth, exploding in a brilliant flash as it crashed into a pale-green pasture.

"Mother Hen, this is Lonestar." Greene put his Sun-Wolf into an exuberant victory roll across the cloud-rippled azure sky. "I've got kill number three, and have made the world safe for democracy. . . ."

"Congrats, Lonestar," Buzz Blaisdale radioed. "Look beneath you and you'll see a grateful, freedom-loving European populus launching fireworks in your honor."

Greene banked his wings in order to view the ground, laughing in delight as beneath him a bright and colorful display of pinwheel fireworks formed a carpet in the sky.

"Is this your doing, Mother Hen?"

"Roger, Lonestar."

"Don't suppose you could conjure up a pretty li'l angel to give me a blow—"

"Negative!" Buzz quickly cut in.

Greene chuckled. "Well, you could at least telephone President Nixon and tell him for me that while I can't help him out concerning that John Dean character, the Prez can at least rest easy on one point: the hammer and sickle will not—I repeat—*will not* be flying over Disneyland."

"I'm sure the President would have been glad to hear that," Buzz Blaisdale said dryly. "Assuming, of course, that those three kills you just scored had been *real*—"

The transmission ended, and the ever-present radio hiss vanished from Greene's headphones as all around him the earth, sky, fireworks—*the world*—flickered like a faulty light bulb. Then the world went dark.

"Well, get me out of here," Greene muttered impatiently as the Sun-Wolf's instrument panel next blinked out, and he was left in total pitch-black oblivion. Greene heard the hiss of pressure valves adjusting, and then the whine of hydraulic lifters kicking in. Greene unbuckled his oxygen mask and removed his helmet as the top half of the clamlike mechanism rose, revealing that all this time Greene had been sitting in the middle of a large, windowless, fluorescent-lit room surrounded by Air Force technicians wearing white lab coats and manning electronic gear. There were keyboard consoles equipped with various scopes and screens; a large glass operations board; lots of blinking lights, and endless rows of computers looking like refrigerator-size reel-to-reel tape recorders. Thick cables linked all this chirping, clattering, whirring gear to the big, matte-black, clamlike gizmo in which Greene was sitting in his mock-up of a Sun-wolf cockpit.

This room was the core of the Flight Simulation Center at Wright-Patterson Air Force Base, near Dayton, Ohio.

Greene unlatched the phony cockpit's canopy and pushed it up on its hinges. He unstrapped himself from his chair, hoisted himself up and out of the bottom half of the simulator. Buzz Blaisdale, wearing brown flight overalls, was seated at the nearby radio transmission console that served as ground control during the simulations.

"Well, you had quite a ride," Buzz remarked, smiling. He was in his mid-twenties, with wavy dark hair and light-brown eyes. "I don't think anyone has ever beat the machine three against one before," Buzz added.

"It's this machine that inspired me to do it," Greene replied, shaking his head. "I just can't get over this toy."

The Simulation Generator System-360 was the latest state-of-the-art result of the Air Force's ongoing effort to supply its fighter pilots with the opportunity to hone their air-combat skills and still live to profit by their mistakes. When a pilot climbed into that big black clamshell and settled into the cockpit, he "flew" against the computers, which could be programmed to present him with any number and variation of Warsaw Pact aircraft. The enemy aircraft behaved within the parameters of their individual specs as if they were being flown by real enemy pilots, because the bogies' attack and defense ploys were drawn from the accumulated data on Red air tactics during the Korean and Vietnam wars, and on the intelligence evaluations garnered from electronic snooping of present-day Warsaw Pact air exercises.

"The more I fly the SGS-360, the better it seems to get," Greene continued. "The only thing missing is physical G-stress on the pilot. Other than that, it's as good as being there. There's little discernible lag time to the display, and the perspective and background detail is just incredible. I swear I could have almost counted the rivets in those MiGs."

"The SGS-360 *is* getting better," one of the nearby computer technicians offered. "We're constantly adding to the data banks. Pretty soon we expect to have the system configured to simulate dusk and night as well as day, and to operate in the air-to-ground weapons-delivery mode in addition to just air combat."

Greene said, "I'm waiting on the twin-tub version, when one real-life pilot will be able to fly against another." He winked at Buzz. "That's when I wax your ass once and for all."

"Tough talk from a guy almost took it up the tail pipe from a Fishbed," Buzz pointed out.

Greene blushed, thinking that Buzz was absolutely right. "Ah, I had him just where I wanted him," he joked, a trifle lamely.

"That reminds me," the technician scowled. "You almost

blew the circuits when you put the Sun-Wolf into that spiral dive."

"Hey, it worked, right?" Greene shrugged. The Sun-Wolf's performance specs were also locked into the simulator's memory banks. If a pilot tried an unrealistic maneuver, the simulator flashed its equivalent of "Tilt," and the game was over.

"Just remember that the computer learns from experience," the technician warned. "Next time you try that stunt, your bogies might have an unpleasant surprise waiting for you."

"I never worry about next time," Greene said, forcing a smile. "That's why I always win *this* time."

He turned away before the technician could reply, thinking that he'd argued this fundamental difference in philosophy before with the boys who baby-sat the computer: fighter jocks took risks; desk jocks went by the book.

Greene guessed that Buzz had picked up on the sudden level of tension in the room. "Hey, the bottom line is that Robbie did a beautiful piece of work this morning," Buzz began, playing the peacemaker role just like always. "I'm looking forward to the playback on the big screen at this week's training debrief."

"I'm not," Green said, smiling ruefully. "I made a couple of real bonehead mistakes. I expect I'll get my ass chewed ragged during the playback." He paused. "Buzz, you scheduled to fly the simulator today?"

"Negative," Buzz replied. "Tomorrow."

"Then you want to grab some lunch?"

"Sure," Buzz said. "But I've got some signing off to do on your simulation. . . ."

"That's okay. I'll stow my gear and stop by my quarters to get cleaned up. I'll meet you at the burger place near the commissary in about half an hour."

Greene left the Flight Simulations Center, which was part of Wright-Patterson's research and development complex, taking the shuttle bus over to bachelor officer quarters, where he showered and changed into a fresh uniform. He was on his way out as they were delivering the mail. That was when Greene got the letter from his uncle Steve.

(Two)

It was the lunch rush, and the Burger Barn was crowded when Greene arrived. The restaurant was done up like a barn, with rough-hewn paneling and cutesy descriptions of the food on the menu, but for all that it was one of the better lunch spots in the on-base shopping mall. There were no tables available, and Buzz hadn't yet arrived, so Greene sat at the counter while he waited, with a mug of coffee and his uncle's letter in front of him. He'd already read the damn thing, but he couldn't help reading it again. The letter was handwritten on plain white paper, as if Steve Gold, an Air Force colonel presently assigned to Los Angeles Air Force Station, understood the enormity of his betrayal and didn't want to use official stationery.

The Burger Barn was noisy with the clattering of silverware and the loud drone of diners' conversation, but the racket seemed to recede as Greene read:

6/11/73

Dear Robbie,

> *I guess I've been putting off writing to tell you this, but now that the time is getting close when the official announcement is going to be made, I figured I better get on the stick and lay it on you before you heard about it from someone else. I've finally decided to make good on that threat I've been making down through the years to leave the Air Force. Next month, I'll be joining in with your stepfather to help run GAT.*
> *I know that you might take this as a shock. Hell, it still comes as a shock to me. . . .*
> *Flying fighters has been my life. I never even went to college or finished high school. Just ran off back in '41 and lied about my age in order to join up with Chennault's Flying Tigers. It's been the "Wild Blue Yonder" for me ever since, and while I can't say that I've never looked back, I do think that the Air Force has given me a good life.*
> *But Robbie, my Air Force career had to come to a*

close, sooner or later. I guess now is as good a time as any.

I know what you're thinking, nephew: "But Steve, you've worn Air Force blue for so long you're not going to recognize yourself out of uniform. . . ."

Am I right? Thought so. You see, Robbie, I know what you're thinking, because it's what I've been thinking. I don't mind telling you that for the first time in a long time I'm scared. (Not even going to War College freaked me out this much!) I know it's not going to be easy giving up my identity and starting something new at my age, but like I said already, it had to be done sooner or later, and it wasn't going to get any easier the longer I waited.

About my new job at GAT: I'll be handling the marketing and sales ends of things, with an emphasis on selling military airplanes. In case you were wondering, I won't be taking orders from Don. Your stepfather and I are going to be equal partners.

Well, I guess that's all I can tell you for now, except for the fact that your mom and your grandmother are all enthusiastic about what I'm doing. I can only hope that you are, as well. . . .

If this letter kind of sounded like I was trying to convince you of something, it's because I was. And trying to convince myself, too, I guess. But hell, you probably guessed that much, right? . . .

The truth is I'm scared, and already lonely and homesick for the only life I've ever known, and I ain't even left it yet! Of course, there's an upside for you, old buddy: In just a couple more weeks, you'll be the senior fighter jock in the Gold clan. How about that?

Seriously, Robbie, there's an upside for me, as well. Nervous as I am about all this, it's what I want to do. The Air Force doesn't have many challenges left for an old bird like me. It's time for me to make my own challenges. Helping to run GAT is going to be a big one.

I hope you wish me luck.

Steve

"Sorry I'm late."

Greene glanced up to see Buzz Blaisdale standing behind him. "No, problem, man. . . ."

Buzz was studying him. "You okay? You look pale. You're not suffering from simulator sickness, are you?"

Greene smiled, shaking his head. "Just some bad news from home. . . ." Greene realized that his friend was waiting for him to elaborate, but he just didn't feel like getting into it right now.

"There's some tables opened up," Buzz said, breaking the awkward silence.

"I guess I'm not that hungry, after all," Greene said. "I'll have another cup of coffee while you eat."

Buzz was frowning in concern. "Look, I had a late breakfast, so I'm cool." He paused. "You want to go work out?"

Greene nodded, sliding off the stool and putting down a buck on the counter to take care of his coffee and a tip. He folded up his uncle's letter and stuffed it into his pocket.

"Gym or *dojo*?" Greene asked. Eighteen months ago both Greene and Buzz had gotten into the martial arts in a big way: karate, aikido, *nunchakus*, *bo* sticks, the whole nine yards. Both of them were now karate brown belts, and had a bet going concerning who was going to make black belt first.

"*Dojo*," Buzz said, winking. "That way if you continue to refuse to tell me what's wrong back home, I can beat it out of you."

(Three)

The *dojo*, or karate training hall, was part of the health club on base. It was a long, wide, brightly lit place with polished wooden floors and mirrored walls. There was an area carpeted with padded mats for judo and aikido practice, racks of plastic and rubber training weapons, and racks of body armor to protect against injury during sparring. There was a karate class just ending when Greene and Buzz left the locker room, so they had the *dojo* to themselves. Both men were barefoot, and both were wearing the floppy white karate suit called a *gi*.

"Hard to believe a guy like your uncle could leave the Air Force," Buzz commented as he and Greene faced the mirror and began their stretching exercises.

Greene just grunted in reply, intent upon his leg lifts and turns. On the way over to the *dojo*, Buzz had managed to badger him into revealing the contents of Steve's letter. Now he was sorry he'd let Buzz grill him. He wanted to put his turncoat uncle out of his mind.

"Wasn't your uncle the guy who wrote the book on the Fishbed?" Buzz asked.

"Literally," Greene replied. "He was the guy the Air Force sent to check out that Arab MiG-21 the Israelis managed to get their hands on back in the 1960s. It was my uncle's actual evaluation sheets that we studied back at fighter pilot's school. Most likely, the computer guys used my uncle's evaluations to program the flight simulator."

They were silent as they warmed up by doing a hundred karate punches and an equal number of snap kicks, watching their form in the mirrors. Greene studied his reflection as he brooded about the news from home: he was just a little under five ten and weighed one sixty-five, all of it muscle, thanks to his frequent workouts. He had green eyes under a shock of black hair. Back in 'Nam he'd worn his mustache with the ends waxed and twirled, but upon coming home he'd trimmed away the handlebars.

They next practiced their *kata*, the series of prearranged movements that formed the bedrock for their karate training, watching and correcting each other's form. They then faced each other to do some basic combination thrusting, kicking, and blocking techniques.

"There's just one thing I don't understand," Buzz suddenly piped up. "Why did you call the fact that your uncle is leaving the Air Force bad news?"

"Why do you think, man?" Greene responded angrily. "I grew up worshiping that guy, and here he is selling out!" He increased the pace and intensity of his thrusts; the smacks echoed in the *dojo* as Buzz managed to deflect Greene's strenuous punches with circular blocks.

"Hey, man, cool out," Buzz complained, stumbling back.
"Sorry . . ."

"You want to spar, let's put on some body armor."

"Yeah, right."

They walked over to the racks, where they selected and strapped on padding to protect their chests and groins, moved To the center of the *dojo*, bowed to each other, and then began their wary circling. Buzz went into a cat's-foot stance, his knees bent, all of his weight on his rear leg so that he could kick out with his front foot. Greene refused to allow himself to be lured into anticipating a kicking attack. Instead, he watched Buzz's eyes.

Buzz skittered forward, feinting a kick and then attacking with a left thrust to Greene's chest. Greene sidestepped to the right, deflecting Buzz's punch, sweeping it away with with his left forearm. As Greene completed the block, he slid his forearm down Buzz's outstretched arm, gripping Buzz's wrist in order to haul Buzz toward him, simultaneously executing a side foot thrust to Buzz's thigh. Buzz freed his wrist using an aikido technique, and pivoted away from Greene's kick.

The two men separated from each other. The entire exchange had lasted only a few seconds.

"God, I love this." Buzz smiled, breathing lightly. Both men were again circling each other, looking for a chink in the other's defenses.

Greene nodded. "This must be like what dogfighting was like in the old days: lots of aerobatics with machine guns blazing.

"Yeah, that's right," Buzz muttered. "Your old man was an RAF World War Two fighter jock. . . ."

Greene hesitated. He didn't like talking about his father. "He flew a Hawker Hurricane against the Germans over Africa," he admitted reluctantly. "He was an ace—"

Greene suddenly lashed out a front snap kick to Buzz's protected belly. Buzz stepped away from the kick and then lunged forward, bending at the waist, making a grab for Greene's outstretched leg. Greene managed to retract his leg just in time and then snapped out a back fist strike to Buzz's padded shoulder.

"Gotcha!" Greene gloated. "Score's one to nothing!"

Buzz stepped in fast, scoring with a foot strike to Greene's upper thigh and then two solid punches to the chest that knocked the wind out of Greene despite his body armor. Greene tried to backpedal away, but he lost his balance and sat down hard on the wooden floor.

Buzz was grinning down at him with his hands on his hips. "You keep making the same mistake, Robbie. You made it in the simulator, and just now. You get so carried away with your initial victory that you leave yourself open for a counterattack."

"Thanks, I'll have to remember that, oh wise one," Greene said dryly as Buzz gave him a hand getting to his feet.

"Score's three to one, my favor," Buzz said as they again began to circle each other. "Now, then, you were telling me about your father . . . ?"

"There's nothing more, except that he died in the war," Greene ended firmly. It just hurt too much to talk about the precious little he knew about his father.

Blaize Greene had died in combat, purposely sacrificing his own life to save others, the day his son was born. What Robbie Greene knew about his father he'd learned from his mother, but when she'd remarried she'd stopped talking about her first husband. She'd even taken on the Harrison name, and had a son with her new husband, leaving Robbie Greene as the outsider in this new family and all alone to carry on the Greene name. For Robert Blaize Greene, so hungry for his mother's recollections, it had all seemed a cruel betrayal, which had festered within him through the years. In retaliation, he'd turned away from his mother and that slimy bastard she'd married, giving his uncle Steve all his affection.

But now Uncle Steve was also betraying Blaize Greene's memory by making peace with Don Harrison; by becoming partners with his father's usurper.

Greene saw an opening and stepped in close, driving his elbow into Buzz's ribs. He knew instantly that he'd hit Buzz too hard, even before his friend cried out, falling to his knees and clutching at his side.

"Goddammit, Robbie . . . ," Buzz grumbled as Greene helped him to his feet.

"I'm sorry, man." Greene shook his head. "Look, that's enough sparring. I'll see you later. I'll pay for the beers tonight to make it up to you. Right now I'm going to go work out on the heavy bag. I'm feeling a little too mean today. I'm not fit for human company."

CHAPTER 3

(One)

**The International Air Transport Committee annual
trade show
Sunshine Convention and Exhibition Center
Los Angeles, California
12 November, 1973**

Steven Gold knew that the IATC trade show was the number-one event in the industry. It was here that the aviation industry offered for sale to the American and foreign airlines everything to do with the commercial air-transport business: jetliner fuselages, engines, avionics, door-latch assemblies, seat-upholstery fabrics, in-flight catering equipment, personnel uniforms, and so on. The trade show had a carnival atmosphere. The vendors spent heavily on elaborate promotions and lures designed to attract the airline purchasing agents to their exhibits. As Gold wandered the maze of aisles formed by the hundreds of elaborate booths, he saw giveaways, sweepstakes, and hucksters dressed up as clowns, birds, and in World War I flying gear; and the largest concentration of platinum-blond "spokes models" in low-cut sequined gowns outside of Hollywood. The manufacturers' sales and marketing departments began preparing for the IATC extravaganza months in advance. Everybody who was anybody in the commercial aviation business was here, but as Gold bleakly returned to GAT's huge booth in a prime spot in the hall, he wondered if anybody in the history of the world had felt so out of place as he did just now.

Gold glanced at Don Harrison, who was standing like the king of the mountain on a raised platform in GAT's multilevel booth. Don was busy chatting with several airline vice presidents. Evidently, one of the prosperous-looking guys had told a joke: Don and the others were all laughing uproariously.

Sons of bitches, Gold thought grimly. Nobody had said two words to *him* all morning, and the times he'd tried to intrude into ongoing conversations, things got strangely quiet. He felt like a wallflower, and felt doubly foolish about his sorry situation because Don had told him his presence at the trade show wasn't necessary. It was Gold who had insisted upon coming. It was his way: when things weren't going well, Gold liked to throw himself wholeheartedly into the fray.

And things definitely *weren't* going well, Gold now brooded. He was loitering in front of the GAT booth, his shiny plastic exhibitor's badge pinned to the lapel of his custom-tailored, three-piece blue flannel suit, standing around playing pocket pool with himself and rocking on his heels like a goddamned department-store floorwalker. It had been a tumultuous five months since he'd turned in his Air Force uniform for executive's pinstripes, and he was having a tough time getting used to the civilian world. For instance, not even in your own office could you just *order* that things be done according to standard operating procedure. No way, pal. Even with your own staff, you had to "communicate," "negotiate," be "considerate," and "compromise." If you didn't, the hippy-dippy bastards would up and quit on you, for chrissakes.

Gold smiled grimly. He would have liked to see somebody on his staff try to quit him in the *Air Force.* . . .

He was comfortable dealing with the DOD military-aviation market because he was an old hand at finding his way through that particular jungle, but the civilian air-transport business was virgin territory. Don Harrison had told Gold he needn't concern himself with that side of the business, but Gold was damned if he was going to be satisfied with half a loaf: Pop had mastered all aspects of the aviation business, so Herman Gold's son was going to do the same, even if it killed him.

And so here Gold was attending this trade show, feeling bored and out of place, wandering the hall until even the would-be starlets in their form-fitting glitter gowns had begun to pale.

And there wasn't one armament or combat avionics vendor in the whole fucking convention center.

"Hello, amigo."

Steve turned. "Tim?" He smiled tenatively. "Tim Campbell?"

"None other, amigo." Campbell grinned.

"Damn, it's been a long time!" Gold exclaimed.

Campbell was in his early seventies. He was short and stocky, but still looked as randy as an old billy goat. Campbell had a full head of gray, auburn-tinged hair that he wore in a Beatles cut, and modishly bushy sideburns. His clothes were 1960s-era, dandified English mod as well: his tan and green windowpane-plaid, double-breasted suit had wide lapels and a nipped-in waist; his tie was a riotous maroon and yellow paisley pattern; his snakeskin boots had zippers on the sides. Campbell may have dressed like a backwater used-car salesman, but he was one of the richest men in America.

And maybe the world, Gold amended to himself as he took in Campbell's diamond-encrusted wristwatch and the glittering rocks set in his pinky ring and his tie's stickpin: the gems were big enough to double as airfield landing lights.

"So, you liking the airplane business, amigo?" Campbell asked.

"Still too soon to tell," Gold replied.

Campbell nodded. "I always knew you'd follow in your father's footsteps."

"You knew more than I did."

"Well, now, amigo." Campbell smiled fondly. "Who's

known you longer than me?'' He reached up to pat Gold's cheek. ''Come on, say it just once like you did way back when?''

Gold blushed. ''Uncle Tim,'' he murmured.

Campbell nodded, pleased. ''*You* may have forgotten how I used to bounce you on my knee, but *I* haven't, amigo. . . .''

Gold nodded, remembering back over thirty years to when Tim Campbell was Pop's close friend and business partner. In those days, Skyworld Airlines had still been a part of Gold Aviation and Transport, but at some point Tim Campbell and Herman Gold had suffered a falling-out. Steve Gold didn't know the details. He'd been a little kid when it happened, and Pop had never talked about it, but whatever it was that had caused the disagreement, its result had been a split in GAT as the two men went their separate ways. Pop had retained control of the aviation design and construction portions of the GAT empire, while Campbell had taken control of the airline. Since then, Campbell had branched out. In addition to his interest in Skyworld, Campbell owned a sizable portion of Amalgamated-Landis Aircraft Corporation, which was exhibiting here at the IATC trade show. Campbell also had other extensive, diversified holdings in America and abroad. Like a spider sitting in the center of its web, Campbell's reach extended to all corners of the globe, which explained why this little old man with the Moe Howard haircut and the bad suit turned up as a regular cover boy for the nation's business magazines.

''Those were the good ole days, all right,'' Campbell said. ''But we can't hold back the clock.'' He paused. ''You know how sorry I was when your father passed away?''

''Of course, Tim.''

''First Hull Stiles dying, and then your father.'' Campbell shook his head. ''I guess Father Time is breakin' up that ole gang of mine. . . .''

Gold sighed. Hull Stiles had been another of Pop's friends and business partners; a fellow barnstormer pilot who had come in on the ground floor of Gold Express, helping Pop to establish the fledgling freight and mail air-transport business.

Campbell briskly decreed, ''But we can't dwell on the past, can we, amigo? How's business here at GAT?''

"Like everywhere, I guess." Gold shrugged. "It isn't a seller's market. President Nixon's Watergate troubles combined with the Arabs' oil embargo has sure put the brakes on the world economy."

"It's all politics, amigo," Campbell said philosophically. "The politics of oil, and the dirty politics in Washington. I reckon ain't nobody's been harder hit than the airlines now that the price of kerojet has skyrocketed."

"Is that what you 'reckon'?" Gold teased. Tim Campbell had been born in Providence, Rhode Island, and knew how to speak perfectly well, but during a sojourn in Texas revolving around the oil business, Campbell had cultivated this half-cowpoke, half-good-ole'-southern-redneck's manner of speech.

"You funnin' me, boy?" Campbell winked to show he was aware of the joke.

"Just a *mite*, Tim." Gold grinned. "But seriously, you're right about the rise in the price of jet engine fuel shaving the airlines' already slender profit margins."

Campbell nodded. "And when a fella feels like he's got a hole in his pocket, he's in no mood to buy," he moped. "Amalgamated-Landis has a paper airplane it's been floating past the airlines, with no luck."

"That's too bad," Gold said. A paper airplane was a jetliner concept still on the drawing boards that a manufacturer promoted to the airlines in order to gauge potential customer reaction before committing the enormous sums required to turn a concept into a prototype. A major trade show like this one was the perfect place to try to get such a ball rolling.

Campbell said, "Of course, I shouldn't be telling you any of this, seeing as how you're now the competition, but what the hell, blood's thicker than water, and we're almost blood, right, amigo?"

"Yeah, sure, Tim." Gold wondered what Campbell's angle was; "Uncle Tim" always had an angle.

"I think I'm going to have A-L concentrate on the military end of the stick," Campbell was confiding. "I've had it with building airliners. In that game, there's only one rule: survival of the fittest, just like in the jungle. Your daddy taught me that—"

"What do you mean?"

"Come on, Stevie," Campbell chided. "Don't kid a kidder. You tryin' to tell me you don't know how your father won the competititon between his GC-909 jetliner and my Amalgamated-Landis AL-12, back in the 1950s?"

Gold shrugged. "I always assumed the 909 got bought by the airlines because it was the better plane. . . . No offense, Tim."

"That's rich." Campbell laughed. "Oh, that's too rich!" He glanced around as if he was worried about being overheard, then took a step closer to whisper, "Your father scuttled my airplane."

"Scuttled it? How?"

"He used his CIA contacts," Campbell whispered.

"What the hell are you talking about?"

Campbell hesitated, studying Gold. "You mean to say you really don't know?"

"Know *what*?" Gold demanded, exasperated.

Campbell shook his head. "You go ask your business partner." He nodded to himself. "Yeah, you go ask Don Harrison how your father got his buddies in Washington to see to it that my jetliner got its wings clipped."

"I *will* ask," Gold said defiantly, thinking there was no way his father could have done something underhanded.

"I hope you do, amigo. It'll be a good lesson for you in your new line of work." Campbell winked. "But now *you* tell *me* something: In this fucked-up economy, it's plain there ain't no manufacturer gonna scare up a launch customer for a new airplane 'less that manufacturer is willing to take on extensive seller financing."

"Well, I suppose you're right," Gold agreed. a "launch customer" was that initial airline that could be persuaded to place a large order for a new jetliner, thereby legitimizing it to the rest of the industry.

"Tell me, amigo,"—Campbell was watching Gold's eyes—"is seller financing what GAT has in mind in order to peddle the Pont 500?"

Gold hesitated. The Pont 500 jetliner was the latest product of the long association between GAT and the European aviation consortium Skytrain Industrie. This new version of the Pont was a smaller, fuel-efficient airplane ideally suited for short hops. It was the right jetliner at the right time in this era of escalating fuel costs, and was selling well in Europe. GAT had a large financial stake in the Pont 500, and hoped to get the airplane accepted by airlines in the United States.

But that was GAT's business, and no one else's, Gold thought. Old family friend or not, Gold wasn't about to be reveal company sales strategy to Tim Campbell.

"I really can't say, Tim—"

"Can't or *won't*?" Campbell pounced, eyes glittering.

"Can't because I don't know," Gold replied, lighting a cigarette to hide his unease at lying. "You see, Don is handling the commercial jetliner side of the business. For the few months since I've joined up, I've been concentrating on the military market." Gold remembered reading somewhere that the best lies had a healthy dose of truth mixed into them.

Campbell was nodding, but Gold couldn't tell if he was convinced. "Well, thanks anyway, amigo," Campbell said. "Now I got to be moseyin' on."

Gold was relieved. "Good to see you again. . . ."

"Uh-huh." Campbell looked amused. "I have me a feelin' we'll be seein' a lot of each other in the future, amigo. Now, don't you forget to ask Don about the GC-909/AL-12 competition."

"I will," Gold promised.

Campbell nodded, looking satisfied. "Yeah, it's 'bout time you had your eyes opened now that you're playin' with the big boys. . . . You give my regards to your sister, and your lovely mama. . . ."

Gold waited until Campbell was gone and then beelined it into the GAT booth, intent upon finding Don, and finding out what Tim had been referring to concerning the jetliner competition. One of the GAT sales executives told Gold that Don was off checking out the competition. Gold left the GAT booth, hurrying as best he could along the narrow, crowded aisles, looking for Don at the Boeing and Lockheed booths; then fighting his way through the crowd to the Brower-Dunn exhibit, where a B-D sales rep told Gold that he'd just missed Don, who'd mentioned that he was heading over to the Pratt & Whitney booth.

Gold headed that way as well, striding down the aisle and turning the corner—

That was when Gold saw Linda Forrester browsing among

the booths, collecting manufacturers' brochures and stuffing them into a canvas shopping tote.

Son of a bitch, what's she doing here? Gold wondered. He saw that she was wearing one of the bright-yellow press badges, and then he remembered that Don Harrison had told him that Linda had left her TV journalist's job in order to write a book on the airline industry. She must have gotten her book publisher to arrange entry credentials. . . .

Linda hadn't yet spotted him. Gold took the opportunity to study her. She looked different than Gold remembered her, but then, a lot of years had passed since that day she'd stormed out of his bed and out of his life, he thought ruefully. Linda was in her forties now. Her brunette hair was cut very short. She was wearing a tan silk suit with her skirt ending well above her knees, patterned stockings, and alligator pumps. For jewelry she wore chunky gold earrings and a gold Tank watch on a brown leather band. The exhibition hall's unforgiving fluorescent lights clearly revealed the laugh lines time had put around her eyes and her mouth, but the years had only transformed rather than robbed her of beauty: Her youthful, carnal sensuality had matured to sexy elegance.

She still had not seen him. Gold knew he could easily avoid her in the large, crowded hall, but what would be the point? She was researching commercial aviation for her book, and he was a GAT chief executive. They were destined to run into each other sooner or later. Anyway, Gold knew that she was married, that she had a couple of kids, for chrissakes.

The bottom line was that if Don Harrison could get over Linda, so could he. No! Make that, so *had* he, Gold amended, walking over to her before he could chicken out.

She still hadn't noticed him when he said, "What's a girl like you doing in a place like this?"

She looked up quickly, her expression blank. For an instant, Gold was acutely embarrassed, thinking: *she doesn't even recognize me*. But then her blue eyes widened.

"Son of a bitch," she murmured sardonically. "They'll let *anybody* in this place, won't they?"

Nodding dumbly, grinning like a fool, he awkwardly took her arm in order to give her a peek on the cheek. He found touching her to still be a thrill, even if she did stiffen slightly. She actually flinched against his touch on her sleeve.

"Long time no see," Gold heard himself blurt to fill the roaring silence between them. *Oh, yeah, just brilliant,* he scornfully thought. "How have you been, Linda?"

"I'm fine," she said adamantly. "I'm terrific!"

She was sounding strident. Clearly, she was just as fucked up over this as he was. Gold hoped the encounter wasn't going to turn out to be a total fiasco. He thought hard for something to say. "I heard you were doing a book."

"Yeah!" She nodded quickly, looking on the verge of hysteria.

Gold was feeling as awkward as a kid on his first date, which was not normally his style with women, to say the least. If his heart pounded any harder, he was going to have to sit down.

"Just look at you! All spiffy in your business suit!" Linda chattered. "I'd heard that you'd left the Air Force to join your father's company—" She stopped short, her expression instantly turning sympathetic. "Oh, Steve, your father! I was so sorry when I heard. . . ." She brightened. "But look at you now! That's a lovely suit." She ran her fingers along his lapel but then jerked her hand back as if she'd been burned. "I almost didn't recognize you out of uniform!"

This was going nowhere, Gold thought, watching her. She looked like she was ready to bolt.

"Come on, Blue Eyes," he kidded softly, knowing that he was taking a risk calling her that: Blue Eyes was what he'd used to call her back when they'd thought they were going to last forever. "*You* of all people have seen me out of uniform the *mostest.*"

She laughed at that, and the ice somewhat broke between them. Gold took out his cigarettes and offered her one, which she accepted. He lit her smoke and then his own. As she exhaled, he could see the tension flowing out of her.

"So, Steve," she began, sounding self-assured and a bit smart-alecky; in other words, like the old Linda. "What's it been like for you now that you're among us mortals in mufti?"

"It's had its ups and downs," Gold told her. "Mostly downs, until *now.* You're the first person I've met here all day that I wanted to talk to. I heard you were married and living in New York? That you had a couple of kids?"

"You're half right," she replied. "I have two boys, seven

and nine years old. But I'm back here in L.A. now. My marriage didn't last," she added evenly.

"Oh, I'm sorry. . . ."

"The divorce went through a couple of years ago," she said, dismissing the matter with a wave of her hand. "My ex now lives in Chicago. It's history." She paused. "Like a lot of things, huh?"

She was contemplating him, that old, devilish smile he remembered so well playing at the corners of her mouth. Gold felt his groin stir as the memory of that smile unleashed a thousand other memories of Linda Forrester that rushed through him. This wasn't going to be as safe as he'd thought. As a matter of fact, Gold realized that he was on very thin ice.

"Where you living?" he asked.

"My boys and I live in Rustic Canyon."

"It's beautiful there."

She nodded. "Good for kids. You still living in Malibu?"

"Uh-huh. Still on the beach."

"My boys like the beach. . . ."

"What kid doesn't?" Gold remarked.

"No matter how old," Linda pointedly commented. "Good old Steve." She laughed in response to his frown. "Some things never change, huh?"

Gold realized he was holding his Pall Mall with his thumb and index finger, like Humphrey Bogart in *Casablanca. Cut it out, before she nails you on it,* he warned himself. "So, your boys are seven and nine?"

"Uh-huh."

She was watching him now with her head cocked, her attention focused. Gold couldn't shake the feeling that every word he was saying carried supreme weight and importance. He could see her evaluating his responses—reevaluating him—and he realized that he had already made his decision about what *he* wanted. *All right, let's get this over with, one way or the other.*

"Boys that age are a real trip," Gold began. "I remember how much fun I had with my nephews when they were that age. God, I had some great times with them camping out, fishing, or just messing around." He paused. "Do your kids get to see their father much?"

She shook her head. "Like I said, he lives in Chicago. My boys see him whenever he's on the West Coast for business, and for two weeks every summer."

"But you take the boys to the beach?

"Every weekend I can."

"Well . . ." Gold hesitated. "Well, maybe next time you're at Malibu you'll stop by the house to introduce me to them? I'm usually home on weekends. . . ."

"Okay." She smiled tentatively, suddenly seeming very shy. "Maybe I will."

"Yeah, that would be great!" Gold said, knowing he was sounding overeager but not caring.

"I know they'd love to meet you," Linda said. "You being an ex–fighter pilot. A war hero and all—"

"And I'd like to meet them," Gold said firmly. "Maybe if we hit it off I could take them fishing sometime. It's not much fun fishing alone."

"No, I suppose it wouldn't be," Linda agreed, watching him very, *very* closely now.

Talk about fishing, Gold thought. He swallowed hard. "Who knows? Maybe they'll have a soft spot in their heart for an old Air Force man?" He pushed the rest of it out. "Like their old lady . . . ?"

Linda's eyes were bright blue beacons. "Anything's possible."

(Two)

Malibu

The beach outside Steve Gold's house was wide and flat. The sand was almost as blindingly white as the pale disc of sun burning through the overcast. There was a cool breeze blowing off the Pacific, creating swirling eddies upon the low, sunbaked dunes. The waves were rolling in very high. The rough blue surf crashed rhythmically as it broke against the beach. Gold, hearing that somber sea song played in counterpoint to the gull's shrill laughter, could let it carry him back in time, to when he was a child, building damp sand castles just out of reach of the foaming swash. But now, in the bedroom of his house, in his big double bed, Steve Gold was lost in another form of time travel as he made love to Linda Forrester.

The wind off the beach rattled the bedroom's jalousie windows, carrying with it the salt tang of the sea as it caressed and cooled the lovers' sheened, naked bodies. The wind moved the windows' lowered bamboo blinds, casting slanted patterns of light and dark on the bedroom's white walls, and on the white bed, and on the lovers' white limbs, entwined.

Gold and Linda were lying on their sides, facing each other. He stroked her supple curves as he moved his lips across her full breasts, pausing to suck her nipples, not stopping until he had her moaning and pleading for mercy, her hip's silken swell writhing beneath his touch. Gold sighed softly as she reached out for him, pulling him closer, one hand on his shoulder and the other gently encircling his erection, drawing him into her smoothly with no fumbling. Gold closed his eyes. The feel of her body was both the same as he remembered and also very different; she was an exotic but familiar land to which he'd returned after being too long away.

They began to move together slowly, silently, gradually speeding up their rhythms until the wind sighing off the roaring ocean mixed its brine scent with Linda's flowery perfume and the sea-salty musk of their lathered, locked-together bodies. The currents of scent and touch swirling around Gold tumbled him into further dizzying waves of exquisite sensation. Linda wrapped her long, tawny legs around his waist to grind herself against him. It went on like that forever, impossibly delicious and unbearably long, until at some point in their dance they found themselves looking into each other's eyes.

"Hello." She laughed breathlessly between nibbling kisses.

"Hello . . ." For some damn reason, he was crying. His tears softly plopping onto her breasts ran a helter-skelter course down her cleavage.

"Welcome," she began, but suddenly her back arched and her mouth stretched wide; in her climax her words melted to an unintelligible moan. It was long moments before she managed within the lessening throes of her orgasm to come to her senses, and then her voice in his ear was the hiss of the wind-wracked sea: *"Welcome home—"*

The two of them lay side by side in Gold's bed, letting the breeze dry them as they shared a cigarette. Gold, watching the ashtray balanced on his stomach rise and fall with his breathing, found himself thinking of Linda's ex-husband. Whoever this guy was, Gold was damned glad he lived in Chicago. It was amazing and a bit frightening how fiercely jealous and protective he felt toward this woman lying beside him.

"Do you want to hear about it?" Linda asked, breaking the silence.

"Hear about what?"

"My marriage."

Gold couldn't help flinching. *What'd she read my mind?* It was damned spooky.

"Well, you're not answering," Linda continued. "But if you don't mind, I'd like to get this out of the way between us once and for all."

"Yeah, sure," Gold hedged. "I mean, if you want to . . ."

She chuckled. "Okay . . . First off, it was a good marriage. We loved each other. I'm not saying we loved each other the way *you* and *I* love each other." She looked at him out of the corner of her eye as she took the cigarette from him. "I hope I'm not making you uncomfortable by saying that?"

"Well, I uh . . ." Gold couldn't seem to get his mouth in gear.

"Because if I did just embarrass you, that's too bad, but I've been putting up with your damned foolishness for what seems to me to be my entire life, and I'm getting too old to go chasing after you or any man with a butterfly net. But that's really neither here nor there at the moment." She paused for a breath and a tug on the cigarette. "Anyway," she pressed on, exhaling smoke toward the bedroom ceiling, *"anyway . . ."*

Gold abruptly realized that Linda was exorcising her husband's ghost more for her own sake than his.

"Anyway, the first couple of years of marriage were fine: my husband, who is an attorney, was doing well at his L.A. law firm, and I was a reporter on the local news broadcast, up for a correspondent's slot on that affiliate's network evening news. Well, I got that job——''

''I seem to remember seeing you on TV once or twice,'' Gold interrupted. ''At least, I don't *think* I switched channels when you came on.''

Linda laughed, and Gold let her think it was a joke. Actually, he had always switched the channel when she came on the air, but it was only just now that he understood why he had. All of his life it had been his way to firmly turn his back on those things he wanted but for some reason couldn't have.

''My husband and I moved to New York in order for me to accept that network job. It was no hassle for him to do that: He had his pick of job offers in the Big Apple. We continued to live happily ever after.'' She paused. ''I mean, I *guess* things were okay, but to be fair I have to add that in those days our individual schedules were so hectic, and we got together so infrequently, that when we *did* see each other it was almost like we were still *dating*. . . .'' She trailed off, lost in private, brooding reveries.

''So what happened?'' Gold demanded, anxious to snatch her back to the here and now.

''What happened was he got a supreme-o job offer in Chicago. I remember how excited he was about it—it meant a senior partnership for him—but all I felt at the time was anger: 'What about my career?' I remember demanding. 'What am I supposed to do? Quit my job and follow you to fucking Chicago with the kids on my hip like some fucking pioneer woman?' ''

Gold, his head beside Linda's on the pillow, could hear the resentment building in her voice as she once again lost her way in the past. He raised himself up on one elbow to look down at her. ''You're just upsetting yourself,'' he warned. ''You yourself told me it was history, right?''

''Right.'' She nodded, mollified.

''Let's not talk about it any more if it upsets you. Okay?''

''Okay.'' She smiled. ''Anyway, you must have the picture by now. We realized our ambitions meant more to us than our marriage. Of course, we were still young——''

''Wrong!'' Gold corrected her. ''You were merely younger.''

"Oh, right," she said, chuckling. "I forgot I was talking to Barrie's original role model for Peter Pan."

"What's that supposed to mean?"

"It means that some things really *never do* change," she countered, amused, and then gestured toward the bedroom doorway. "Like, for instance, when are you going to break down and buy some furniture?"

Gold shrugged. Pop had bought up a bunch of Malibu oceanfront back during the Second World War, when people were worried about the Japanese invading California. Herman Gold had put up houses on most of the lots, including this house with its three bedrooms and a double garage, one of the largest on the beach. Herman Gold's estate had left this house to his son, but Steve Gold had been living in it for several years previous to that, ever since he'd been reassigned to the Los Angeles Air Force Station. Despite the length of time Gold had been living here, the only real furniture in the house was the stuff in the bedroom. The other rooms were empty of furnishings, except for some rattan-woven rugs on the teakwood floors, and, in the living room, some beach chairs, a liquor cabinet, and a wall unit to hold Gold's extensive stereo equipment and the TV.

"I bought furniture once," Gold joked. "A set of custom bucket seats for my Corvette . . ."

"And this bed," Linda added.

"Well, sure, this bed," he agreed.

She sat up, reaching across Gold in order to retrieve her watch from the night table. Her breasts brushed his chest as she grabbed the watch, and Gold stroked the small of her back. She sighed, wiggling under his touch. Gold could feel himself thickening in response; his erection was nudging insistently at her thigh.

"My God!" she exclaimed. "It's almost four o'clock! What's happened to the afternoon?"

Gold smiled. Hours ago they'd left the trade show to get some lunch, and then one thing had led to another until they'd ended up here. Linda had followed him to Malibu in her own car, a '71 silver Mercedes 280 SL ragtop.

Gold reached for her, murmuring, "Time flies when you're having fun."

She patted his bobbing erection. "Hold that thought."

"Why don't *you* hold it?"

"Because I have to use your phone," she fretted, snaring the telephone from the night table and putting it like a wall between them on the bed. "I've got to call my housekeeper and tell her when I'll be home. I promised my boys I wouldn't be late this evening."

She paused in her dialing. "What's that sour look for?"

"Nothing, I guess . . ."

"Spit it out, buster."

"It's nothing really," Gold said reluctantly. "I guess it's just that *I* grew up with housekeepers. . . . *My* mom was hardly ever home."

"Hey," she began, looking very serious as she hung up the phone. "Let's get one thing straight right now. I'm a *superior* mother."

"I'm sure you are," Gold placated.

She stopped him. "No offense, cutie, but I don't need you to be sure, because *I'm* sure. I have made some *supreme-o* sacrifices for my kids. When the network wanted to bump me up to be their Paris correspondent—a job my professional peers would have killed for—I turned it down because I didn't want to raise my kids outside of the U.S.A., and because as a single parent I didn't want to be apart from them for months at a time. It was for the sake of my kids that I decided to leave New York: I wanted them to have a goddamned back-yard to play in. It was for them that I decided to try my hand at free-lancing, so that I could be there for them."

Gold held up his hands in surrender. "Okay! You've convinced me! I apologize."

Linda smiled, calming down. "Apology accepted."

Gold listened as she made her call, telling her housekeeper in fluent Spanish that she would be home in about an hour, depending on the traffic. When she'd hung up, Gold moved the telephone back to the nightstand, saying, "You know, it's funny you talking about being there for your kids, and your kids being there for you. I just found out something about my own father I never knew. Before I ran into you this morning, Tim Campbell put this bug in my ear about something he and Pop were involved in a lot of years back. Campbell told me to ask Don Harrison about it, so just before we left the trade show—while you were finishing up your note-gathering—I managed to collar Don long enough to get the story."

"Story about what?"

Gold paused. "This is probably going to piss you off, but I've got to say it: What I'm about to tell you now is not for publication. It's totally off the record, or whatever the phrase is, okay?"

Linda spread her arms wide, her breasts rising, her nipples looking rouged against her pale skin "In case you haven't noticed, I don't have my notebook and pen," she said coolly. "But would you like to frisk me for a wire?"

"Come on, Linda. You know what I mean."

"I suggest you thoroughly explore all the usual hiding places . . ." She went up on her hands and knees to present him with her heart-shaped bottom.

Gold lunged and bit her on the ass. She squawked in outrage, spinning away to the foot of the bed and facing him.

"Now that I have your attention," he began, exasperated. "Once upon a time we tried not to keep secrets from one another, but this is different. I've got responsibilities to the company. I need to know the ground rules on what I can tell you concerning GAT, and what I can't."

Linda thought about it. "Fair enough, considering what I do for a living, and the book I'm currently working on," she admitted. "How's this: Unless you tell me otherwise, or I specifically ask, I'll always assume that our conversations are off the record."

"Okay . . ." Gold reached for his cigarettes. "As I was saying, this all took place back in the fifties, when GAT and Amalgamated-Landis had individually come up with the industry's first jetliner prototypes, and both firms were competing for orders from the airlines. It was about this same time that the CIA and the Air Force approached my father about the possibility of GAT designing and building a high-altitude spy plane that could be used over the Soviet Union. . . ."

He hesitated, watching Linda, wondering just how much detail about this to go into with her, because it was this same spy-plane project that had broken up their romance back when Gold had been a lieutenant colonel in the Air Force. Gold had been set to leave the military in order to settle down with

Linda in Los Angeles, but then the CIA had tapped him, borrowing him from the Air Force in order to put him in charge of the spy-plane pilot-recruitment program. The day he'd backed out of his promise to resign from the Air Force without being able to tell Linda why—the spy-plane project was ultra top secret—was the day she'd stormed out of his life.

"I remember the Mayfly MR-1 spy plane program very well," Linda was saying. "Especially the flap when the Russians managed to shoot one down, and how embarrassed Eisenhower and the country was when the Reds put our pilot who'd been captured alive on trial for espionage."

"That's right," Gold said. "Well, anyway, it was GAT who built that spy plane for the government. Back then, as always, GAT had the best research-and-design department, and at that point the company already had a long history of working with the government on top-secret—or, more to the point, clandestine—programs concerning aeronautical espionage."

"What does this have to do with GAT's jetliner competition against Amalgamated-Landis?"

"Everything." Gold sighed. "The AL-12 jetliner was luring away the airlines from the GAT GC-909, the production costs for which had been enormous. My father was financially over extended. If the GC-909 didn't emerge triumphant in this competition, GAT was finished. Meanwhile, concerning the spy plane, Pop knew that he had the government over a barrel. GAT had the best engineering talent in the industry for that sort of project. If GAT couldn't—or *wouldn't*—build the spy plane, the CIA would have to go without."

"And?"

"And so Herman Gold cut a deal. He agreed to build the spy plane if the CIA used its influence with the Civil Aeronautics Board to get CAB to reconsider its prior approval of the AL-12's design specs." He shook his head. "As you can imagine, the news scared the airlines right off the AL-12 and right into the waiting arms of GAT. The GC-909 was a success. The AL-12 was sucker-punched into history. Amalgamated-Landis's perfectly good airplane suffered such a tarnished-by-innuendo reputation that it never even made it into production. End of story."

"Wow . . . ," Linda said slowly. "Double-wow . . . That's a best-seller's worth of airline industry dirt right there."

"Hey!" Gold exclaimed accusingly.

She winked. "Just kidding, cutie."

Gold nodded, feeling bad.

"Hey, come on now," Linda comforted. "It was a long time ago, and your father just did what he had to do in order to save his company."

"I guess."

"And from what I know about Tim Campbell, that guy's no angel." She took Gold's hand. "Steve, it was business, that's all."

"Yeah, I know that," Gold replied. "It's just that I grew up with this image of Pop as always being on the up-and-up. A guy in a white hat, you know? But I guess I never really knew him. We started to communicate once the Air Force transferred me to L.A., but there was so much ground to cover between us, and so little time. . . ." He trailed off.

"And now it's too late," Linda finished for him.

Gold frowned, angry and frustrated. "I can't help thinking about all that wasted time when I was growing up and could have gotten to know my father. What the hell use is hindsight when we can't go back to amend our mistakes?"

Linda kissed him. "Sometimes you can."

CHAPTER 4

(One)

Gold Aviation and Transport
Burbank, California
12 February, 1974

Don Harrison was seated at the head of the table in the empty executive conference room. The room was windowless and darkly paneled, illuminated by brass wall sconces and ceiling fixtures with green glass shades, and dominated by the massive, rectangular mahogany conference table surrounded by leather chairs. The conference room had always reminded Harrison of the interior of the New York Public Library. Herman Gold had favored this men's-club look with lots of brass, dark wood, and antiques. Harrison preferred a lighter touch, and eventually intended to have the conference room redecorated, but today he had more important matters on his mind.

The door opened, and Steve Gold entered the room with a thick stack of folders under his arm. Harrison and Steve chaired this weekly meeting of department heads and project managers scheduled to begin in twenty minutes, and Harrison felt the lengthy meeting progressed more smoothly when he and Steve could take a few minutes beforehand to set the agenda.

"Good morning." Steve settled into the chair at the opposite end of the table.

Harrison glowered. "Why do you always choose to sit down there?"

Steve glanced up from shuffling papers. "Pardon?"

"Why don't you sit beside me for once?" Harrison said irritably. "Say, here on my right?"

"Because I'm not your right-hand man," Steve replied agreeably. "I'm your partner."

"But it would look better to the others if we weren't facing each other like opposing forces."

"The others care more about how we act together than where we sit," Steve countered, lighting a cigarette.

Harrison shook his head. "I still say it speaks volumes the way you insist upon sitting down there, like . . ." He thought about it. ". . . like an opposing king on a chessboard."

"Why think of it that way?" Steve shrugged. "Why not think of us as, say, a pair of aircraft engines? You're on the starboard wing and I'm on the port wing, simple as that. We're not opposing one another, we're working in tandem." He winked at Harrison. "At least, that's the way I see it. Now, can we get on with this?" He glanced at his watch. "The others are going to be here soon."

"All right," Harrison said grudgingly. He wasn't sure how much his perceptions were being tainted by his own foul mood, or if Steve was pulling his leg concerning all of that tandem-engine stuff. . . . He glanced at his agenda sheet. "What's happening with the GXF-66?"

Steve said, "Well, as you know, the Stiletto suffered a temporary setback last month—"

"Yes," Harrison cut in impatiently. "Tell me something I don't know!"

"My mistake," Steve said gently. He was gazing inquisitively at Harrison as if to ask: *What the fuck is your problem this morning?*

"Go on," Harrison said, regretting his harsh tone as he ducked the unspoken question in Steve's eyes. Harrison knew he had a bad habit of venting his anger on others when the person he was really mad at was himself.

"As I was saying," Steve continued, "I was hoping to clinch the deal directly with the Air Force, but the Department of Defense intervened, requiring us to enter the Stiletto into the interservice Lightweight Air Combat Fighter competition. My contact has since notified me that the DOD has received competing submissions from General Dynamics, Dunn-Brower, Amalgamated-Landis, Grumman, and McDonnell Douglas."

"How many of those are paper airplanes?" Harrison asked.

"I know for sure that Dunn-Brower's and Amalgamated's are paper, but the others . . . ?" Steve shrugged. "It's been no secret that the Air Force and the Navy have for some time been looking to fill their niche for a cheaper fighter. Those two branches of the military could have been funding research on any number of projects in addition to ours."

"So now everyone's thrown their hat into the ring," Harrison muttered. "Who knows what the others have up their sleeves? By allowing this to turn into a competition, GAT has lost whatever advantage it had in already being able to field a prototype," Harrison accused.

Steve smiled. "Someone's gotten up on the wrong side of the bed today," he said lightly.

Harrison glared at him a moment, and then sighed. "I suppose . . . I'm sorry. I'm not angry at you."

"For what it's worth, a little bird at the Air Force tells me they're leaning toward the Stiletto," Steve offered. "The Navy, on the other hand, is said to like something one of our competitors—I don't know which one—has cooked up."

"That's good information," Harrison said quickly, anxious to make amends to Steve for the way he'd been acting.

"All we can do now is watch and wait," Steve finished.

"All right," Harrison signed. "Now on to my baby, the Skytrain Industrie Pont 500 jetliner that GAT has agreed to market in this country." He sheepishly confessed, "The Pont 500 is the reason why I'm in such a foul mood. I'm having trouble getting a launch customer."

"I've been so busy hawking the Stiletto that I'm still not totally up to speed on the Pont," Steve said.

"The Pont 500 was originally designed to meet European

air-travel needs," Harrison explained. "But GAT's fellow members in the Skytrain consortium strongly felt that the jetliner could be positioned to satisfy the U.S. market's demands for an intermediate-size, wide-body, double-aisle aircraft that is both fuel-efficient and suitable for operation on short trips." He paused. "You see, every airline wants to own its share of glamorous jumbo jets, but the mainstay workhorse of the industry is the smaller jetliner that can profitably fly short hops."

"So what's the problem?" Steve asked. "It sounds to me like we've got just what the doctor ordered: a product ready at the right time to meet the customers' current and future needs. The airlines ought to be lining up to buy the Pont." He added pointedly, "I wish *I* had it so easy peddling the Stiletto to the military. . . ."

Harrison struggled to retain his composure, reminding himself that Steve "Caustic Loudmouth" Gold was new to this game. Sure, Harrison knew that he himself had a short fuse, but since Steve had joined GAT the guy had earned himself a reputation for having about as much diplomatic style and tact as a sledgehammer meeting a plate-glass window.

Harrison said tensely, "Selling airplanes on the commercial market is very different from selling them to the military." He sighed in frustration. "Take it from me, it's a *lot* more complicated. For one thing, in your end of the game the military funds start-up costs. For example, the Air Force has bankrolled the to-date R and D on the Stiletto."

Steve smiled. "The military has always bankrolled its suppliers because the start-up costs are so enormous."

"As they are in the commercial aviation market," Harrison replied. "But in the commercial market, the *supplier* has to absorb all of the start-up costs. Not only that, but those costs can be even higher in the commercial market due to the highly competitive nature of the game. If the military finally does decide on the Stiletto, it'll lock into GAT for a large number of units over a period of years, right? But the airlines constantly add to their fleets by buying from everybody; they don't lock into one plane or manufacturer for more than one order at a time, an order they can cancel. Accordingly, if GAT doesn't keep its commercial customers happy, some other supplier is positioned to be ready to try. That means we have to be flexible and competitive on pricing, on financing, and on modifying our airplanes to suit each customer in order to get them to sign on the dotted line, and stay signed.''

"That's something else I've never understood," Steve groused. "It seems to me the commercial suppliers have been playing patsy to the airlines for years. You oughtn't let them dictate price or demand changes in the specs at no additional cost."

Harrison smiled ruefully. "You don't understand because you've been an Air Force man all your life. Thanks to the taxpayers, the military has deep pockets, something the airlines sadly lack. The airlines survive by pinching pennies, and their most effective way to cut costs is to play one airplane supplier against the other."

"It sounds terrible." Steve frowned. "And I'm glad I'm not working your side of the street, but if it's that bad, then why the hell is GAT even in the commercial game? Maybe we ought to specialize in the military market."

"Well, the jetliner business does have its up side," Harrison said, smiling. "Sure the military market's profitable when you've got what the military wants, but things can get pretty lean when your only customer is Uncle Sam and he turns his back on you. For the sake of this discussion, let's say GAT *was* only in the military business, and the Stiletto happened to lose out in this fighter competition the DOD has going. We'd be in pretty tough shape trying to survive until the next contract competition came around."

Steve nodded. "But in the commercial aviation business, you can always go knocking on another door if one customer freezes you out."

"That's right." Harrison leaned back in his chair. "And there are also real satisfactions to be found in the design aspects of the commercial end of the business. . . ." He trailed off, fondly remembering back to the days when he could concentrate on his drafting board and let Herman Gold assume the primary worry of selling what Harrison and the rest of the design department dreamed up. "Sure, the military demands state-of-the-art technology, but so do the airlines, in their way."

"What could be more state-of-the-art than a high-performance fighter?" Steve challenged.

Harrison countered, "A jetliner designed to carry hundreds of people in comfort and safety every day over fifteen or twenty years. Meeting the commercial market's demand for reliability is every bit as challenging as meeting the military's demand for cutting-edge performance. As a matter of fact, as an engineer I can tell you that in many ways the military's challenge is the easier one to meet: The military doesn't expect to get more than a thousand or so hours of flying time out of its warbirds. We can pack all of that cutting-edge stuff into an airplane like the Stiletto because we know that the thoroughbred fighter will spend so much time in the shop being fine-tuned to function briefly but superbly in a war that hopefully will never come. If a GAT commercial jetliner were ever to suffer that much downtime, the airlines' legal departments would be on us like ugly on an ape."

"I never thought of it that way," Steve admitted. "But getting back to the Pont, why can't GAT find a launch customer?"

"There's two basic reasons," Harrison remarked. "One applies to the market in general. The other specifically to the Pont. In general, the airlines are waiting to see which supplier will come up with the most attractive financing package. Dunn-Brower has an intermediate size fuel-efficient jetliner it's trying to peddle. Boeing and some others are trying to fill the niche as well. It's no secret these various airplanes are all essentially similar to the Pont. Any one of them would fulfill the airlines' requirements. Price is the airlines' main concern at this point."

"You said there was a specific reason for the lack of sales pertaining to the Pont?"

"Yeah, right," Harrison said, feeling disgusted. "The airlines' purchasing agents have been waving the Stars and Stripes, objecting to the fact that the Pont is European." Harrison made a face. "The airlines have been asking me why they should buy foreign when there are so many 'American-built' jetliners on the table."

"Wow, that's a tough objection to overcome," Steve remarked.

"It's bullshit," Harrison dismissed it. "This has nothing to do with patriotism. All the airlines are trying to do is soften us or our competition for a price break. As I told you, the airlines like nothing better than to sit back and watch companies like GAT, Boeing, and the others undercut each other's prices to the fucking bone."

Steve looked unconvinced. "Nevertheless, the politicians, the public, and the airline industry's unions might have something to say about the notion of the airlines buying European instead of American."

That's a very perceptive comment, Harrison thought appreciatively. "That's good thinking. I'm sure you'll be pleased to know that GAT had anticipated that particular argument. The Pont may be foreign-born, but she's got a lot of America in her bloodline. GAT designed and currently builds the Pont wing, which is the most important part of the airplane, and we required that all Ponts destined for the American market undergo final assembly and quality-control testing right here in Burbank. Most important, we mitigated the European origins of the airplane by requiring that Skytrain award Rogers and Simpson the contract to design and build the Pont engine."

"That was especially smart concerning the engines," Steve said. "Rogers and Simpson is right up there with Pratt and Whitney and General Electric as one of America's premier aviation engine-building concerns. The airlines can't question Rogers and Simpson's reputation for reliability and for providing good after-sales service and an extensive spare-parts inventory."

Harrison nodded. "That reputation proved to be necessary, since the Pont has only two engines, and the airlines' engineers complained that they wanted a trijet to satisfy their own and the public's concerns about safety in the event of an engine failure." Harrison paused. "But Rogers and Simpson's reputation didn't come cheap. They didn't like the idea of designing a new engine for a foreign airplane. They'd been approached by Dunn-Brower concerning building the engines for the new D-B plane, and they were leaning that way when I prevailed upon the firm to go with Skytrain. I reminded Rogers and Simpson of their long association with GAT, and finally got them to come aboard the Pont project by underwriting their engine research-and-development costs.''

''Holy shit,'' Steve breathed. ''Engine R and D can cost almost as much as airplane R and D. No wonder you're sweating not being able to scare up a launch customer for the Pont. The only bright spot is that the Skytrain consortium is absorbing the Pont's start-up costs.''

''It might seem so, wouldn't it?'' Harrison nodded wryly. ''Trouble is, GAT is responsible for fifty percent of those costs. Our share comes to around one billion in American dollars.''

Steve looked aghast. ''We're carrying half of Skytrain's *and* Rogers and Simpson's nut? How the fuck did that happen?''

''There was precedent for the Skytrain part of the arrangement,'' Harrison said hastily. ''From the start of The GAT/Skytrain transatlantic partnership, GAT has periodically played banker to the consortium. Back in 1957, when your father originally entered into the agreement with the British aircraft firm of Stoat-Black and the French firm Aérosens Aviation to form Skytrain, it was GAT that financed the lion's share of the costs to build a first-generation short-hop jetliner for the European market.''

''That was the Pont I,'' Steve volunteered.

Harrison nodded. ''It was important to Herman Gold that GAT establish a beachhead in the European commercial market. At the time I disagreed, but in hindsight I must say I've come to see the wisdom of your father's actions. Skytrain Industrie had made GAT a lot of money, and earned the company a lot of international goodwill. Our partnership with the Europeans is going to be even more important in the future if GAT wants to be a major player in the rapidly expanding Third World market.''

''Yeah, I suppose . . . .'' Steve grinned. ''The second thing a banana republic *does do* after designing its flag is set up its airline.''

Harrison continued: ''And our partnership abroad will remain vital in the face of our own country's softening domestic economy and our industry's ever-escalating start-up costs. Finding a way to spread the burden of those crippling start-up costs is especially crucial since our own government, concerned about monopolies, has seen fit to forbid American-owned aircraft concerns to enter into partnerships with each other.''

"But all that doesn't explain why we're taking it up the ass dollars-wise concerning the Pont 500," Steve interjected.

Harrison, nodding, sagged back in his chair. "I'm afraid that I wasn't at my sharpest when I negotiated the agreement with Skytrain concerning the Pont 500. You see, your father had just suffered his second heart attack and I was feeling overwhelmed here in the office." He anxiously tried to read some reaction into Steve's poker-faced expression. "But I realize that's no excuse," he added hastily. "I totally blame myself for the unfavorable terms that GAT has ended up with."

"Hey, that's my father you're talking about," Steve said evenly. "I'd be mad at you if his illness *hadn't* upset you. Now, then, what bad terms are you referring to, besides mortgaging the farm to build the Pont, that is?"

Harrison looked down, unable to face Steve as he said, "I let the French and British structure the deal so that GAT would receive its share of revenue from the sale of the Pont in Europe on a sliding scale, a scale that is dependent on the number of airplanes sold in America. In other words, partner, we don't get back a dime unless we can sell the airplane in this country."

"Goddammit, Don!" Steve exclaimed, making Harrison flinch. "European sales of the jetliner were the only sure thing in the deal! Government ownership of most of the European airlines guaranteed Skytrain's home countries sales!"

Harrison mutely nodded, feeling like an ass. "At the time, it didn't seem like such a bad arrangement." He sighed. "The Vietnam thing was winding down, this Watergate business hadn't yet started, and who could have anticipated the Arabs' oil embargo against the West? I felt confident that with Rogers and Simpson on board, the Pont was going to be a grand success here in America." He shrugged. "But at this point, what I thought *then* is no longer important. The reality now is that GAT doesn't start to recoup until the Pont penetrates the U.S. market. The only bright spot is that at that point we *do* recoup at an accelerated schedule."

"So everything really does come down to getting a launch customer," Steve mused.

"There's more," Harrison muttered. "You might as well know it all. Skytrain wanted a British engine firm to supply the Pont with its fan power plants. I knew how essential it would be to the U.S. airlines that an American company supply the engines, so in order to get the consortium to endorse Rogers and Simpson, I had to trade off some of GAT's Third World profits on the Pont.

"Jesus," Steve groaned. "Why didn't you just put on a pair of black fishnets and *charge* people to screw you?"

"Taken by itself, it was a reasonable arrangement," Harrison said defensively. "GAT had to compensate Skytrain because the consortium had to in turn compensate the foreign and Third World airlines. Skytrain had to cover those airlines' cash outlays concerning the cost to them for the American engine spare-parts inventory they would have to carry in order to keep their Ponts airborne."

"So GAT had to *pay* Rogers and Simpson to come into the deal, and had to pay the *deal* to let Rogers and Simpson in," Steve said slowly. "All of that, in addition to GAT shouldering half the Pont's start-up costs, while putting itself at the very end of the line when payday came around. Talk about getting it coming and going . . ."

"I took a risk," Harrison admitted.

Steve burst out laughing. "Talk about understatement! You call this a *risk*? Then what's your idea of a long shot: playing Russian roulette with a fully loaded gun? You've put this company on the brink! We've got to be in hock up to our necks?"

"Okay, so I took a *large* risk." Harrison sulked, thinking that if Steve knew more about this business he'd know that it was a cutthroat game of poker that called for the guts to put everything you had on the table to back up your hand. Harrison had not been flying totally on instruments when he'd entered into this deal. Part of his strategy had been to recruit Steve into GAT, and he'd succeeded in that. The fly in the ointment, the "unk-unk" as aviation engineers called those unknown and unforeseen problems that can crop up in a design, was the unexpected move by the DOD to run a fighter competition. Harrison had been counting on an ex-Pentagon heavyweight like Steve being able to muscle the Air Force into buying the Stiletto. That influx of Air Force dollars, combined with another stock offering propelled by the afterburn of positive publicity surrounding the new military contract, was to have temporarily pulled GAT out of the red until the Pont could be successfully launched in America.

Of course, Harrison was not about to tell Steve how he had expected the ex-Air Force man to be GAT's white knight riding to the rescue. This mess the company was in was Harrison's doing, and he was not about to off-load the responsibility for it on anyone else.

Harrison said, "All I can tell you is that at the time I felt the potential reward to GAT was worth the risk. I still feel that way. If the Pont is an American success, we'll see the return on our investment, plus enjoy a sustained substantial cash flow to finance other projects. And consider the prestige. GAT will tower over its competitors. The company will have taken a giant step toward being an international aviation concern. If we can get the Pont accepted in America, it will mean—"

"Not 'if,' " Steve suddenly and firmly interrupted. "You keep saying 'if' when you ought to be saying 'when.' The existence of our company depends on us succeeding. We can't afford to voice doubt, even among ourselves. With the economy the way it is, some of our smarter people must already be wondering about their futures at GAT. If our fears concerning this deal should leak, we'd suffer a mass exodus. We can't afford that kind of talent drain. There's something Pop told me years ago: A company like GAT is only as good as the brains of the people who work for it."

Harrison, gratified, stared at Steve in admiration. "Son of a gun, every time I think I have you pegged, you surprise me."

"No wonder you've been prowling around here like a bear all this while." Steve smiled. "I thought you were mad at *me*, that maybe you were sorry you had me come into the business. . . ."

"No way," Harrison said. "You may still have a few Air Force rough edges on you, but I'm very pleased with the job you've been doing. Convincing you to join GAT was the soundest damned business decision I ever made." He shook his head. "I've just been pissed at myself, Steve. And at the way our luck has been breaking."

"Listen up," Steve demanded. "I've got something to say to you, because I think in all your worrying you've forgotten it. My father literally bet this company on nothing more substantial than a wing and a prayer any *number* of times."

"But Herman always won."

"So will we," Steve said. "Next to building airplanes, winning is what Herman Gold's sons do best."

Jesus Christ, Harrison thought. *He sounded just like his father when he said that.*

The telephone rang. Harrison went over to the antique sideboard to pick up the receiver.

(Two)

Steve Gold watched Don answer the phone, thinking ruefully of how comparatively sedate life had been in the Air Force. Don had sure as fuck made some bad mistakes concerning this Skytrain/Pont situation; hell, the whole thing was a fiasco. On the other hand, Gold realized that it was vital that GAT's position as a member in good standing in the consortium be preserved. That position would be vital in the future just as it had been vital in the past, in ways that GAT's stockholders and the general public could never imagine.

For example, it had been GAT's participation in Skytrain Industrie that had allowed Herman Gold to come to the aid of the nation of Israel prior to that country's 1967 Six-Day War. Back then, Aérosens Aviation, the French company in the Skytrain consortium, was supplying Israel with Tyran II jet fighters. The Tyran II was a good warbird, but it needed aftermarket, sophisticated combat avionics: specifically, the Vector-A radar-ranging weapons-firing system that GAT was manufacturing in a co-venture with another firm. The United States government had a foreign export restriction in place on the Vector-A when Steve Gold's old war buddy turned political lobbyist asked Steve to intercede on Israel's behalf with Herman Gold. The official U.S. government stance on the matter was that it was a nonstarter, but the CIA and the

USAF persuaded GAT to do the deal—at the company's own risk—because in exchange the Israelis had offered the Air Force a peek at a Russian-built MiG-21 the Israelis had managed to purloin from Iraq. In those days, the MiG-21 was the Russians' top-of-the-line fighter. The U.S. Air Force was drooling over the chance to check one out.

Gold remembered how much his father had wanted to help Israel. Pop, who most of his life had been something of a lapsed Jew, had seen it as a chance to get back to his roots. Pop had risked his company, breaking the law by smuggling the Vector-A's to Israel by way of France. The combat avionics systems left America hidden in GAT shipments to Skytrain Industrie.

Fortunately, the caper went smoothly, and in response the grateful Israelis made good on their offer to let the U.S. check out their stolen MiG. Not only that, but the Israelis, in appreciation for what GAT had done, required that none other than Herman Gold's fighter-pilot son be sent to do the checking. Colonel Steve Gold went to Israel, where he spent several wonderful months putting the MiG-21 through her paces.

It all worked out well for everyone. Pop got his chance to do something important for Israel, and in the process revitalized his own spirit. Israel was helped to win the Six-Day War thanks to the Vector-A's installed in their Tyran II warbirds. And GAT earned itself brownie points with an appreciative USAF that were still paying off. Just the other day, Gold's contact at the Air Force had confided to him that they were leaning toward buying the Stiletto in some part due to the good feeling toward GAT concerning the Vector A/MiG-21 trade that still existed at the highest levels of that branch of the service. The Air Force had received invaluable information on the state of Russian aviation thanks to the reports Gold had filed on the MiG-21.

And Gold himself had gotten something personally important out of the deal: his name in the Air Force's history books. It was Colonel Steven Gold's notes and evaluations on the MiG-21 that comprised one of the textbooks that every fledgling pilot studied in Fighter Training School.

All of those unexpected benefits had accrued thanks to GAT's membership in Skytrain, Gold now realized. Pop could never have smuggled the Vector-A's to Israel if he hadn't had a working relationship with Aérosens, getting that company to serve as a conduit. Who knew what other unknown benefits were waiting in the future for GAT thanks to Skytrain?

Or for the American company that replaced GAT in Skytrain Industrie if this Pont 500 situation was allowed to get out of control?

"It's my secretary on the phone," Don said, breaking through Gold's reveries. "She's got Jack Rosa on the line. Rosa is the president of TransWest, a smaller airline operating west of the Rockies. The Pont is the perfect airplane for TransWest, and the airline would be the perfect launch customer for the Pont. I've been working on Jack for months to get him to put in an order. I told my secretary to cancel our meeting with the department heads, and that I'd take Rosa's call here. I'll use the speakerphone so that you can listen in."

Gold watched Don fiddle with some buttons on the telephone console. There was some crackling as the small rectangular speakers and omnidirectional mikes built into the walls came to life, and then the secretary's voice was clearly broadcast into the conference room: "Mr. Harrison? Here's Mr. Rosa."

"Jack," Don said in conversational tones, returning to his chair.

"Hello, Don," Jack Rosa's hearty voice came booming through the wall speakers.

"Jack, how are you?" Don said.

Gold listened idly as the two men proceeded to exchange pleasantries concerning the weather, current events, and their current golf handicaps. The sound of Rosa's voice had jogged his memory. Gold remembered that he'd met Jack Rosa at the IATC trade show back in November. Rosa was short, fat, and in his late fifties, with white hair and a beard. Gold recalled thinking at the time that Jack Rosa looked like Santa Claus in cowboy boots and three-piece glen plaid.

"Don, I called to talk to you about the Pont deal."

Gold nervously lit a cigarette. Don looked at him, holding up both hands and crossing his fingers.

"I hope you've got good news for me," Don said jovially.

Gold had to give Don credit: he sounded relaxed and on top of the world about the whole thing, as if it didn't really matter one way or the other.

"Well, it's good news all right, Don, but for us, not for GAT."

Gold's heart sank. He heard Don say, "Oh? Tell me about it." Don's voice was calm, but he was leaning back in his chair and his eyes were closed, a man in pain.

"It's like this, Don," Rosa was saying. "TransWest and the other airlines have received an offer from a new outfit on the block: Agatha Holding Company."

"I don't think I've ever heard of them," Don said slowly.

"Like I said, they're new. . . ."

Rosa was sounding evasive, Gold thought. Don must have sensed Rosa's unease as well, for he smoothly changed his line of questioning.

"You said they made you an offer?" Don began. "I'm not sure I understand. They sure can't be manufacturing airplanes?"

"No, not planes," Rosa answered. "Engines. Agatha Holding contacted us representing the British engine firm of Payn-Reese in regards to our power plant choice should we go with the Pont—"

"Wait a minute, Jack," Don interrupted. "What do you mean by *choice* of engines for the Pont? You know she was designed to hang Rogers and Simpson's new fan jet?"

"Come on, Don." Gold heard Rosa's laugh hiss forth from the wall speakers. "We've both been in this game too long to be jerking each other around. You know as well as I do that most airplanes can be equipped with a choice of engines. Take Boeing's 747: it comes with a choice of GE, Pratt and Whitney, or Rolls-Royce power plants."

"But the Pont was designed for the Rogers and Simpson . . ." Don was repeating icily. Gold frowned. Don was beginning to lose his composure.

"Maybe," Rosa said noncommittally. "But the engineering representatives from Agatha Holding made quite a convincing presentation to my own engineers about how the Payn-Reese power plant could be fitted to the Pont."

"But it's all bullshit!" Don exploded. "Jack, get it through your head that GAT is licensed by Skytrain Industrie to be the exclusive supplier of the Pont in the United States. You buy it from us or you don't buy it at all, and if you buy it from us, that plane will come with Rogers and Simpson engines.''

"I look at it this way," Rosa said. "Say we decide to go with the Pont, but with the Payn-Reese engine. You know the competition that exists for you out in the marketplace. Do you mean to tell me that GAT is in a financial position to withhold the airplane from those customers who demand a change in the engine?''

Gold watched as Don opened his mouth to say something but then closed it.

"I thought not." Rosa chuckled. "Look, Don. The bottom line is that Agatha Holding has offered a superior financing package to any airline that decides to go with the Payn-Reese equipped Ponts. Agatha will attractively seller-finance the initial purchase price of the engine portion of the airplane, and also guarantee and attractively finance the after-sale service and spare-parts inventory for ten years.''

"You're going to need that guarantee," Don rallied valiantly, "if you decide to trust a British-based company to keep your planes flying.''

Jack Rosa said, "And we've got that guarantee. From Agatha Holding, an *American-based* company," he emphasized. "They're right here in L.A.—'' Rosa stopped abruptly, as if he'd belatedly realized he'd said too much.

Who are *these Agatha fuckers?* Gold wondered, savagely grinding out his cigarette in the ashtray.

"You know how damned arrogant Rogers and Simpson has been getting concerning prepayment on after-sales service and spare parts," Rosa was continuing. "The consensus among the airlines is that Rogers and Simpson has gotten too big for its britches, and that part of that is GAT's fault. For too long they've been your sole engine supplier. They need to be shaken up a little. It will do Rogers and Simpson—not to mention us airlines—a world of good to have a little competition concerning who supplies the engine for a GAT jetliner.''

And "competition" is the airlines' word for price-cutting, Gold thought, remembering what Don had just told him about the nature of the business.

"But what about all that flag-waving you and the others were doing?" Don asked weakly. "You said the only way you would buy a foreign airplane was if it came with American engines?"

"Well, now, we did say that, didn't we?" Rosa clucked. "And that brings me to the real purpose of this call. You offered us a nice enough price on the Rogers and Simpson/Pont combo, but that price is now yesterday's news in light of this new offer from Agatha Holding. There's a lot of good airplanes out there waiting to be bought. If you want us to keep considering the Pont, you're going to have to come back with a lower unit price and sweeter finance deal on the Rogers and Simpson/Pont combo, and a *drastically* lower price/financing package to make up for the bad press we'll receive if we go with the all foreign combinations of the Pont equipped with Payn-Reese engines. If you can't, or won't, it'll mean the Pont is knocked out of the running, and TransWest will have to make its selection from the other available jetliners."

"I hear you, Jack," Don said tiredly, getting to his feet and moving toward the telephone console on the sideboard. "I'll get back to you."

"Sure, Don." Rosa must have picked up on the dejection in Don's voice. The airline executive suddenly sounded oddly different as he added, "Don? It's just business, you know?"

"I'll get back to you." Don pushed the button on the console that broke the connection, and then shut off the speakerphone. "Jack's sounding guilty," Harrison said to Gold. "He knows something he's not telling us."

"You have any idea at all who Agatha Holding might be?" Gold asked.

Don shook his head. "But I'm going to find out." He picked up the telephone and rang his secretary: "Get me Otto Lane at Lane Associates."

"Who's that?" Gold asked as Don waited for the call to go through.

"They're an investigations firm based in L.A., with offices in Chicago and on Wall Street," Don explained. "They've been handling GAT's business for years—"

"What sort of business?"

"The Lane group supplies us with corporate intelligence,"

Don replied. "They're private detectives who know how to use a computer instead of a gun to discover corporate malfeasance. When GAT considers, say, advancing an airline a substantial line of credit, or is interested in taking over a smaller company, we use Otto Lane and his people to make sure we're not about to bite into a wormy apple—" Don held up his hand to Gold. "Hello, Otto? How are you? I'm fine. Listen, Otto, I need a favor, and I need it immediately. I need to know who's behind an L.A.–based outfit called Agatha Holding Company. Yes, I guess it is spelled like the woman's name . . ."

"The woman's name Agatha," Gold muttered. Something about that rang a bell . . .

"No, Otto, I'm sorry," Don was saying. "I don't have any Social Security numbers to give you. Realize I'm not asking for an in-depth report. I just want to know who runs the damn thing. Yes, I need the information immediately. Really? That quickly? That's wonderful! I'll be waiting for your call." Don hung up the phone. "He said he can get back to us with the information in just a few minutes."

"I wonder who they're going to turn out to be?" Gold mused. "The name Agatha sounds familiar to me."

"Really?" Don returned to his chair. "Well, whoever they are, they're the fucking angels of death as far as GAT is concerned. They've obviously made the same offer to the other airlines that they made to TransWest."

"Do we have any room for financial maneuvering?" Gold asked worriedly. "*Can* we do better on the price/financing deal?"

"We've got no choice, but that alone won't get us out of this jam. You see, the fact that these bastards at Agatha have muddied the waters concerning the Pont is bound to cost us orders, and some of those orders we do keep will likely require the Payn-Reese engines."

"An airline would be crazy not to specify them considering the deal Agatha is offering," Gold had to agree. "And that will further delay our break-even point."

"Delay it!" Don laughed thinly. "Hell, at this stage of the game, GAT's so far in the hole the break-even point has become largely theoretical. The break-even point moves into the next *century* if we have to pay out to Payn-Reese that portion of income that was originally going to go to recouping the R and D costs we sank into Rogers and Simpson.''

"I'm getting a headache." Gold sighed.

"I'm getting into my car and driving off a cliff," Don replied. "That way *you'll* be the one who'll have to finagle the books, deferring expenses while desperately hoping the Stiletto project comes to fruition." He paused, smiling sadly. "So, Steve? How do you like the corporate world so far? Aren't you glad you let me talk you into leaving the Air Force for this snake pit?"

Gold winked. "I'll get you for this, Harrison."

Don waved him quiet. "You'll have to stand in line. First dibs on my hide will go to the stockholders, the IRS, the—''

The telephone rang. Gold watched as Don bolted out of his chair and over to the sideboard to snatch up the receiver.

"Yes," Don said impatiently into the telephone. "Of course put him through! Hello, Otto? Yes? It is? *Who?* I'll be *damned*! Thanks, Otto. Talk to you soon. Bye."

"Well, don't keep me in suspense," Gold implored as Don hung up the telephone.

"It's Tim Campbell," Don said fiercely. "What's with this Agatha bullshit, I'd like to know? Did Campbell think we wouldn't be able to see through it?"

He wants us to know, Gold thought. "He wants us to know. Agatha was Tim's wife's name. That's why the name sounded so familiar to me. This was just Tim's little joke on us. Like a child's riddle, you know? He'd probably laugh his head off if he found out we had to call your high-powered private eye to figure it out."

"Well, I'm not laughing," Don said. "He wants to ruin this company, you know?"

"I know he had this love-hate thing going with my father for over forty years. Ever since they disbanded their partnership . . .''

"He couldn't bring GAT to its knees while your father was alive," Don muttered. "So he's trying again now."

Steve said, "Listen, Don. I want to work with you on this. Tim Campbell is one tough son of a bitch. You're going to need somebody flying on your wing—watching your back— if you intend to take him on."

"I could use the help." Don nodded. "We're way out on a limb on this one. The wind is blowing and the bough is starting to break."

Steve nodded grimly. "And old 'Uncle Tim' is the tree surgeon."

CHAPTER 5

(One)

Agatha Holding Company
BADCO Towers
Los Angeles, California
4 March, 1974

Tim Campbell's huge corner office was on the fiftieth floor, with sky-blue carpeting and walls of translucent frosted glass framing dramatic, panoramic views of downtown L.A. There were no file cabinets or bookcases in this office, and minimal furniture: just a set of sleek chrome-and-leather armchairs arranged in front of Campbell's long desk with its gracefully carved redwood pedestal and thick glass top. There were no folders or papers on the desk. Not even a pen. Just photographs of Campbell's wife, his children and grandchildren, and a large, sophisticated telephone console. The telephone was Campbell's weapon of choice—with a phone he could move mountains—but the phone was it. Campbell had other offices scattered around the country and the world, and they were all just as Spartan. At one point in his life Campbell had coveted *things,* the pricier the better, but not anymore. Anyway, Campbell's spiritual adviser had stressed the importance of lack of clutter as well as transcendental meditation if Campbell wanted to lower his blood pressure without resorting to medication.

Campbell didn't believe in pill popping, and he didn't believe in doctors. He believed in mind over matter. Thought into action. "Will to power," as that kraut Nietzsche put it. Campbell thought about Nietzsche a lot, just like he thought a lot about that other kraut son of a bitch who'd so influenced his life: Herman Gold.

Campbell was seated behind his desk in his big leather swivel chair. He was wearing a green silk turtleneck and a tan gabardine suit. He should have been meditating on his mantra, but instead he contemplated an imminent, sublime victory. Thanks to Campbell, Gold Aviation and Transport was about to join its founder in the hereafter, or at the very least, became a crippled shadow of its former self.

Campbell smiled in anticipation of this crowning achievement in a life that had been dedicated to the art of coming from behind in order to even the score. . . .

Campbell was born in Providence, Rhode Island, the youngest of seven children. His father spent his days slaving away in a textile mill, and his nights getting drunk, coming home to rage and swear and beat his wife, while the children watched, cowering. It was during those nightmarish outbursts of domestic violence that young Tim Campbell, huddled in the corner of that shabby living room, learned what it was to be powerless. It was then that he swore that someday he would be the hammer, not the nail.

He ran away when he was twelve, riding the rails to Boston, where he joined a gang of older boys who found his big, dark eyes and winning smile useful in panhandling. The gang took care of him, taught him how to survive on the streets, to be a pickpocket and con artist, to take what he wanted through stealth and guile.

Once Campbell felt he'd learned all that the older boys could teach him, he ran away from them. He preferred being a loner. He rode the rails for a while, making the freight boxcars his home. He was little and fast, and knew how to hide when it suited his purposes, so he managed to stay one step ahead of the railroad-yard bulls for over a year, until the odds finally caught up with him in Tulsa, Oklahoma. The railroad cops turned him over to the Tulsa police, who didn't know what to do with him since Campbell refused to tell them where he was from: There was no way he was going back to that hellhole in Providence. In 1913, the Tulsa authorities put him in a nearby work farm run by the Protestant Church.

The work farm turned out to be Campbell's first lucky break. He could have done without the preaching, but they gave him a warm bed, clothes, three square meals a day—and an education. Campbell came to love learning, especially arithmetic. By the time he was fifteen, he'd earned his high-school diploma. He asked the supervisors if there wasn't some work he could do on the farm that would let him use his book learning as opposed to working in the fields, which he loathed. They let him teach reading and numbers to the youngest boys, who called him "Mister" and "Sir." Tim Campbell reveled in the status and respect that his cleverness won. He knew that he was on the right track, that knowledge was the way to power, to paraphrase Francis Bacon.

When he turned sixteen, the work farm arranged a job for him as an office boy at the Western Union office in Tulsa. He worked there for a year, taking night-school courses in accounting and hearing a lot about California as the new land of opportunity. When a slot opened up in the Los Angeles Western Union office, Campbell applied for it, and was transferred to L.A. Within a month of the move, Tim Campbell left Western Union, landing a job as a teller at Pacific Coast Bank.

He resumed his night-school education, intent upon earning a college degree in accounting. On his eighteenth birthday, after finishing his day at the bank, Campbell decided to treat himself to a steak dinner before accounting class. He went into a café near the school and sat at the counter, where he was served by a slim, dark-haired waitress with big blue eyes and a shy smile. It was a slow night, and she tarried to chat with him while he ate. Her name was Agatha Wilcox, and within a few years time she was to become his wife. . . .

Campbell gazed at the photograph of his wife on his desk

taken on their fiftieth wedding anniversary. Aggie had passed away two years ago.

When the United States entered World War I, Campbell was drafted but turned down as physically unfit due to a heart murmur. When Campbell was twenty, after three years at the bank, he was promoted to head teller. The increase in salary meant he and Agatha could be married, and soon they were. A little while later, Aggie became pregnant. That was a dark time for Campbell. He was ecstatic over the prospects of having a family, but money was tight. He was resigned to quitting night school and moonlighting at a second job in order to make ends meet, but Aggie wouldn't hear of it, so the family suffered through some lean years while Campbell pressed on, finally earning his bachelor's degree in accounting in 1923. That same year, the bank moved him out of his teller's cage, promoting him to junior loan officer. The new desk job was gratifying, but money was still as tight as ever, especially when the Campbells had their second child.

Time passed as Campbell cooled his heels at his desk at the Western Pacific bank headquarters in downtown L.A. Then one morning while Campbell was thinking about how lousy it was to always be a dollar short, and that it would be another three years at best before he could even hope that he might be promoted to senior loan officer, into the bank walked Herman Gold. Campbell recognized Gold immediately from his photo, which regularly appeared in the newspapers. Gold had curly red hair and a bushy mustache. He was tall and broad-shouldered, and looked on top of the world in his fancy suit and snappy fedora. Back then, Herman Gold was barely thirty years old, but he was already a somebody in L.A., thanks to his air-transport business that moved people, mail, and freight up and down the West Coast.

Knowledge is power. Junior loan officers had access to the bank's files, so Campbell made it a practice to stick around after closing in order to study up on Western Pacific's most important clientele—the real VIPs—just in case the information should ever come in handy. From having read Herman Gold's file, Campbell knew that Gold was here at the bank to see the bigwigs about getting some extensions on his considerable loans. Campbell also knew that Gold was going to be turned down, because Gold Aviation was in tough financial straits. This was no surprise to Campbell. He had seen Herman Gold's type before. Gold's first and only love was airplanes. He was an innovator, a creative entrepreneur. Dreary day-to-day details were the bane of Herman Gold's existence and always would be. Campbell was willing to wager that Herman Gold had never even balanced his personal checkbook, never mind his company's ledgers.

The bank did turn down Gold's request, and that night Campbell let Herman Gold stew in his own juices a while before telephoning him at the Gold residence, using the unlisted number that he got out of Gold's file. Campbell did some fast talking and managed to win himself a meeting with Herman Gold for the next day, in order to make his *real* pitch. . . .

"You know about airplanes, but you must put your company on a more businesslike footing," Campbell told Herman Gold on that sunny Tuesday morning in August 1925. They met in Gold's rough-hewn office, on the top floor of the Santa Monica waterfront warehouse that in those days housed the fledging company. "You and your staff have the ideas, but ideas need organization to turn them into reality," Campbell argued. "I'm suggesting that I come to work for you as CEO of your company in order to supply that organization. I can run the air-transport side of the business for you. I can straighten out your books, control your expenditures, and keep track of your billing. I can supply you the firm foundation Gold Aviation needs to reach the heavens on the wings of your revolutionary airplane designs."

Herman Gold laughed appreciatively at that last line, as Campbell had thought he would the night before when Campbell had been endlessly rehearsing this spiel.

"The first thing we do is set up a holding company for the airplane-manufacturing division and the air-transport line," Campbell continued. "We could call it Gold Aviation and Transport."

Herman laughed a second time. "GAT, huh?"

"GAT." Campbell nodded.

And the rest, as they say, was history. . . .

The first thing Campbell did after coming to work at Gold Aviation was to get the firm some much-needed interim relief from its creditors. Next, Campbell convinced Herman to take GAT public. Herman retained a 35-percent controlling interest and Campbell used his bank contacts to borrow the money to buy 3 percent. The remaining shares were offered to the general public, bringing in a little over a hundred thousand dollars.

A hundred grand, Campbell now thought, laughing to himself, looking around his office. *A hundred grand was chicken feed these days. It was less than half a year's rent for the office space here at Agatha Holding, but back in 1927 it had seemed like all the money in the world. . . .*

And back in those days, that hundred grand had been enough to get built Herman Gold's first airplane design, the G-1 Yellowjacket mail plane. The United States Post Office and the private air-transport industry ended up buying about a zillion G-1s, and that cash flow funded the other airplane designs and allowed the company to buy the original patch of Burbank desert on which it now stood.

Thanks to Tim Campbell, the rejuvenated Gold Aviation and Transport was flying high, and by then Campbell and Herman Gold had become solid friends. It turned out that Campbell's and Herman's origins were very similar. Herman Gold had been born Hermann Goldstein in Germany. An orphaned Jew, Herman had also endured a hard childhood on the streets of Berlin. During the First World War, Herman served as a fighter pilot, flying with the Red Baron and becoming an ace. After the war, Herman immigrated to America, where he'd worked as a truck mechanic and a barnstorming pilot before a dangerous stint flying booze from Mexico to California during Prohibition earned him the start-up capital to establish Gold Aviation.

Yeah, we were a lot alike, Campbell now brooded. *Too much alike . . .*

When the Depression hit, GAT, like most of the other big aviation concerns, emerged relatively unscathed. Once things began to return to normal, Campbell got Herman Gold's blessing to again restructure GAT in order to raise operating capital. Campbell split the firm into two companies with separate stock offerings. GAT remained the airplane design and manufacturing concern, while the newly severed Gold Transport changed its name to Skyworld Airline. Herman Gold kept a controlling interest in both companies, but Campbell sold all of his GAT holdings in order to buy enough Skyworld stock to be able to wrangle himself the job of president of the new airline. It was a momentous decision on Campbell's part. For years, Campbell and Herman Gold had fulfilled their dreams of being wealthy, but now, for the first time, Campbell felt that he had become Herman's equal in the business. In his own mind, Campbell thought he had moved from being Herman's employee to becoming his partner. . . .

That was when the trouble started.

On Campbell's desk, the telephone console beeped. Campbell pressed the talk button. "Yes?"

"Mr. Layten to see you," the secretary announced.

"Send him in."

The door opened and in came Turner Layten, Campbell's personal assistant at Agatha Holding. Layten was in his early fifties. He was pear-shaped, with rounded shoulders, baby-smooth jowls, small gray eyes, and black hair seeded with gray, waxed and parted on the side. He was dressed in a gray suit, white shirt, and red tie.

Still dressing like a government bureaucrat, Campbell thought as he watched Layten standing in front of his desk. *Got to get this boy to loosen up, put a little flash in his wardrobe.* . . .

"Jack Rosa just phoned to say he still hasn't heard from Don Harrison concerning the Pont," Layten began.

"That's good." Campbell gestured to his assistant to take a seat.

Layten looked perplexed as he sat down. "Sir, Mr. Rosa seemed extremely concerned that his call to Don Harrison some weeks ago may well serve to goad GAT into withdrawing its Pont jetliner from the market."

"That's bullshit," Campbell declared. "GAT ain't never withdrawn from nothing." Campbell enjoyed Layten's involuntary grimace at his use of a double negative. It was part of the fun of being as rich as Midas that you could be as crude as you wanted, scraping your nails along the blackboard of life, and folks had to take it. "GAT ain't never backed down when Herman Gold was running it," Campbell reiterated. "Don Harrison ain't about to start now."

"Yes, sir." Layten nodded. "But Jack Rosa fears that if GAT *should* withdraw, the reduced competition would automatically drive up the price of the remaining aviation companies' jetliner offerings."

"Jack Rosa ought to know better than to fret like an old lady," Campbell snorted. "He knows I've guaranteed that TransWest will come out of this smelling like a rose no matter *what* happens in the marketplace in exchange for his having made that call to GAT." Campbell frowned. "But if I'd known old Jack was going to be such a lily-liver, I would've had some other airline exec phone Harrison at GAT to give him the advance word about Agatha Holding."

"Sir, why *did* you want Don Harrison to know what we were up to?" Layten asked, looking puzzled.

Campbell laughed. "So Harrison would know who it is about to do him in! I want that boy to *see* GAT tied to the railroad track, to *see* that locomotive bearing down with *me* at the throttle, and for him to know there isn't a damned thing he can do about it."

Layten asked, "But by giving advance warning of what we intend to do, haven't we given Don Harrison time to find a way out of the predicament we've put him in?"

"How?" Campbell demanded impatiently. "How's he gonna do that, son, you tell me?" Campbell shook his head. "I swear, Turner, you were in the CIA *too long*. All that slinking around on your belly you had to do, it's no wonder your balls got rubbed clean off."

Turner Layten had turned bright red. He cleared his throat, clearly anxious to change the subject. "You've never told me, sir, why *do* you hate Herman Gold so much?"

Campbell was amused. "Why do *you* hate Steve Gold?" he asked rhetorically.

(Two)

"Why do *you* hate Steve Gold?" Mr. Campbell asked.

Turner Layten barely noticed that the man behind the desk was grinning like a wolf as Layten surrendered himself to his ever-constant, deep, and abiding hatred of Steven Gold. . . .

Layten and Gold met back in 1957, and disliked each other from the first. In those days, Steve Gold was an Air Force lieutenant colonel, a cocky maverick who thought he could have things all his own way. Layten was just as young, bright, and ambitious, but he didn't subscribe to the notion that the way to get noticed was by having a smart mouth and a swagger. Turner Layten was *proud* to be a team player.

In those days, Layten was assistant to Jack Horton, an associate deputy director at the CIA. Back then, the smart money had it that Horton was being groomed to one day assume the Agency's directorship, and Horton might well have made it, taking Layten along with him to the very top, if it hadn't been for Steve Gold's meddling in the aftermath of the Mayfly MR-1 spy-plane disaster.

The MR-1 had been Jack Horton's project from its inception. It was Horton who convinced Herman Gold at GAT to design and build the spy-plane fleet for the CIA. When it became evident that a war-hero-type Air Force fly-boy was going to be needed to front the spy-plane pilot-recruitment program, Herman Gold suggested to Horton that his son, Steve, be given the job. The Air Force was agreeable, so Jack Horton had the CIA borrow Steve, who plunged wholeheartedly into his new assignment.

In retrospect, Layten had to admit that Steve Gold did an exemplary job of convincing top-drawer, young Air Force pilots to volunteer to fly the MR-1 over the Soviet Union. Steve Gold also did a fine job of motivating those men during their training. The trouble arose once the MR-1 spy planes began making their flights. The goddamned Boy Scout in Lieutenant Colonel Gold wouldn't let the man simply walk away from a job well done. Steve Gold couldn't leave well enough alone; he had to feel *responsible* for the men he'd recruited.

In 1960, an MR-1 spy plane was shot down over Russia, its pilot captured alive by the Reds. There was a huge international diplomatic stink over the matter. The United States' official line was that the MR-1 was nothing but a meteorological research plane, but the Reds put the pilot on trial for espionage, found him guilty, and sentenced him to ten years. The CIA's position on the matter was that the pilot knew the risks when he'd signed on, that he'd been equipped with devices to take his own life to avoid being captured alive, and that if he'd chosen not to use them that was his business.

Thinking back on it, Layten still believed that the Agency's position had been sound. The CIA had just been newly installed in its Langley, Virginia, headquarters and preferred to look toward its bright future rather than the past, and Jack Horton didn't want this unfortunate spy-plane business to muck up his record. Accordingly, Horton lobbied hard on Capitol Hill that it would be in the national interest to put the incident behind the country, to let the imprisoned pilot fade away forgotten.

The politicians seemed willing to go along with the idea. Everything might have gone smashingly . . .

If it hadn't been for Steve Gold.

Lieutenant Colonel Gold got it into his head that since *he* had gotten the imprisoned ex–Air Force pilot into this mess by recruiting him, it was up to him to get the sap out of that Russian prison cell. Gold began lobbying on Capitol Hill to arrange a spy swap. When Jack Horton tried to put a lid on the idea—and on Gold—the impudent lieutenant colonel went so far as to threaten that he was willing to destroy his own career by going public concerning all the dirt he had on the spy-plane program. Horton couldn't take the chance that Gold was bluffing, so he reversed his stance and began lobbying for the pilot's release, and a spy swap to free the pilot between the United States and the Soviet Union was eventually arranged. Trouble was, all that noise Steve Gold had made inspired the Senate Intelligence Committee to investigate the MR-1 matter. Jack Horton was dragged through the mud, his career destroyed, while Layten himself suffered taint through association. Horton ended up resigning from the Agency, and Layten found his own ticket to the top abruptly canceled. Layten lost all the marvelous perks and privileges—*the power*—that came from being Jack Horton's right-hand man, and was transferred to a dead-end job in the Agency, where it was made clear to him that he was on the shelf for the duration of his career.

Layten contemplated resigning from the Agency, but he couldn't. He had nowhere to go. There was certainly no place for him in his father's prestigious law firm, nor any position at an appropriate level available to him in the private sector after the public scouring he'd endured in the press—in the *tabloids*, for heaven's sake—during the MR-1 investigation. Layten found himself ostracized from his crowd, dropped by his friends, and only tolerated by his scandalized family.

Layten remained in his dead-end job at the Agency for nine years, daily pushing papers, watching others with less talent pass him up the ladder, and every second of his life deeply cursing Steven Gold for doing this to him. It was Gold who had caused him to be plucked from the heights and buried in a windowless cubicle in Data Storage and Records.

Mr. Campbell nodded somberly. "Son, you asked me why I hate Herman Gold, and now I'm going to tell you. The bad blood came about in 1933, after we'd been together seven years." Mr. Campbell thumbed his chest. "Thanks to me, GAT come out of the Depression tempered by the flames, stronger than ever and poised for even greater growth. You see, I understood that the key to the future was to expand into the vacuum that had been left by so many smaller aviation firms that had gone under during the Depression."

"But Mr. Gold refused to follow your strategy?" Layten asked.

"He refused, and we quarreled," Mr. Campbell replied. "But I always managed to win our arguments. You see, Herman was a genius and a risk taker when it came to designing and building his airplanes, but he was a timid old lady when it came to spending money on anything *but* aviation research and design. Herman didn't understand finances. He called what I did money mumbo-jumbo." Mr. Campbell's fists clenched. "Can you beat that, son? Can you imagine my hurt and insult when he said that to *me*, the man who'd saved his fucking company for him when it was about to go under?"

Layten thought back over the years to the initial planning sessions concerning the MR-1 project when he'd met Herman Gold. . . . "Yes, sir, Mr. Gold was a man who could be terribly blunt and impatient with others."

"The ornery son of a bitch called what I did mumbo-jumbo," Mr. Campbell muttered. "But that was Herman's way: What he didn't understand or didn't care about he turned his back on, dismissing it as unimportant." He smiled grimly.

"That was also Herman's Achilles' heel. His weak spot. And I used it. I set up new, separate lines of communications at Skyworld Airlines, cutting Herman out of the loop. I played it smart, son. I was always careful not to go too far, and I always made sure that there was plenty of money available for Herman to spend on new airplane designs." Mr. Campbell closed his eyes. "I seem to recall that in those days Herman was all wrapped up in his Monarch GC-1 airliner."

"Yes, sir. Back in the mid-thirties all the airplane builders were scrambling to come up with the replacement for the Ford 'Tin Goose' Trimotor."

"Yeah." Mr. Campbell nodded, opening his eyes. "That's right. . . . Very good, Turner."

Layten beamed. He prided himself on being a quick study. Since coming to work for Mr. Campbell, he'd been reading up on the airliner business.

Mr. Campbell said, "The final straw came when I had the chance to buy out a small midwestern air-cargo outfit. They flew a route between Chicago and New York that I coveted: That route would have been the last piece in the puzzle to make Skyworld a coast-to-coast airline." He pounded his desktop. "That was my dream, Turner. In those days all I lived for was the chance to make Skyworld a major player, and not just for me, son. For both me *and* Herman." Mr. Campbell scowled. "But Herman said no. Said that Skyworld had the money, but he didn't want it spent in case he needed it transferred to GAT to fund unanticipated R and D problems with that fucking Monarch GC-1." Mr. Campbell's voice rose. "Herman said that Skyworld would *always* come second to Gold Aviation, because that's the way *he* wanted it. That they were both *his* companies and that I better get that straight in my head!"

"Yes, sir, I understand," Layten said hurriedly, trying to placate Mr. Campbell, worried that the man would have a stroke or a heart attack, or something. The doctors had warned Mr. Campbell about his high blood pressure. . . .

"But what Herman Gold forgot was that public companies belong to their stockholders." Mr. Campbell chuckled, abruptly calming down. "Behind Herman's back I put together an investor group to buy up GAT shares, and then waged a proxy battle for control of the company. Herman and I fought hard, we fought nasty, and in the end we each came away with half a loaf. He kept GAT. I kept Skyworld.''

"So you got what you wanted," Layten heard himself blurt.

"What *I* wanted?" Mr. Campbell echoed, again becoming livid. What I. . . ? No, son! What I wanted was for the company I helped to build to remain *whole*!'' he sputtered, a white froth of spittle collecting at the corners of his trembling mouth. "All I wanted was for Herman and me to stay together as partners! Together we could have gone all the way until GAT was, was . . ." He shook his head, suddenly at a loss. ". . . until it was bigger than anything. Until GAT was *supreme*!''

Mr. Campbell paused to take a deep breath. Layten hoped the man would use the moment's respite to regain his composure.

"But Herman didn't want that." Mr. Campbell sighed. "He thought he could do it alone, or with the help of people like Teddy Quinn, and when Quinn died, Don Harrison.'' His voice hardened to steel. His eyes turned cold. "And all this time since we split up, I've been doing my damndest to see to it that Herman and his clan *don't* do it alone. I bide my time, Turner. I strike only when the odds are with me. Herman and I have had our skirmishes down through the years. Some he's won. Some I've won. But the victories on either side have never proved decisive.''

"But hopefully this one shall, Mr. Campbell," Layten said encouragingly.

"This one shall, there's no doubt about it, Turner! For me, Herman won't be dead and buried until I can wipe the monument he left for himself and his heirs off the face of the earth.'' He nodded vigorously. "Until I've destroyed or humbled GAT, the war will go on." He grinned. "But at long last, it looks as if my V-J Day is about to dawn.''

"And Steve Gold?'' Layten asked hopefully.

"When we take GAT down, Steve will go with it,'' Mr. Campbell said reassuringly. "*And GAT is going down!* Don't forget, I know Don Harrison. He was head of engineering at Amalgamated-Landis back when I outright owned that company, back before Herman stole Harrison away from me. I know how Harrison thinks: that's why I know his options are limited. He can withdraw the Pont from the market, but that's the equivalent of putting a gun to GAT's head and putting the company out of its misery once and for all. He can shave the airplane's unit price until the Pont becomes a loss leader, then dutifully supply the airplane with Payn-Reese engines when the airlines demand it, but that will still be financially devastating for GAT.''

"There is the GAT Stiletto project, sir," Layten pointed out.

Mr. Campbell waved the objection aside. "Oh, sure, GAT might be able to limp along if it wins that DOD contract, but the days of GAT reigning supreme, the era of Herman Gold, will be over. And not only that''—Mr. Campbell licked his lips—''GAT will no longer be in a position to meet its financial obligations to retain its membership in Skytrain Industrie. The Europeans will be looking for a new American partner—''

"And I'm sure Amalgamated-Landis will be the perfect replacement for GAT.'' Layten smiled.

Mr. Campbell nodded, beaming. "That's the icing on the cake. I get my revenge and in the process make a bundle. I still have a substantial stock holding in A-L—'' He snapped his fingers. "You know, Turner, *you* ought to be buying up all the A-L you can while the stock price is still low due to the news circulating that A-L doesn't have a snowball's chance in hell of winning the military lightweight fighter competition.''

"Yes, sir. I *have* been buying stock in the company,'' Layten replied. "A-L stock is going to go through the roof when the company joins Skytrain.''

Mr. Campbell gloated: "Thanks to Agatha Holding's business dealings with Payn-Reese, when the time comes we'll have laid the groundwork to pitch Amalgamated-Landis to the Europeans. I've already got those Brits at Payn-Reese kissing my ass for giving them a chance to penetrate the American market through this Pont deal.''

"And Payn-Reese has a long history of supplying aircraft engines to Stoat-Black, which is the British partner in the consortium,'' Layten elaborated. "Amalgamated is a shoe-in once GAT folds its tent and slinks away.'' Layten stood up. "Well, sir. I'll be going. I have a lot to do." He was heading for the door when Mr. Campbell stopped him.

"Turner!"

"Yes, sir?" Layten grew apprehensive when he saw Mr. Campbell's frown.

"Whatever you got to do around here today, cancel it, or postpone it, or whatever," Mr. Campbell ordered. "I want you to take the afternoon off to go shopping for clothes. Stuff with a little more pizzazz . . ."

Layten, bewildered, looked down at himself: gray suit, white shirt, gray socks, black shoes. But his tie was red. . . .

I swear to God, Turner," Mr. Campbell was muttering. "Every time you come in here I worry I've dropped dead and you're the fucking undertaker. You go see what they got that might tickle your fancy at Mister Fred's on Rodeo Drive. Or maybe try Ted Rutledge, Limited. They sell some of that tweedy shit you like. You tell 'em I sent you. No! Better yet, I'll call them and let them know you're coming. That way you'll be sure to get the same VIP treatment they give *me*."

"Thank you, sir," Layten murmured, swallowing hard as he took in Mr. Campbell's Kelly-green turtleneck and his tan suit with the contrasting turquoise stitching on the lapels and pocket corners.

"And Turner?"

"Yes, sir, Mr. Campbell?"

"It's about time you cut that 'sir' and 'mister' crap. Sir is what I always had to call my father. . . ." He trailed off, looking sour. "You just call me Tim."

"Yes . . . Tim," Layten said, thrilled.

"That will be all, Turner. Git shoppin', son."

Layten left the office, shutting the door softly behind him, wondering if Mister Fred's stocked gray turtlenecks.

CHAPTER 6

(One)

In the skies near Wright-Patterson AFB
25 April, 1974

Captain Robert Greene's GXF-66 Stiletto turned a lazy corkscrew through the scattered clouds over the Ohio countryside. Greene leveled out at 45,000 feet, marveling at the Stiletto's smooth response to the controls. The new fly-by-wire computer-augmented control technology the Stiletto incorporated was definitely where it was at, and the Stiletto's cockpit design was also a joy: There were far fewer dials and displays in the Stiletto than, say, the F-12B Sun-Wolf or F-15 Eagle. The prototype's HOTAS hands on throttle and stick arrangement had more buttons and switches than an accordion, but once Greene had gotten used to them he found that he was able to operate the HOTAS arrangements instinctively, without feeling like a piano player straining to stretch his fingers across the keyboard. Even the Stiletto's pilot's chair was revolutionary. Greene was almost lying down in the cockpit—the reclining posture was supposed to aid the pilot in withstanding G force—but he still had an outstanding 360-degree view out the Stiletto's bulging teardrop canopy.

This bird was a keeper, all right, Greene thought as he did a barrel roll, watching tendrils of cloud flit past the canopy's curved expanse of Plexi. Below him was the gray-ribbon tangle of roadways leading into the urban sprawl of Dayton, ten miles southwest of Wright-Patterson Air Force Base.

The official reason for this flight was that Greene was evaluating this new GAT prototype fighter for the DOD's Lightweight Fighter competition. Of course, that was bullshit. Even if he were a test pilot, he'd have to disqualify himself from evaluating this particular scarlet and turquoise painted bird, since the prototype was built by his grandfather's company. But anyway, Greene wasn't assigned to aircraft testing. He was still locked into his assignment serving as a guinea pig for the lab coats who were perfecting the Simulator Generator System-369. During the past several months, Greene had flown more combat missions in more exotic places than Terry and the Pirates, but only on the flight simulator. Greene appreciated the fact that the lab coats insisted upon using him because he was one of the few pilots on base who was able to give their computers a proper workout, but he was nevertheless getting antsy: He belonged in the sky, but due to his present assignment he only got to take the bare minimum of check rides necessary to hold on to his fighter pilot's rating.

Greene had heard so many good things about the Stiletto from the other pilots that he'd been dying to take her up and check her out, so he'd prevailed upon Colonel Wyatt Dougan to let him take this ride. Dougan owed him a favor in return for the way Greene had been behaving himself with the lab coats.

"Ice Pick, this is Snowbird—"

The ever-present hiss in Greene's helmet was broken by Lieutenant Buzz Blaisdale's voice coming through the headset. Buzz was flying chase escort in an F-5E Tiger II.

"Ice-Pick, do you read? Over."

Greene thumbed his mike switch. "Roger, Snowbird." He looked around and spotted Buzz's camo-painted ghost-gray Tiger II off to his left, about 3,000 feet away at two-o'clock level.

"How do you like your bird, Ice Pick?" Buzz called.

"Have you flown her?" Greene asked.

"Negative."

"Well, in some ways she's a lot like your Tiger," Greene began, thinking that the F-5E Tiger II was a sexy little sports car of a fighter jet, with a needle nose and stubby, straight-edged, razor-thin wings. Greene had seen stereo receivers with more complex control panels, the Tiger's avionics were almost nil, and her twin GE turbojets could take her supersonic during afterburn only briefly and at great fuel cost. Still, the little Tiger II was an absolute ball to fly, and in the hands of a competent pilot could tie knots around larger, more powerful and sophisticated airplanes. If, say, the F-15 was a majestic and powerful S-class Mercedes of the sky, than the Tiger II was the airborne version of a ragtop, bug-eyed Triumph TR-2: two very different and very unequal machines, but each affording its own pleasures and advantages.

"Yeah, Snowbird," Greene continued. "This GXF is a lot like the Tiger, but with none of that bird's limitations. She's definitely a knife fighter, but with enough electronics to get the job done long-distance if need be. I can't swear to it now since this prototype is unarmed, but her eventual air-combat maneuverability should be outstanding."

"It might be too much to hope for," Buzz replied. "But maybe the big shots are ready to come back to the KISS principal in fighter technology."

Greene smiled. KISS was the acronym for Keep It Simple, Stupid. Like most fighter jocks, he and Buzz believed that what the Air Force needed were not multicrew, black-box-laden dodo birds masquerading as fighters, but stripped-down birds of prey that would allow the pilot to see the enemy, kill him, and get away.

Birds like the Stiletto, for example, Greene thought with pleasure as he tooled the prototype into a vertical reverse, flying straight up until all forward speed was lost and the jet was in danger of stalling, and then ruddering the bird around into a sharp dive, regaining speed as he plummeted toward the earth.

Atta boy, Grandpa, you did good, Greene smiled to himself as he pulled out of the dive, resuming steady flight. *This is how they ought to be built.*

The Stiletto had remained controllable throughout the low-speed phases of the vertical reverse, passing the difficult maneuver with flying colors. Grandpa had definitely known what he was doing when he stitched this one together. It made Greene feel good inside to think that at the very end of Herman Gold's career the old man had returned to the fold by building an airplane any fighter jock would feel proud to fly.

Greene's headset crackled. "It looks like you had no trouble in that stall turn," Buzz remarked.

"None at all," Greene replied. "A baby could have done it. This is the first bird I've flown—besides the Tiger II—that can execute a vertical reverse without threatening to fall out of the sky. She's really something, Buzz. This bird can do anything your Tiger can do, and do it better."

"You sure about that?" Buzz drawled.

Greene smiled. His friend was sounding playful.

"Consider the simplicity of my Tiger II," Buzz continued. "She's got just enough juice and agility to make for a steady gun platform for Sidewinders and twin 20MM cannons." He paused. "Which, if this airplane of mine happened to have any, would be drilling your ass at this very moment, since I am locked onto your six o'clock."

Greene checked his six and saw Buzz sitting on his tail. "Locks are made to be picked, Snowbird."

"This lock is burglar-proof."

"Do I hear a challenge, Lieutenant?"

"What you hear is the truth, Captain." Buzz laughed. I've got you where I want you."

"That'll be the day." Greene zoomed up and away, thinking Buzz would back off, but instead, the nimble little Tiger II went to afterburn, rising up on twin fiery-orange cones and rolling over as it duplicated the Stiletto's climb, so that the two jets were flying canopy to canopy. Greene saw Buzz giving him the finger.

Greene mashed his radio transmit button. "Well, if that's how you want to play, you Sunday driver, you. . . ." He closed the lateral separation gap between his and Buzz's parallel climbs, until the two planes were so close together that their canopies were almost touching. The two pilots flew like that for ten long seconds, mirror images of each other, exaulting in their respective control over their machines, close enough to read each other's lips if they weren't both wearing oxygen masks:

Greene offered Buzz a jaunty wave, and then abruptly pitched over into a high-G turn. Greene's G-suit squeezed him tight as he winced from the stress. He was at full afterburn, and the Stiletto was rocketing toward the earth. The altimeter was unwinding so fast it was starting to sizzle. The airspeed indicator read 350 knots, 400 knots, 500 . . .

"Son of a bitch . . ." Greene heard Buzz wince as the Tiger II followed the Stiletto over the top. "You crazy son of a bitch!" Buzz moaned as the G force flattened him.

Hey, sonny, Greene thought, as his own G stress eased off now that he was in a dive. *You want to play, you've got to pay.*

Greene looked out to see Buzz following him down on his eight o'clock. He maintained his 500-knot speed, holding top rudder, gritting his teeth, trying not to think about burying his Stiletto like her dagger namesake deep into the heart of suburban Dayton. The ground reached up for him as he waited for Buzz to draw a bit closer.

"Ice Pick, this is ground control. Are you in distress? Ice Pick! Come in . . ."

Greene ignored the radio transmission, watching and waiting as he lured in the Tiger II angled off his tail. *Just a little closer, Buzz . . .*

"Ice Pick, this is ground." The controller was starting to sound a little perturbed, Greene thought absently. "Ice Pick, what's your status?"

Now! Greene thought, continuing to ignore the radio transmission as he rolled out of his dive with wings level and then went to afterburn, pulling into a vertical. He grinned savagely, both from the renewed G-stress pain he was enduring and the satisfaction of seeing Buzz's Tiger II continuing its dive, overshooting the Stiletto.

"Ice Pick, come in!" ground control shrilly commanded, breaking into Greene's concentration. "Cease air-combat maneuvers. Do you read? You will cease ACM!"

Ground, I can't let you spoil my fun, Greene thought. *Not when I'm about to show Buzz who's top dog around here.*

Greene pressed his radio transmit button. "Ground, Ice Pick. Come again. Ground. . . ?" He purposely repeatedly clicked his talk switch to break up his transmission, mimicking radio trouble. "You're coming in broken up," he informed ground, stalling for time. "I'm not reading you."

Meanwhile, Buzz was still committed to his dive, so Greene worked stick and rudder to abruptly skid over the top of his climb, whipping the Stiletto back into an accelerating dive of its own. Now he was 3,000 feet behind and above the Tiger II, angled in on Buzz's six o'clock.

Don't look now, Lieutenant, Greene thought. *But somebody's about to send an imaginary Sidewinder up your tail pipes.*

"Ice Pick, ground. You are ordered to cease air-combat maneuvers immediately! Cease ACM and return to base, Ice Pick. Do you read? Return to base!"

Somebody down there is awfully pissed, Green thought idly. Then again, high-speed, high-risk ACM was forbidden over populated areas.

Guess, I'd better be a good boy, or somebody will sprinkle salt on my tail, Greene decided. He was about to radio an acknowledgment to ground control that he was returning to base when Buzz suddenly rolled his Tiger II's wings level, pulling a vertical climb that forced Greene to overshoot.

"Guess who's back," Buzz chuckled as he dropped down onto Greene's tail.

"Can't let you have the last word, Buzz boy," Greene radioed. He forgot his good intentions toward ground control as he rolled level, pulling into a vertical climb of his own that forced Buzz to overshoot, and then again slid his Stiletto over the top, dropping her nose back onto Buzz's six.

"Gotcha now!" Greene couldn't resist transmitting to Buzz.

"Not for long," Buzz replied, countering by repeating his own level-off/vertical climb/up-and-over three-step.

We've stalemated each other, Greene realized, the horizon spinning like an old-fashioned airplane prop as he repeated his own version of the three-step. *Neither one of us can get more than a split-second advantage on the other.*

Meanwhile, the ground was getting closer all the time as the two descending jet fighters remained locked in their vertical rolling-scissors ballet, one of the most spectacular and dangerous duets two airplanes can attempt. They were down around 10,000 feet when Greene's radio literally shook with angry force.

"This is ground control! Ice Pick! Snowbird! You two *will* cease what you're doing and return to base!"

Again, Greene ignored the transmission. He was a fighter jock, dammit! Buzz had challenged him, and he was going to win! He guessed that Buzz was feeling the same sense of urgency to decisively finish their game as Greene repeated the leveling-off/climbing maneuver. As he'd hoped, this time Buzz was ready for him. The Tiger II almost exactly followed the Stiletto's maneuver, pulling into Greene, who let his counterpart have a little taste of his six o'clock, just enough to keep Buzz interested, while remaining just out of the Tiger II's firing envelope. As the two jets banked shrieking through the sky at 7,000 feet, Greene suddenly unloaded in a full-afterburn shallow dive, leaving the less powerful, panting Tiger II far behind. Once Greene was safely out of range, he made a low turn back toward the Tiger II. Buzz was using the respite to climb, intent upon regaining the altitude necessary to maneuver in a renewed tussle. Greene angled the Stiletto's needle nose up toward the other jet's ghost-gray belly and streaked forward, intent upon a kill.

Greene was not surprised that now neither man was breaking his concentration through banter. This was a game, but one that was deadly serious. Fighter jocks played to win.

As Greene closed the gap, he pulled back on the stick to approximately equal Buzz's climbing trajectory, then popped his speed brakes to avoid overshooting the Tiger II, hopefully making Buzz think that he intended to repeat their initial parallel climb. Greene then suddenly rolled the Stiletto hard to the right, skidding across Buzz's six o'clock and out of his line of sight. *Gotcha again, old buddy*, Greene thought as he watched Buzz's Tiger II desperately barrel-roll in an attempt to find Greene.

"*Lose sight, lose the fight*," Greene thought savagely. Having experienced air combat over Vietnam, he knew how heartstopping it was during a furball mix-up to suddenly lose sight of your adversary. Just now, under the circumstances, Buzz was doing the intelligent thing by breaking off the engagement in order to come around into a more advantageous position where he would again have tallyho with

Greene. As Buzz broke right, Greene followed, dropping down into a six-o'clock low position, shadowing Buzz but still keeping out of his line of sight. The Tiger II went to afterburn as Buzz tried to beeline it out of weapons range. Greene used the Stiletto's superior speed to control the situation, carefully working the throttle to maintain optimum missile-firing range as he angled toward the Tiger II, gradually closing the lateral separation between the two warbirds until the Tiger II was enclosed in the Stiletto's firing envelope. Greene was relaxed now. It was over. He knew it, and he guessed Buzz knew it as well.

Greene's finger rested lightly on his radio transmit button as if it were his missile-firing control. When he was ten to twenty degrees off the Tiger's right wing, following his prey down toward the earth in an almost genteel dive, Greene mashed the transmit button and said, "Snowbird, I'm 3,000 feet behind you, on your six. *Wooosh!* is the sound of the heat-seeker I've just launched, old buddy."

"Taking evasive action," Buzz growled as he just about cartwheeled his doomed gray bird through the blue in his attempt to get away.

Greene watched grimly, thinking about how it felt to know that in your desperate, last-ditch attempt to lose the Sidewinder homing in, you were dissipating the precious speed and altitude essential if you were going to shake your adversary.

"Snowbird, I'm firing a second heat-seeker," Greene began.

"Save it," Buzz chuckled ruefully. "I concede I either have been or am about to be french fried—"

"When I get through with you two, you're going to *wish* you'd shot each other down!" the radio suddenly erupted in fury. "This is ground control. Colonel Dougan speaking. You two hotshots get yourself back to base. And I mean *right now*, misters!"

He sounds mad, Greene thought. He listened to Buzz transmit, "Ground, this is Snowbird. I copy. Am coming home."

Greene saw the Tiger II disengage in a split-S turn, coming around and heading back to base.

"Ground, this is Ice Pick," Greene radioed. "I'm on my way back."

As Greene brought his own bird around, flying at 5,000 feet, he noticed that along both sides of U.S. 40 leading into Dayton the traffic had stopped dead. Clumps of people were out of their cars and looking up at him.

Guess we put on quite a show, Greene thought nervously. He remembered how angry Colonel Dougan had sounded. *Well, Buzz and I had our fun. Guess now it's time to pay the piper.*

(Two)

Pilots Equipment Room
Wright-Patterson AFB

"Who do you guys think you are?" Dougan thundered.

I, for one, think we are extremely positively fucked, Greene thought in reply. He and Buzz Blaisdale were standing at attention beside the row of pea-green enameled personal-gear lockers in the equipment room. The two pilots were still in their sage-colored flight overalls, parachute harnesses, and G-Suits. Their orange-and-white-swirled flight helmets and attached oxygen masks were lying on the long bench where they'd hastily dropped them. Colonel Wyatt Dougan had been here when Greene and Buzz had entered the equipment room, coming directly from the flight line. The colonel had immediately ordered them to attention.

Out of Greene's range of vision, he could hear Buzz Blaisdale's rapid, shallow breathing. *Poor guy was probably shaking in his boots,* Greene thought, but then, his own legs were feeling a bit rubbery.

"Maybe you guys think you're the Lone Ranger and Tonto?" Dougan demanded. He was a short, broad-shouldered man in his forties, with a shaved head and a thick reddish-gray mustache. Some twenty odd years ago, before Dougan had joined the Air Force, he'd had a short career as a professional boxer during which his nose had been flattened so many times it now resembled an eagle's curved bill.

"Maybe you think you're Batman and Robin?" Dougan was scowling. He paced back and forth in front of the two pilots like an enraged tiger prodded one too many times through the bars of its cage.

Greene had never seen the colonel so angry. *Yes, we are fucked to the nth power unless I figure out something.* His mind worked furiously as he stared straight ahead at the clock on the wall, which was above the dirty towel bin, which was alongside the door that led to the showers. *Dougan's an ex–fighter jock*, Greene thought. *Early in the Vietnam War he'd served a tour of duty flying close-air support missions in an F-100 Super Sabre. Combat pilots appreciated bravado. Maybe a brazen, balls-out attitude would get him and Buzz out of this?*

What the hell, Greene pondered. *There was nothing much to lose. . . .*

"Or maybe you two guys think you're Dean Martin and Jerry Lewis?"

Greene smiled tentatively, a wisecrack on the tip of his tongue.

Dougan was on him like a shot. "Wipe that smile off your face, Captain!"

Greene wiped the smile off his face. *So much for plan A.*

Dougan roared, "I am very angry with you two! I am so angry that words fail me! Do you read me, Captain?"

"Yes, sir."

"You *sure* you read me?" Dougan was standing about an inch away from Greene, shouting into his face as he prodded Greene's chest with a finger that felt like a steel bar. "You're not having radio trouble *now*, are you, Captain?"

"No, sir."

Dougan backed off a bit. Greene watched out of the corner of his eye as the colonel shook his nasty old cauliflowered bullet of a head.

"You guys probably think what you did was funny," Dougan continued, his voice calmer but still throbbing with anger. "Well, it wasn't funny. It was stupid, thoughtless. . . ." Dougan ticked the points off on his fingers. "It needlessly jeopardized your own lives, the countless lives of the people of Dayton, and about a hundred million dollars' worth of airplanes. Tiger IIs we've got, but that GXF *you* were flying, Captain Greene, happens to be an irreplaceable prototype."

Shit, I never thought of that, Greene realized, abashed. *If anything had happened to the Stiletto prototype, the bad publicity would have most likely served to put GAT out of the lightweight-fighter competition.*

"Yeah, what you did was totally moronic on every level and in every aspect," Colonel Dougan continued. "But it sure as fuck wasn't *funny.*"

"Sir, if I could just say one thing," Buzz suddenly spoke up. "This was all my fault. I challenged the captain to a dogfight—"

"But I accepted the challenge," Greene quickly said. "It's really my fault, sir. I was the superior officer involved. The lieutenant would never have done it if I hadn't set a bad example."

"Keep quiet, both of you," Dougan ordered. "This time there's no need for you two Katzenjammer Kids to butt heads over the right to fall on the grenade." The colonel's smile was an evil, awful thing to behold. "This time there's *plenty* of grenades to go around, gentlemen."

"Sir," Greene tried again. "It was just a little fooling around that got out of hand."

"Is *that* all you think it was?" Dougan cut in, silencing Greene. "The telephones have been ringing off the hook! I've got newspaper reporters and TV news crews from all over the country crawling up my asshole to get the lowdown on you two guys! I can see tomorrow's headlines now: 'Mayor Expresses Outrage At Dogfight Over Dayton' or some such shit! The Community Relations department here on base is backhanding civilian complaints about noise pollution, traffic jams, and similar such bullshit all the time, but this time the shit is *really* gonna hit the fan, and the worst of it is that this time the complaints are *justified.* You two cowboys really put on one helluva show!"

"It *was* some fancy flying, sir," Greene suggested. "You have to give us that much?"

Dougan glared, but then his expression softened. "Yeah, Captain. It was fine flying. Nobody's arguing that. But there's a time and a place for everything." He paused, seeming to study Greene, and then glanced at Buzz. "Lieutenant, you're dismissed."

"Yes, sir," Buzz replied. "I'll just change and—"

"You're dismissed *now,* Lieutenant," Colonel Dougan

said sharply. "Go take a walk for about ten minutes, *then* you can come back and change."

"Yes, sir."

Well, at least one of us will live to fly another day, Greene thought enviously as Buzz hurried out of the equipment room.

Dougan waited until Buzz was gone, and then said, "At ease, Captain."

"Yes, sir. Thank you." Greene relaxed slightly, hopefully thinking that maybe the worst was over.

"I have no doubt that Blaisdale was telling the truth when he said he challenged you to the dogfight," the colonel announced. "But I also have no doubt that you were being honest when you said that you egged him on. I know Buzz. He's a balls-out, aggressive flier, but he's not the type to rock the boat. Challenge authority, and all that. . . ." Dougan balefully eyed Greene. "*You,* however, are the original rebel without a cause."

Greene decided that didn't really call for a reply.

"You know, Captain," Dougan continued, "after I came Stateside from Vietnam, I was assigned to General Howard Simon's staff here at Wright-Patterson. I'd just been promoted to Major. I worked under a light colonel named Steve Gold." He paused. "That's your uncle, isn't it?"

"Yes, Colonel, Steve Gold is my uncle. He's left the service, sir. He's gone into private industry."

"Yeah, I heard that." Dougan nodded. "But you know what I remember best about Steve Gold? That he was a boat rocker, a rebel, just like you've been acting lately. It wouldn't be that you somehow feel compelled to carry on in Steve's tradition now that he's left the Air Force?"

I don't want to be like Uncle Steve, Greene thought. *I used to, but that was before he sold out, teaming up with my stepfather . . .*

He said, "Begging the colonel's pardon, but you're reading too much into all this. I'm a fighter pilot, sir. That's the beginning and end of the explanation of why I did what I did. Put me in a fast mover and I do what comes naturally, just like if you take a bird dog out into the field, that animal is going to point. Simple as that."

Dougan, pondering Greene, nodded. He glanced at his wristwatch. "Look, Buzz is going to be back here any minute,

and there's something I want to discuss with you in private."
He frowned. "I've got a busy afternoon ahead of me shoveling us out of the shit pile you've dumped us in, so you meet me in my office tonight at nineteen hundred hours. Sharp."

Goddamn, Greene thought glumly. *I've got a date* . . .

He'd have to cancel. Colonel Dougan may have cooled down, but he sure as fuck didn't look like he was ready to take a raincheck.

"Yes, sir, I'll be there. Nineteen hundred. Sharp."

(Three)

That evening, Greene put on his best uniform, hoping that a spiffy appearance along with the sight of his ribbons grouped above his coat's left breast pocket beneath his silver wings might help to mitigate Colonel Dougan's ire over the morning's airborne hi-jinks. He left his quarters a half hour early to make sure he wouldn't be late for his appointment. He was already in up to his neck in shit; no way was he getting in any deeper by keeping Dougan waiting.

There wasn't much going on at the administration complex when Greene arrived there. Dougan's office was on the first floor of a long, low, cinder-block wing surrounded by a vast expanse of hot-topped parking area. Inside, the administration wing reminded Greene of a fifties-era high school in a predominantly blue-collar suburban town. As he made his way through the quiet, fluorescent-lit hallways, past the maple veneer hollow-core doors, he now and again heard the sound of a typewriter clacking, or a voice murmuring into a telephone.

There was no one on duty at the clerk's desk outside the colonel's office, so Greene knocked on the door.

"Come in," Dougan called.

Greene, unsure how to play this, stepped into the office, closed the door behind him, came smartly to attention, and said, "Captain Greene reporting as ordered, sir."

Dougan, who was wearing an open-collared duty uniform, looked amused as he leaned back in his swivel chair, eyeing

Greene. The colonel's office was small, with turquoise painted cinder-block walls, gray metal office furniture, and a window overlooking the parking lot. On a filing cabinet a small, sickly-looking yellow-green cactus plant shared space with a tiny plastic watering can. The office's walls were decorated with several posters showing jet fighters in flight; a movie poster for *Somebody Up There Likes Me*, starring Paul Newman; and a framed, yellowed, cardboard fight card. Down near the bottom of the card, a bout description read "Dukes Dougan vs. Slammer McCoy."

Colonel Dougan must have noticed Greene looking at the fight card. "I'll never forget that guy McCoy," he said. "He wasn't that big. Just a welterweight like me, but one minute into the first round and I knew I was in trouble. I gave that son of a bitch my best punch, and it hurt him. I know it did, because he spat blood. But then he just smiled at me with his fucking bloody teeth. He looked positively gleeful. . . ." Dougan trailed off, shaking his head. "Scariest thing I ever saw. I'll never fucking forget it."

"What happened, sir?" Greene asked. "Did he win?"

The colonel nodded. "Third round, they stopped the fight. My fucking nose was bleeding too much." He shrugged. "I didn't give a shit. I knew that was my last fight as soon as I saw that son of a bitch McCoy laughing off my punch." He snapped his fingers. "I just knew it like that. The thing was, I knew I couldn't take this guy, and he was a nobody! A . . . a . . ."

"A palooka?" Greene offered.

Dougan laughed. "Yeah, a palooka." He gestured to the fight card hanging on the wall. "After that fight, I knew I wasn't gonna get any closer to the top of the card than right there, and that wasn't high enough for me. Next day, I hung up my gloves and enlisted in the Air Force."

"It turned out to be a good move for you, sir."

"Yeah, it was." Dougan nodded. "But I want to talk to you about *your* next move, Captain. Pull up a chair."

As Greene sat down, he saw the colonel take a fifth of Jack Daniel's and two glasses out of his desk drawer. *This is turning out all right, after all,* Greene thought, beginning to feel relieved.

Dougan poured a couple of shots. "Got no ice, but there's some water in that watering can by the cactus . . . ?"

"I like it fine, straight up, sir." Greene waited for Dougan to take a swallow of whiskey, and then sipped at his own.

"All right, let's get old business done with," Dougan began. "I called in some favors, and managed to get you and Blaisdale out of the deep serious over that stunt you two pulled today."

"Thanks, Colonel."

"Fuck thanks," Dougan scowled. "I didn't do it only for you guys. It was my ass out on the line, as well. Don't forget, it was me that let you take that prototype up in the first place."

"God, that's right," Greene remarked. "Gee, I really am sorry, sir," he said sincerely. "I never meant for you to get in trouble. I guess that in the heat of the moment I just didn't think—"

"That's it exactly," Dougan cut him off sharply. "You didn't! You've got the classic successful fighter jock's inclination to act instinctively. That's an admirable trait to have in a dogfight, Captain, but it can really put you in the deep serious when it comes to life."

"Yes, sir," Greene said, although he wasn't really clear as to what the colonel was talking about.

"Fuck it, though," Dougan said, mellowing. "What happened today is over now as far as I'm concerned." He raised his whiskey glass. "Let's just forget about it."

Fine with me, Greene thought as he clinked glasses with the colonel.

"All right," Dougan continued gruffly. "After today I think you've about worn out your welcome around here, and the lab coats are ready to use a new pilot to shake the bugs out of their simulator's computer programs. It's time to talk about your next assignment."

"Sir, as you know, I was hoping to be assigned to a tactical fighter wing."

"I know that," Dougan said, pouring them both another drink. "And it's a possibility, but I heard about something else you might be interested in. It's kind of an unusual assignment, but one that might lead to something for you."

Greene shrugged. "I'm listening, Colonel."

"You and I were both in Vietnam," Dougan began. "My tour was over before there was much air-to-air action, but I understand you saw some?"

"Yes, sir. Mostly the F-4s flew MiGCap, but now and again us Thud drivers got the chance to tangle with gomer."

"You bag any?"

"I sparked one once, Colonel. It was a MiG-17. I managed to land some hits with my cannon before the damned gun jammed on me." Greene sighed. "Gomer got to suck down his fish sauce that day, sir."

Dougan seemed to wave the matter aside. "You were flying bombing missions anyway, son. Not MiGCap. You were lucky to get the taste you did."

Greene nodded. "I guess, sir. A little while after that incident, I was offered the chance to transition into a Phantom fighter squadron, but I declined. Those twin-seaters never appealed to me. I guess I'm kind of antisocial when it comes to flying." He smiled ruefully. "But every now and again, especially since I've been doing so much simulator ACM, I find myself thinking about my Fishbed, the one that got away. I can still see that MiG-17 framed in my gunsight. I fire. The sparks rise off his wings, but then the gun jams, and I can't do anything but watch my kill fly away home."

"That's an experience a lot of fighter pilots who served in Vietnam have had," Dougan remarked sadly, sipping at his whiskey. "And their weapons functioned."

"I'm not sure I follow you, Colonel."

"It's like this, son," Dougan explained. "During World War Two and in Korea, the U.S. military air-combat kill ratio was something on the order of ten to one: For every one of *us* the enemy got, we knocked down *ten* of them. That was good, but then along came Vietnam. We went into it full of piss and vinegar: After all, we were flying state-of-the-art airplanes, and gomer was fielding for the most part twenty-year-old subsonic MiGs. But then a funny thing happened. We found that our kill ratio dropped to two to one. That was unacceptable. We couldn't continue to trade a multimillion-dollar Phantom jet and its even more precious two-man crew for every pair of crappy old MiGs we managed to bag. Both the Air Force and the Navy knew what was wrong: crummy missile performance, crippling rules of engagement—"

"Yes, sir," Greene interrupted. "There were more places we couldn't hit the enemy than places we could."

Dougan nodded. "But the most important missing element in our bag of tricks was decent training in ACM. The brass thought the day of the dogfight was over, but they were wrong, and our guys were frying, or ending up in the Hanoi Hilton because of their mistake. The Navy did something about this. In 1969 they established a kind of fighter pilot's Ph.D. program in ACM for their F-4 Phantom crews. They called it The United States Navy Postgraduate Course in Fighter Weapons Tactics and Doctrine."

Greene nodded. "Top Gun."

Dougan smiled. "Funny nickname for that outfit, considering that the Navy's Phantoms weren't armed with guns, but Top Gun it was, and it did the trick. Before Top Gun, the Navy's kill ratio was two to one. After Top Gun, it jumped to around thirteen to one. Meanwhile, the Air Force's kill ratio actually got a little worse as the war progressed, until we initiated our own tactical training programs."

"Yes, sir." Greene vaguely nodded, sipping at his drink, wondering where this conversation was headed. "We've got our Fighter Weapons School. . . ." FWS was a course in ACM given to selected Air Force pilots who were supposed to take what they'd learned back to their squadrons.

"We've got that, and a few other programs," Dougan said. "But what we've got doesn't go far enough. The feeling is that the Air Force needs something akin to the all-encompassing experience of computerized flight-simulation scenarios, but in out in the *real* world, in *real* airplanes. To that end, something new is in the preliminary planning stages" —the colonel's eyes gleamed—"something that will make Top Gun look like a game of dodge ball in comparison."

"What is it, Colonel?" Greene asked quickly, catching a bit of the colonel's enthusiasm.

"It's not anything definite, *yet*, son. The pieces haven't all been cut out, let alone put together, at this point. I *do* know this much, the whole shebang is code-named 'Red Sky,' and a chunk of it is based on Top Gun's idea of having a core of instructor pilots flying full-time ACM against visiting groups of experienced pilots."

"Full-time ACM?" Greene gasped. "Holy shit, sir . . ."

Dougan laughed. "I thought you'd like the sound of that, Captain. Imagine, those instructors will be mock dogfighting most every day." He winked. "The way you and Lieutenant Blaisdale were doing this morning."

"It sounds like hog heaven, Colonel."

"Figured you'd say that." Dougan smiled. "Now, here's the good part. Senior officers like myself have been asked to keep an eye out for likely candidates to participate in Red Sky's eventual implementation."

"I'd like to volunteer," Greene said instantly.

Dougan nodded. "And I have it in mind to recommend you, and I'm considering Buzz Blaisdale, but that's another story. So, then, you think you'd like a piece of what I've been describing?"

"Yes, sir!"

The colonel warned, "Before you sign on the dotted line, you'd best know that there's a catch."

Greene sighed, thinking, *there always is.* "What do I have to do, Colonel?"

Dougan said it absolutely deadpan: "Join the Navy."

Greene laughed. "Come on. Seriously, sir?"

"Never more serious in my life, Captain," Dougan replied. "You want this, you're going to have to join the Navy to get it." He held up his hand to stop Greene before he could reply. "I don't mean literally, but you will be assigned aircraft-carrier duty, assuming you can hack carrier landing training."

"Sir, slow down!" Greene pleaded. He set his glass on Dougan's desk. "Either I've had too much sour mash, or something here isn't making sense."

"Okay." Dougan nodded. "I'll start from the beginning. On one hand, the Air Force wants to build on what the Navy has accomplished through Top Gun. On the other hand, the Air Force is a little touchy about perpetuating the widely held notion that the Navy flew rings around us over Vietnam."

Greene nodded. "In Vietnam, I remember I heard a lot of disillusioned griping about how the Air Force had become a bombing outfit, and that when it came to ACM the time had come to face reality and let the Navy handle it."

"It's not that we've got a lot to learn, so much as we've got a lot to *relearn*," Dougan replied. "When it came to dogfighting the Air Force used to have it, but we've lost it, and now we want to get it back. The Air Force wants to benefit from the Navy's training and ACM procedures. The question is how to do that without humiliating ourselves in the process. Toward the end of the Vietnam War, small detachments of Navy fighter pilots who'd graduated Top Gun visited Air Force fighter squadrons in Thailand to try to teach them ACM tactics. The Navy guys supposedly did their best, but our own men were simply too uptight over the notion of being tutored by squids to really profit from the experience. This time around, the Air Force thinks the tutelage process might work better if the situation is reversed: if a couple of Air Force hotshots are dropped into a squid environment. Accordingly, they and the Navy came up with Operation Indian Giver."

"Kerrist!" Greene scowled. "I'd like to meet the guy who comes up with the names for this stuff."

"That guy's ultra top secret," Dougan muttered, nodding in bemused agreement.

"Why not just send me to Top Gun School?" Greene asked.

"Senior-level personnel *will* be attending Miramar," Dougan replied. "But the Air Force wants to do it the other way, as well." He shrugged. "If you want to read between the lines, I figure that what the Air Force wants is to see how good the *average* Navy fighter pilot is."

"You mean the guy who never gets to Top Gun," Greene mused.

"Right on," Dougan said. "Anyway, as you can imagine, there's no shortage of Air Force fighter jocks who'd like to get in on the ground floor of Red Sky. I'd like to see you make the cut, because I think you've got the makings of an excellent ACM instructor. I could put you on the list of guys who'd like to take a Top Gun tour, but you'd be farther down on that sheet than I was on that fight card I've got hanging."

"I read you, Colonel," Greene said glumly.

"I think your best chance would be if you volunteered for the least popular aspect of the preliminary program."

"Which is Indian Giver." Green sighed. "Long-term bunking with the squids on a flattop."

Dougan nodded. ''The word is that there's been a deafening silence of guys volunteering for Indian Giver. It means eight months, or maybe longer, cruising on a flattop, and before that an extended period of training in order to qualify to land on a carrier.'' Dougan's expression turned sour. ''The squid fighter jocks have always lorded it over us blue-suiters on the topic of carrier landings. As far as the squids are concerned, they can do something we can't. Just between us, I agree that they've got something worthwhile to crow about. We've got some fine fighter pilots, but not a one of them has ever had to prove himself by setting down a screaming jet on a little scrap of metal moving and tilting on a big ocean.''

''I can do it, sir, given the training,'' Greene declared adamantly. ''If it can be done, I can do it.''

''I figured you were sure enough of yourself to at least give it a shot,'' Dougan smiled.

Greene asked, ''You said you were also thinking about recommending Lieutenant Blaisdale for Indian Giver?''

''Indian Giver calls for several *two-man* Air Force evaluation teams,'' Dougan acknowledged.

''Colonel, it sure would be be a lot easier to handle being surrounded by all those squids if I had my buddy along.''

''I'll take that under advisement,'' Dougan said wryly. ''Captain Greene, you now know the whole of it. Or at least as much about Red Sky as I do. So how about it? You want in or out of Indian Giver? If you're willing to volunteer, I'll start the paperwork. Assuming approval, you'll be temporarily reassigned to a paper Tactical Fighter Training Group and released to Indian Giver. First off, the Air Force will teach you how to keep detailed notes on everything you'll be learning. Next you'll be sent to Pensacola so that the squids can start checking you out. Eventually, assuming you do hack the squids' program, you'll be flying alongside our web-footed friends on training operations.'' He paused. ''But don't forget, Captain, you've got other options. I could still likely get you assigned to a traditional fighter squadron.''

Screw that, Greene thought as he briefly allowed himself the luxury of daydreaming of a time when he was somewhere happily ensconced as a Red Sky instructor, with nothing to do but fly ACM against the best and the brightest, every blessed day of his life.

"I'll go with Indian Giver, sir, assuming they'll have me." Greene laughed. "I'd do *submarine duty* if it offered me a way into Red Sky."

CHAPTER 7

(One)

New York City
8 May, 1974

Don Harrison's cab ride seemed to take forever. It was a Wednesday morning, the midtown traffic was bad, and the rumpled Checker cab was uncomfortable. But then, Harrison rarely rode in cabs. They were an endangered species in car-crazy L.A.

Lucky Los Angelenos, he thought sourly as the cab squeaked and rattled like a bucket of bolts over the infamously cratered Manhattan streets. The Checker smelled of urine. Its black leatherette upholstery was torn, with silverduct tape patching the spots where the springs poked through. The bulletproof glass driver's partition was plastered over with red-on-white stickers telling Harrison all the things he couldn't do: smoke; eat or drink; play a radio; or expect the driver to carry more than five dollars in change. What Harrison did expect the driver to be carrying was a switchblade and a hypodermic loaded with dope. The guy was unshaven, and dressed in rags. He spoke no English and would have made a good fighter pilot if only he could have toned down his driving aggressiveness.

This was the cab from hell, but Harrison would have been ornery even if he'd been lounging in a stretch limo's glove-leather interior. Harrison was on his way to the most important business meeting in his life. He knew that he was supposed to be feeling poised and aggressive, but instead he felt like throwing up, and his queasiness had nothing to do with the cab's putrid odors or its pitching and swaying due to its worn-out shocks . . .

Last week Harrison had been in his office at GAT, thinking that things couldn't get any worse concerning the Pont jetliner, when he'd received a telephone call from Roland Tolliver. Tolliver was Harrison's contact at the Aviation Venture Group, the Manhattan-based syndicate of investment banks that specialized in funding commercial-aircraft project start-ups. The AVG syndicate had worked extensively with GAT during Herman Gold's reign, and had most recently loaned the company $400 million to partially finance GAT's share of Skytrain Industrie's development costs on the Pont. Tolliver's call had concerned that $400 million loan.

Thinking back on it now, Harrison realized that on the telephone Tolliver had been deft as a surgeon. With typical understatement, Tolliver had delineated what he termed the "circulating troubling rumors" regarding the domestic air-lines' position on the Pont vis-à-vis its engine controversy, and had sounded solicitous and sympathetic as he'd discussed GAT's problems. It had almost given Harrison hope.

But then Tolliver had sunk the hook, "inviting" Harrison to New York in order to discuss the matter. At that moment in the background behind Tolliver's unctuous voice, Harrison could have sworn that he'd heard the shriek of the grinding wheel as AVG's on-staff, hooded executioner sharpened his ax. Harrison had no desire to march like a lemming to New York in order to leap off Tolliver's cliff, but he knew he had no choice: AVG could decimate GAT's credit rating at any time.

Harrison readily agreed with Tolliver that it would be best if he hopped a flight to the Big Apple in order to soothe the bankers' jitters.

Trouble was, now that Harrison was here, he still couldn't shake the notion that this was a kamikaze mission, even as he hated himself for being so pessimistic. Hadn't Herman Gold long ago taught him that if you thought like a winner it helped you to look like a winner, which more often than not *made* you a winner.

Herman, how I wish you were here now, Harrison thought as the cab pulled up in front of the midtown building where AVG had its offices. Sunday night he'd taken the red-eye to LaGuardia, and since then he'd been holed up at the Plaza Hotel, chowing down on room service and going over his notes, refining his last-ditch strategy intended to get the AVG banking syndicate back into GAT's cheerleading section.

Harrison dolefully stuffed some bills through the cab's partition and got out, clutching his briefcase. The office building was a looming, black glass rectangle that reminded Harrison of a huge version of the monolith in the movie *2001*.

That's fitting, Harrison thought, pushing his way through the revolving doors into the busy atrium lobby. *In that flick the astronauts couldn't communicate with the aliens, and I'm going to have just about as much luck communicating with these bankers.* Bankers were infamous for only wanting to lend you money when you didn't need it. Right now, Harrison guessed he felt more down and out than the bums congregated at the Fifty-ninth Street entrance to Central Park across from his hotel.

He took an express elevator up to AVG's eagles' aerie, the sensation of rapidly rising forty-three stories adding to the butterflies floating in Harrison's stomach. The elevator's doors opened on a vast expanse of pearl-gray lobby furnished with ultrasuede upholstered modular seating. One curved expanse of wall was taken up with a large, free-form metal sculpture that spelled out AVG in silvery two-foot-tall letters above a stylized jetliner. Beneath the logo sat a blond ice queen seated behind a swoopy expanse of gray Formica. Harrison identified himself to her and then waited while she telephoned Tolliver's secretary. Then, incredibly, the receptionist smiled sweetly and asked Harrison "to have a seat and wait," like he was a goddamned salesman here on a cold call.

Harrison had a seat, but he was fuming: Who did Tolliver and the rest of these AVG banditos think they were?

They're the guys who lent you 400 million bucks. They're the guys who can shut off the cash spigot and demand back what they already lent you at any time. They're the guys that hold your future in the palm of their hands.

The minutes ticked by. The receptionist's telephone warbled. She picked it up and began chatting with someone she was evidently meeting for lunch. The conversation got personal. The blonde laughed and murmured into the telephone like Harrison wasn't even there.

Think like a winner, Herman Gold's ghost whispered in Harrison's ear, and Harrison wanted to do like Herman said, but even the most substantial of ghosts had a way of disappearing in the cold hard light of judgment day.

A sleek brunette came out from behind a door and told Harrison, "Mr. Tolliver will see you now."

Harrison stood up, feeling absolutely pathetic. Whatever weak resolve he'd had coming into this situation had dissipated itself during his wait. That bastard Tolliver probably intended as much, Harrison thought. Tolliver knew his stuff, knew how to throw off a man's timing.

Snap out of it, Harrison commanded himself. *Show a little cool, for chrissakes. Herman would have been amused at Tolliver's obvious tactic.*

But Herman Gold would not have been in this position in the first place, Harrison realized. Herman had always been in control.

The secretary led Harrison into AVG's inner-sanctum maze of corridors lined with offices, finally coming to a set of teak, ornately carved double doors. "In here, sir," the secretary said, opening the double doors for him and then standing aside.

Harrison gaped. The doors had opened up on a large, glassed-in terrace. A profusion of bright flowers and lush shrubs and palms in redwood tubs created an exotic jungle upon the gray slate patio floor. There were colorful songbirds chirping in scattered cages, and a green-tinged copper fountain gurgling soothingly into its stone basin. Roland Tolliver, flanked by a pair of assistants, sat at a large, round, glass table on a wrought-iron stand, surrounded by black metal chairs with pastel striped cushions and backrests. Behind Tolliver stretched a dramatic view of Park Avenue and the Pan Am Building, glinting in the sun.

"Gentlemen, Mr. Harrison," the secretary announced.

"Donald, so good of you to come," Tolliver said softly, standing up to shake hands. "I hope you don't mind if we have our meeting here in the solarium. I find these surroundings so tranquil and soothing."

"It's a nice setup," Harrison agreed, looking around. "Where's Bambi?"

Tolliver smiled. "Kimberly," he addressed the Secretary, "would you bring us coffee?"

Harrison looked Tolliver over, thinking that it had been a while since they'd met person to person. Tolliver was a tall, thin man in his mid-fifties. He'd been with AVG for the past five years, Harrison remembered. Tolliver had a long, pinched face, brown hair worn slicked down and parted on the side, and horn-rimmed glasses that he liked to perch on the tip of his nose, so that he could peer over the tops of the tortoise frames in a kindly, country-doctor manner while he drove a stake through your heart.

"Donald, please make yourself comfortable," Tolliver invited. "Take off your jacket if you like."

Harrison considered it. It was somewhat humid in the greenhouse, and Tolliver's own suit jacket was off. Tolliver was wearing a light blue shirt with white collar and cuffs, a finely patterned maroon and gold tie, and matching suspenders that held up blue flannel trousers with knife-edge creases.

Harrison both envied and despised Tolliver's projected unstudied perfection; that insufferable coolness that stems from old money. For Harrison, who'd been the first of his hardworking blue-collar family to go to college, Tolliver was everything he aspired to but knew he could never be. It wasn't just money; Harrison *had* money; it was that noble birthright honeyed in gold that kept you cool, calm, and collected in any situation, like genetic deodorant: Harrison was dressed every bit as tastefully and expensively as Tolliver, but beneath *his* Sulka custom-tailored charcoal-gray tropical wool suit and made-to-measure Turnbull & Asser Egyptian cotton shirt he was sweating like a schoolboy called into the principal's office.

Of course, maybe even a guy like Tolliver would be nervous if he was 400 million plus interest in the hole.

"Thanks, Roland, but I'll keep my jacket on," Harrison decided, keenly aware of the sweat rings under his arms.

"Donald, allow me to introduce my associates," Tolliver said.

Harrison paid scant attention as Tolliver presented his two flunkies in Brooks Brothers blue. For one thing, Harrison was busy thinking about how he abhorred being called "Donald" as in Duck. For another, from past experience he knew that these two guys didn't count. They probably would not even speak during the meeting.

Tolliver was the big cheese. It was going to be up to Tolliver whether AVG stayed at GAT's elaborately set table, or whisked the damask out from under everything Harrison had planned, sending the fragile crystal that was Gold Aviation and Transport crashing to the floor.

They took seats around the table and chatted about non-business matters until the secretary returned with a Wedgwood coffee service on a silver tray. Harrison sipped his coffee black, waiting as Tolliver dismissed her. As she left the greenhouse, Harrison decided to take the initiative.

"Roland, I appreciate this opportunity to set your mind at ease concerning the Pont situation."

Tolliver nodded. "We've been hearing some disquieting things . . . ?" He paused expectantly.

I'm sure you have, Harrison thought. *But there's no way I'm going to blab to you about problems of which you may not yet be aware.* "Why don't you enumerate your concerns, and I'll address them one by one."

Tolliver's long, slender fingers came together to make a steeple on which he rested his chin. "We've heard that TransWest, Atlantic Air, and a host of other airlines are leaning toward choosing Payn-Reese to supply the engines for their Ponts, assuming, of course, that they even decide to *buy* Ponts. We've heard that Rogers and Simpson are very angry at GAT for tarnishing their company's reputation by involving them in this affair. We've heard that GAT's position in Skytrain is in jeopardy over this fiasco, and that Tim Campbell, who, it seems, has outfoxed you concerning the Pont matter, is now moving to replace GAT in Skytrain with Amalgamated-Landis.''

"You've heard a lot," Harrison observed evenly.

"Ah, well, you know how it is," Tolliver lightly replied. "From time to time, a little bird lands on my shoulder to whisper a something in my ear."

"Must have been a flock of pigeons that landed on your shoulder."

"They may have *landed* on my shoulder," Tolliver said, "but they've *shat* on yours, Donald."

Harrison paused as one of the assistants began whispering something in Tolliver's ear. Harrison, waiting, reminded himself to at least try to *sound* as if he was in control of the situation. Tolliver and his people were like a pack of dogs that could smell fear. If they smelled it on Harrison, they'd be tearing at his jugular in an instant.

"Yes, Donald, you were about to say?" Tolliver was peering at him from over the tops of his eyeglasses.

"GAT and AVG have been doing business together for years."

"When Herman Gold was running things," Tolliver emphasized.

What the fuck is that crack supposed to mean? Harrison forced a smile. "It's no different now than when Herman was running things. GAT has always met its loan obligations in the past, and will do so in the future."

"That you were going to meet your obligations is not the issue," Tolliver said. "You will meet them one way or the other." He paused. "The issue is how you intend to do it."

Here goes nothing—and everything, Harrison thought. He took a deep breath. "I want your syndicate to advance GAT an open-ended line of credit."

Tolliver looked astonished. "You've actually come here to ask for more money?"

Harrison nodded. "Which I intend to use to capitalize a new subsidiary. Gold Aviation and Transport Credit Corporation." Harris opened his briefcase and extracted several sheets of figures, which he handed across the table to Tolliver. "GATCC is the weapon GAT intends to use to defend itself from Tim Campbell. The plan would work this way: GAT would go to the airlines and offer each one one-hundred-percent seller financing for a term of ten years in exchange for a minimum order of twelve Ponts *with* Rogers and Simpson engines.''

Tolliver pursed his lips thoughtfully. ''What you're suggesting is that AVG allow you the financial means to fight fire with fire. You want to throw Tim Campbell's tactics right back into his face.''

''Exactly,'' Harrison said. ''The airlines buy price, not brand name. If GAT undercuts Agatha Holding's financial inducement to go with Payn-Reese Motor Works, Tim Campbell's fabled deal of the century becomes history.''

''Campbell's undercut you before,'' Tolliver said. ''What's to stop him from doing it again?''

''Two things,'' Harrison replied. ''First off, Tim's not crazy. He's too good a businessman to self-destruct by staying in a grudge-match poker game if GAT can raise the stakes too high.''

''Campbell doesn't like to lose,'' Tolliver said.

''That's the beauty part,'' Harrison replied. ''He *won't* lose. You know how the market has been reacting to this battle. You said yourself that the talk on the Street is that Amalgamated-Landis is GAT's most likely successor in Skytrain, should we be forced to withdraw from the consortium. A-L stock has gone through the roof.''

''Campbell is a major player at A-L.'' Tolliver nodded. ''He's made himself a bundle on his holdings, but I still don't see what that has to do with this vendetta he seems to have against GAT.''

''Tim's gotten where he is today by being cagey, by knowing how to play the percentages. In his own way, he plays fair. In this case, if it becomes clear to Tim that he can't bring GAT to its knees, his A-L profits will allow him to walk away with his chin held high. As much as he hates GAT, he loves money more.''

Tolliver looked unconvinced. ''You mentioned *two* things that would stop Campbell?''

''GAT is fighting this war on two fronts,'' Harrison declared. ''Right now my partner Steven Gold is in London, scheduled to meet with representatives of Payn-Reese Motor

'Works, and Stoat-Black, the British partner in the Skytrain Industrie consortium. GAT's relationship with Stoat-Black dates back to the thirties. We're confident that we can persuade that firm to use its influence to get Payn-Reese to toe the party line.''

''You're confident, all right.'' Tolliver sighed. ''That's your problem, Donald. You've always been *too* confident.''

Grin it and bear it, Harrison thought. *You can take a little dressing-down if it means you get what you need.*

''You've already put GAT in a deep financial hole,'' Tolliver said. ''Now you're asking AVG to supply you with a shovel to dig yourself in deeper.''

''You see it as a shovel, maybe,'' Harrison smiled. ''But I see it as a ladder.''

''Up onto a tightrope,'' Tolliver countered neatly. ''Where's AVG's safety net in this high-wire act?''

''Well, as GATCC's creditor, you'd hold title to the Ponts.''

Tolliver shook his head. ''That doesn't ring my chimes, Donald. We're in the money-lending business, not the airplane-repossession business. What the hell would we do with a fleet of used airplanes if we did take them back? Anyway, you already owe us 400 million plus interest. How do you intend to pay back the original loan, never mind make good on this proposed line of credit?''

''It's all there in that proposal I gave you, but basically, we'd have to come to an arrangement where AVG let the principal GAT owes ride for the time being. GAT would then meet its interest payments in two ways: Number one, we'd make AVG the direct third-party recipient of the airlines' semiannual payments on their GATCC loans.''

''The more I hear, the less I like,'' Tolliver pronounced. ''I'm disappointed in you, Donald. You're Herman Gold's protégé, but all you can come up with is a tired rehash of Tim Campbell's original plan.''

''You said it yourself,'' Harrison replied defensively. ''I intend to fight fire with fire.''

''No.'' Tolliver pointed an accusing finger. ''You're *reacting* instead of acting. It seems to me that Campbell has you on the ropes, and now you're trying to hide behind AVG's skirts.''

"That's not a fair assessement of the situation," Harrison said.

"It isn't?" Tolliver looked skeptical. "Aren't you suggesting that AVG take on exactly the same role as Tim Campbell's Agatha Holding company?"

"It's not at all the same role."

"You want this syndicate to become some sort of indirect third-party creditor to the airlines, don't you?"

"All I want is for AVG to lend money to GAT, just like the syndicate always has," Harrison stubbornly repeated, even as he realized that Tolliver was right.

"You said you'd advance the airline's loan payments directly to AVG." Tolliver paused. "What will that do to your own cash flow?"

"GAT will enjoy a huge influx of operating capital from the government, thanks to the Stiletto."

Tolliver looked sour. "There's that confidence again."

"It's not confidence, it's certainty."

"Donald, it's bad enough the way you've spent the money you've borrowed." Tolliver lectured primly. "You *certainly* shouldn't be spending money you haven't yet earned. There's no guarantee that the government will choose your fighter."

"There *is* a guarantee," Harrison declared. "The certainty born of quality. The government will buy the Stiletto because GAT's new fighter is the best there is."

Tolliver held up his hand. "Just for the moment, let's assume that GAT does *not* win the fighter competition. What then?"

Harrison shrugged. "Then we'll come to a new financial arrangement, of course. As I said at the beginning of this conversation, GAT has always met its obligations and will continue to do so in the future."

"And as I said at the beginning," Tolliver replied, "the question was not *if*, but *how*?"

"I can't operate on 'ifs and hows' that far down the road," Harrison snapped, feeling exhausted. For a while there he'd been hopeful he was persuading Tolliver to go along with his plan, but now it looked like he was losing ground.

"But it's *my* responsibility to formulate varying strategies taking into account all the ifs," Tolliver said. "To that end,

AVG had taken the liberty of working up a corporate restructuring plan for GAT.''

"What?" Harrison blurted, astonished.

Tolliver nodded to one of his assistants, who produced a manila folder from out of a briefcase and pushed it across the table toward Harrison, who eyed it like it was something dead he'd spotted on the side of the road. From all Harrison's years spent watching and listening to Herman Gold negotiate deals, he knew that it was a bad mistake to let the other side of the table take control of the agenda, but that was happening now, and Harrison didn't know what to do about it. He was fresh out of ideas.

Tolliver said, "We'll certainly take GAT's debt-restructuring proposal under advisement, and get back to you on it—"

Yeah, and the check is in the mail, Harrison thought dismally.

"—with the understanding that your proposal is predicated upon GAT being awarded the DOD's fighter contract," Tolliver was continuing. "If you should win the contract, all well and good, but if not, AVG believes that there would be no more auspicious time for GAT to, shall we say, draw in its horns."

"Roland, say what you mean," Harrison replied wearily. His throat was dry and his voice was hoarse from talking. He sipped at his coffee, but it had gone cold.

"What we've done is draw up a plan to reduce GAT's overhead by eliminating six thousand to eight thousand jobs."

Harrison was horrified. "You're talking about an almost thirty-percent reduction in the work force!"

"Of your military aviation specialists." Tolliver nodded. "On both the corporate and operating-unit level. We'd also assist you in selling off your military avionics and related subsidiaries."

"What you're suggesting is that GAT quit the military aviation market," Harrison challenged.

"What we're suggesting is a way for GAT to meet its debt obligations to AVG," Tolliver argued.

"Castrating my company is not the way to go about it, Roland."

"Why think of it that way?" Tolliver soothed, smiling. "As the saying goes, 'Small is beautiful.' "

"Not *that* small." Harrison watched Tolliver's smile fade along with his own hopes that AVG was ever going to ease his company out of this jam.

"In any event, small is better than oblivion," Tolliver observed dispassionately. "In AVG's opinion, this partial dismantling of GAT is preferable to a total dismantling through bankruptcy. But one way or another, we intend to get back our investment."

"You're not talking about money any longer," Harrison complained. "Now you're talking about a pound of flesh."

Tolliver actually looked hurt. "I suppose it's every money lender's fate to be called a Shylock at some point."

"That's who you're acting like."

Tolliver wagged a finger at Harrison. "What we're trying to do is save GAT, not kill it." He gestured to a nearby shrub. "The plants in this solarium are healthy in part because they are regularly pruned back. That's all AVG intends for GAT, a good, healthy pruning."

Harrison scowled. "Sure, starting with my company's balls. Look, Roland, GAT has a tradition to be maintained. When Herman Gold founded his company, he intended it to supply airplanes to both the civilian *and* military markets. GAT is not going to swallow your so-called restructuring without a fight."

"Oh, Donald," Tolliver looked wistful. "GAT currently has enough fights on its hands, don't you think?"

The bluster went out of Harrison. Talk about castration: AVG had GAT by the short hairs, and that was that.

Tolliver eyed Harrison from over the tops of his horn-rims. "GAT's pruning is a prerequisite if you wish AVG to extend the line of credit you're going to need to beat Tim Campbell at his own game. The choice is yours."

"It's no choice at all," Harrison said. "Don't you see, Roland, either way Tim will get what he wants: the legs chopped out from under GAT."

Tolliver said brightly. "There is your fighter contract. Perhaps it will come through for GAT." He smiled thinly. "You seemed so certain of it just a few moments ago."

"GAT is going to get that contract," Harrison vowed. "My company is going to come out of this smelling like a rose! Bigger and better than ever. When that happens, you'll be begging me to let you lend me money!" He slipped his left hand into his jacket pocket and crossed his fingers.

Tolliver looked bored. "Well, then. The sooner the DOD makes its decision, the sooner AVG can make its decision concerning your proposal to us. Meanwhile, you might as well explore our suggestions for getting GAT into fighting trim." Tolliver looked philosophical. "Just in case . . ."

"GAT's dismemberment won't be necessary. You'll see."

"We certainly shall." Tolliver stood up. His two assistants sprang to their feet. "Donald, thank you so much for coming."

(Two)

British Ministry of Aeronautical Science
Whitehall
London, England
10 May, 1974

Steve Gold considered Sir Lyndon Tobray's office to be a temple to aviation. The elegantly furnished office in the ministry building that overlooked St. James Park in the heart of London was overflowing with memorabilia representing the grand tradition of British aeronautics. Gold saw scale models and framed, detailed three-view spec sheets of British-built military aircraft from World War I to the present; from the famous Sopwith Camel biplane fighter and circa forties Fairey Swordfish open cockpit bomber, to the contemporary, extraordinarily unique STOVL Short Take Off/Vertical Landing Harrier jump jet multirole warbird.

The commercial side of British aviation was also well represented within the mahogany display cases and upon the beige walls of Sir Lyndon's office. There were models and drawings of the early, Spartan, Bristol 170 Freighter, and the luxurious Vickers Viscount turboprop of 1950, among others.

"Mr. Gold, I don't know what could be keeping the

others," Sir Lyndon apologized as he guided Gold past the collection. "Perhaps you wouldn't mind waiting a few more moments?"

"No problem." Gold smiled.

Sir Lyndon looked relieved. He was a short, somewhat frail-looking man in his early seventies, with a silvery fringe of beard and hair, and very bad teeth. He was dressed in a three-piece, black, chalk-striped suit with all four buttons of his jacket primly done up, a striped regimental tie, and a blindingly white shirt with a detachable collar.

Sir Lyndon said: "I do think it would be rather pointless to begin our discussion without a representative on hand from Payn-Reese, and someone present from Stoat-Black."

"I agree, and I don't mind waiting at all," Gold reassured Sir Lyndon. "To tell you the truth, I'm enjoying myself. I could poke around your office for days."

"It is rather a tidy little exhibition of the air, eh?" Sir Lyndon smiled proudly.

"The equal of the RAF Museum," Gold flattered.

"Ah, not quite, I'm afraid." Sir Lyndon laughed appreciatively. "Have you been to the RAF Museum, then?"

"In Hendon?" Gold nodded.

Sir Lyndon eyed him. "Hendon is rather off the beaten path. It takes an effort to get there."

"True enough." Gold smiled. "But I had a personal reason for making the pilgrimage. You see, my late brother-in-law, Captain Blaize Greene, was an Englishman and an RAF ace."

"Ah, yes, of course," Sir Lyndon said, flustered. "Lord Blaize Greene, the young undergraduate engineer who worked with Whittle at Oxford on the gas turbine project, and then took up air racing for Stoat-Black."

"And after that, Greene came to work at GAT," Gold added.

"Until the War." Sir Lyndon shook his head. "Lord Greene's death was a tragic loss, but then England lost so many of her finest young lads to the War."

"I'll never forget how important it was to Blaize that he join the RAF," Gold began, and then paused. "Sir Lyndon, by any chance did you know my father?"

"I had the pleasure of working with Herman Gold on several occasions."

Gold nodded. "Then you're no doubt aware that my father could be a very forceful man when he wanted something. Back during the first years of the war, what my father wanted was for his new son-in-law Blaize Greene to remain in America, at GAT, in order to complete his pioneering research on developing a jet engine. Blaize wanted to serve his country as an RAF fighter pilot, but my father put many obstacles, both personal and professional, in Blaize's path. Blaize had to overcome a lot to make his dream a reality." Gold smiled. "Ironically, my father forced me to confront many similar obstacles on my own way to a flying career."

Gold abruptly paused, embarrassed to be revealing so much about himself. He wasn't usually so talkative. Chalk it up to nervousness about this upcoming meeting, he decided, telling Sir Lyndon, "Anyway, although I hardly knew Blaize at the time, I now feel very close to him, or at least my memory of the man."

Sir Lyndon grew quiet. Gold took the opportunity to study a fabulous, two-foot-long cutaway model of the Hawker Siddeley D.H. 106 Comet, the world's first jetliner. In 1954, the U.S. airlines were lining up to buy the Comet, but the aviation firm of Hawker Siddeley saw its bright future turn dark after a series of mysterious midair breakups caused the Comet to be grounded. A lengthy and meticulous investigation turned up the cause of the problem, and an improved version of the Comet eventually saw service, but by then Hawker Siddeley had lost its lead advantage. The Comet never lived up to its full potential, unable to enter the American market due to the competition from American-built jetliners from Douglas, Boeing, Lockheed, and, of course, GAT's own offerings.

Let's hope the Pont's performance in the marketplace doesn't parallel that of the Comet, Gold thought. Well, that's why he was here, to *make sure* the Pont reigned supreme in America's skies by getting Payn-Reese to back off. Gold was prepared to do whatever was necessary today to make the British engine firm think twice about trying to muscle in on the Pont deal, even if Payn-Reese's play was being backed by Tim Campbell. Gold was confident he was going to be able to take control of the situation, and looked forward to reporting back to Don Harrison that this mission had turned out to be a piece of cake.

And Don could certainly do with an up, Gold thought. A couple of days ago, Don, who was still in New York, had telephoned Gold in London to give him the bad news concerning AVG's reaction to the GAT Credit Corporation proposal. On the telephone, Don had tried to put the best face on it he could, calling Roland Tolliver's reaction "mixed," but by now Gold had worked with his partner long enough to be able to read Don Harrison: There wasn't a snowball's chance in hell that AVG would advance GAT the line of credit necessary for the plan unless the Stiletto won the fighter competition, or, barring that, GAT agreed to AVG's restructuring proposal. Don was still in New York, trying to drum up some enthusiasm at AVG, and among the rest of the investment community for GAT's defensive strategy against Tim Campbell, but Gold didn't think much of Don's chances for success. The other financial underwriters would take their lead from AVG; if Tolliver and his bunch vetoed GAT's plan, that would be that.

The office intercom buzzed. Sir Lyndon went to the antique, gateleg oak dining table he used as a desk and spoke to his secretary.

"Ah, they're here at last, Mr. Gold." Sir Lyndon smiled. "Thank you for your patience."

The door opened, and in they came. *Talk about Mutt and Jeff,* Gold thought.

Lord Geoffrey Glass, Stoat-Black's chairman, was an English nobleman by way of Shakespeare: a large, rotund man in his fifties, with curly gray hair and a bushy salt-and-pepper beard. He was wearing a three-piece suit cut from scratchy-looking green tweed, and was carrying a walking stick with an ivory carved dog's head—some sort of spaniel it looked like—for a handle.

On the other hand, Quint Peters, the senior sales director for Payn-Reese Motor Works, looked like a racetrack tout. He was fortyish, and sleek as an otter in his skimpy, Italian designer sharkskin suit. Peters had thinning, slicked-back dark hair, and one of those pencil mustaches like David Niven wore.

"Sorry to have kept you," Lord Glass said after Sir Tobray had made the introductions all around and then retreated behind his desk. "Peters here wanted me to take a look at something Payn-Reese has in development." He sighed. "The traffic between here and the Works was just horrendous."

Gold nodded. Payn-Reese Motor Works was located in an industrial park twenty miles outside of London. Stoat-Black, on the other hand, had its administrative offices right here in town. Gold thought it interesting that Lord Glass felt the need to go all the way out to Payn-Reese today when he knew he had to be back in London for this meeting. What was so important to see at Payn-Reese?

Gold saw a glimmer of hope. Was Payn-Reese experiencing production difficulties concerning the engine they'd designed for the Pont and intended to sell to the U.S. airlines in lieu of the Rogers and Simpson turbofan?

"Gentlemen, please sit down," Sir Lyndon invited, gesturing toward a trio of spindly, uncomfortable-looking Sheraton armchairs arranged in a semicircle in front of his desk.

Gold instantly understood the symbolism: Sir Lyndon, by sheltering himself behind his desk, was signaling that he intended merely to play the role of referee during this furball mix-up. Gold had been halfheartedly hoping for an ally in Sir Lyndon; that the British government had realized how disastrously shortsighted Payn-Reese and S-B were being.

But it looks like this dogfight is going to be two against one after all, Gold decided, *with Sir Lyndon acting merely as an observer on the ground to keep score.*

"I'm rather surprised you felt it necessary to make this trip, Mr. Gold," Quint Peters began. He took out a cigarette case and opened it, politely holding it out to Gold, who saw that Peters's cigarettes were filter-tipped. Gold shook his head, extracted a pack of Pall Malls from his coat pocket, and lit one.

Peters was smiling. "Unless, of course, you've decided to submit to the inevitable concerning the Pont, and you've come to visit Payn-Reese in order to commission us to design an engine for some new project GAT has in mind?"

Gold had no patience for this sort of coy bullshit. He'd been a fighter pilot, trained to hit and run. The tactic had always served him well in the sky. He saw no reason to abandon the trait in the combat of negotiation.

"I'm here to keep Payn-Reese from making a big mistake," Gold told Peters. "I'm here to tell you that GAT has a long memory. You cross us now by muscling in on the Pont, you'll be looking over your shoulder for some time to come."

"Looking over our shoulder at you *behind us in success*, perhaps," Quint Peters snapped, his eyes flashing. "But as for Payn-Reese being afraid of GAT"—his thin mustache wiggled into a sneer—"I hardly think so, Mr. Gold. Like your country so recently in Indochina, GAT has become something of a paper tiger—"

"Here, now," Sir Lyndon dutifully tried to break in, but Peters was on a roll.

"Rattle your saber all you wish, Mr. Gold," the representative from Payn-Reese continued. "But don't be surprised if the other side is armed with machine guns!"

"No need for tempers to flare," Sir Lyndon interjected.

"That's all right." Gold nodded calmly. "I expected a bit of bluster from Payn-Reese. Maybe you're trying to compensate for your guilty conscience, Mr. Peters?"

"Guilty conscience over *what*?" Peters demanded. "My company was presented with a business opportunity and moved to take advantage of it. End of the matter."

"I quite agree with Peters," Lord Glass announced. He'd puffed alight a short-stemmed black briar pipe and was now sending aromatic blue clouds of smoke wafting toward Sir Lyndon's plaster-decorated ceiling. "This is just business, Mr. Gold."

"Don't hand me that cop-out!"

Lord Glass rolled his eyes. "I'd hoped that Donald Harrison might have seen fit to attend this meeting."

"Mr. Harrison is attending to business in New York," Gold said.

"Regrettable," Lord Glass mumbled from around his pipe. "Mr. Harrison was involved in the Pont project from its beginning. He *understands* the situation," he added pointedly.

Meaning I don't? Gold thought, riled. "The situation as I see it is cut-and-dry," he calmly replied.

Peters laughed sharply. "Yanks!" He shook his head.

Lord Glass said: "You see the situation wrongly, Mr. Gold, for it is neither cut nor dry. From the start of the Pont project, there was ambiguity and controversy, protracted and at times heated discussion concerning the jetliner's engines. Since the French were doing the lion's share of the work on the fuselage, and GAT was in charge of preliminary design and building the wing, the British viewpoint was that an English company be given the opportunity to design and build the engine. It was GAT that insisted that the job be given to an American firm, specifically Rogers and Simpson. At the time, GAT made several persuasive arguments to that end that there was real doubt whether Payn-Reese or any other British motor works could produce a sufficiently powerful engine within the desired time frame. Also, Aérosens was keen on the idea of involving an American engine concern that our French partner might do business with on their own at some later time. Finally, we British accepted GAT's argument that if your firm was to be able to market the Pont in America, the jetliner would have to be perceived as a more American product. Skytrain wanted the Pont jetliner to symbolize the post war reemergence of the European community as an industrial power." He shrugged, sighing. "But at GAT's behest it was reluctantly decided to blur the Pont's European origins." Lord Glass frowned at his pipe, which had gone out while he was busy talking. "Mr. Harrison would attest to as much *if* he were here."

"I don't dispute what you've said," Gold replied. "On the contrary, I would only add that in exchange for getting what it wanted, GAT allowed its consortium partners an extremely advantageous financial arrangement."

"Quite so," Lord Glass sanguinely acquiesced, stoking his pipe.

Gold shrugged. "So as I said, it's cut and dry. You're the one who said that this is just business. A deal's a deal. The question is, will Skytrain live up to it's agreement?"

"Skytrain is living up to its agreement," Lord Glass said. "GAT wanted Rogers and Simpson to build the Pont's engines. That company did. The fact that an English firm has since decided to venture into the market by offering an alternative engine has nothing whatsoever to do with Skytrain."

What a duplicitous crock of shit! Gold thought. "Lord Glass, I'm prepared to leave that questionable statement on your part unchallenged for the moment, because now I'd like to speak to you as the director of Stoat-Black rather than the British representative in Skytrain."

Gold glimpsed Peters casting a worried look at Glass. *All right,* Gold thought. *It's about time we got down to the nitty-gritty.*

"For years Payn-Reese has been the exclusive supplier of aircraft engines to Stoat-Black," Gold continued. "It's perfectly obvious that if your firm chose to do so, it could influence Payn-Reese to withdraw their proposed Pont engine. Why haven't you done that?"

"Stoat-Black has no desire to interfere in this matter," Lord Glass said. "Why should we? Stoat-Black and Payn-Reese have everything to gain and nothing to lose. The entire venture is being funded by an American company, Agatha Holding."

"You know who that is," Gold accused.

"I do indeed!" Lord Glass vigorously nodded. "What's more, since I'm aware of the history between Mr. Campbell and your late father, I know *why* Mr. Campbell has seen fit to wiggle his toes in GAT's previously pristine pond, but that holds no relevance to us. Meanwhile, if Payn-Reese should succeed in penetrating the American market, its enhanced cash flow will make it possible for the firm to develop more advanced engines that will in the future power Stoat-Black's airplanes. Also, if Payn-Reese's venture is successful, the company's enhanced status as an international engine concern will make Stoat-Black's current and future airplane offerings more desirable to the American domestic market."

"And that's why you're willing to stab GAT in the back?" Gold asked fiercely. He gestured to the display cases lining Sir Lyndon's office. "Over there are models and drawings of the Supershark World War Two pursuit plane and the GAT-SB Sea Dragon flying boat, the first two products of the early collaboration between GAT and Stoat-Black. Back then, my father and Stoat-Black's own Sir Hugh Luddy created a revolutionary mutually advantageous partnership across the sea that has since flowered into Skytrain." Gold paused. "Lord Glass, a few moments ago you spoke of tradition: Are you now prepared to turn your back on the long tradition between your company and mine?''

Lord Glass had been listening intently. Gold had high hopes that his remarks had hit home.

Lord Glass studied his pipe as he answered: ''What has gone before does mean a great deal to me, Mr. Gold. Your father was a great man.'' His eyes flicked up to pinion Gold. ''But your father is dead. Sir Hugh is dead. It is one thing to honor the past, quite another to wallow in it. I count myself among the many in my country who believe that for too long the European community has done just that: mourn past glory. If you'll forgive me for saying this, Mr. Gold, I think that these days GAT is also guilty of wallowing in the past.''

''You're tragically mistaken,'' Gold said fiercely. ''You're as wrong as Peters here was a minute ago: GAT is no paper tiger.''

Lord Glass looked embarrassed. ''My information has it that your chief creditor, AVG, has become concerned about GAT's ability to repay its outstanding loan. That GAT has requested AVG to issue the company an extensive line of credit intended to counter Tim Campbell's offer to the airlines. That AVG is unlikely to do so.''

''That's not true!'' Gold lied bravely. ''AVG and GAT are in negotiations concerning the matter, and GAT is in negotiations with another investment syndicate,'' he added forcefully, remembering what Don had said during their last telephone conversation: If Gold could bluff the English into backing down by making them *believe* that GAT had the financial resources to do battle with Tim Campbell, GAT would no longer *need* AVG to advance the line of credit. The first rule of threat management was that the bigger your gun, the less likely it was that your adversary would force you to fire a shot.

''I think you're mistaken on that, Mr. Gold,'' Lord Glass said diplomatically. ''You see, Mr. Gold, I also know that AVG is pressuring you to pursue a cost-saving corporate restructuring that would drastically reduce—perhaps even eliminate—GAT's presence in the military market.''

More lies were rising up on Gold's tongue, but he swallowed them down. Lord Glass clearly had his act together concerning GAT's financial situation. Bluffing was one thing;

trying to convince a sane man that night was day was something else entirely.

"GAT has no intention of accepting AVG's recommendations," Gold said, and left it at that.

Lord Glass shrugged. "GAT is a company on the rocks, but Skytrain desires to extend a helping hand."

"Meaning what?" Gold tried hard not to sound eager.

"I have spoken to my counterpart at Aérosens," Lord Glass began. "In exchange for GAT withdrawing its opposition to Payn-Reese in the American market, Skytrain will renegotiate the original profit-sharing agreement. GAT will be allowed to participate in the Pont's European and Third World markets' payback in order to give GAT some interim relief from its financial woes."

"You see the beauty of it, Mr. Gold," Quint Peters spoke up. "Skytrain is prepared to help shoulder GAT's financial burden by allowing you a slice of the *whole* pie, not just that portion baked in America."

Lord Glass said, "My advice to you, and to Mr. Harrison, is that you accept our offer, and live to fight another day."

Skytrain's offering a bribe to get GAT to back off, Gold thought. *Why? It's painfully obvious they're holding all the cards, so what are they afraid of?*

Gold glanced at Quint Peters. The Payn-Reese sales exec was watching him closely. Their eyes met, and Peters smiled, nodding encouragement.

Gold thought: The cash flow to GAT from the Pont's existing European and Third World sales would only serve to temporarily balance the company's books. GAT would gain only a little breathing room in which to figure out what to do next, or until the DOD did or didn't pull GAT's bacon out of the fire. GAT was dying of thirst, but all Skytrain was willing to give was a swallow of water to keep GAT alive a bit longer, while it hoped for rain.

The sad part was how much Gold wanted to accept the crummy little offer. How much he wanted to be able to telephone Don Harrison and relay even this meager scrap of positive news that a backlog of funds from the Pont's existing sales was forthcoming, and that the wolf at GAT's door might be temporarily appeased.

Lord Glass said, "Before you reply, Mr. Gold, you'd best

realize that you've heard Stoat-Black's final opinion on the matter, and Skytrain's best offer.''

Gold said, ''Your offer is not acceptable, Lord Glass. GAT will abide by its original agreement with Skytrain, and GAT expects Stoat-Black to abide by its moral responsibility to bring Payn-Reese to heel concerning this matter.''

''Why, of all the bloody gall,'' Lord Glass murmured in astonished consternation as Gold stood up and strode out of the office.

CHAPTER 8

(One)

London, the West End

"So why didn't you accept Lord Glass's offer?" Linda Forrester asked.

"Pride, I guess," Gold said, rehashing in his mind the day's earlier meeting at the Air Ministry. "They were offering me an ultimatum, and nothing gets my back up quicker than someone telling me I've got no choice in a matter."

Gold leaned toward her across their small table, so that she could hear him over the surrounding noise. They were in a pub off Piccadilly Circus. It was Friday evening, and the place was bustling. Earlier, he and Linda had left their suite at Claridge's on Brook Street to wander the West End, until they'd discovered this pub called the Winged Bull. Considering the state of things at GAT, and the tone of today's meeting at the Air Ministry, the Winged Bull had struck Gold as an appropriate place to grab a bite, so they'd gone in.

Now Gold signaled the waitress and ordered another steak-

and-kidney pie for himself. "How about you?" he asked Linda.

She shook her head, smiling. "One's my limit. But I'll have another glass of wine," she told the waitress.

"And another pint of Guinness for me." Gold said. As the waitress left, he confided to Linda, "I'm really enjoying this, especially after all those fancy, stuffy restaurants where we've been having dinner since we got here."

She laughed. "To tell you the truth, I've also been getting a little sick of prime rib carved at your table from the trolley, or the British idea of classic French cuisine."

Gold smiled at her, thinking how pretty she looked. Linda was wearing a dark-blue skirt, a tan, cashmere turtleneck, high brown boots, and the small, gold, hooped earings he'd recently given her. Gold wore cordovan oxfords, brown corduroys, a muted plaid flannel shirt, and a tan tweed jacket. Both of them had new Burberry trench coats purchased the other day on Oxford Street, where Linda had tried without success to convince Gold to buy a derby.

"I'm very glad you decided to come with me on this trip," Gold said. He reached across the table to take Linda's hand, feeling that tingle of electricity he always felt when they touched.

"I'm glad, too," Linda said, her blue eyes very large and serious. "I'm glad you asked me, and I'm glad I could find a way to arrange my schedule to come. For so many years that we've known each other, we've decided to go our separate ways. . . . That makes our present time together seem especially delicious."

"As usual, you seem to be able to say exactly what I'm feeling," Gold murmured.

She winked at him. "Words are my business."

Gold relinquished her hand as the waitress arrived with the food and their drinks.

"Steak-and-kidney pie can certainly turn a man's thoughts away from romance," Linda wryly observed.

"Can't help it," Gold confessed, digging in. "I love this stuff! Do you think you might cook this for me back home?"

"Not a chance, dear heart."

Gold poked at the crust. "I don't think they put deer heart in it."

"Steven, what did you mean when you said it was pride that kept you from accepting Skytrain's offer?"

Gold took a long pull of stout. "If I'd taken Lord Glass's handout, GAT's reputation would have been ruined. GAT would have been forever consigned to second-class citizenship in Skytrain, and in the American aviation industry for that matter."

"Why?" Linda sipped at her wine. "Skytrain was offering GAT a better profit-sharing deal than your company now enjoys. How could improving GAT's position have hurt its reputation?"

"A couple of ways," Gold said. "For one thing, in the aviation business deals are sacrosanct. The tradition stems from the early days of the business, when the sky was still a forbidding place, and aviators had to count on one another for survival."

"That's interesting," Linda said. "Can I quote you on that for my book?"

"Don't quote me, but you can use it for background."

Linda laughed. "You've been hanging around with me for too long."

"The best is yet to come."

"Have you a specific point in the future in mind, dearest?" Linda asked sweetly.

"Now that you mention it, yes, I do," Gold said, nodding. "I was thinking of later this evening, in the privacy of our bedroom." He finished his stout and signaled to the waitress for another by holding up his empty glass.

"Where are you putting all that liquid, Colonel?"

"It's all that steak-and-kidney pie I ate," Gold explained. "All those kidneys are acting like auxiliary fuel tanks, siphoning off the load. Anyway, you know what they say: Guinness is good for you." He leered. "It puts the lead in a man's pencil."

"Uh-huh." Linda smiled. "Let's return to the topic at hand, or later on this evening you shall find yourself with all that lead and no place to write."

"Okay. As I was saying, in the early days of this business

a man's word and his handshake counted for something. If after the fact you were unhappy with what you negotiated for yourself, you didn't renege and you didn't complain. You just bit the bullet and lived with the pain.''

"How macho."

"I try." Gold grinned. "Having said that, I have to admit that I still might have accepted Skytrain's offer, *if* the deal held out to me had been a better one. As it stood, GAT had little to gain beyond some financial breathing room, and a lot of prestige to lose. To use a phrase from the sixties, the whole world is watching GAT to see how the company is going to weather its first crisis without my father around to lend his hand. Herman Gold would never have countenanced GAT being thrown a bone and then slinking away from the confrontation with its tail between its legs, so neither was I."

Gold finished the last of his pie and set down his knife and fork as the waitress came with his stout. When she'd cleared away the dishes and left, Linda said, "So, to save face you've declared war on Skytrain."

"You sound disapproving."

Linda shrugged, taking a package of Salems from out of her purse. Gold held his lighter across the table to light her cigarette for her.

"I just hope that in this case pride *doesn't* come before the fall," she said, exhaling smoke. "No matter how poorly the world might have thought of you and Don if you'd capitulated to Skytrain or Tim Campbell or whomever, the world is going to think even less of you two guys if you let your company be hacked into little pieces by AVG" She paused. "Also, I wonder how wise it was of you to have so rudely stormed out of today's meeting with the Air Ministry."

"I wanted to shake them up," Gold explained. "Make them think I had an ace up my sleeve I hadn't yet played." He took a swallow of Guinness, then took out his own cigarettes and lit one.

"Granted, it was a dramatic gesture," Linda admitted. "But the English put a lot of stock in etiquette and protocol. Your brash behavior might backfire. Instead of intimidating your partners in Skytrain, you may have insulted them into being your enemies."

"Well, you might be right," Gold mused. "I'm just not sure it matters. We're in the midst of a major battle, one that GAT didn't start, I might add. We might as well sally forth with our colors flying."

"You are a wonderful man," Linda said. "And very strong . . ."

"Some parts are stronger than others. Later on, I'll let you feel my best muscle."

Linda smiled, but Gold could tell by the look in her eyes that she was onto something serious.

"Sometimes I think you might be too strong," she warned. "Maybe it has to do with the fact that you spent your life in the military, that you're a warrior, but you tend to see everything as black and white, in terms of winning and losing, in terms of combat—"

"But combat is exactly what this is about," Gold protested. "GAT is locked in mortal combat with Skytrain and Tim Campbell. And now it looks like AVG is about to gang up on us, as well."

"That's exactly what I mean," Linda said. "You're seeing what's happening as some kind of personal attack, but really, what's going on is just business as usual."

"Everybody's saying that to me." Gold frowned. "Don Harrison said it to me a couple of days ago on the telephone when he called to tell me AVG's reaction to our plan. Lord Glass said it to me today in explanation of Skytrain and Stoat-Black's betrayal, and now you."

"Because it's true."

"No, it's not true." Gold shook his head. "Maybe the peripheral players in this drama are being motivated by the almighty dollar, but don't forget who started this rock rolling downhill toward GAT."

"You mean Tim Campbell," Linda said.

Gold nodded. "Don thinks that Tim will be satisfied with making a buck off of GAT's troubles, but he doesn't know Tim like I do." He paused. "They say that 'hell hath no fury like a woman scorned.' "

"Which you'd better not forget," Linda warned playfully.

"No, ma'am." Gold smiled. "But what I was getting at was that the relationship between my father and Tim Campbell was like a marriage that went sour. Tim loved my father, then he hated him." He shook his head. "Maybe we ought to amend that saying to 'Hell hath no fury like a *business partner* scorned. . . .'"

Linda started to say something, but she was drowned out by raucous laughter washing over the room. The tumult was coming from the bar, near where a cutthroat game of darts was being played.

"It's getting late," Linda said. "And this place is getting rowdier by the second. What do you say we leave?"

"I don't know." Gold looked at his empty glass. "I'm sure they probably have a couple of barrels of Guinness left. Nobody likes a quitter."

"What a pity. You see, while you were busy jousting with Skytrain today, I took the opportunity to do some shopping. I came across some rather unique lingerie. . . ."

"On the other hand, if my pencil gets any sharper, the point's going to break off."

Gold got the check and paid it, and then helped Linda on with her coat. He grabbed his own trench coat and they left the pub.

They walked slowly arm in arm through the soft spring night. The West End theaters were letting out, and the square was crowded with traffic and pedestrians. A mist was falling, shrouding the streetlights and the statue of winged Eros in the center of the square. The theaters' neon marquees reflected against the glistening streets, turning Piccadilly into an Impressionist's whirl of color.

"When we get back to the hotel, I'll see about booking us on a flight home," Gold said as they turned up Regent Street.

Linda sighed. "You don't think there's any point to you recontacting Lord Glass?"

"None that I can think of." Gold shrugged. "I feel I've done the best I could with what amounted to a very weak hand of cards."

"Nevertheless, maybe if you spoke to him again the two of you could come to some arrangement," Linda coaxed. "After all, it's in everybody's best interest that this mess be settled peacefully."

"Not really," Gold told her. "I would have agreed with

you on that before today's meeting at the Air Ministry, but no longer. You see, Lord Glass said something very interesting to me: That Skytrain had wanted the Pont to symbolize Europe's postwar reemergence as an industrial power.''

''Meaning?''

''Meaning that Skytrain probably welcomes this opportunity to rid itself of GAT. Back when my father pitched the idea of an international consortium to S-B and Aérosens, the English and the French needed American aviation know-how, but they don't need it any longer, and now probably resent the fact that GAT still insists upon trying to run the show.''

''You're saying that the Europeans would prefer a new American partner,'' Linda mused. ''One that wasn't around when they were weak. An American company that's willing to be their equal as opposed to their leader.''

''Or to be their weak sister,'' Gold added. He sighed. ''In other words, a company like Amalgamated-Landis. ''I've gotta hand it to Tim Campbell. That old son of a bitch has really stuck it to us this time.'' He paused. ''And now that I think about it, you're probably right that I made a mistake to go stomping out of Sir Lyndon's office.''

''All you accomplished was to give Lord Glass an excuse for feeling righteous about stabbing GAT in the back,'' Linda agreed.

''Where were you when I needed you?'' Gold asked.

''You've always needed me.'' She hugged him more tightly. ''You were just too dense to realize it until now.'' They strolled on silently for a few moments, and then Linda said, ''Look, you know that I've been doing a lot of research on the aviation business for my book?''

''Yep.''

''Well, something I came across in my reading has given me an idea concerning GAT's predicament: Have you considered approaching the federal government for a bailout loan?''

Gold said, ''You must have come across the inside story concerning the loan guarantee Uncle Sam gave Lockheed back in 1971. . . .''

''Yeah,'' Linda said. ''Maybe that's an avenue GAT ought to explore. In many ways, Lockheed's situation back then parallels GAT's currently. Lockheed has a large military program just like GAT does, and back in the early seventies Lockheed was also financially overextended due to production problems with its L-1011 airliner—''

Gold stopped her. ''We're way ahead of you. Don moved to explore the likelihood of getting a federal loan guarantee to keep AVG happy directly after his meeting with Tolliver. Don pointed out to California's congressional delegation that the employee cutbacks GAT might be forced to make would prove devastating for the California economy, and Don suggested to our on-staff lobbyist in Washington that GAT's forced shut down of its military research-and-design operation would be detrimental to national security.''

''And?'' Linda asked as they turned left on Brook Street, approaching the hotel.

Gold shook his head. ''We got shot down.'' He sighed. ''Nobody questioned the validity of our arguments, but the current political situation in Washington is a lot different than what it was back in 'seventy-one.''

''Ah, shit,'' Linda cursed softly. ''You mean Watergate?''

''Yep. Our congressmen said both Houses are in no mood to take up consideration of a bailout bill, not when they're confronting the real possibility that a United States president might be impeached.'' Gold laughed thinly. ''They said there might be something they could do for us in the fall.''

''Great,'' Linda muttered. ''By then, GAT will be like Humpty-Dumpty; nobody will be able to put all the pieces back together again.'' She brightened. ''But what about that lobbyist of yours?''

''He felt—and by the way, we agreed with him—that things are currently too sensitive concerning the DOD lightweight fighter competition to go rocking the boat. Who knows what little thing might tip the scale for or against the Stiletto?''

''I see.'' Linda nodded. ''If your lobbyist goes to the DOD and starts making noises about what bad shape financially GAT is in, that might be sufficient grounds for the Stiletto to be rejected due to questions about the reliability of its supplier.''

''You got it.''

''Well, I thought my idea was a good one at the time,'' Linda said lamely.

"It was a swell idea," Gold assured her. "One that might have worked if the timing for GAT had been better."

"So what's left?"

"For me?" Gold shrugged. "To fly home, supervise the destruction of my father's dream, and then open up a model-airplane hobbyists' shop in a modest suburb of Los Angeles." He winked at her as they came up on Claridge's dignified, Victorian entrance. "Or maybe I'll let *you* support me. I could hang around the house and be your stud. . . ."

Linda said: "Well, let's get upstairs and I'll begin my job interview."

The doorman tipped his visored cap to them as they entered the hotel, crossing the elegant lobby with its gleaming black and white marble floor and its mammoth red leather armchairs invitingly arranged around the crackling hearth.

"Just a moment," Gold told Linda. "I want to see the concierge about booking our flight."

"Ah, Mr. Gold," the concierge said as Gold approached the desk. "I believe there's a message for you." He handed Gold a sheet of stationery folded in half.

"What is it?" Linda asked, coming up behind Gold as he unfolded the note.

"It's from Don. He wants me to call him at the office immediately." Gold glanced at his watch. "It'd be about one in the afternoon in L.A., right?"

Linda nodded. "What do you suppose he wants?"

He tapped the sheet of paper. "Whatever it is, this says that it's urgent. . . ."

Fifteen minutes later, they were upstairs in their suite. Gold was in the bedroom, seated in the armchair alongside the big double bed. He had his shoes off and was chain-smoking, watching the clock on the mantel above the fireplace and staring at the telephone on the nightstand, wondering how long it was going to take the hotel switchboard to put the call through.

The telephone rang.

He lunged for the receiver. "Steve Gold here!"

"Mr. Gold," the operator said. "Your call to America."

There was some clicking on the line, and then Gold heard: "Hello? Hello, Steve?"

"Yes, Don! It's me. What's up?"

"Steve, I've got great news!" Don laughed.

Out of the corner of his eye, Gold saw Linda bring him a scotch on the rocks nightcap from the wet bar in the living room. He smiled at her gratefully as she set the drink down on the nightstand, blew him a silent kiss, and then went padding off into the big, marbled, master bath adjoining the bedroom. A moment later, Gold heard the shower running.

"What's the good news, Don? Did you manage to arrange our line of credit financing, after all?"

"Better than that!" Don crowed. "We got it, partner! We won the DOD competition! The Air Force wants the Stiletto!"

Gold found himself unable to speak. *Thanks, Pop,* he thought as his eyes filled. *Thanks for saving our asses one last time. I promise you—I swear it—from here on in we'll handle things the way we ought to.*

"Steve? Are you there?" Don demanded. "Did you hear what I said?"

"Yeah," Gold responded huskily. "That's great, partner!"

"You know who we *really* have to thank for this?" Don began.

Steve smiled. "Yeah, I do, and I appreciate the fact that you realize it as well."

"From here on in, our troubles are solved," Don said. "Thanks to the Stiletto contract, we'll have the financial credibility to borrow money from AVG on our own terms! I can't wait to contact that asshole Tolliver and rub it in."

"Hold off on that," Gold said.

"Huh?"

"Hold off initiating any further negotiations with AVG."

"But why?" Don demanded.

"I've got an alternative idea." Gold heard the shower being shut off in the bathroom. He smiled. "Actually, it was Linda's idea."

"What is it?"

"Trust me," Gold said. "When you hear it, you'll love it." He laughed. "After all, you're a vindictive son of a bitch just like I am, and this is going to be the sweetest revenge we ever could have hoped for. How soon can you be here?"

"In London, you mean?" Don sounded baffled.

"I need you here to help me work out the details of what I have in mind."

"Okay . . ." Don hesitated. "I guess I can be there Sunday."

"Great," Gold said. "First thing Monday morning, we'll telephone Sir Lyndon Tobray at the Air Ministry to set up another meeting for us with Stoat-Black and Payn-Reese." Gold paused. "I think we also better have somebody from Aérosens there, as well."

"Steve, just give me a hint!" Don pleaded. "What have you got up your sleeve?"

"It's too complicated to go into over the phone," Gold began.

Just then the bathroom door opened and out came Linda. "We got the Stiletto contract!" Gold began to tell her, but the words died in his throat.

". . . *unique lingerie* . . ." Gold remembered Linda saying, as his eyes widened and his heart began to pound.

She was fresh from the shower, her short-cut dark hair touseled into damp ringlets, her skin glowing pink from toweling. She was wearing silk stockings, a black lace corset shot through with fiery-red satin ribbon, and black, patent-leather high heels.

"Steve?" Don was calling. "Are you still there, Steve?"

Linda was pirouetting. Her high, rounded bottom framed by the garter straps holding up her seamed stockings jutted lewdly from beneath the tight corset. Then she was coming toward Gold, meanwhile tugging down on the corset to allow her lush, creamy breasts to pop free.

"What do you think, Colonel?" Linda asked slyly.

"Where the hell did you *find* something like that?"

Linda winked. "England swings like a pendulum do." She looked down at herself, murmuring. "I just hope I can get it past Customs. . . ."

"Hello, Steve?" Don shouted insistently.

"Bye, Don," Gold said.

"But—"

"See you on Sunday," Gold cut him off as Linda knelt before him, reaching for his zipper. "Can't talk now, partner," he added, hanging up the phone. "Something's come up."

(Two)

British Ministry of Aeronautical Science
Whitehall
16 May, 1974

Steve Gold surveyed the men assembled in Sir Lyndon Tobray's office. "By now, gentlemen, I'm sure you're aware of GAT's latest success concerning the American military's decision to purchase the Stiletto fighter plane."

"Yes, quite," Lord Glass said.

"Stunning achievement," Quint Peters added.

"Aérosens conveys its congratulations," said Andre Duvalle in his thickly accented English. The director of Aérosens was a tall, imposing figure in his sixties, with snow-white hair and brilliant blue eyes. He was impeccably dressed in a charcoal-gray double-breasted suit.

"And the Prime Minister asked me to relay his personal congratulations," Sir Lyndon chimed in from behind his desk.

Gold smiled. It was Thursday morning, six days after Don had telephoned with the news that GAT had won the DOD fighter competition, and all the players, with the addition of Andre Duvalle, were back in Sir Lyndon's office. Just like last time, Sir Lyndon was playing the role of referee, hiding behind his desk, and everyone else was sitting in these damned uncomfortable, spindly armchairs.

Except that this time Gold had his partner, Don Harrison, by his side. And this time it was GAT that had Skytrain and Payn-Reese on the defensive.

Don Harrison said, "What you gentlemen might not have heard is that the French government and the other NATO powers are interested in the Stiletto, as well."

Duvalle asked, "Perhaps GAT will consider involving Skytrain Industrie in a joint construction effort to manufacture the Stiletto fighters destined for the European market. . . ?"

"That's an interesting suggestion." Gold tried not to gloat, but it was hard. Duvalle had claimed he was too busy to attend the first meeting, but that had been before the DOD had made its announcement. Duvalle had been only too eager to find the time to wend his way across the Channel in order to attend *this* get-together.

"Monsieur Duvalle," Don Harrison said evenly. "Before GAT and Skytrain can discuss any new business, we must first settle the Pont matter at hand."

"But I should think the Pont affair has been settled nicely." Lord Glass laughed, a bit too heartily Gold thought. "After all, now that GAT can count on the cash flow from the Stiletto, your company can certainly arrange the financing to weather Payn-Reese's foray into the U.S. market."

"Lord Glass, nothing has changed since we last met," Gold said, lighting a cigarette. He was aware of Don's eyes on him, but studiously avoided meeting his partner's gaze. During the past week in which he and Gold had planned the strategy for this meeting, Don had been steadfastly doubtful and extremely nervous about what Gold wanted to do. Now Gold, who was aware of his partner's uncertainties, rushed to get all of GAT's cards on the table before Don could say or do anything to mitigate the situation.

"Lord Glass," Gold firmly began. "Last week, from a position of relative weakness, I told you that Skytrain's offer to renegotiate profit sharing was not acceptable, that GAT intended to abide by its original agreement with Skytrain."

"Yes, well," Quint Peters, the sales director for Payn-Reese, interrupted, smiling anxiously. "Now at least you can certainly afford to abide by the original agreement, thanks to your government."

Gold nodded. "However, last week I also made it clear that GAT expects Stoat-Black to abide by its moral responsibility to bring your Motor Works firm to heel, Mr. Peters."

Lord Glass spoke up. "And last week I said that was not in our interest."

"So be it." Gold nodded. "GAT and Skytrain agree to let their old agreement concerning the Pont stand. However, in light of Stoat-Black and Payn-Reese's insistence upon compromising the situation, GAT finds it necessary to open up a new negotiation on a related but separate matter—"

"Excuse me, Steve," Don Harrison politely interrupted, taking some papers from out of his briefcase. "Perhaps it would be best if you allowed me to run through the details."

Gold nodded. "Go right ahead, Don."

"Gentlemen," Don began. "GAT requires that Skytrain Industrie extend to our firm's newly formed subsidiary, GAT Credit Corporation, an interest-free, open-ended line of credit—the first such installment of which will amount to five hundred million dollars—which GATCC will in turn extend to the U.S. airlines in the form of hundred-percent seller financing at a below-market interest rate on any minimum purchase of twelve Ponts, regardless of whatever engine a particular airline chooses: be it Rogers and Simpson's turbofan or the power plant manufactured by Payn-Reese—"

"How outrageous!" Lord Glass sputtered.

"Excuse me," Harrison firmly cut him off, "but there's more. Skytrain must agree to underwrite GATCC in such a manner to be detailed later that GAT's own credit rating is not affected, so that GAT will be able to use its own credit in other ways if it so wishes. . . ."

Gold, listening, was proud of Don, who was articulating the various terms of GAT's demands with authority. Don's performance was all the more impressive because these were the very demands that Gold had insisted upon, against Don's judgment.

"For its part," Don continued, "GAT will make no further attempt to prejudice the U.S. airlines against Payn-Reese. Furthermore, GAT will enter into a sidebar agreement with Payn-Reese to grant it full R and D input and favored subcontractor status in all future GAT commercial-jetliner proposals."

"This is just too ridiculous for words," Lord Glass scoffed.

"It's our deal to you, take it or leave it," Gold interjected.

"Take it or leave it?" Lord Glass echoed in astonishment. "Did you say take it or—"

"But don't you see?" Quint Peters cut him off. "No U.S. airline would choose a British-manufactured engine over one made in America unless they got the favorable financing terms that Agatha Holding is offering."

Don shrugged. "That's fine with us if you have an agreement with Agatha Holding for the latter to *further* subsidize that portion of buyer financing relating to engine costs, should a customer choose a Payn-Reese–equipped Pont."

"But, but . . ." Peters sputtered.

Gold enjoyed Quint Peters's look of consternation. The Payn-Reese sales exec was likely realizing that Tim Campbell would marshal all of his legal talent to get Agatha Holding out of the deal as soon as Campbell realized that his scheme was not going to bring GAT down.

Don continued. "Look, GAT realizes that Payn-Reese may well find itself at a disadvantage to Rogers and Simpson concerning the U.S. market in light of GAT's demands. In order to level the playing field for Payn-Reese, GAT is prepared to cooperate with you on redesigning the Pont's engine nacelle to accommodate your engine. You know as well as I do, Mr. Peters, that the engine pod is a tricky component, that the matching of engine, nacelle, and wing is crucial to airplane performance and safety. Your engine option will be a lot more palatable to the U.S. airlines if they can be assured that GAT stands behind the redesign to accommodate the Payn-Reese power plant."

Peters was looking somewhat appeased, Gold thought. And no wonder. Coming on board GAT as an approved subcontractor, and receiving GAT's indirect endorsement by GAT's agreeing to cooperate with Payn-Reese in the Pont's nacelle modifications were important breakthroughs for the British company. Gold didn't think Rogers and Simpson would be giving GAT much guff concerning Payn-Reese's proposed elevation in status. The American engine firm was going to be enjoying a lucrative future for some time to come supplying Stiletto engines and spare parts to the military.

"I say," Lord Glass was fuming. "Last week I said you had bloody gall, but this . . ." He trailed off darkly, shaking his head. "The *cheek* of you bloody Yank chaps! How could you ever imagine Skytrain would accept your proposal?"

Here goes bomb number one, Gold thought, saying, "Because if Skytrain doesn't accept our proposal, GAT is prepared to withdraw the Pont from the U.S. market as it is within GAT's rights to do. Furthermore, if Skytrain doesn't cede to our wishes, GAT is prepared to withdraw from Skytrain Industrie."

"Voluntarily withdraw from Skytrain, you say?" Lord Glass exploded. "You're bluffing!"

Gold's eyes swept the room the way he'd once scanned the sky from inside the cockpit of a fighter plane in order to pin down his enemies' positions. Good old Don Harrison was looking detatched and alert: the quintessential wingman, watching Gold's back. Sir Lyndon was sitting slumped behind his desk, looking sick. Quint Peters was chain-smoking, looking sweaty and anxious; Gold figured the sales exec had finally realized what everyone else had known all along: that Payn-Reese Motor Works was just a pawn in a much larger game.

The major wild card in the lineup was Andre Duvalle of Aérosens, but he seemed detatched from the matter at hand. *But in a way, that makes sense*, Gold thought, remembering that from the beginning this had been a grudge match between GAT and Skytrain's English faction. Gold guessed that the Frenchman was at present too busy calculating the future profits to be made by supplying the Stiletto fighter to Europe to be much concerned about what happened concerning the Pont.

The only adversary in the room who still looked defiant was Lord Glass. Gold thought, *Time to let the air out of his balloon.*

"GAT is not bluffing," Gold said. "Far from it. Thanks to our new military contract, we can endure the financial losses that would stem from our canceling U.S. distribution of the Pont." He paused. "But can Skytrain withstand the loss of prestige? Last week, you told me Skytrain intended the Pont to symbolize the dawning of a new industrial age in Europe. How will the European aviation industry look to the world after GAT blackens Skytrain's eye by deeming the consortium's best ever jetliner too inferior for the U.S. market?"

"We wouldn't allow you to get away with that!" Lord Glass vowed. "We'd fight you in the courts! If not for breach of contract, on some other grounds. Meanwhile, we'd get some other American aviation firm to sell the Pont in your country."

"Yes!" Quint Peters piped up hopefully. "Perhaps Amalgamated-Landis!"

"Precisely!" Lord Glass nodded. "A-L will do quite nicely as Skytrain's new American partner! There you have it, Mr. Gold. That is Skytrain's response to your attempted highway robbery."

Don Harrison said: "Lord Glass, trust me when I suggest to you that you may not be as familiar with American courts as I am. The litigation you're contemplating would drag on for years. Meanwhile, you'd experience little success trying to market the Pont through some other vendor. Don't you realize that when GAT refuses to sell the Pont, dark clouds of doubt will gather around the jetliner? The airlines will wonder: Why did GAT withdraw the airplane? Is there something wrong with it? Quality-control problems, perhaps? Maybe we'd better buy another manufacturer's offering, just to be safe. . . ."

"My God," Lord Glass murmured. "You mean you'd go so far as to smear by innuendo the airplane's reputation?"

Gold shrugged. "We'd make no public judgment on the Pont. But what any particular airline might think of GAT's refusal to sell the Pont and the ensuing litigation would be that customer's own business."

Lord Glass, scowling, looked away. No one else spoke. For a few moments the room positively ticked with silence.

Gold listened to the street traffic occasionally rattling the office windows. He busied himself lighting a cigarette. He glanced at Don, who was pretending to study the papers on his lap. By prior arrangement, both Gold and Don were prepared to sit quietly, all day if necessary; both men knew it was of the utmost importance strategically that they not be the ones to break the deadlock of silence.

Surprisingly, it was Andre Duvalle who spoke up. "Mr. Gold, Mr. Harrison. As you are no doubt aware, your partners in Skytrain are nationally funded. Speaking for Aérosens, I must tell you that I do not have the authority to agree to your proposal without conferring with my government."

"Yes, it's quite the same for us," Sir Lyndon said, looking pained. "Most likely the Prime Minister himself will be directly involved."

"Gentlemen, let's not try to hide behind international bureaucracy," Gold said. "GAT will not accept your feeble excuses concerning 'my government this' or 'my government that.' "

Don Harrison picked up where Gold left off. "You're suggesting that Skytrain treat GAT's demands as a financial-appropriations matter, which would allow you to use the excuse that you must take the matter to your respective governments. You are at liberty to do that, of course, but you only further jeopardize the Pont's fate in America by your procrastinations. The U.S. market is continually in flux. If Skytrain dithers, if it hems and haws, trying to stall, the consortium may find that it has cut its own throat concerning the Pont's success in the United States because some other American manufacturer of jetliners has moved to fill the void. Meanwhile, we all know that Skytrain Industrie has autonomy concerning airplane design, production, and marketing strategies. It is GAT's position that what we're requesting from Skytrain falls within that third category: marketing. The funds necessary to advance GATCC its line of credit should come from the profits already on Skytrain's books from those European and Third World sales of the Pont, and should simply be chalked up to marketing."

"I see," Lord Glass said bitterly. "You expect us to take the money out of our own pockets to line yours."

"We expect Skytrain to move quickly on our proposal for its own good," Gold said. "We've just provided you with a credible explanation to your governments for making that quick decision."

"This isn't only highway robbery," Lord Glass muttered. "It's blackmail!"

"Enough bickering," Andre Duvalle spoke up, staring sternly at Lord Glass. "Mr. Gold, I believe you have made GAT's position crystal clear. When do you wish our answer?"

"We're returning to the United States this evening," Gold said, standing up. Out of the corner of his eye, he saw Don packing up his briefcase and getting to his feet. "We regret that we can't stay longer, but we have pressing business to attend to at GAT."

"Yes, of course," Duvalle said. "Your military contract for the Stiletto . . ."

Don said, "We would like your answer to reach us at Claridge's by five o'clock."

"That's less than three hours from now!" Lord Glass grumbled.

Gold shrugged. "Frankly, Lord Glass, I don't see why you'd need more than three seconds to accede to our terms."

"To accede to the inevitable," Don added quietly.

Gold headed for the door with his partner on his heels.

They were quiet as they left the Air Ministry building and while they were busy flagging a cab. It was only once they were settled into a taxi and on their way back to Claridge's that Don said, "I still think we were too hard on them."

"No." Gold adamantly shook his head. "They started this, we didn't."

"Actually, Tim Campbell started this," Don corrected gently.

"Okay, so maybe Tim *did* start it." Gold admitted. He leaned back tiredly against the cab's burnished leather upholstry, watching London roll past. "But Skytrain thought we were weak, that they could kick us while we were down. I wanted to prove them wrong."

"Which you did, in spades," Don replied wryly. "You really rubbed their noses in it."

"My father had a reputation for being a bad man to cross," Gold said. "Since he died, and I joined the company, Skytrain has been constantly gauging our corporate leadership to see how we measure up to Herman Gold."

"I suppose you're right." Don sighed. "If we *had* shown mercy, I suppose it would have been interpreted as a sign of weakness on our part."

Gold, nodding grimly, said: "Now Skytrain knows what everyone is going to know sooner or later: that despite my father's passing, GAT remains a power to be reckoned with."

"Even Tim Campbell?" Don wondered.

"Even Tim, partner. Even Tim."

(Three)

TEA Flight #429: Heathrow to JFK
In the night skies over the Atlantic Ocean

Gold considered it fortunate that the Trans-European Airlines GAT-built GC-999 jumbo jetliner was less than one-third filled for this midweek, late-night flight. In his tired, pent-up state, the quiet, roomy, first-class cabin helped to make bearable this first leg of the journey home.

Gold stretched in his seat as best he could without disturbing Linda Forrester, who was dozing with her head leaning against his shoulder. Across the aisle, Don Harrison was stretched across two seats, snoring lightly.

Lucky ducks, Gold thought, enviously eyeing his sleeping companions. He was feeling exhausted, but he knew that there was no way he was going to be able to sleep.

The flight roared on. Dinner had already been served and cleared away. Gold had already disinterestedly leafed through all the magazines to be had on board. He thought about signaling the stewardess for another scotch, but decided against it. They still had a connecting nonstop flight to Los Angeles to go before they'd be home, and Gold knew there was plenty of work piled up on his desk in Burbank. The jet lag was going to be bad enough to deal with without his getting drunk while traversing half the world's time zones.

Gold lit a cigarette, glanced at Linda, and snapped his lighter closed just a little too loudly. Linda stirred, coming awake.

"Gee, I didn't mean to wake you."

"Hi," she mumbled sleepily.

"Hi." Gold smiled, thinking that he'd been with a lot of women in his life, but hadn't known many who could look good sleeping or just after they'd slept. Linda was one of them.

"Have you slept at all?" Linda asked thickly.

"No . . ."

"Oh, right." She yawned. She was still only half awake, and cuddled against him. "You never sleep on airplanes, do you?"

"No."

"It's probably because you think you ought to be in the cockpit. . . ." Her voice faded, as if she were about to drop off again.

"Hey." Gold gave her a gentle nudge. "Stay awake, keep me company."

"Yes, sir!" Linda blinked, opened her eyes. "Okay . . . I'm up!"

She sat up and stretched. Gold watched her breasts rise and fall beneath her thin cotton sweater. He wished they could make love right now. It wasn't lust as much as it was his desire to stop thinking for a little bit.

"Do you think you could get us some tea?" Linda asked.

Gold pushed the call button to summon the stewardess, and when she came he asked for a cup of tea for Linda and a scotch on the rocks—screw the jet lag—for himself.

"You look sad," Linda observed, coming fully awake now. "Now that I think about it, you've been glum ever since you came back from your meeting today. How come?" She paused, smiling tenatively. "I'd think you'd be elated over your victory."

"I am," Gold said, and then shrugged. The message from Skytrain capitulating to all of GAT's demands had reached them at Claridge's at four-thirty that afternoon.

"So what's wrong?" Linda persisted. "What's going on?"

The stewardess came with Linda's tea and Gold's drink. The scotch tasted cool, clean, medicinal, but Gold doubted whether all the whiskey in the world could ever banish the bad taste in his mouth that had been left by Gold's response to this latest attack on GAT by Tim Campbell.

As the stewardess left, Gold murmured, "I guess that now that the heat of the battle is over, I'm feeling a little depressed by what I had to do to win."

"Meaning?" Linda watched him closely as she squeezed some lemon into her tea and then took a sip.

"I guess I'm thinking about what you said to me last week about seeing everything in terms of combat."

"About you being a samurai businessman, you mean?

"Yeah." Gold nodded. "It ain't easy ruling with an iron fist."

"If it was, everybody would do it, big guy."

"Don't sound so smug," Gold said. "After all, I creamed the opposition using your idea."

"Oh, sure, pin it on me," Linda scolded, but then paused, thoughtfully musing. "Although I must say it is gratifying to be recognized as the woman who stands behind the throne."

Gold chuckled. "Your idea to secure GAT a United States government loan guarantee was a good one. Don and I just modified it: instead of the U.S. backing GAT financially, we got the governments of France and England to do it.

"But I thought Skytrain Industrie is writing off the cost as a marketing expense?"

"Ah, that's just a creative-accounting rationalization we provided to Skytrain, one that they in turn could provide to their home governments." Gold scowled. "What you have to understand is that from the European perspective there really is no such thing as Skytrain Industrie. It's just a kind of international steering committee for multinational aviation projects. Skytrain pays no taxes and shows no profits. All monies in and expenditures out go directly to the firms that are partners in the consortium. In the cases of Stoat-Black and Aérosens, which are nationalized companies, that means that all profits and expenses end up with their respective governments."

"So the treasuries of France and England will ultimately bear the burden of GAT's financial bailout?"

Gold nodded.

"Son of a bitch," Linda whispered, licking Gold's ear. "You're one smart cookie for a love stud."

"Well, I just had the general idea," Gold demurred. "Don's the one who was able to supply the financial specifics that turned my concept into a reality." He paused. "Of course, the love-stud part is all my own."

"You practice a lot?" Linda asked, her lips still nuzzling his ear.

"Whenever I'm alone."

Linda laughed, moving away from him to rummage through her purse for her cigarettes. "But what I still don't understand is why you seem to have such mixed emotions about your victory. It was a tremendous coup on your part, but from the way you're acting someone would think that you were the one who lost."

"Maybe I did lose in a way. . . ."

"What's that supposed to mean?" Linda demanded as Gold lit her cigarette.

"I didn't play fair, Linda."

She nodded. "Okay, then. Let's go through it. Was what you did necessary to win this battle or negotiation or whatever you want to call it?"

"Yes."

"Can you think of any other way you could have won?"

"No."

"Then there you go," Linda said. "At the risk of sounding

overly western, a man's got to do what a man's got to do" She winked. "*Capeesh?*"

"*Capeesh*," Gold echoed, smiling slightly. "What kind of western lingo is that?"

"Spaghetti western," she said brightly.

"Ah." Gold took a swallow of scotch.

Linda, watching him, suddenly said, "I know what's *really* bothering you."

"You do, huh?" Gold looked at her.

"Uh-huh." She kissed him lightly on the cheek. "You see, I remember what you told me that afternoon we ran into each other at the trade show six months ago; what you told me after we made love at your beach house. You told me about how Tim Campbell had implied that back in the fifties your father had played dirty pool, using his CIA connections to win the competition between his GAT 909 jetliner and Tim Campbell's perfectly good Amalgamated Landis AL-12 by unjustly tarnishing that airplane's reputation. You'd checked the story out with Don and had found out it was true."

"You've got a very good memory, young lady," Gold said sourly.

"Reporters need to remember most everything they hear," Linda replied. "Anyway, back then your father indulged in mudslinging because the stakes were high and his company's survival was at stake. Today, you threatened to use the same mudslinging tactics against Skytrain's Pont jetliner."

"Pretty rotten of me, huh?"

"It depends on how you look at it," Linda said. "This time around the stakes were equally high for GAT, but only you can decide if you did the right thing by doing what you had to do for the sake of your company."

Gold felt like crying. "All my life I've lived according to a personal moral construct."

"A code of honor," Linda suggested.

"Yeah, a military code of honor, I guess you'd call it," Gold murmured. "It worked for me because in the Air Force it was easy for me to see things in terms of black and white." He smiled wistfully. "Out here in the civilian world, the lighting isn't so good. White is becoming increasingly gray." He took Linda's hand. "There's who I always tried to be, and who I seem to have become. The difference between the two frightens me, and I'm not used to being afraid.''

"Like I said before, you did what you had to do," Linda told him. "And like I've said before, you're a strong man. The question becomes, are you strong enough to keep what you've done from eating you up inside?''

Gold didn't immediately answer. Instead, he turned toward the jetliner's window. The plastic oval looking out onto the night reflected the lit cabin's interior, and within that murky cameo of plastic Gold saw his own features. The cabin's recessed, dimmed lighting bleached the little color that was left to his thinning, blond hair, and brought out the lines in his face, so that Gold could hardly recognize the man staring back at him. . . .

I look so old, Gold brooded as he studied the image caught against the blackness some 40,000 feet above the turbulent Atlantic. *My God, I look like my father.* . . .

Gold, turning away from his reflection, said, "I'll get over it."

"Promise?" Linda coaxed.

"It's only business," Gold said.

Linda laughed, squeezing his hand. For her sake, Gold forced a smile, not that he thought anything was particularly funny.

CHAPTER 9

(One)

Downtown Los Angeles, California
11 September, 1974

The fire-engine-red Corvette convertible's twin exhausts rumbled like thunder as Steve Gold weaved his way through the tangled downtown traffic. Gold, the wind blowing through his hair as he cruised along Sunset Boulevard, saw a clear stretch of left lane and got the 'Vette up to fifty, but then some clown up ahead doing thirty in a shit-brown Mercedes evidently spotted Gold coming, and decided to appoint himself traffic cop. As the Corvette approached, the Mercedes veered left while maintaining its sedate speed to keep Gold from passing. Shut down, Gold hit the brakes, downshifting and cursing, but then he saw that he had just enough room to squeeze by on the right, and made his move.

The Stingray's tires squealed, leaving rubber patches as the roadster's rear end fishtailed. Gold felt the kick in his pants reminiscent of a jet fighter's afterburn as he was pressed back against the custom-installed Recaro racing bucket. The

Mercedes driver, some old dude in a plaid golf cap, leaned on his horn, glaring at Gold as the Sting Ray zoomed past with just inches to spare between the Mercedes' passenger side and a big yellow fire hydrant sticking out from the curb. Gold cut in sharply in front of the Mercedes, then glanced in his rearview mirror to check his six. He saw the Mercedes driver waving his fist. Gold waved back jauntily as he turned off the boulevard.

Passing on the right like that was certainly stupid and childish, Gold thought, feeling a twinge of conscience. Then he smiled: *But that's what made it fun.* After all, there was nothing quite as exhilarating as driving a powerful convertible on a sunny California day when you were in a good mood.

First off, the 1971 Stingray certainly fit the definition of powerful. Gold had bought the 'Vette new when he'd still been in the Air Force and assigned to L.A. He'd stayed with the car because it had a big block engine with mechanical lifters; 1971 being the last year before the namby-pamby federal safety czars citing the oil embargo did their best to neuter the marque.

Secondly, it was certainly a doozy of a day: warm and sunny, with a hint of cooling breeze.

And thirdly, I'm certainly in a good mood, Gold thought as he slowed to tool the Corvette down the ramp that led into the BADCO Towers underground parking garage. He took off his Ray-Ban gold-rimmed Aviators as he went from the bright sunlight to the garage's fluorescent lighting, thinking: *Oh, I'm in a wonderful mood. I've been looking forward to this for the entire summer.*

He nosed the 'Vette into a corner slot to protect it as best he could against dinks in her door panels from other drivers who were careless getting out of their cars, and set the anti-theft alarm. He then took the elevator from the garage up to the main lobby, where he switched to an express to the fiftieth floor. While he was riding up, he ran his fingers through his sparse, close-cut hair and straightened his tie. He tried to smooth out some of the wrinkles in his tan linen suit, but then he remembered that Linda had said these natural-fiber deals were supposed to look rumpled.

The elevator came to a stop and its doors opened. Gold stepped out and wandered down the corridor past various

office suites until he came to a glass door lettered: AGATHA
HOLDING COMPANY.

Grinning savagely, Gold opened the door and strode inside.
He looked around, gleefully satisfied to see the bare white
walls marked with ghostly rectangles where framed pictures
had recently hung. A frazzled-looking but pretty freckle-faced
redhead was manning the reception desk which was surrounded by office furniture on dollies and cardboard packing
boxes.

"Sir? Can I help you?" She looked surprised to see Gold,
or any visitor for that matter, Gold surmised, but she was
smiling tentatively. Probably my animal magnetism, Gold
thought. That, or the wrinkles in my suit.

"I'd like to see Tim Campbell."

The redhead's smile reversed into a puzzled frown. "But
Mr. Campbell no longer . . ." She trailed off, flipping
through the pages of her appointment book. "Was Mr. Campbell expecting you?"

"No, but if you tell him Steven Gold is here, he'll see
me."

"Just a moment, sir."

Gold watched her reach for the telephone. She certainly
had a lot of freckles, Gold thought. She was wearing a light-
blue patterned sundress with a scooped neckline that revealed
her extensive cleavage. Gold could see a scattering of freckles
across the tops of her breasts, which made him wonder about
the freckles he couldn't see.

The redhead punched a three-digit extension number into
the telephone and then held the receiver to her ear while she
waited for somebody on the other end to pick up. She noticed
Gold gazing at her and smiled. Yes, definitely a lot of freckles, Gold decided. It'd be a tough job counting them all,
but somebody had to do it.

"Sir?" the redhead suddenly said into the receiver.
"There's a Mr. Steven Gold here to see Mr. Campbell. I
don't have him in the appointment book. . . ." She listened
a moment and then hung up the telephone. "Mr. Campbell
isn't in—" she began.

Gold interrupted. "I bet he hasn't been in for a while,
right?"

She paused thoughtfully. "I really don't know if I should

say. . . ." Gold saw her looking him over, taking in the expensive cut of his suit, her eyes tarrying at the gold Rolex on his wrist. "Then again, this is my last week here. . . ." she trailed off expectantly.

Gold took out his wallet and extracted a business card. He picked up a pen from her desk and jotted on the back of the card the name and phone number of a personnel manager at GAT.

"You call this person and mention my name," Gold said. "I'm sure we can find something for you at my company."

"Any strings attached to this offer, Mr. Gold?"

"No."

"Oh." She pouted, expertly using her blue eyes as she reached for the card. "Too bad."

Gold grinned at her. She was cute, all right, and ripe for the taking, but since Linda Forrester had come back into his life, Gold had amazingly found himself behaving in a monogamous fashion. Even more amazingly, he was liking it. Oh, sure, he still liked to ogle, but he no longer had the desire to score on each day's passing pretties. It had to be that he was in love with Linda, Gold mused. Or burgeoning old age.

"You were going to tell me when Tim Campbell was here last," Gold coaxed.

The redhead tucked his business card into her purse, confiding, "He hasn't been in since midsummer."

Gold nodded. Now that he thought about it, it made sense that Campbell, who had other fish to fry throughout the world, would have long ago deserted this sinking ship. Meanwhile, it had been an exciting and lucrative summer for GAT.

The airlines had enthusiastically embraced GAT Credit Corporation's financing offer. GAT didn't come close to cornering the jetliner market with the Pont, but then, there were a lot of good airplanes out there available from various manufacturers. GAT did get enough orders to feel confident about eventually turning a profit on the Pont, and for at least the next eighteen months to two years, GAT's commercial aircraft division's assembly lines would be operating full-time building the Skytrain jetliner. That happy situation, combined with GAT's military contract firmed up over the summer to supply the Air Force with six hundred Stiletto fighters over a five-year period, had the company sitting pretty.

"The fact that Mr. Campbell hasn't been here in so long was why I was so surprised when you asked for him, Mr. Gold," the redhead was explaining. "But Mr. Layten will see you."

"That's right." Gold chuckled. "I heard Turner Layten had signed on with Campbell. Yeah, old Turner will do just fine."

"It's just through that door, sir," the receptionist said, pointing over her shoulder. "Then you go down the hall. Mr. Layten's office is on the left." She smiled apologetically. "I'd show you the way, but I have to stay at my desk in case the movers come."

"No one else here but you and Layten?" Gold asked.

"No, sir. We're shutting down operations, you see. . . ."

"You call that number I gave you," Gold reminded her. "We'll get you set up at a *decent* place for a change."

He went through the door she'd indicated. His footsteps echoed in the carpetless corridor which was lined with more packing cases on both sides, so that Gold had to walk sideways through the narrowed passage.

"In here," Turner Layten called as Gold sidled past his open doorway.

"Hello, Turner." Gold stepped inside the large office.

Layten nodded warily. He'd stood up behind his desk, but made no offer to shake hands.

Gold looked around. Like the rest of Agatha Holding, the place was in a shambles. There were large, potted palms on dollies, rolled-up Oriental scatter rugs, more of the ubiquitous cardboard shipping crates, and a partially disassembled glass display case filled with intricately detailed miniature soldiers.

"I see you're dressing more casually than I remember." Gold gestured at Layten's yellow, short-sleeve, open-neck shirt-jac, and muted plaid green-and-black slacks. "That's a new look for you, huh?"

Gold hadn't seen Turner Layten for over ten years, and was shocked at how much the man had aged. *But then, haven't we all*, Gold thought sadly. Layten was still built wide in the hips and narrow in the shoulders, with lank dark hair and a jowled baby face, but these days there was gray seeding Layten's hair, and the guy had grown a couple more double chins.

"Well! What can I do for you, Steven?" Layten asked brusquely, settling back into his desk chair. "I'm very busy."

"Oh, yeah, I can see that," Gold remarked, perching on a stack of packing cases. He looked out through the office windows, which afforded a sweeping view of downtown, dominated by ARCO Plaza's twin monoliths. "Nice office you have. Or should I say, nice office you *used* to have . . . ?"

"These offices are expensive to maintain, and are no longer necessary," Layten said stiffly.

"So Agatha Holding is folding up its tent and slinking out of town, eh?"

Layten smiled indulgently. "That's hardly the way I'd put it," he sniffed. "Now that the airlines have placed their jetliner orders, Agatha Holding has become a mostly bookkeeping and inventory-control operation. For that reason, Mr. Campbell had decided to combine it with his existing accounting operation."

"I must confess I was surprised when Tim didn't try to renege on his Payn-Reese financing and spare-parts-inventory offer to the airlines," Gold acknowledged. "I guess he couldn't get out of the deal, huh?"

"Tim Campbell stands by his word," Layten replied archly.

"Yeah, sure," Gold said, taking quiet satisfaction in what he'd heard through the grapevine: that Tim had moved to abrogate Agatha Holding's marketing agreement with Payn-Reese and the airlines, but that Campbell's lawyers had warned that litigating to get out of the deal would have cost Campbell more than honoring it. "Tim must really be pissed that he got stuck paying the piper without being able to call the tune?"

"Is that why you're here, Steven?" Layten asked coldly. "To nose around in other people's business? To gloat?"

"Well, yeah, sure." Gold shrugged. "Gloating is definitely on my list. . . ."

"I suppose you think you've won!" Layten snapped.

"I'll presume that's a rhetorical question," Gold replied. "No, on second thought, I'll answer it." He stroked his chin.

"Let's see: GAT ended up with everything it wanted, and you and Tim got screwed royally."

"That's not true!" Layten protested, adding lamely, "I made a lot of money trading Amalgamated-Landis stock!"

Gold nodded. "Okay, so you made some money. But we both know that money wasn't what this was about. We both know what you wanted, and we both know that you didn't get it, so on the whole I'd say GAT won."

"And here you are to crow about it, like the immature, overblown jerk you are," Layten smirked.

"You tried to destroy my company," Gold said, growing angry at being talked down to by this son of a bitch.

"So what?" Layten scowled. "Sure Tim Campbell and I tried to take you down, and we came damn near close to pulling it off, too."

"Not close enough, Turner," Gold laughed, regaining his composure.

"There's always next time."

"There won't *be* a next time."

"Fuck you," Layten scoffed. "That just shows how little you know! Tim has a lot more ideas up his sleeve—" He stopped abruptly, his eyes narrowing slyly as he regarded Gold. "But then, you'd like me to talk about that, wouldn't you?"

Too bad, Gold thought. *The loudmouth was just beginning to get interesting.* "Talk about what?" He shrugged, trying to play innocent.

Layten laughed. "Give it up, Steven. Subtlety was never your strong point."

"I don't think you and Tim have shit up your sleeve," Gold tried again, but Layten dismissed the attempt to ferret out information with a wave of his hand.

"You know, Tim was absolutely right about you," Layten mused. "He said that I should expect a visit like this from you. I said no, that while I had no use for Steve Gold, I had to give him *some* credit. That he had to have more class than *that*."

"Thanks for sticking up for me, old buddy," Gold said wryly.

Layten shook his head in mock sorrow. "But I was wrong,

huh?'' He paused, his smile hardening. ''What's the matter, Steven? Are you here because your partner at GAT—the brains of the organization—hasn't seen fit to give you any more busy work to do?''

Don't get mad, get even, Gold reminded himself. He patted the packing box on which he was sitting. ''Some things never change. When you were Jack Horton's CIA stooge, he had you following him around to clean up his messes. Now that you're Tim Campbell's stooge, I guess it makes sense that while Tim's moved on to other, *important* things, he'd keep you hanging around here to sweep out this failed venture.''

Layten jumped out of his chair and came around his desk. ''You've got a lot of balls to come here and talk to me like that. . . .''

Gold slid off the packing cases and took several steps toward Layten, until their faces were scant inches apart. ''Yeah, I do have a lot of balls, Turner. You should have remembered that before you let Tim Campbell talk you into trying to ambush me.''

''Talk me *into* it?'' Layten echoed, amused. ''Nobody had to talk me into anything. I was *glad* to do it.''

''That's because you're an ambusher by nature,'' Gold said.

''Shut up,'' Layten warned.

''You're a back-shooter. . . .''

''You son of a bitch!'' Layten was shaking with anger.

Gold said, ''Your trouble all along has been that you've blamed *me* for the mess you and your CIA honcho Jack Horton got yourselves into over the MR-1 spy-plane project.''

''*You're* the one who fucked things up!'' Layten's jowls were crimson. His eyes were wild.

''No.'' Gold shook his head. ''You're wrong. You and Horton fucked it, but then, your kind *always* wants to blame someone else for your own failings.''

''Get out!'' Layten demanded, his voice rising. ''Get out of here before I throw you out!''

''What are you going to do, Turner? Call Security?'' Gold winked. ''Why don't you call that redhead you've got sitting out front?''

''Shut up, you bastard!''

Layten lunged, taking Gold by surprise. He grabbed hold of Gold's wrist and tried to twist Gold's arm up and around behind his back.

"Nice try," Gold muttered, stepping away from Layten to rob him of any leverage advantage. Gold brought his arm up and around in front of him, twisting his wrist free of Layten's grip using an *aikido*-derived unarmed-combat technique he'd been taught in the Air Force.

Layten reached a second time for Gold's wrist. This time, Gold simply batted Layten's hands away.

"Get real, Turner. You and your whole family going back to the Mayflower couldn't take me."

Layten looked frenzied. "You think you've got it covered, huh?" He took several steps backward, pawing at his right hip beneath the hem of his shirt-jac.

Gun, Gold thought, tensing. *Jesus Christ, he's got a gun.*

Time seemed to slow for Gold, the way it always had in air combat through three wars. For an instant Gold found himself back in 1966, crouching fearfully beneath the palm fronds in a North Vietnamese jungle: Several hundred yards away his shot-down Thud fighter lay in flaming wreckage while looming over Gold's hiding place was a Vietcong soldier armed with an AK-47.

Layten had produced a small, blued, snub-nosed revolver from out of a high-ride hip holster.

Gold moved instinctively, catching hold of Layten's gun with both of his own hands and then bending Layten's wrist around so that the revolver's snout was shoved into Layten's protruding gut. Layten, grunting in shock and pain, tried to twist free, but Gold hung on, keeping the gun jammed against Layten's stomach while his fingers spread over Layten's hands. Then Gold found the revolver's hammer and managed to thumb it back with a loud *click!*

At the sound, Layten froze, his eyes widening in alarm. "D-don't," he whispered, looking very pale. "D-don't shoot. . . ."

Layten winced as Gold drove the revolver's snubbed snout deeper into his gut. At the same time, Gold surreptitiously put a finger in front of the cocked hammer to keep it from falling in case the trigger got pulled. He despised Layten, but he didn't want to shoot the guy. Anyway, it was probably impossible to get bloodstains out of a hundred-percent-natural-fibers linen suit.

"I've got to say, old buddy, for an ex-CIA man you are one sorry tub of lard when it comes to throwing down on a guy," Gold observed. "Didn't they teach you *anything* useful at spook school?"

"Let go of me," Layten demanded.

"What the fuck are you doing carrying a piece in the first place?" Gold wondered. "It's not your style, Turner. It smacks of prowess."

Layten tried to pull away.

"Easy now," Gold warned. "Single-action, these babies can have a hair trigger."

Layten again froze. "Let go . . ." he began to whine.

Gold, his pulse racing, feeling giddy from adrenaline, couldn't resist taunting, "*Does* this gun have a hair trigger? Have you ever even fired it, Turner? You hunk of shit!"

"Let go of me!" Layten repeated, shouting.

"Or what?" Gold sneered. "You'll shoot yourself?"

Gold roughly tore the gun out of Layten's grasp and looked at it. It was a Smith & Wesson, a five-shot .38 special. Gold had known fighter jocks in Korea and in 'Nam who'd carried similar revolvers as backup guns to their standard-issue sidearms.

Gold opened the Smith's cylinder and dumped out the rounds onto the carpet. He then tossed the gun into a large potted palm in the far corner of Layten's office.

"You get out of here," Layten ordered.

"Oh, shut up," Gold said tiredly. "You couldn't manhandle me, and now I've taken away your gun. Don't you know when to quit?"

Layten actually stamped his foot. "I said get *out*!"

Gold, gathering up a handful of Layten's shirtfront, lifted him and spun him around, slamming him against the wall.

"You clearly *don't* know when to quit, you little shit," Gold swore, shaking Layten. "So I'll tell you that the time to quit gunning for me and my company is *now*. You reading me, Turner? It's *now*! You'd better get yourself a new job, because staying on with Tim Campbell is going to be hazardous to your health."

"You don't scare me," Layten said. He tried to wriggle free, but Gold kept him pinned. "I'll never quit watching you," Layten defiantly vowed. "I'll always be watching and waiting for my chance to bring you down the way you did me! Tim Campbell and I make a *great* team! Together we've got what it takes to lay waste to everything you and your asshole *kike* father—"

Kike? Gold savagely punched Layten in the stomach, and felt his fist sink into Layten's gut up to his wrist.

Layten cried out, his face twisting in pain. Gold stepped back, turning him loose. Layten, moaning, dribbled down the wall like splattered molasses. He slumped to his green-and-black-plaid knees, and then doubled over with his hands laced across his belly until his face was pressed against the carpet.

Gold nudged him in the ribs with the toe of his shoe. "Give it up, Turner," he muttered. "You aren't built to take the kind of punishment I can mete out."

Layten, wheezing, was curled up in a fetal position, but he slowly turned his head to look up at Gold with malevolent eyes.

"You're looking a little green around the edges, Turner," Gold said. "I hope you aren't going to be sick. . . . Oh, and you've got some lint sticking to your upper lip."

"This isn't over," Layten gasped, pushing himself up to a sitting position on the floor. "It will *never* be over, not until one of us is broken once and for all! Now, *get out* of my office!"

"Yeah, sure, I'll leave." Gold sighed. "Don't bother to get up."

Gold left the office and headed back down the corridor. He'd anticipated feeling great after coming here, but instead he felt depressed and somehow degraded, like a man who'd given in to a tawdry temptation.

It had been a childish, stupid stunt he'd pulled when he'd passed that Mercedes, Gold brooded. It had been even more reckless to have come here in the first place. *Turner Layten had been right to ridicule me for gloating*, Gold brooded. *What the fuck was I thinking of?* He shuddered as he replayed in his mind the tussle for control of Layten's revolver. How easily either he or Layten could have died in that office!

Gold's dark thoughts once again found their way back through the years to 1966 and that North Vietnamese jungle. The Vietcong soldier that had stood over Gold's hiding place had left Gold with no choice, so Gold had killed him, rising up from out of his hiding place with his pistol to blow off the top of the enemy soldier's head at point-blank range.

That had been the first and only time that Gold had killed at close quarters, and the memory of the look in that soldier's almond-shaped eyes just before Gold blew his brains out had haunted Gold's dreams for months. After that incident, Gold had thanked God that as a warrior his chosen weapon was the fighter plane, that he could wage war for his country without ever having to see his enemy's face. . . .

Until now, Gold brooded. *Now you have very clearly seen the enemies' faces; they belong to Tim Campbell and Turner Layten. And don't kid yourself: this war is not over, and it is every bit as bloodthirsty and potentially violent as any you've survived in the past. . . .*

Yeah, it had been very foolish and childish to come here today. As was so often the case, Gold had done it without thinking through the ramifications of his actions. Now he would have to prepare himself for the consequences, whatever they might be.

"Have a nice day, Mr. Gold!" the receptionist said brightly as he came through the door into the lobby.

"Some turn out better than others, Red," Gold said, passing her desk and continuing to the elevators, where he punched the Down button. While he was waiting, he tried to light a cigarette.

He couldn't do it. His hands were shaking too much.

(Two)

Turner Layten remained on the carpet in his office. His back was against the wall and his knees were drawn up to his chest. He was breathing deeply, waiting for the pain in his belly to subside as he listened to Steven Gold's footsteps receding down the hallway.

Then, suddenly, Steve Gold was back in the office standing over Layten.

Gold began, "I came back to make sure you understand my position—"

Layten didn't wait for Gold to finish. He moved fast, pushing off from the wall and barreling into Gold's knees, sweeping Gold's legs out from under him to topple him. Gold cried out shrilly as he sprawled belly-down on the carpet. Layten rose up on his knees and clipped Gold on the jaw, just to quiet him down a bit. As Gold rose groggily to his hands and knees, trying to shake off Layten's powerful punch, Layten got to his feet and sauntered over to his desk, where he kept his backup gun, a .32-caliber Walther PPK.

Layten always kept a round chambered in the Walther, so after taking the gun from his top desk drawer he had only to thumb the safety, revealing the red dot on the side of the sleek, black pistol that meant the weapon was "hot" and ready to fire.

"Don't shoot me, Turner!" Gold pleaded, staring at the Walther held casually in Layten's hand. "I beg you, don't do it!"

Gold frantically crawled to the office's far corner, upending the potted palm in order to retrieve the .38 Smith & Wesson. Layten watched as Gold then scrabbled across the carpet, fingers clawing around the bases of the packing cases in order to gather up a couple of the spilt .38-caliber rounds. He began clumsily jamming them into the revolver's cylinder.

"Take your time, Steven," Layten said coolly as Gold managed to load the Smith. "I want to give you the fairest possible chance against me. You're going to need it. . . ."

Gold, his face twisted into a hideous grimace of fear, rose up to his knees, grasping the revolver with trembling hands as he brought it to bear on Layten.

"Go ahead," Layten told him while still holding his Walther at his side. "Shoot, if you've got the balls."

Gold, bellowing in fear, started to press the Smith's trigger. Layten smoothly extended his right hand holding the Walther. Gold fired the Smith. Layten squeezed off his own shot. . . .

Gold's round went wild, plowing an ugly furrow in Layten's desktop. Meanwhile, the Walther had bucked in Layten's hand, ejecting a brass shell casing that chimed musically as it bounced off the desk and then landed on the carpet. The guns' twin sharp reports had sounded very loud within the confines of the office, but not as loud as Gold's despairing howl as the crimson flower of death blossomed on his shirt-front.

Gold's revolver drooped. His eyes glassed over. "Help me," Gold begged piteously, his earlier arrogant tone now reduced to a hoarse whisper. "Call an ambulance. . . . Please! . . . Help me, Turner. . . ."

But it was too late.

"It's too late," Layten said, not unkindly, for he could afford pity for a vanquished foe. "I aimed for your heart, and I never miss." Layten shook his head. "Steven, Steven, Steven . . . You should have listened when I told you that someday I'd even the score between us."

"Should . . . have . . ." Gold nodded, pausing to cough bright scarlet bubbles of blood. "Should have listened—"

Layten watched Gold pitch forward to settle into the oblivion of death. Then Layten heard footsteps clattering down the corridor.

"Mr. Layten!"

Layten looked up to see Clarice, his sultry redhead receptionist, standing in the doorway. Clarice pressed the back of her hand to her mouth as she stared with horrified, widened eyes at Gold's corpse lying curled on the carpet.

"M-Mr. Layten— Turner!" she amended shyly. "W-What happened?"

"It was self-defense, Clarice." Layten calmly gestured with his Walther to the smoking revolver still lying curled in Gold's fingers. "As you can plainly see, I had no choice. . . ."

"Yes, sir!" Clarice seemed to be calming. "But Turner, are you all right?"

Layten, studying her, saw the smoldering passion in her blue eyes. It was a look he'd been aware of for months but had chosen to ignore.

But no longer, he thought, feeling his own passion flaming his loins. *Clarice, I will make you mine, for to the victor belongs the spoils.*

"I'm fine, baby . . . ," Layten murmured, beckoning her. "At least, there's nothing wrong with me you can't kiss and make better."

"Oh, yes, Turner." Clarice sighed happily. She hurried across the room—stepping nimbly over Gold's corpse—to fold herself within Layten's strong embrace. . . .

The telephone on Layten's desk rang, startling him out of his fantasy.

"Yeah, it could have happened like that," Layten told his empty office and the ringing telephone. "*If* Gold had come back, and *if* I had a backup gun . . ."

Layten guessed that by now Gold was in an elevator and on his way down to the lobby. Layten was still on the floor, where Gold had left him. He was still leaning against the wall, hugging his knees and breathing deeply, focused on his throbbing gut, waiting for the radiating circles of pain and the waves of nausea to subside. He wanted to answer the shrilly insistent telephone, but he didn't think he was ready to get up yet.

"Got to get into shape," Layten muttered. "Ridiculous for one punch to have wiped me out like this . . ."

Then again, it wasn't as if he were used to physical violence. The CIA didn't train you in firearms or unarmed combat unless you were designated likely material for certain kinds of field assignments, and from the beginning of his Agency career it had been clear that Layten's future lay in administration.

Really ought to answer that telephone, Layten thought. Then, mercifully, the damned thing stopped ringing.

Haven't been struck since I was a youngster, Layten remembered. That last time had been in prep school, during some altercation over a close call in a game of lacrosse. Ironically, back then as now, Layten had been punched in the stomach, and back then as now, he'd found the experience to be excruciatingly painful, humiliating . . .

Enraging.

Layten had been unable to exact his revenge upon that schoolyard bully, but *this* time things would turn out differently, because this time he had far more offensive options at his disposal.

He was feeling better and got up slowly, groaning. He felt like he had a white-hot coal smoldering in his gut. He managed to hobble over to his desk and collapse in his chair.

The telephone again began to ring. Layten wearily picked it up. "Yes?"

"Mr. Layten?"

"Yes, Clarice—I mean, Miss O'Brien," Layten hastily corrected himself. *Clarice, Clarice, Clarice.* He'd had a crush on the redheaded receptionist for months, but had been unable to bring himself to do anything about it. It was too late now, he supposed with some relief. In a couple more days these offices would be closed, and he would never see her again. Just as well. He wasn't good with women. Never had been . . .

"Mr. Campbell has been trying to reach you," the receptionist said.

"Oh, did he just call?"

"Yes, sir. Mr. Campbell said your phone rang and rang, and then he called me."

"Ah, well, I was . . . indisposed," Layten said. "Did he leave a number?"

"Mr. Campbell said you could reach him on his private line in New York."

"Thank you," Layten said, and broke the connection. He then dialed Campbell direct, punching in the long-distance number from memory. He was very good with numbers.

Campbell picked up on the fifth ring. "Yes?"

"It's me," Layten said. "You wanted to speak to me, sir?"

"Yeah, I did, Turner. I have some further ideas on the Amalgamated-Landis expansion we discussed—"

"Excuse me, Tim, but before we get into that, I think I should tell you that Steven Gold was just here to see me."

"Hah! I told you so, Turner!" Campbell said, sounding pleased.

"Actually, sir, he came to see *you*," Turner amended respectfully.

"Obviously, Turner," Campbell said impatiently. "Well, what did Steve want? What did he say? Tell me everything!"

Layten told him, leaving out the part about the gun. Layten

was ashamed of how he'd fubbed that, and anyway, Campbell would never have approved if he knew Layten carried one.

"He actually struck you, Turner?" Campbell asked when Layten had finished his account of what took place. "You're not exaggerating, now?" he cautioned. "Steven actually hauled off and punched you in the stomach?"

"Yes, Tim." Layten was feeling a bit affronted at the way Campbell was sounding so amused about the incident.

"Well, you did call his father a despicable name," Campbell scolded mildly.

"With all due respect, Tim, I called Herman Gold exactly what he was."

Campbell chuckled. "In any event, you got off lucky with just a sore belly, Turner, boy. Many, many years ago I witnessed Herman Gold *kill* a man who called him a kike."

"Killed . . . ?" Layten echoed feebly, shuddering as he remembered how easily Steve Gold had taken control of the revolver. Layten often had fantasies in which he violently triumphed over his enemies, but the notion that he himself might be seriously hurt scared the daylights out of him.

"Anyway," Campbell said. "Let's look on the bright side of this here juicy li'l contretempts between you and Steven."

"I didn't think there was a bright side," Layten said sourly.

"There's always a bright side," Campbell lectured. "What separates the men from the boys in our line of work is the ability to discover it and use it to one's advantage."

"Yes, sir," Layten said happily. He loved it when Campbell got off on the Machiavellian thing.

Campbell said: "Now, what we can infer from Steven's belligerence today is that he's been riled by his clash with us, or rather to the lengths to which he had to go to counter our threat." He cackled. "In a word, son, poor ole Steven's *remorseful*."

He didn't seem very remorseful to me," Layten muttered, rubbing his aching belly.

"That's 'cause you don't know 'em like I do, son," Campbell assured.

I don't? Layten thought glumly. *I've only spent the last ten years of my life obsessed with getting even with the man.*

"Oh, sure, Turner. You *think* about Steven a lot," Campbell said, as if he'd read Layten's mind or something. Campbell did it a lot, and it never failed to spook Layten.

"You think about Steve and have studied up on 'im," Campbell was continuing. "But you don't know him personally, the way I do, son. I watched Steven grow up, and I can tell you that he's just like his father. Like Herman, Steven has a conscience. In other words, like his father, Steven has the brains to figure out what needs to be done in a specific situation, and the ability to do it, but he hasn't got the willpower to put out of his mind the less savory aspects of what he's done." Campbell paused, sighing. "It was Herman's inability to take pleasure in his ruthlessness that kept him from true greatness."

Layten smiled, forgetting his physical discomfort at Steven Gold's hands in the rush he felt at chatting so intimately with Tim Campbell. "But ruthlessness like so many of the finer things in life is an acquired taste, isn't that so, sir?"

"Indeed it is, Turner, old boy." Campbell chuckled. "Indeed it is. You know what they said about the gunfighters of the Old West? That the best of 'em didn't think twice about killing an adversary. They just drew and shot: That was what made 'em the fastest. Flying way up high in the sky in his fighter planes, Steven Gold had always considered himself above the fray, but we made 'im get down and dirty this time, Turner."

"But, Tim . . ." Layten paused, afraid to say it. "Sir . . . GAT won. They cost you a lot of money."

"Steve knows money don't mean shit to me anymore," Campbell said. "I got so much money I could catch me a dose a dysentery, wipe my ass with thousand-dollar bills, and never feel the pinch. As far as I'm concerned, money is just a raw material, like clay to a sculptor. Money's just the medium in which I work my art."

"Just the same, sir," Layten said. "They did win?"

"Yeah, sure, GAT won," Campbell muttered. "Steve Gold and Don Harrison did what they had to do, but like I said, I know those hombres. I'll betcha anything they didn't *like* doing it."

"They were reluctant gunfighters," Layten murmured, shivering with pleasure as he began to understand.

"*Now* you're with the program, son," Campbell laughed.

"Reluctant gunfighters was *just* what they were. Next time we go toe-to-toe with GAT, Steven Gold and Don Harrison just might flinch before they make their move."

"But we never flinch," Layten boasted.

"And that's the advantage we'll use to finish 'em," Campbell concluded.

It was all so obvious, Layten thought. "Thank you, Tim."

"My pleasure, son," Campbell said. "You're a fast learner. Now, then, getting back to the Amalgamated-Landis expansion. I've decided to move you over to our El Segundo facility. Your title at A-L will be executive director of marketing and sales, reporting directly to me. Your cover will be that you're at A-L to monitor the industry competition in the marketplace, but the only company I want you to keep your eye on is GAT. I want you to continue to devote yourself to information gathering on our friends in Burbank, is that clear?"

"Yes, sir."

"All right, then," Campbell said. "I'll be back in L.A. next week. For now, is there anything else?"

Layten briefly considered asking if he could bring along the redheaded receptionist to be his secretary. That would give Layten more time to get to know her. Perhaps he and Clarice could have lunch together—maybe even dinner—to discuss the job?

"Turner?" Campbell spoke up impatiently. "You still there?"

"Yes, sir," Layten said. "No, Tim, there's nothing I need." He paused. "Except for Steve Gold's head, mounted above my mantel."

Campbell laughed. "That's my boy!"

CHAPTER 10

(One)

**Gold Estate
Bel-Air, California
7 April, 1974**

It was a Sunday morning. Erica Gold was sitting in the quiet of her bedroom, remembering her wedding day.

The mirrored vanity reflected Erica's surroundings. There was the large, circular bed she had shared with her husband, Herman, who'd been gone these past two and a half years. The French doors leading out to the balcony were framed in draperies of embroidered, emerald satin, and the bedroom's scrolled, gilt-bronze furniture reposed on lion's paws upon the plush, ivy-green carpeting.

Erica Gold saw all these fine trappings, but when she looked at her own reflection she did not see a slim, white-haired woman of seventy-two, elegantly attired in a gray silk suit. Instead, she saw a twenty-year-old bride, a long-legged, coltish girl with blonde hair plaited into thick braids, brown eyes set far apart, and a slightly crooked nose.

She'd broken her nose when she was very little; a tomboy, as her mother used to scold. One day her brothers had dared her to leap across the stream behind the farmhouse, and she'd done it, leaping farther than any of them, until she'd slipped on a slick stone and ended up walking back to the house with her brother Arnold's blue neckerchief pressed against her face. . . .

Such memories! Erica absently fingered the plain gold wedding band on her left hand. She had boxes and boxes of jewelry here at the house and in various safe-deposit vaults. She had elaborate gold and silver ornaments; diamonds, rubies, emeralds: over the years Herman had graced her with some of all the world's glittering, precious things. . . . She wore none of it anymore. She couldn't be bothered. She'd worn it all in the first place because it had made Herman happy. Now there was just her wedding band.

Anyway, memories were life's true jewels, and she had so many splendid ones from which to choose. . . .

She was born Erica Schuler, in rural Nebraska, the only girl among five boys in a German immigrant farm family. Erica's father early on became a wealthy man and showered her with the best of everything. But all the expensive diversions couldn't distract her from the infuriating awareness that women were supposed to stand by and watch while menfolk did the important things. What Erica wanted was to remain forever a tomboy, to soar on her abilities. But she knew that meant that she would first have to find a man, a soul mate, who was self-confident enough to allow her free rein. . . .

It was July 1921. Summer in Nebraska, and the sky was a faded blue above the amber and green vastness of the plain. Erica was nineteen, and becoming resigned to being just like all the other girls she knew, when a barnstorming troupe rolled into town and a tall, lanky, twenty-two-year-old pilot named Herman Gold came into her life, changing everything. When Erica's father found out that Herman Gold was also a German immigrant, her father invited the boy to supper. The next day, to repay the kindness, Herman took Erica for a ride in his rickety old Curtiss JN-4D "Jenny" biplane. Together she and Herman banked and pinwheeled across the sky, until Erica, laughing and crying, felt like she'd flown with the angels. After they landed, she told Herman as much, and he shyly murmured that *she* was the angel. And she kissed him. . . .

Thinking back on it now, Erica wasn't sure which she had fallen in love with first: that noisy, old biplane, or the man who flew it. It was funny how shy Herman had been with her, considering his reckless bravery in the sky, but gradually during their courtship he confessed to her his dream of starting his own aviation company, of becoming an emperor of the air. . . .

And he did it, with my help, Erica now thought proudly.

From outside her bedroom windows overlooking the pool, came the sounds of the family and friends gathering for to-day's grand occasion. The Gold estate was hidden behind stone walls and wrought-iron gates in Bel-Air. The house was a rambling English Colonial with a vine-covered, gray stone exterior, black iron casement windows, and a green copper mansard roof. Behind the house was a four-car garage, broad expanses of rolling lawn, a tennis court, the pool, and the stables where the family had kept Shetland ponies when the children were young. A full-time caretaker lived above the garage and kept everything running smoothly. Live-in servants tended to the house itself.

Erica and Herman had lived here with their two children, Susan and Steven, since 1928. They'd enjoyed decades of happiness within this house. . . .

A knock at the bedroom door startled Erica.

"Mother, it's Susan. Are you all right?"

"Yes, darling." Erica, looking in the mirror, saw that her eyes were wet, and daubed them with a tissue from the vanity. "Come in, Susan."

Susan Harrison came into the bedroom carrying an orchid corsage like the one she was wearing. Erica's firstborn was a brown-eyed blonde of forty-seven, wearing a green silk party dress with puffy sleeves that showed off her wide, tanned shoulders. Erica thought her daughter looked smash-ing, but then, Susan had always been a big, athletic girl, with her mother's coloring and her father's sturdy build.

"Mother, everyone's arrived," Susan said. "They're wait-ing for you." She studied Erica. "Have you been crying?"

Erica shook her head, smiling. "No, just thinking." She got up from the vanity, slipping her stockinged feet into a pair of black pumps as Susan came over to fasten the corsage to her lapel.

"There," Susan said, giving Erica a peek on the cheek. "It looks lovely on you."

"Thank you, dear. Shall we go downstairs?"

They left the bedroom, walking arm-in-arm along the third-floor hallway, and then downstairs via the central, curved marble staircase. Susan was quiet until they reached the first floor, and then she asked, "Were you thinking about Daddy?"

Erica nodded, giving Susan's hand an affectionate squeeze.

"I wish Daddy could have been here today." Susan sighed as they moved through the big, quiet house with its high, gilded ceilings and mahogany paneling. "I'm sure he would have thought Linda Forrester was just wonderful. How happy he would have been to see Steve getting married at last."

They went out through the solarium's French doors to the terraced, flagstone patio. The patio was landscaped with shrubbery and redwood flower boxes and overlooked the Olympic-size swimming pool. Erica, who'd been preoccupied with planning the wedding, now carefully surveyed the scene. As she'd decreed, the patio was an extravaganza of floral arrangements, and the caterer had set out the cold buffet in the patio's screened dining area near the bar, where the four-piece chamber-music ensemble was playing softly.

Only the immediate family and a few close friends had been invited to the wedding, and now those guests were having drinks, chatting in clusters. Erica saw her son-in-law, Don Harrison, the best man, standing with Steve, who was looking exceedingly nervous. Both men were wearing business suits with boutonnieres pinned to their lapels. Erica had lobbied for more formal attire, but Linda Forrester, who would be married wearing a turquoise suit with a small beaded veil pinned to her hair, had wanted things kept simple.

Erica supposed she understood. This was Linda's second marriage, after all, and neither she nor Steve was exactly a kid anymore. . . .

Erica smiled at Andrew Harrison, who was chatting with friends of the family near the pool. Andy was Susan's youngest son by her second husband, Don. He was a handsome, blond-haired, brown-eyed young man who was presently wearing a suit and tie, but yesterday Erica's grandson had come to visit her wearing his cadet's uniform. Andy was in for the wedding from the Air Force Academy in Colorado Springs, where he was in his second year. The only member of the immediate family not here was Robert Greene, Erica's first grandchild and Susan's oldest son by her first husband. Robbie, an Air Force captain, had sent his regrets. He was currently somewhere far away, involved in some sort of fighter-pilot exchange program between the Armed Services.

Linda Forrester was an only child, and both her parents had passed away, so she had no family in attendance today beyond her two children from her first marriage. Chad, thirteen, and Thomas, eleven, looking preppy in their double-breasted blue blazers and chinos, were chasing each other around the pool. Erica smiled as she watched them, pleased at the prospect of acquiring another set of young grandsons now that Robbie and Andrew were all grown up. Erica knew Steve adored Linda's boys, and that they adored him. Linda had joked that she wasn't sure who held the greater attraction for Steve: herself or her sons. There was nothing Steve liked better than to take the boys flying in one of the company's private planes, or for a camping weekend.

"Everything looks lovely, Mother," Susan complimented.

"I suppose," Erica commented wryly. "For a 'laid back' kind of an affair, as Steven and Linda stipulated, that is."

Beyond the patio, a striped awning had been erected on the lawn to afford shelter from the sun during the ceremony. Beneath that awning, almost hidden by still more flowers, a justice of the peace now stood, prepared to conduct the ceremony. Erica searched out her butler, caught his eye, and signaled with a subtle nod that things could begin. The butler relayed the message to a number of young Air Force officers who had served under Steven in the military and had volunteered to honor their ex—superior officer by acting as ushers. The young men in their slate-blue dress uniforms now began conducting the guests to their seats beneath the awning. Once everyone was seated, Erica, escorted by her daughter, took their places in the front row of folding chairs.

"Linda will be good for Steven." Erica whispered to Susan. "She's tough. She'll know how to keep him in line."

Susan giggled. "The way you kept Daddy in line?"

Erica shook her head. "Your father didn't need me for that. He grew up in difficult times. Long before he met me, the circumstances of his birth had tempered him. There was only one way for him to go, and that was up. But Steven was born into the lap of luxury. As you were. As I was." She paused, smiling wistfully, as the wedding march began. "I've come to realize it's far harder to maintain one's balance at the pinnacle than it is to climb there in the first place."

(Two)

During the reception after the ceremony, Steven Gold asked his bride, "So how does it feel to be married, Mrs. Gold?"

"That's Forrester-Gold to you, chum," Linda remarked.

Gold winced. "That sounds like a brand of rum."

Linda thought about it. "Maybe I'll just stick with Forrester. . . ."

They were at the bar, sipping mimosas, ogling their shiny new wedding bands. Gold was feeling relieved it was over. He hated ceremony of any kind, and was grateful that Linda had kept everything as low-key as possible, given the fact his mother was involved in the planning.

"My mother looked happy, don't you think?" Gold asked.

Linda nodded. "I'm glad. I've come to really like Erica."

"You sound surprised."

"Well, when I began getting to know her, I didn't know what to expect. Here she was, the white-haired, Bel-Air matriarch locked up in this castle. . . ." Linda shrugged. "But as I got to know her, I realized how together she is. She really knows what's going on."

"She always has," Gold agreed. "She was an aviatrix back in the twenties, you know."

"Come on." Linda looked skeptical. "Your mom, a *flier*?"

"Yep. You should get her to tell you about it sometime. It might make a good book. She took flying lessons with Amelia Earhart, and then got involved in air racing. She has a whole collection of trophies and plaques she won. Pop used to keep them in his office to show off to people, but now they must be somewhere around the house. She was pretty famous in her day, featured in newsreels and on magazine covers. Back when Pop and Tim Campbell were still partners, they convinced her to represent the company in an advertising campaign—''

"Holy shit!" Linda interrupted, laughing. "You mean *Erica* was the 'GAT girl'?"

Steve nodded proudly. "I couldn't have been more than five or six at the time, but I still remember that poster showing the airplanes flying above the Gold Aviation hangar, and my mom in her flying suit, with a big smile on her face, and all those blond ringlets sticking out from underneath her leather flying helmet.''

Linda said: "That was one of the most successful early campaigns in advertising history."

"I remember Pop telling me once that Gold Transport's passenger volume soared whenever my mom was featured in an ad." Gold paused as his nephew Andrew came over to them.

"Congratulations, Uncle Steve, ma'am," Andy said, shaking hands with them both.

Linda said, "Thanks, Andy, but please call me Linda." She winked. "Take it from me, no woman, married or single, wants to be called 'ma'am.' ''

"Suppose not," Andy murmured.

"Not that you're going to have any trouble with women, Andy," Linda continued. "Not with those looks."

Andy was blushing. Smiling shyly.

"Now that I think about it, you're the spitting image of your uncle Steve, about twenty years ago. . . ." Linda paused. "You wouldn't know it to look at old baldie today, but back then he had thick blond hair just like yours."

Gold rolled his eyes, complaining to Andy: "Women: You can't live with 'em, and you can't strafe 'em."

Linda asked, "Did you enjoy the ceremony?"

"Sure," Andy replied.

"Have enough champagne?" Gold coaxed.

"I don't drink, Uncle Steve."

"Oh, yeah . . . I forgot." Gold hesitated, feeling awkward, feeling sad. He used to know just what to say to make his nephew smile. "Well! How's the Academy treating you?"

"Things are great there, Uncle Steve," Andy said politely. "I've been doing a lot of flying."

"Just wait 'til you solo in a jet," Gold enthused. "It's something else! It'll make flying a prop plane feel like driving a golf cart." He told Linda: "I used to take Andy flying when he was a kid. I had him doing stunts in the company Cessna when he was no more than twelve." He grinned at his nephew. "Right, kid?"

Andrew nodded politely. "Right, Uncle Steve."

"I never saw anybody take to flying so quickly, except maybe your brother Robbie."

"Half brother," Andy corrected firmly.

"Right . . ." Gold thought sadly that the look in Andy's eyes was hard far beyond his years.

"I'm pleased to see the company is doing so well," Andy said, changing the subject.

Gold nodded. "It looks like we're going to sell a whole bunch of Stiletto fighters to our NATO allies through Skytrain Industrie."

Andy said, "Speaking of the Stiletto, it's a real feather in both yours and my dad's caps that GAT was able to report increased earnings and revenues this quarter. The fact that you were able to announce an increase in stock dividends to forty-five cents a share, up from forty cents, and a three-for-two stock split really shut up those loudmouth industry analysts who were claiming that GAT would go down the tubes without Grandpa."

Gold's jaw had dropped. "You really *have* been following the business, haven't you kid?"

"Well, after all . . ." Andy shrugged modestly. "I *do* expect to be in the pilot's seat at GAT someday."

Gold chuckled. "Your dad and I had better start checking our sixes a little more often now that we know we've got *you* gunning for us."

Andy laughed. "Oh, I'm not in competition with *you* two guys, Uncle Steve." He glanced at his watch. "Look, I've got a flight to catch in about an hour."

"Back to Colorado Springs?" Linda asked.

"I've got classes first thing tomorrow morning," Andy replied. "But I want to spend a little more time with Grandma."

"Take off, then," Steve said.

"Yeah, I guess I'd better." Andy grinned at Linda. "Welcome to the family."

"Thank you," Linda smiled. She waited for Andy to walk away before telling Gold: "If you ask me, that young buck has grown up and is looking to lock antlers with the resident stag."

"What? You mean all that showing off the kid was doing spouting those numbers concerning GAT?" Gold shook his head. "He gets that kind of talk from his old man. And he was just kidding around when he threatened to bump Don and me out of the cockpit at GAT."

Linda, smiling, shook her head, squeezing his arm. "No offense, darling, but you're not the resident stag to whom I was referring. I think Andy meant it when he said he didn't see himself in competition with you or his father." She paused. "But didn't you see the way you wiped the smile off his face when you mentioned his brother Robbie?"

"*Half* brother," Gold remarked dourly. "Yeah, I did, but I was hoping it was my imagination. There's been bad blood between Robbie and Andy for a long time. Now I don't think my two nephews exchange half a dozen words a year. It's like they don't exist for one another, except as thorns in each other's sides. The only thing that's kept the family peace is the fact that chance has kept them geographically apart."

"I wouldn't count on chance for much longer," Linda said. "The world can get very small very quickly once *both* of them are Air Force fighter pilots."

"Tell me about it," Gold grumbled. "I hate to admit it, but I was somewhat relieved when I found out Robbie wasn't going to be able to attend the wedding. I love both my nephews dearly, but I really wasn't in the mood to be stuck refereeing a furball mix-up between those two on my wedding day."

"Where is Robbie?"

"Somewhere he can't get into trouble," Gold said firmly.

"What do you mean by that?" Linda laughed.

"It's really not a laughing matter," Gold replied, frowning. "I've been hearing things about Captain Greene. Things that aren't so good. For instance, there was that blowout at Wright-Patterson when he and some buddy of his dive-bombed the city of Dayton or some such crapola, and that wasn't the first time he broke the rules."

Linda looked at Gold in mock horror. "He broke the *rules*? *Your* nephew broke the *rules*? Now who do you suppose taught him to do something like *that*?" She laughed. "Steve, in your career you must have fractured every regulation in the Air Force's book!"

"Maybe so." Gold chuckled. I guess I was something of a wild card, but the thing is, in *my* heyday there were usually a war going on. Being needed on the front line in combat cuts a guy a considerable amount of slack, but things are different in peacetime. The brass tends to take the rules and regs a lot more seriously when they don't have a shooting war to distract them. That's why I'm worried about Robbie. The Air Force is getting buttoned down. It isn't the sanctuary for rogues and wild cards that it used to be." Gold smiled. "But now Robbie's on an aircraft carrier, stuck out in the middle of nowhere. Like I said, for once I can breathe easy. Robbie Greene is somewhere where even *he* can't get himself into trouble."

CHAPTER 11

(One)

USS
Sea Bear CV-22
South China Sea
12 May, 1975

It was just past noon. Robbie Greene wasn't scheduled to fly today, so he was in the flattop's officer-rec room, having a cup of coffee and playing solitaire, when he heard about how the Commies in Cambodia had grabbed the *Mayaguez*.

The rec room was windowless. It had flat fluorescent lighting, a green vinyl tile floor, gray metal furniture, and two tones of gray paint on its curved steel walls. The room was decorated with posters of sleek Navy jets like the F-4 Phantom and F-7 Corsair; and even sleeker female rock stars like Linda Ronstadt, beckoning with soulful brown eyes, and Tina Turner making love to the microphone from the movie *Woodstock*. There was a bookcase that held a selection of tattered paperbacks, metal shelves stacked with the usual suburban rumpus-room assortment of board games, and a boom-box portable cassette player. There was also an ever-flickering TV mounted high up on the wall on one of those hospital-room-type swivel brackets. The carrier's closed-circuit facility was broadcasting an old movie, *Mutiny on the Bounty* with Charles Laughton, which Greene thought was a weird choice for programming on a United States Navy military vessel. The TV's volume was turned low, because Greene wasn't watching the movie, and the only other person in the rec room, a lieutenant JG by the name of Gillis, was dozing in his chair.

Greene put away the cards midway through his game, bored out of his skull. He'd been on this flattop three months now, and couldn't wait for this tour to be over. He'd felt some initial excitement when he'd first come aboard—"yo-ho-ho and a bottle of rum,'' and all that—and things had picked up at the end of last month, when the *Sea Bear* had participated in the American evacuation of Saigon. Other than that, as far as Greene was concerned Operation Indian Giver had turned out to be a bust.

Things started out okay back at Wright-Patterson. Colonel Dougan came through, arranging it so that both Greene and his buddy Buzz Blaisdale could participate in Indian Giver. The two pilots left Dayton, feeling on top of the world and looking forward to whatever it was the Navy thought it could dish out. Greene and Blaisdale arrived at the naval air station at Pensacola, Florida, grimly determined, expecting to be treated like lepers. So they were surprised and gratified at their cordial reception from the instructors and fledgling-winged squids here for "Jets" training: the fundamentals of jet flight.

Settling into Pensacola, the two Air Force pilots had themselves a problem dealing with their living condition. The Navy, claiming a lack of room, stuck them out in the boondocks of the base, in a beer can of a trailer surrounded by rusted-out abandoned vehicles, scrub brush, and palm trees. The only thing missing was a junkyard dog, but then, the alligators probably ate it. Blaisdale had a really tough time with the cockroaches. The Floridians called them palmetto bugs, but the fuckers were cockroaches, plain and simple, except that they were on average two inches long and faster off the mark than a Harrier jump jet. Greene himself wasn't much fond of bugs, but he'd served his time in hell at Phanrat AFB in Thailand; once you'd dealt with the creepy-crawlies of Indochina, no bug smaller than a mountain lion indigenous to the States was going to much upset you.

Accommodations and vermin aside, those first few weeks in Pensacola among the squids were an A-1 blast. Greene and Blaisdale totally enjoyed "regressing," tooling around in the "turbofan tricycle," dual-seat, T-1 Buckeye primary jet Trainers while their backseater pilot instructors went through the motions of checking them out on the basics. Pretty quickly the two Air Force pilots were bumped into the accelerated course to qualify them for carrier ops. The first stage of the training involved making simulated arrested landing on a "carrier flight deck" painted on a shore runway.

Throughout their intitial stints flying the basics for their appreciative instructors, Greene and Blaisdale kept remarking to each other on how they couldn't get over how nice everyone was being to them. The squid pilots were going out of their way to include them in the late-night bull sessions and the occasional beer blast, and Greene was even encouraged to tell war stories. All in all, their easy acceptance into the naval frat of fliers was eerie. It was a dream too good to be true. . . .

The honeymoon ended the night before carrier flight training began. On that evening, Blaisdale came stomping into the trailer to complain that he had accidentally overheard a couple of squid instructors laughing among themselves about the "tiger trap" betting pool. The betting wasn't *if* the Air Force "tigers" would wash out during carrier training, but *when.*

That night, Greene and Blaisdale glumly put two and two together in their humid, sticky trailer, drinking Coke and listening to the bugs thumping the window screens. They realized that the squids' seeming civility was really a form of mockery. Everyone was being so nice to them because none of the Navy personnel thought a couple of Air Force jocks had a chance in hell of making it through CARQUAL, carrier qualification. The damn Navy had kissed them hello, all right, but in gleeful anticipation of kissing them goodbye. They hadn't been accepted into the naval aviators' fraternity; far from it, the real hazing had only just begun.

That night, Greene and Blaisdale vowed they'd show the Navy what a couple of Air Force jocks could do. Thinking back, Greene knew that Buzz had tried as hard as he could to keep that vow.

It was only in retrospect that Greene came to understand the enormity of the training problem that had faced him and Blaisdale. Carrier ops was like no other kind of flying. The squid pilots taking carrier training had been flying only a short while, so for them it was comparatively easy to modify the basic flying techniques they had so recently learned. Unfortunately, it was an entirely different story for Greene and Blaisdale. They were experienced military fliers, which meant that they had long ago formed ingrained habits that would die hard. Greene and Blaisdale became the proverbial old dogs, straining to learn new tricks.

New tricks that Buzz Blaisdale proved incapable of learning.

Everything that the Air Force had drummed into them concerning flared, nose-high, easy-does-it touchdowns had to be erased from Greene's and Blaisdale's memory banks. When you landed on the flight deck of a carrier at 150 miles per hour, you had to slap down hard, like slamming your fist on the table, So that one of the four arresting cables strung across the deck trapped your bird's tailhook, stopping the airplane the way spider's silk stops a fly. Anything less than that brutal collision with the runaway and you'd run out of carrier deck and into a whole lot of ocean before you could say "Oh, shitttt—"

Now maybe it was the fact that Greene had been in combat while Blaisdale had missed out on 'Nam that had made the difference between them. Maybe the experience of having an enemy doing everything it could to knock Greene's Thud out of the sky during his bombing runs had served to teach him to blank out his mind, to put himself in the zen warrior state in order to accomplish whatever it was that had to be done. Then again, maybe it was just that Buzz Blaisdale had a better imagination than Greene. Maybe poor old Buzz wasn't able to stop himself from visualizing all the things that could go wrong when you tried to land on a heaving carrier by rabbit-punching the deck with your airplane.

Or maybe it was that Greene was more ornery. That he was crazier. Or maybe he just wanted it more. . . .

For whatever reason, that first time out trying a simulated carrier landing on dry land, Greene was able to put aside everything he'd learned about the Air Force way of landing a jet. As he angled his Buckeye trainer down toward that impossibly small-seeming rectangle painted on the tarmac, he just cleared his mind of distractions and kept his eyes moving between the Fresnel light landing aid, his instruments, and the looming ground. The Fresnel light landing aid, called "the ball," was set up along the side of the runway to give the pilot a point of reference for setting up his glide path. The ball looked something like a traffic light, with a horizontal bank of lenses extending on both sides to form a cross. If the pilot was making his approach properly, he'd see the middle vertical lens illuminated in relation to the horizontal lights. Too high and one of the upper lenses would glimmer; too low and one of the bottom lights would show.

"Pay attention to me first, and the ball second," Greene's backseater pilot instructor warned on that first flight. The Buckeye was arrowing toward the earth. The ground was coming up so fast that Greene was sure they were going to auger in, but then the PI ordered, "Put her down—now!"

Greene, gritting his teeth, slammed that Buckeye down where the instructor told him to. As the arrestor cable grabbed the Buckeye's tailhook, Greene's harness straps bit into his shoulders and the moleskin protective strip mohawking the top of his helmet scraped the inside top of the canopy. The Buck left rubber scorches on the tarmac, but Greene got the fucking job done.

"That was okay . . . for a first time," the instructor muttered through the cockpit intercom.

Damn right it was okay, Greene thought. *Ain't nothing the Navy can do the Air Force can't do better.*

But when it came time for it to be Blaisdale's turn, Buzz froze up. By then, Greene had finished for the day, and was watching from the sidelines as Buzz's sleek little T-2 Buck made its first approach toward that rectangle painted on the tarmac, shimmering in the Florida heat.

"He's coming in too low," remarked one of the squid pilots standing around watching along with Greene.

"He'll do okay," Greene muttered hopefully.

But Buzz didn't do okay at all. He bounced the airstrip, touching down too early and then rising up and dropping down again, totally missing the painted rectangle that represented the carrier's flight deck.

"If that had been the real thing . . ." The squid pilot trailed off, shaking his head.

"Hey, it wasn't the real thing," Greene said, feeling defensive. "Cut the guy some slack. It was his first try. He'll do better."

To the squid's credit, he didn't say anything further, not even when Buzz proceeded to botch his remaining landing attempts. Greene felt embarrassed for his friend. That kind of initial performance might have been excusable for an inexperienced pilot, but it was searingly humiliating for Blaisdale.

From then on, Blaisdale was shook. For a fighter jock there is nothing worse than a loss of confidence. Buzz knew what he had to do, but it was as if his reflexes conspired against him. He never did get the hang of hammering his plane into the landing rectangle. For a while, Blaisdale tried talking it out with Greene, but there are some things—the really important things—that talk can't fix. Eventually, Blaisdale just got kind of quiet and moody. Greene recognized the symptoms. He'd seen them before. Blaisdale may not have known it himself yet, but he'd given up.

The weeks passed. Greene moved ahead in his training. Blaisdale didn't. He was like a man with a critical illness, lingering on by a thread. Each day the squid instructors took him up and tried to teach him what he couldn't seem to learn. Sometimes different instructors took him up during the same day. It wasn't about cruelty on the part of the Navy; the squids didn't know what else to do. They would have washed out one of their own—plenty of squids did wash out—but in this case the touchy interservice politics of the situation didn't allow for giving Blaisdale the boot. The Navy wasn't about to kick Buzz Blaisdale out of Indian Giver; he would have to take himself out of it. By this point, all of the Navy's efforts were directed toward giving Blaisdale a nudge in that direction.

Finally, the the day came around for Greene to get his feet wet landing on a training carrier. He awoke that morning to find Buzz in his Air Force service uniform: slate-blue trousers and tunic; light-blue shirt and dark-blue tie; visored cap. Buzz was packing his bags.

"Well." Buzz shrugged, smiling thinly when he saw that Greene was awake. "I'm out of here."

Greene sat up in bed, scratching, and yawning. "I guess that makes sense," he said.

He felt terrible, but what could he say? *Sorry you didn't make the cut?* Buzz was doing the right thing. His only mistake had been waiting as long as he had. If Blaisdale couldn't hack the basic necessary flight procedures during Visual Flight Rules, how would he ever manage the rest of CARQUAL? Carrier qualification required proficiency in ILS Instrument Landing System carrier approaches. And what about the night landings?

Outside the trailer, a jeep's headlights flashed against the curtains, illuminating the gray Florida dawn. A horn honked.

"That's my ride," Buzz said, hefting his bags. "See you around, Robbie."

"Yeah, see you," Greene murmured.

Blaisdale looked supremely uncomfortable. "I'll let you know where I'm reassigned," he said.

"Good," Greene said, although he knew it was unlikely Blaisdale would do any such thing. Greene had been witness to his friend's great humiliating failure. Buzz would be anxious to put the shame behind him, and that meant disassociating with everyone who'd been on the scene when he'd failed to make the cut. This was good-bye.

Their eyes never met as Greene rolled out of bed and padded toward the trailer's narrow stall shower. By the time he was done showering, Buzz was gone.

A couple of hours later, Greene was adorned in his olive-drab, Nomex fire-retardant flight overalls and "speed jeans" G-suit. He was cinched into his parachute harness, wearing his helmet and oxygen mask; strapped into the Buckeye's pilot's seat. For a change, his backseater PI on this trip, Lieutenant Commander Bill "Popeye" Popovich, was quiet as they soared past the Florida coastline and out over the blue water, toward the training carrier.

Greene felt surprisingly calm considering the momentousness of what he was about to attempt. After all, successfully setting a jet down on a flattop was a true rite of passage. Greene guessed that the pain he'd felt on Buzz Blaisdale's behalf earlier that day had served to numb his emotions concerning himself.

Greene was also feeling good about that fact that he had Popeye Popovich along as his backseater this first time getting his feet wet. Greene had flown with Lieutenant Commander Popovich a couple of times; the senior instructor had come along on most of Greene's check rides. Popeye, who'd gotten his Navy call-sign nickname for obvious reasons, was in his late forties, with a gray crewcut and light-blue eyes. Of all the squid instructors, Greene liked Popeye the best. Unlike some of the other PIs, the lieutenant commander didn't have an attitude problem. Popeye didn't seem to care who you were or where you were from. If you flew the airplane okay, you were okay in his book.

Greene's radio headset crackled. "This landing should be a piece of cake for a hotshot like you, Air Force," Popeye said over the cockpit intercom. "My fucking grandmother could land on a flattop on a *bee-yuutiful* day like today."

"I didn't know your fucking grandmother was in the Navy, Popeye," Greene muttered. "Of course it's a beautiful day with A-1 flying conditions. Otherwise, I wouldn't be out here in the first place. . . ."

Greene had no trouble locating the carrier. From three miles away and three thousand feet in the air, the flattop looked like a scant smudge of gray trailing a comet's tail of white wake across the surface of the blue ocean. Landings on a carrier were made into the wind, so Greene circled the flattop, passing it downwind.

"You know, you young guys today got things *sooo* easy," Popeye announced.

Uh-oh, here we go, Greene thought affectionately. Popeye could chew your ear off reminiscing about the old days.

"Back in Korea, this kind of work was still dangerous," Popeye rambled. "*We* didn't have the precision instruments you pussies got now, and those Panthers *we* flew weren't anywhere near as throttle responsive—"

"Hey, Popeye," Greene interrupted as he put the Buckeye into a crosswind turn toward the carrier's stern. "Didn't I see you in that flick *The Bridge at Toko-Ri*?"

"Huh?" Popeye demanded. "What's that?"

"Yeah, man . . . ." Greene finished his crosswind turn and dirtied up his airplane by lowering his landing gear, flaps, and tailhook as he began his landing approach. "You were in that movie, Popeye. . . . Weren't you the guy who held William Holden's leather jacket for him?"

"Kids today," Popeye snorted dolefully. "Can't tell 'em shit."

A new voice crackled through Greene's helmet. "Five five five, clear deck, clear deck," the CATCC Carrier Air Traffic Control Center officer on board the carrier radioed, watching Greene's approach on his radar screen. The message directed to Greene's jet number 555 was that the carrier's deck was cleared for his landing.

"Now, don't you go spotting that deck, Air Force," Popeye cautioned.

"Roger." Greene nodded absently, his mind on the task ahead of him. His tendency to concentrate on the deck to the exclusion of all else was the biggest problem Greene had faced during his training, and "spotting the deck" had been Buzz Blaisdale's insurmountable error, as well. As an Air Force pilot, it was second nature for Greene during a VFI landing to fixate on the approaching runway, but when you did that trying to land on a carrier, the optical perspective invariably served to convince you that you were coming in too high. It was all an illusion, and if you gave in to it and came in too low, you'd hit the ramp and turn yourself into barbecue. The way to fight the optical illusion was not to steadily eyeball the deck in the first place. Instead, you listened up to your carrier-based controllers and kept your eyes moving across your instruments, as well as peering out your canopy at that itty bit of metal that was home sweet home.

The carrier loomed. That smudge of gray had grown into a narrow strip of hot-topped parking lot sliced from some suburban shopping mall and set afloat in the glinting blue Atlantic. Greene could clearly see the white striping that outlined the five-hundred-foot-long angled flight deck. True to habit, he felt he was coming in too high, but let his angle of attack indicator persuade him otherwise. He glanced at the ocean skimming past beneath his wings. *I go any lower, I'll need windshield wipers to clear the salt spray.*

"Five five five, on line, one mile," said the carrier's air controller. He was informing Greene that he was flying a correct approach toward the carrier, and that he was a mile away.

"R-Roger," Greene managed. His mouth had suddenly gone so dry that he had difficulty getting the word out.

"You're sounding tense, there, Air Force," Popeye said lightly. "You don't want to hit that ramp now. . . . If you bolt the carrier, I can take control of the airplane and get us out of it. You trap a little too much to the right or left, we'll merely slide off the deck and into the nets, and probably come out of this with just a couple of broken necks. But you hit that ramp, and we become deep-fried food for the fishes."

"Thanks, Popeye, I really needed to hear that right now," Greene snapped.

"No problem, Air Force." Popeye chuckled. "Did I mention that my fucking grandmother could set her down on a *bee-yuutiful* day like today?"

"This is where I came in," Greene said. He heard himself laugh.

"There you, go, Air Force," Popeye said. "Smile and the world smiles with you . . ."

Son of a bitch, I do feel better, Greene thought gratefully. Talk about stress, he wondered how a guy like Popeye could take so many backseat rides with first-timers and still find it within himself to joke the novice pilot out of his funk.

"Five five five, all down, call the ball," said another voice from the carrier, that of the landing signal officer. The LSO would be in charge of Greene's landing during its final moments, talking him down with last-second corrections if necessary, or, if the LSO didn't like the look of Greene's approach, waving him off. Just now, the LSO had told Greene that his landing-gear flaps and tailhook were down, and had asked Greene if he had visual contact with the LLD Light Landing Device.

"Five five five on the ball," Greene said, telling the LSO that he had visual contact with the LLD.

"Roger, ball," the LSO said.

Greene's touchdown aimpoint was the center of the four arresting cables that bisected the angled flight deck, roughly parallel to the carrier's superstructure. The cables were spaced forty feet apart: 120 feet of sanctuary in all, hence the 120-foot training rectangle painted on the tarmac way back when all this was just make-believe.

"Five five five on line, very slightly right, one half mile, call the ball."

Greene nudged the Buckeye starboard as he replied, "Five, five five. I've got center ball."

The carrier was coming up fast now. *Just another few seconds*, Greene thought.

The instant before Greene touched down, he would have to go to full throttle—full military power—so that his bird would have the energy to make it back into the sky in case Greene "bolted," missing all four cables, or in case something else went wrong. At full throttle, he'd travel from the first cable to the fourth in less than a half second.

"You ideally want that number-three wire, Air Force," Popeye said calmly.

"Five five five on line," the LSO radioed. "Good luck, Air Force."

"Well, well, well," Popeye laughed appreciatively. "Looks like you provisionally got yourself your call-sign moniker."

"Provisionally?"

"Sure," Popeye said. "You've got to earn it to keep it."

Don't think, Greene warned himself, pushing out of his mind the cautionary films they'd shown the pilots during training of those who'd done this wrong, in the process transforming themselves into fireballs. *Don't think. Do.*

The carrier was rocketing toward him with incredible speed. Greene's stomach was doing nervous flip-flops. *Come onnnn*, he thought, his eyes flitting from the ball, the expanding carrier deck, and his instruments. *Popeye's fucking grandmother could do it on such a bee-yuutiful day*.

Greene glimpsed the LSO officer and his people on their platform cantilevered off the carrier's aft port side, and then his bird's nose crossed the ramp—

He was over the ship!

Greene pushed forward his throttle to full military power, hearing the Buckeye's shrill scream as he slammed his bird down, transforming the silky rush of flight into a roaring, vibrating nightmare. "Trapped!" somebody yelled into his headset as Greene felt his harness straps bite his shoulders the way his tires were biting the nonskid coating of the deck.

"Power at idle. Feet off the brakes," Popeye calmly reminded Greene.

Greene didn't reply. He was flattened against his seatback, willing the plane to stop its forward rush, too busy staring wide-eyed at the fast-approaching front edge of the angled flight deck—and the *sea!*

"P-Popeye! W-We're going over into the nets!" Greene gasped.

"Nah," Popeye replied. He was sounding bored. "There, see?"

The trapped bird had rolled forward about three hundred feet before coming to a halt; its forward velocity had stretched the one-and-a-half-inch-diameter arresting cable as if it were an elastic band. Greene started to relax as the Buckeye came to a halt, and then began to roll backward a few feet, due to the arresting cable's rebound.

"Five five five, OK," the LSO radioed.

Greene smiled. "OK" indicated that Greene had made a perfect landing, trapping the number-three cable.

"Welcome aboard, Air Force," the LSO signed off.

"Not bad," Popeye commented. "Welcome to the Navy."

"Welcome to the Navy," Greene now murmured out loud, staring blindly at the deck of cards in his hand. Over on the far side of the rec room, the TV still offered Captain Bly in counterpoint to Gillis's snoring.

That first time out landing on a carrier had kind of been like Greene's first time going all the way with a girl: Driving that initial glide path was scary as hell, but once you'd been through the routine, the rest was just perfecting your technique.

In the weeks after, Greene completed CARQUAL. He progressed to solo VFI landings in his Buckeye, practiced IFS instrument and night landings in the simulator and then did the real thing with a backseater, and finally soloed at night. Then he went through the whole training schedule again, this time in the far more grown-up A-4 Skyhawk. The humpbacked, short-tempered "Scooter" truly made the lovable little Buck seem like a child's three-wheeler.

In addition, Greene learned how to take off from a carrier flight deck, which was a snap compared to setting down on one. After all, when you were strapped into a trimmed-for-takeoff bird with a wide-open throttle and then catapulted away, doing zero to 170 miles per hour in two seconds, you were pretty much just along for the ride.

From Pensacola, Greene moved on to Corpus Christi, Texas, into a Replacement Air Group for a stint familiarizing himself with the plane he'd be flying during his carrier tour. That was when interservice jealousy on the part of the Navy first reared its ugly head, and Air Force Captain Robbie Greene, for the first time in his military career, found himself a victim of the infamous military catch-22 mentality. All along Greene had expected to be destined for the front seat of a carrier based F-4 Phantom: the core jet fighter shared by both the Air Force and Navy. After all, the whole purpose of the Indian Giver project was to acquaint Greene with Navy air-combat tactics. Unfortunately, each gentleman on the list of naval flight officers available to crew with Greene in the tandem-seat Phantom made it clear that he was not interested in becoming famous—or infamous—as the only naval aviator to serve as the backseat "bear" radar intercept officer to an Air Force pilot. Now, any one of those RIOs in waiting could have been *ordered* to fly with Greene, but everyone involved realized that forcing an RIO into Greene's backseat would have defeated the whole purpose of Indian Giver. You needed the spirit of teamwork to excel with the Phantom: why else was the "Double Ugly" a two-man airplane in the first place? Anything less than wholehearted support from his bear and Greene might just as well go back home to the Air Force, because he was not going to be in a position to apply himself to learning anything about Navy air-combat manuevers.

There *was* a single-seat supersonic jet fighter in the Navy's arsenal: the shit-hot F-8 Crusader. Greene hungered for it. The F-8 was fast, carried a gun, and Greene had never liked the idea of flying with backseaters in the first place. The problem—enter catch-22—was that Greene had already been slotted for duty aboard carrier CV-22, the USS *Sea Bear*, and the *Sea Bear* didn't fly Crusaders, just dual-seat F-4 Phantoms, A-6 Intruders, and single-seat A-7 Corsair IIs. The tandem-seat A-6 Intruder was a subsonic attack-bomber, which made it totally unsuitable for Greene, even if the Navy could have come up with an NFO to fly with him. The A-7 Corsair was a subsonic version of the F-8 Crusader fighter that Greene had wanted but couldn't get. The A-7 was a visual-flight-rules-only operable light attack craft that would have been right at home flying close-support missions for the infantry back in Korea. It was a totally unsuitable airplane for a fighter-jock participant in Indian Giver to fly, but the Navy argued that at least it carried a gun, and, at times, a pair of fuselage-mounted Sidewinder heat-seekers—to be used only for self-defense, of course.

And so, Greene, kicking and screaming, was assigned to an A-7 RAG for six weeks of training in the cuddly, low-level "Mud Mover" Corsair. Greene continued to complain his head off about the stupidity of the assignment: why not just issue him a grenade launcher and assign him to the Marines if ground support was what the Navy had in mind for him? His complaints were duly noted, but nothing happened in response to them. Finally, a kindly CO advised Greene to save his breath. It seemed that the Air Force and Navy brass were so pleased with how smoothly the "important" Air Force personnel had been integrated into the Top Gun school at Miramar that nobody was in the least interested in spoiling the interservice love fest by heeding Captain Greene's mayday.

When Greene's RAG time was done, he was airlifted onto the *Sea Bear*, where for the past three months he'd been flying regular cyclic ops in the A-7, puttering around subsonically, strafing towed targets and the like, while high above him the elite, supersonic Phantoms were mixing it up in practice furballs. Talk about being the ugly duckling!

On the TV, the movie abruptly went off in midscene, followed by static hissing from the speaker and filling the screen.

Gillis snorted awake. He was a sandy-haired, soft-featured man in his twenties, wearing the Navy's summer-issue uniform of tan cotton trousers and a short-sleeve, open-neck shirt. Gillis sat up, blinking and yawning, staring at the TV, and then, accusingly, at Greene.

"Hey," Gillis said. "I was watching that."

Greene shrugged. "I didn't touch it. It just went off."

The television's sound and picture returned, but instead of the movie the TV showed a nervous-looking junior officer seated behind a desk. Behind the officer was the world map divided into a time zones backdrop they used for the daily news broadcasts.

"This is a special bulletin," announced the TV anchorman, reading from a stack of papers on his desk. "We have been informed that early this morning an American container ship, the merchantman *Mayaguez*, en route across the Gulf of Thailand, has been fired upon and boarded by Cambodian forces."

"Holy shit," Gillis breathed, getting out of his chair to turn up the volume.

The TV anchorman continued: ". . . President Ford and the National Security Council have met, and the White House has since issued the following statement. I quote: 'The President, concerned that the *Mayaguez* has been seized on the high seas, condemns the Cambodians for this act of piracy, and further demands the immediate release of the ship. Failure to do so will have the utmost serious consequences.' End of quote."

The reporter paused. "The *Sea Bear* has been ordered to the Gulf of Thailand concerning this matter. The skipper anticipates that the *Sea Bear* will be operational to the vicinity in approximately forty-eight hours, and has authorized further news bulletins to be broadcast as they come in." The newscaster smiled shyly. "Now, back to the movie."

Greene jumped up to turn down the sound. "What a break!" he said excitedly. "We're going to see some action!"

"Bullshit." Gillis shook his head. "No way is it going to come to that. The Commies will back down." He looked thoughtful. "I think that diplomacy will resolve the issue."

"Maybe it will," Greene said. "On the other hand, the *Sea Bear*, and who knows how many other ships are heading into the area . . ."

Greene glanced at his watch. It was a little after 1600 hours. The flights would be wrapping up for the afternoon. He headed for the door, thinking that now was a perfect time to start the ball rolling if he wanted a piece of the possible action to come.

The man to see was Gil Brody, the carrier's air boss.

* * *

Greene didn't get to see Brody until late the next day. As the chief officer in charge of supervising all air operations, Brody ended up spending the rest of Monday and most of Tuesday tied up in meetings with the skipper and the rest of the executive officers concerning the *Mayaguez* incident. Greene alternately checked in with the air boss's clerk and cooled his heels waiting, brooding anxiously over his chance to get a piece of the increasingly likely action as more developments concerning the *Mayaguez* were announced.

Late Monday night it was revealed that at about the same time the *Sea Bear* had been ordered to make full speed toward the Gulf of Thailand, Navy reconnaissance aircraft from out of Subic Bay, the Philippines, had been ordered to locate the captured American ship and keep it under surveillance. The planes had found the *Mayaguez*, reporting it anchored off the Cambodian mainland, near the port of Kompong Som. The excitement level on board the *Sea Bear* was raised a notch when it became known that the Navy's unarmed reconnaissance planes had been fired upon by the Cambodian patrol boats ringing the *Mayaguez*. Fortunately, none of the high-flying planes had been hit.

Tuesday morning it was reported that the Third Marine Division on Okinawa had been alerted. Over a thousand marines were being flown to Utapao Air Base in Thailand. Later that day, reports came in that the President had ordered armed USAF aircraft from out of Utapao to protect the Navy's surveillance craft from the Cambodian gunboats, and that the Cambodians had been warned that the use of force by the United States was becoming increasingly likely unless the *Mayaguez* and its crew were released.

Clearly, the *Mayaguez* situation's status had been upgraded from "incident" to "crisis."

(Two)

"What's the matter, Air Force?" Gil Brody, the *Sea Bear*'s air officer sarcastically asked Robbie Greene. Brody was a trim, muscular man in his forties, with thick black eyebrows, dark hair gone silver at the temples, and a salt-and-pepper mustache. On his open-neck shirt collar he wore a naval commander's oak leaves.

Brody leaned back in his swivel chair behind his gray metal desk. "You look like a man who's got his pecker caught in the catapult."

It was a little after seven on Tuesday night. The latest on the *Mayaguez* was that USAF warplanes were on the scene and drawing heavy machine-gun fire from the Cambodian patrol boats. So far no airplanes had been hit. Upon the President's orders, the Air Force planes had refrained from firing back at the Cambodians.

At seven o'clock, Greene had been notified that the air boss had a few minutes free in which to see him, and so Greene had come charging into Brody's office, which was small and windowless, like most everything else on this carrier. A poster taped to the wall behind Brody's desk showed a snowcapped mountain in Japan. Surrounding the poster were plaques Brody had won in various martial arts tournaments. More awards and trophies for placing in various martial-arts competitions filled several bracket shelves. Brody was known to be a martial-arts fanatic. He'd spent a year studying in Japan, and in his spare time ran classes on board the *Sea Bear*. Greene, wanting to pursue the martial-arts studies he'd begun at Wright-Patterson AFB, had taken some of Brody's classes for a while, but then he'd dropped out.

"Speak up, Air Force!" Brody was demanding. "What's on your mind?"

Greene didn't know how to begin. He'd come in here like gangbusters, his heart pounding and his pulse racing, thinking he was all charged up to make his case. Trouble was, Greene had spent the past sixteen hours rehearsing his piece. Now that he was actually in Brody's office, he found himself gone stale, with all of his pretty speeches gone out of his head.

Brody took a pack of Marlboros from out of his shirt pocket and lit one with a banged-up-looking Zippo. "Past day and a half, I've been up to my ass with meetings concerning how we might have to put the hurt on the Cambodians," he muttered.

Greene nodded. Brody and his people were the supreme

traffic cops for all the activity on the carrier's flight deck. During aircraft launches and recoveries, it was Brody and his gang who occupied Pri-Fly, or Primary Flight Control, a glassed-in balcony just beneath the carrier's bridge. Everyone—CCATC air controllers, LSO officers and staff, catapult crews, deck supervisors, and aircraft handlers (responsible for maneuvering the airplanes about the crowded deck)—answered to the air boss. From what Greene had been told, even the carrier's skipper made it a point to quietly occupy himself with steering his boat when the air boss was doing his thing.

"Finally, I get a little breather from all those meetings," Brody muttered. "But then, I find out that *you* got some sort of bone to pick with me."

"No way, Boss," Greene said. Everybody called the air officer "Boss". Personally, the practice made Greene feel like he was in *Cool Hand Luke*.

Greene forced a nervous smile. "Boss, I've got no problem. I'm here to make a request."

"I'm listening." Brody was slumped in his swivel chair with his eyes closed and his feet up on his desk. Every now and then, he took a puff off his cigarette and then flicked the ash in the general direction of a scummy-looking Blue Angels coffee mug.

Brody sure was looking tired and pale, Green thought. But then, the ever-present fluorescent lighting bleached the hell out of everyone's skin tone. What a joke Greene had played on himself when he'd imagined that his stint on board the *Sea Bear* would entail lots of salt breezes and sunshine. Coal miners got more fresh air and had better suntans than carrier crews. Living on an aircraft carrier was like inhabiting the subbasement levels of an office building, with only occasional, brief forays to the building's flat roof: the carrier's flight deck.

Greene began, "It's about this military action concerning the *Mayaguez*—"

"*Possible* military action," Brody corrected, sounding half asleep. "The latest out of CINCPAC is that the Chinese are going to intercede on our behalf with the Cambodians." He opened one eye. "Not that you heard that from me, Air Force . . ."

"I don't think the Chinese are going to do shit, one way or the other, Boss."

"Oh, do tell, Mr. Kissinger," Brody said sarcastically. His eyes again closed.

"Hey, I may not be the secretary of state, but I keep up with current events," Greene said. "Since the Khmer Rouge took over in Cambodia last month, those dudes have shown themselves to be pretty mean."

"Mmm." Brody's head was beginning to loll. His cigarette had burned down to its filter. Without seeming to look, Brody expertly flipped it into the coffee mug.

That was precision bombing for you, Greene thought. Just then the office's ventilator came on, clattering like marbles on tin. Greene grimaced at the racket. The *Sea Bear* dated from World War II. Nothing on board the old boat worked one hundred percent of the time.

"Maybe the Khmer Rouge might like to tweak the imperialist paper tiger's tail," Greene suggested. "Especially after the Vietcong seemed to have gotten away with it."

"Yeah, maybe . . ." Brody sounded bored. "But if they do, we got the men and machines to point out the error of their ways."

"That's right, Boss." Greene took a deep breath. "And I want a piece of it when it happens."

That got his attention, Greene thought. The air boss had sat bolt upright, his eyes snapping open.

"Are you nuts?" Brody demanded. "What's wrong with you, Air Force? I can't let you fly an actual combat mission!"

"Why not? With all due respect, Boss, I'm as good as any of the guys in your A-7 squadrons."

"Are you?" Brody's bushy eyebrows arched. "My feeling all along has been that you've been stroking it. You're an experienced combat pilot. A Vietnam-vet Thud driver who flew bombing runs against heavily defended targets. You could be bringing a lot more savvy to your training flights in the A-7. But you're holding back. You've got an attitude problem. You think you're too *good* to be flying a Mud Mover."

"I don't *think* I'm too good, Boss," Greene muttered. "I *know* I am."

Brody studied him, looking troubled. "Tell me something, what's the goal of Indian Giver?"

"I'm here to observe and learn from the Navy," Greene replied.

"There you go," Brody said. "Observe and learn: Can you honestly say you're doing either to the best of your ability?"

Greene frowned. "You're missing the point, Boss. I got a raw deal when they stuck me on this boat. I was supposed to be in a fighter squadron. Instead, I end up piloting an A-7, a Mud Mover."

"What's that got to do with anything?" Brody asked.

"It's got plenty to do with it," Greene said. "The Air Force and Navy made a deal with me when I joined Indian Giver, and now they're reneging."

"That's not so," Brody argued. "The Navy offered to share its aviation combat procedures with the Air Force through you, and it's doing that."

"I came into Indian Giver to learn ACM, not air/ground attack procedures!" Greene protested.

"*Any* hard-won combat acumen is worth sharing among the various branches of the services," Brody said. "It's *all* valuable knowledge."

"It's not valuable knowledge to *me*."

Brody's eyes narrowed. "Is that so?"

"Flying ground support and attack missions is not what I want to do," Greene said. "It's not why I agreed to come into Indian Giver. I came into the program thinking I'd come out on a career path to being an ACM instructor in the Air Force's hot new fighter-training program, but now that isn't likely to happen, is it?" Greene waited. "Is it, Boss?" he insisted.

Brody shrugged. "I can't answer that."

Greene wryly nodded. "Well, then, let *me* answer it. What's happened is that I've been shunted off into some kind of dead end. I was a good fighter pilot, Boss, but I haven't flown ACM for months, and you know as well as I do that a fighter jock needs constant practice or else his skills are going to rust."

"Yeah, I know that."

"Boss, I think you also know what's likely to happen to me when my tour on board the *Sea Bear* finally ends."

"I guess I do." Brody nodded wearily. "The Air Force flies A-7s just like the Navy does. What'll likely happen is that the Air Force will stick you into one of their own A-7 squadrons," Brody brightened. "Or maybe make you an A-7 instructor. . . ?"

Green firmly shook his head. "I'd sooner turn in my wings than be a permanent Mud Mover—"

Brody slammed his palm on his desk. "That's just the attitude on your part that pisses me off about you, Air Force!"

"Huh?" Greene was startled.

"You're a quitter!" Brody accused. "Things don't go all your own way, you fold and walk."

"That's not true!" Greene protested.

"Bullshit!" Brody scoffed. "The Air Force has invested well over a million bucks training you, but now, just because they might have different ideas than you on how you might best serve your country, you're ready to take your ball and go home."

"Try to see it from my point of view."

"Why should I?" Brody scowled. "That's all you do is see things from your point of view!" He paused. "You know, I've been watching you—"

"Then you know how good I am!" Greene countered.

"Yeah, you're good." Brody nodded. "But not as good as you think you are. You could be one of the best, if you could get your fucking ego out of the way." He paused. "And while we're at it, why'd you quit taking my karate class?"

What the hell? Greene thought. "What's that got to do with anything?"

"Answer the question, Captain Greene," Brody ordered.

Greene shrugged. "I guess I just didn't feel comfortable taking it."

"Because?"

"Because I was the outsider in your class." Greene hesitated. "Just like I am elsewhere on this boat."

"Hmm." Brody smiled thinly. "So you quit, right? The going got tough, so you got going, right?"

"To hell with this, Boss." Greene stood up, feeling angry

and defensive. "I come here to ask to be allowed to fly a combat mission, and you keep changing the subject."

"Sit down!"

"I don't need this!"

"I said sit down!" Brody barked. "That's an order!"

Greene sat. He waited as Brody pondered him.

"Refresh my memory," Brody began, quiet now. "How long did you study karate before coming aboard the *Sea Bear*?"

"A year."

"What rank did you reach?"

"Brown belt."

"That's pretty rapid progress," Brody acknowledged.

Greene couldn't resist a cocky smile. "What can I say?"

Brody ignored the remark. "What style did you study?"

"Okinawan," Greene said. "*Uechi*-style."

Brody nodded. "No offense meant to your instructor, but some teachers hand out belts easier than others, and finally, anybody can wear any colored belt." He paused. "In your case, were you *really* any good?"

Greene opened his mouth to reply, then shut it, feeling embarrassed.

Brody grinned. "I saw it right there on the tip of your tongue before you swallowed it down. You were going to say you were the best, weren't you?"

"Yeah, Boss." Greene nodded, adding defiantly, "You make it sound silly, but that doesn't mean it's not true."

"Bad answer, Air Force," Brody sighed. "You may have trained your body in the martial arts, but what about your spirit?"

"With all due respect, Boss, I'm not really into that mystical stuff."

"Now, how did I know that?" Brody shook his head. "You do any work with karate weapons?"

"Some."

"Okay." Brody nodded. "I want you to meet me at the gym tonight. Wear workout clothes. You and I are going to do some sparring."

Greene shook his head. "Why should I?"

"You want you to fly some combat in the unlikely event we get any, right?"

"Yeah," Greene said warily.

"Okay. Then you do like I say and meet me at the gym at midnight for some sparring. If you can beat me, or just manage to remain on the mat with me, I'll let you fly combat. Fair enough?"

Greene asked, "And if I lose?"

"You lose, you forget about flying combat, and you agree to apply yourself wholeheartedly to learning everything there is to know about flying the A-7. Finally, you agree to give yourself the chance to get into whatever assignment the Air Force gives you once your stint in Indian Giver is over. Agreed?"

Greene thought about it. It was awfully tempting. Brody was a second dan black belt, and highly proficient in all the martial arts, but he was also over ten years older than Greene. And Greene had trained hard back at Wright-Patterson. He'd had a good teacher, despite what Brody had intimated.

And Brody smoked, Greene reminded himself, watching as the air boss lit up another Marlboro. And speaking of lighting up, lately the air boss had been burning the candle at both ends. Poor old Brody was looking exhausted. . . .

I can take him, Greene decided. He says I'm cocky and conceited, but he's the one . . . Hell, the least I should be able to do is hold my own, and that's all it would take to win a combat slot.

"You've got yourself a sparring partner, Boss."

CHAPTER 12

(One)

USS *Sea Bear*
14 May, 1975

Greene, wearing sneakers, a T-shirt, and sweat pants, arrived at the gym at precisely 2400 hours to find Brody waiting for him. The gym was a large space filled with athletic equipment on Deck 1, one level below the main hangar deck where the aircraft were housed. The carrier's steel structure transmitted noise easily, and the hangar deck was busy twenty-four hours a day, so in the midnight quiet Greene could hear coming from above the gym the whine and clang of the hangar's hydraulic elevators, the shouts and laughter of the aircraft maintenance crews, and the rumble of the tractors that towed the airplanes.

"Right on time," Brody welcomed Greene. The air boss was reclining on a weight bench, about to do presses. Brody was barefoot, dressed in karate pants and a gray sweatshirt that had "AIR BOSS" stenciled across the front. The sweatshirt's sleeves had been cut off, revealing Brody's ropey arms. "You ready to get your ass kicked into the wild blue yonder, Air Force?"

"We'll see who kicks whose ass," Greene said, but he was not feeling all that cocky as he watched Brody easily knock off a set of twelve bench presses. *He's lifting about two hundred,* Greene estimated. Suddenly, Brody did not look so old, and those coffin nails he puffed on hadn't seemed to do much to cramp his style.

"What will it be?" Brody asked, getting up from the weight bench and sauntering over to the corner of the gym devoted to martial-arts practice. The floor here was carpeted with thick canvas-covered mats. The walls were lined with racks of body armor and racks of various practice versions of karate weapons. "You want to spar empty-handed, or use weapons?"

"Let's use *jō* sticks," Greene said, walking over to the rack of forty-inch-long, polished hardwood sticks, each of them an inch and a half in diameter. Greene had done a lot of studying of *jōjutsu*—the art of stick fighting—and guessed that he'd have a better chance against Brody, who was a second dan black belt in karate, with something in his hands.

"*Jō* sticks it is," Brody said. "You put on some body armor."

Greene went over to the racks and began strapping on chest and rib protection. He saw Brody watching him. "You're not wearing any?" Greene asked.

Brody shook his head as he went over to select a *jō* stick from the rack.

"Your funeral," Greene muttered. He donned a padded red leather head guard and selected a *jō* stick. He kicked off his sneakers and then joined Brody on the mats.

All right, Greene thought as he and Brody faced off. *He may be a second dan black belt, but you're a fighter pilot. You've got a chance here. This takes the same elements vital to combat flying: kime and mushin. Kime* was the martial-arts term for the focusing of all mental and physical energies on the job at hand. *Mushin* alluded to that state of relaxed no-mindedness that allowed for instinctive action in response to a threat.

"Okay, Air Force," Brody said cheerfully. "Let's see what you've got."

The two men began circling on the mats. As Brody drew back his stick, Greene pivoted to face him. Brody swung his stick up over his shoulder and then brought it down, slicing in like a Sabre jet toward Greene's head. Greene countered with a horizontal block, gripping the *jō* stick with both hands and pushing up against Brody's stick with everything he had, stopping Brody's swipe from knocking his head off his shoulders, but just barely. Brody threw his weight into breaking down Greene's defensive block, and Greene's knees began to buckle. Greene shifted into a karate cat's-foot stance, putting all of his weight on his rear leg. He danced away from Brody, taking the opportunity to deliver a series of snap kicks to the air boss's unprotected belly. They were solid kicks, and landed squarely on target, but Greene felt like his bare toes were striking thinly padded steel.

Brody took Greene's kicks with hardly a grimace, and then took Greene by surprise, landing a powerful sideways kick against Greene's head guard. The force of Brody's kick stunned and staggered Greene; he dropped his *jō* stick. While Greene was seeing stars, Brody used his momentary advantage to maneuver around behind Greene's and slap the side of his *jō* stick against the backs of Greene's knees.

Greene cried out; Brody's stick had felt like a branding iron. Greene's knees buckled and he went down into a kneeling position. He hunched his shoulders, waiting for the blow that would finish him, but Brody backed off, giving up his offensive.

"Is that all you've got, Air Force?" Brody asked, breathing lightly. "Have I seen it all?"

Son of a bitch, Greene thought, humiliated. He grabbed his stick and furiously launched himself up from the mat, whipping his stick sideways to thwack Brody's ankles, intending to pay Brody back for his throbbing knees.

Brody hopped into the air so that Greene's stick sliced empty space. Greene, cursing, rose up from his crouch to swing his stick like a sledgehammer at Brody's head, but Brody calmly moved his head out of the way, letting Greene's stick miss him by a fraction of an inch.

Greene's momentum put him slightly off balance. Brody jammed his stick between Greene's legs, tripping him. As Greene stumbled forward, Brody stepped in close and delivered a closed-fist, corkscrew karate thrust to Greene's solar plexus. Greene's body armor cushioned the blow, but the force behind Brody's punch still made Greene feel like he'd been hit by a battering ram. The punch pushed Greene backward. He again lost his stick as he windmilled his arms to regain balance. Brody prodded Greene gently in the chest with his stick and Greene fell flat on his ass, the wind knocked out of him.

Brody stepped back, twirling his *jō* stick between his fingers like it was a cane. "Well, Mr. Quitter, you want to quit now?"

"No way," Greene muttered, slowly getting to his feet. His battered knees were loudly complaining, his head throbbed, and his buttocks were cramping up. "I'm just getting started," Greene warned.

"You look like you want to cry," Brody said mockingly. "Sure you don't want to call it quits?"

Greene tried not to wince as he bent to pick up his stick. "I don't lose. . . ."

"We'll see, Air Force." Brody performed an elaborate *jōjutsu kata* exercise. His weapon seemed to break the sound barrier, snapping like a whip as it whirled through the air to come to rest in a present-arms position across Brody's chest. "Well, son?" Brody's thick eyebrows arched. "You going to attack? Or is it your strategy to win this match by waiting until I die of old age?"

Banzai! Greene thought ruefully, moving in against Brody. Brody, grinning savagely, lunged forward, holding his stick as if it were a foil, intending to drive the tip of his *jō* into Greene's chest. Greene countered with a *gyaku-nigiri* reverse hold on his *jō*, placing his hands approximately shoulder-width apart along the length of the stick. He held it horizontally, his palms facing the ground. As Brody's stick lanced toward him, Greene pivoted, so that Brody's stick barely scraped along his chest. At the same time, Greene stepped into Brody's attack and quickly thrust upward his own stick, the middle area of the *jō* clipping Brody's jaw.

Brody's stick clattered to the mat as his head snapped back and he did a backflip, falling hard against the mat. The air boss lay spread-eagled for a moment, obviously stunned. Greene stepped back, feeling supremely satisfied.

Brody rose into a sitting position and experimentally moved his jaw. "Nice shot, Air Force," he said, gingerly holding his chin. "Maybe I should have worn a head guard, after all."

"Want to quit, Boss?" Greene asked.

Brody just laughed. He grabbed his stick and smoothly rose to his feet as if he were a marionette being pulled aloft by strings.

Oh shit, Greene worried. *If he'd hit me the way I just hit him, I'd be on a stretcher on my way to sick bay by now.*

"Let's spar, Air Force. . . ."

Greene jabbed his *jō* stick at Brody's face. Brody easily deflected Greene's thrust, and then, holding his stick by its end, began to twirl it in a blurringly fast figure-eight pattern. Greene, psyched out by the display, stepped back, letting his own stick sag. Brody stepped in, rapping his stick against the padding over Greene's ribs. Greene fell sideways to the mat.

"Stay down," Brody said.

"No way." Greene got up, bringing his stick up over his right shoulder, intending to execute an overhead strike against Brody's neck. Brody stepped sideways, holding his stick with both hands to execute his own vertical block.

There was a loud report like that of a pistol shot as Greene's stick connected with Brody's. Greene's stick was deflected; he felt the vibration travel along the stick's length and thought it was going to shake the fillings out of his teeth.

Brody, bending his knees but keeping his torso erect, as if he were staddling a very wide horse, lunged to thrust his stick into Greene's lower belly. Greene felt pain at the impact despite his body armor, and doubled over, clutching at his abdomen. Brody brought his own stick up over his head in a powerful arc that finished with the business end whipping against the back of Greene's head guard.

It felt like a cherry bomb had exploded inside Greene's skull. His vision purpled and sound seemed to recede as he slo-mo nosedived to the mat.

"Stay down," Brody said, sounding like he was somewhere very far away.

Greene groggily pushed himself to his hands and knees.

"Damnit," Brody swore, standing over him. "Stay down."

Greene didn't look for his fallen stick; it hurt too much to try and move his head. He gauged the distance and then rolled sideways into Brody. Brody stepped back, but Greene skittered around on his spine to use his legs, scissoring Brody's knees and twisting Brody off his feet.

Brody hit the mat hard, losing his stick, but easily kicked his legs free and rose up, to walk away from Greene without looking back at him. "The hell with you, Air Force. You're beaten, you're just too stubborn to admit it."

"No!" Greene launched himself off the mat as if he'd been strapped into a jet and catapulted off the *Sea Bear's* flight deck. He came at Brody from behind, looping his arms around him. Then Brody thrust his elbow into Greene's solar plexus.

Greene grunted in pain as his arms went limp, suddenly encompassing nothing but thin air. He had a moment to ponder how it could be that Brody had the ability to inflict such punishment through the body armor Greene was wearing, and then Brody was on the attack, slamming his elbow into Greene's ribs. Greene, wincing, staggered against Brody, who used his foot to sweep Greene's legs out from under him the way a broom sweeps litter. Greene hit the mat on his hip and rolled onto his back, rasping for breath as he clutched at his chest and side.

Brody knelt beside him. "Stay there," he warned. "Stay down . . ."

Greene began to push himself up on his elbows.

With exquisite gracefulness, Brody rapped Greene's head guard with the back of his fist. Greene's head bounced against the mat, his skull rattling inside his head guard like a nut meat inside its shell.

"Stay down!" Brody got to his feet, watching and waiting. "Stay down," the Air Boss repeated, more quietly this time, almost as if in supplication.

Stay down, Greene mused. *What a lovely thought*. There wasn't a bone in his body that wasn't wholeheartedly endorsing the notion.

Greene, his head hanging like that of a poleaxed steer, slowly rolled onto his side. Then up onto his knees. Then up on one leg. Then up on the other leg. *Look at me, Ma, I'm standing*.

Greene balled his hands into fists and tottered forward, dimly aware that he was moving like Frankenstein and that the fucking aircraft carrier could have gotten out of his way. He fully expected Brody to knock him flat yet another time, but Brody didn't. The air boss just extended his right hand palm forward, straight-arming Greene to a stop.

Greene muttered, "Ah, so you've had enough, have you?" He was slumped forward against Brody's arm. If Brody had moved his palm away from Greene's chest, Greene would have fallen on his face.

"What is it with you, Air Force?"

Greene's head was down. He couldn't fight and lift his head at the same time, simple as that. He was staring at Brody's hairy toes as he said, "Told you . . . I . . . don't . . . lose. . . ."

Brody didn't reply for a moment. Then he said, "Okay. We'll call it a draw."

"Huh?"

"I can't beat you, Air Force." Brody chuckled. "I can *kill* you, but I can't beat you."

"Let that be a lesson to you." Greene nodded, sagging at the knees. Brody moved quickly to catch him and hold him up. "I told you I'm no quitter."

"I knew that all the time," Brody murmured. "I just wanted you to realize it."

"I fly combat if we get any, right?" Greene demanded.

"That's the deal," Brody nodded. "If that's what you want."

"That's what I want," Greene murmured.

"Even in a Mud Mover?" Brody asked wryly. "There's no substantial air resistance expected," he cautioned. "Intelligence reports the Cambodians have nothing but light training aircraft. And even if there were MiGs or whatever, Mud Movers don't get any. MiGs are Phantom meat."

"I don't care," Greene said. "Any kind of action is better than nothing."

Brody nodded. "Good answer, Air Force." He began walking Greene off the mats.

"Where we going?" Greene asked. His feet were dragging. Brody was mostly carrying him.

"We're going to the showers," Brody said. "You grab yourself a hot one and you'll feel better. You'll be a little black and blue, maybe, but none the worse for wear."

"Oh, yeah? How about you, Boss?" Greene asked gamely. "How's your jaw?"

Brody laughed. "I'll feel it when I chew for the next couple of days, don't worry about that, Air Force. . . . But tell me one thing. How'd you get to be so stubborn?"

"Runs in the family," Greene said.

"Uh-huh . . ."

"Boss? Why'd you take it so poorly when I put down flying a Mud-Mover?"

"I flew an A-7 in Vietnam," Brody replied. "That's why I know she can be a damn fine bird if you're willing to give her half a chance. Why, I could tell you some stories . . ."

"Later, Boss," Greene pleaded. "Right now it hurts too much to listen."

(Two)

USS *Sea Bear*, the flight deck
16 May 1975

Greene spooled up his A-7's turbofan power plant, rolling forward in order to be hooked up to one of the *Sea Bear*'s bow catapults. The cats were steam-powered. They looked like three-hundred-foot-long slots in the deck. Greene's Mud Mover was painted blue on top, with a white underbelly. Her vertical tail carried the red hourglass logo of the *Sea Bear*'s Black Widow squadron. She was one of a half-dozen A-7s, four A-6 Intruders, and four Phantoms being sent by the carrier to put a serious hurt on Cambodia for not releasing the *Mayaguez*.

It was Thursday, and a lot had happened concerning the captured American merchant ship since Greene and Brody had rattled their sticks in the gym. In the early hours of Wednesday morning, while Greene was busy anointing himself with Ben-Gay and listening to the radio, he'd heard that the Air Force's warplanes had opened up on the Cambodian patrol boats, sinking several of them. Greene realized that his earlier hunch had proved right. There was more at stake here than the fate of the *Mayaguez* and its crew. President Ford intended to use the situation to clear the air after the disheartening turn of events in Saigon. The United States was going to show the world that it was not a paper tiger, that the country had the will and ability to respond to provocation.

As Greene's roaring A-7 rolled into position on the catapult, the jet exhaust-blast deflector rose up out of the flight deck behind his bird. By the nose of the A-7 there knelt a hookup man wearing a green jacket. Like everyone else on deck exposed to the horrific racket of the gathered jets spooling their engines, the hookup man's ears were protected by a thickly padded radio headset. The hookup man engaged the A-7's nosewheel strut to the cat shuttle and then signaled the cat crew to tighten the pressure according to the weight of Greene's bird.

Wednesday afternoon, the level of preparation had risen on board the *Sea Bear* once the Skipper had announced that the carrier was within air-strike range of the Cambodian coast. Greene took part in briefings outlining the timing and details of the rescue mission. The *Mayaguez* was being held off the coast of Tang Island, which was itself approximately sixty miles off the Cambodian mainland. The rescue mission entailed airlifted marine assaults on Tang Island and on the *Mayaguez*, backed up by U.S. Navy destroyer escorts. The assaults would be further supported by air strikes against Tang Island and by diversionary air strikes against the Cambodian mainland, all of which would be flown from the *Sea Bear* and by Air Force warplanes from out of Utapao AFB in Thailand. Some of the USAF planes and some of the *Sea Bear*'s contingent would attack the Kompong Som oil depot, where there was believed to be a large concentration of enemy troops. A trio of the *Sea Bear*'s A-7s—Greene's included—would attack the Cambodians' Tien Air Base, where a number of light aircraft were supposedly located. It would be the Mud Movers' job, backed up by a duce of Phantoms, to keep the Cambodian Air Force such as it was from taking to the sky to attack the marines.

Late Wednesday night, the *Sea Bear* had received its orders to initiate its phase of the rescue operation. Now it was a beautiful Thursday afternoon. The *Sea Bear*'s planes had been launching for the past hour. Greene's would be the last to take to the sky.

Greene looked out through the A-7's canopy to where the flight-deck director in his yellow jacket was standing with his clenched fists upraised. Now the deck director opened his fists: This was Greene's signal to release his brakes and bring his throttle up to full military power. Greene also scrutinized his instruments and panel trouble-light indicators and worked his flight controls, so that the white jackets in their checkered helmets could look over his airplane for malfunctions. Meanwhile, the red-jacket-wearing weapons handlers gave his ordnance a final check.

Greene's A-7 was loaded for bear. Her ordnance was all the more impressive due to the A-7's small size: With a wingspan of under thirty-nine feet, the A-7 was hardly larger than the four-seat Cessna GAT company airplane in which Grandpa Herman had used to take Greene for rides when he'd been just a kid.

The A-7's 20MM M61 cannon was crammed with one thousand rounds for strafing. Her wing pylons dangled triple clusters of Snakeye bombs, twelve in all, to crater runways and flatten hangars. Her outer-wing pylons carried a brace of rocket pods: six 100MM rockets packed into each launcher. The only weapon system the A-7 was lacking as far as Greene was concerned were Sidewinder air-to-air heat-seekers. The A-7 was equipped with fuselage side rails to carry a pair, but none of the A-7s had been issued any. The Mud Movers' orders were to take care of the enemy aircraft on the ground. If any gomers got airborne, the A-7s were to let the Phantoms take care of them.

Greene saluted the cat officer, signaling that he was ready to be launched. He had his engine spooled up to full military power and the bird trimmed for flight with his control stick full back. Greene saw the cat officer give him the final okay signal. Greene braced himself, pressing his helmet against his headrest. It would be only a few more seconds before the signal to fire the cat was relayed to the cat controller below the flight deck. Even now the catapult was reaching full pressure. Greene glimpsed the tendrils of steam rising up around his trembling bird—

And then he was launched! The heavily loaded, twenty-one-ton A-7 was hurled off the bow of the carrier as if it were a child's toy airplane. Green's stomach braided itself around his spine as he was catapulted to 170 miles per hour in less than two seconds. Greene, grimacing from the stress of the launch, eased forward the stick, bringing down the A-7's stubby nose to aid his shrieking bird in her quest for the sky.

Airborne, Greene banked as the carrier rapidly receded in the distance. The A-7 was subsonic, but in her low- or moderate-altitude combat element she could do 560 knots and turn on a dime; specifically, her turning radius was 5,500 feet, which was an attack or fighter jet's equivalent of a ten-cent piece. As Greene came around over the flattop, he saw the sun glint on the glass windows of the air boss's station just below the carrier's bridge. Greene felt the force of Gil Brody's warrior spirit going along with him for the ride.

Greene rose to 10,000 feet and took his place off the starboard wing of the flight leader. The three-abreast formation of A-7s then began beelining it for Tien Air Base. Up above, a duo of the ship's F-4 Phantoms flew protective escort.

"Wolf lead to Wolf flight," Lieutenant Ernesto "Taco" Rodriguez radioed, cutting through the random ship-to-air communications that cluttered up the frequency. "Wolf flight check," Rodriguez demanded, wanting to make sure that everybody's radio was working properly and that it was tuned to the proper flight frequency.

"Wolf two—" An ensign by the name of Sweeny sounded off, his A-7 flying off Rodriguez's port side.

Greene clicked his own mike, saying, "Wolf three."

"Roger, Wolf flight," Rodriguez said. "Papa lead, you with us?"

"Roger, Wolf lead," the lead Phantom driver, a lieutenant named Saunders radioed. "Over target we'll stay high to make sure you're not bounced. After you've dropped your ordnance, we'll come down to lay our own eggs."

Greene, listening, nodded to himself. The Phantoms were carrying bombs as well as air-to-air missiles.

"Twenty minutes to target," Rodriguez said.

* * *

Wolf flight's ride to the Cambodian mainland passed uneventfully. As they closed on the coastline, they gradually reduced altitude to five thousand feet. The escort Phantoms remained high, so they were first to spot the signs of the battle going on at Tang Island.

"Wolf flight, Papa lead," Lieutenant Saunders radioed. "Check out the fire works on your port side."

Wow, Greene thought as he tipped his wings to get a better view of the action. From his perspective, Tang Island looked like the mossy green shell of a tortoise rising up out of the blue water. Fires were sprouting all over the island, and gray clouds of smoke were wafting in the breeze across the beach. The island had taken a pounding from the Phantoms, A-6s, and A-7s that had gone in to soften the Cambodian resistance for the Marines.

Air power did its best, Greene thought. *But it's just like Vietnam. When the planes were done shooting their wad, it still remained for the foot soldier to do the messy and dangerous mopping up.*

Despite the extensive air strikes, there was still orange 50-caliber tracer fire rising up from out of the trees near the beach. The Cambodians were shooting at the big CH-53 and HH-53 troop carrying helicopters hanging in the air above the surf in preparation for off-loading the Marines. The Jolly Green Giant helios were returning fire with with their door-mounted M-60 miniguns. People on both sides were definitely getting killed down there, Greene knew.

"There's the *Mayaguez*," somebody said. Greene looked down at the rather modest-looking freighter wallowing in the ocean just offshore the island. The *Mayaguez* was a container ship. Her bow deck was stacked high with drab aluminum boxes, each the size of a truck trailer. Approaching the *Mayaguez* was a USN destroyer carrying a Marine force.

Not much of a boat to start a shooting war over, Greene thought. Up ahead he could see the looming Cambodian coast, a line of tan beach backed by an emerald wall of jungle.

"Wolf flight, green 'em up and go to strike frequency," Rodriguez ordered.

But what the hey, Greene thought as he activated his weapons systems and tuned his radio to channel seven. *This was the only war he had, so he might as well enjoy it.*

"Rubber Duckie, Wolf flight's feet are dry," Wolf lead transmitted back to the *Sea Bear* as the strike force crossed over to dry land. "Wolf flight, go to angel three."

Greene and the rest of the A-7s dropped down to three thousand feet. The flight was traveling at five hundred knots. The Cambodians had likely been expecting an assault on Tang Island and the *Mayaguez*, but there was no reason for them to expect Tien Air Field to be hit. Accordingly, it was Wolf flight's strategy to hit and run before the Cambodians could marshal their defenses. Up until now, the pilots on board the *Sea Bear* had been making light of what the Cambodians might have to throw back at their air assault, but after seeing the effort the Cambodians were making to defend Tang Island, Greene, for one, didn't much feel like laughing.

"Here we go," Rodriguez radioed the flight.

Greene got ready for action, dropping down with the rest of the flight to treetop level to initiate the strike. Tien Air Field was situated in a cove. The plan was for the Mud Movers to go inland and then bank around, to attack from the land as opposed to from the sea, in order to further increase the element of surprise. The order of attack would be as follows: Wolf lead, then Wolf two, and Wolf three; two passes each to drop their ordnance. Both Wolf lead and Wolf two piloted by Rodriguez and Sweeny were carrying AGM-62 Walleye TV-directed smart bombs in addition to their Snakeye load, so they were going in first to lessen the strain on their A-7s. Greene didn't have any Walleyes because as an Air Force fighter pilot he'd never been trained to use the complex air/ground Electro-Optical Guided Bombs, and he hadn't had time in his abbreviated RAG tour flying the A-7 to become acquainted with the EOGB system. The Walleye was designed for surgical strikes, to take out a specific target. Wolf lead and Wolf two had Walleyes on board in case the Cambodians tried the old North Vietnamese trick of surrounding its military targets with "noncombatant civilians" in order to sway world opinion against the United States. The Walleye was a one-ton bomb with a TV camera in its nose. The camera transmitted a cross hair–type picture of what the bomb was "looking at" to the five-inch black-and-white Sony mounted on the pilot's panel. The pilot locked the Walleye on target by sighting in on the cross hairs superimposed on the TV screen. Once the bomb was released, it guided itself to aim-point as long as those cross hairs stayed aligned. It was a good weapon, but not at its best during low-level attacks, because it needed time to make course corrections. Also, clouds could fuck it up; if the Walleye couldn't see it, it couldn't hit it.

After the A-7s were done dropping their ordnance, the Phantoms would go in to drop their bombs. Then, if there was anything left of Tien Air Base, the Mud Movers would go back to mop up with cannons and rockets.

Wolf flight was approaching Tien Air Field. It was a com-pound cut into the dense jungle. There were a half-dozen rusting, white and orange hangars and several interlocking tan airstrips angled to lead out over the water. There were maybe a dozen U.S.-built, dark-green, combat-modified, prop-driven T-28 trainers parked in muddy, earth-embank-ment revetments along the runways, but none of the airplanes looked to be in a state approaching takeoff status.

That was too bad, Greene thought. He knew the combat-modified T-28. The Air Force had used them during the Vietnam War for close ground-support work when the job called for a rugged bird that could operate out of a primitive airfield. The T-28 had self-sealing fuel tanks, armor plating around the cockpit, and underwing pylons capable of mount-ing 50-caliber gun pods, napalm, bombs, rockets, and so on. The T-28 could be an agile and dangerous bird at low altitude in the hands of a competent pilot. Knocking the enemy's planes out of the sky one by one would have been challenging, enjoyable work for Greene and his buddies in their gun-toting, subsonic A-7s.

The Cambodian airfield began bustling with people and battered-looking, olive-drab military vehicles as the strike force closed in. Beyond the field Greene saw the timeless, peaceful, blue-gray ocean lapping the sandy beach.

"Looks like we got us a welcoming committee," Ensign Sweeny said matter-of-factly as the Cambodian antiaircraft emplacements around the airfield commenced firing.

Greene said: "Not surprising now that I think about it. The

Cambodians must have anticipated we'd try something, and put this base on alert."

He stared mesmerized at the tracer fire lanquidly reaching up to caress his bird. The incendiary display was as lovely as it was frightening, and watching it, Greene was immediately enveloped in an intense déjà vu. It was 1965, and he was back over Hanoi in his Thud, about to put the hurt on Uncle Ho—*Watch out for SAMs!*

"Wolf lead, Papa lead."

"Go ahead, Papa lead," Rodriguez told Lieutenant Saunders in the lead Phantom circling high above them.

"We picked up a mayday transmission," Saunders said. "A couple of Marine choppers went down off the coast of Tang Island."

"Enemy fire?" Ensign Sweeny in Wolf two asked, concerned.

"Negative," Papa lead replied. "Both went down from rotor malfunction."

Goddamn, Greene thought, listening. *If God had wanted helicopters to fly, He would have given them wings.*

"The rescue operation could use our help flying RES-CAP," Papa lead said. "We thought we'd mosey along that way . . . ?"

"You do that," Rodriguez agreed. "We'll be fine here. It's obvious the Cambodians have no planes ready to fly." Wolf lead paused as the duo of Phantoms banked away from the airfield to join the air net searching for survivors from the copter crashes. "Okay, Wolf flight. Let's do it. I'm going in."

Greene watched as Wolf lead's A-7 attacked fast and low. Rodriguez expertly weaved his way through the antiaircraft tracer and cannon fire arcing up like scarlet, jeweled beads from the sandbag emplacements scattered around the airfield and from the gun sites hidden in the surrounding jungle. When Rodriguez was over the runways he released his load of Snakeyes, which fell leisurely toward the target. The Snakeye retarded bomb was especially designed for low-level delivery. It was equipped with automatically extending tail fins that acted as air brakes on the falling bomb, slowing its descent so that the aircraft dropping it would have time to clear the explosion.

The Snakeyes erupted in fireballs and gray smoke well after Wolf lead had banked away from the airfield. The initial explosions began a chain reaction of blasts as the parked T-28s' fuel tanks began to ignite.

"Your turn, Wolf two," Rodriguez said.

Greene watched as Ensign Sweeny made his pass. The airfields were now pockmarked with smoking craters, but there was still plenty of antiaircraft activity tearing up the sky. Greene was amused when Sweeny took the time to go chasing after an olive-drab truck careening around the airstrip complex with maybe half a dozen twin .50-calibers bolted to its flatbed. It wasn't as if Sweeny was in danger from the truck. The flatbed gunners didn't have a chance in hell of hitting anything as long as their chauffeur kept driving his frantic circles. The gunners were bouncing like jumping beans and hanging on to their guns for dear life. Greene guessed that Sweeny just wanted to have a little fun. . . .

Wolf two popped his speed brakes so as not to overshoot the truck too quickly. When the gunners saw that their truck had attracted the A-7's attention, they jumped ship, hopping off the flatbed. Greene thought Sweeny would open up with his cannon, but instead Wolf two rippled off a salvo of 100MM rockets. The rockets left the pod trailing flame, which transformed to wiggling tails of white smoke as the rockets streaked toward the truck, which was entirely sans gunners now; the silent .50-caliber machine guns mounted on the flatbed were swinging in the breeze. The truck driver must have seen the rockets coming. He tried to get out of their way, but he didn't have a chance since the salvo had spread out to effectively cage his vehicle. The rockets impacted in a high-explosive curtain around the enemy truck, transforming it to tortured, flaming scrap metal.

"Somebody better call the Automobile Club of Cambodia." Sweeny chuckled gleefully as he dropped his Snakeyes on the hangar complex. "Something tells me that truck's got a flat tire or two. . . ."

What a wise guy, Green thought, smiling. Thanks to Sweeny's precision bombing, the hangar complex had vanished in smoke and fire. It was now time for Greene to begin his own run. Remarkably, despite all the destruction that had been caused to the airfield, there was still defensive fire coming up from it, and especially from the surrounding jungle.

A stream of tracers cut across the nose of Greene's bird: .50 cal, he guessed. When the rounds were coming at you, they looked like white hot Ping-Pong balls lobbed in rapid succession.

Greene felt his bird shudder and heard a rattling like pebbles being thrown against the A-7's skin: Several .50-cal rounds had impacted. Greene didn't like being hit, but he wasn't terribly worried. The A-7 was tough as nails. The cockpit and all vital systems were armored, with critical flight components and systems duplicated or triplicated to make sure a shot-up Mud Mover had what it took to get its job done and then get on home to its Rubber Duckie.

However, I wouldn't want to take too many of those, Greene thought as a flurry of what looked like red golf balls floated up at him from out of the jungle. Those were 37MM cannon rounds.

Greene resisted the urge to drop some Snakeyes on the foliage in an effort to silence the more potent gun. Letting the enemy seduce you into expending your ordnance on defenses instead of the primary target was one of the oldest ruses in the Indochinese Commies' bag of tricks.

"Wolf three, Wolf lead," Rodriguez radioed.

"Rog, lead," Greene replied.

"Three, drop all your bombs in an extended run, then we'll get out of here. This field is history, and with all that defensive fire coming up from the palm trees there's no point in us repeatedly exposing ourselves to it just to break big pieces of wreckage into little pieces."

"Rog lead."

Greene flew his attack trajectory, doing the best he could to ignore the fiery AA net of death the Cambodians were weaving to pluck his bird from out of the sky. Fortunately, billowing clouds of oily black smoke were now rising up from the burning airfield. As Greene entered into it, he felt relieved. He couldn't see his dick in front of him, but at least now the enemy gunners couldn't spot him.

He watched his instruments, letting his navigation/weapon delivery computer select the opportune moment to drop his bomb load. When he did trigger off his bombs, he felt his bird rise up, unfettered from over three tons of ordnance. Behind Greene, the roiling smoke cloud cleared just long enough for him to see his bombs going off in a rapid succession of blinking light. From his vantage point, the dozen Snakeyes exploding looked like an oversize string of Chinese firecrackers. Abruptly the field was shaken by a tremendous explosion that sent an anvil-shaped orange fire cloud high up into the sky. The shock wave from the blast buffeted Greene's bird, and for a moment he thought he was going to lose control, but then he had his A-7 reined in. He arrowed out of the smoke cloud, up into the clear blue upper reaches of the sky.

"Woo-whee!" Rodriguez yodeled cowboy style. "That's getting some bang for the buck, Air Force!"

"I must have hit an underground fuel tank," Greene chortled excitedly. "Back in 'Nam, the POL sites used to go up just like that!"

Greene's A-7 was still rising. Now that he'd dropped his bombs, Greene could have flown rings around Wolf lead and Wolf two, both of which were still burdened with heavy, cumbersome, Walleye TV bombs.

"Okay, Wolf three," Rodriguez radioed to Greene. He and Wolf two were already winging out over the cove. "Come on down into formation and let's get out of here."

"Roger, lead," Greene began, but then, as he leveled out at 10,000 feet and prepared to descend, he was distracted by movement glimpsed out of the corner of his eye. He gasped, thinking he was seeing things, that he was having another Viet flashback. "Wolf lead. We've got bogies."

"What? Where?" Rodriguez demanded skeptically. "Air Force, check your oxygen level. You sound a little loco to me, *muchacho*."

"I'm telling you I see three of them!" Greene chattered excitedly. "Check it out! They're at my four o'clock low! You're ten o'clock level. See them? They're skimming the trees, heading out from the jungle—yeah!—they've crossed the beach and now they're over the water!"

"Got them!" Sweeny said.

"Roger, I see them now," Rodriguez agreed. "Where the fuck did they come from?"

"Who knows?" Greene replied. "Maybe the Cambodians have underground hangars. . . ."

Rodriguez said, "I can see plenty of ordnance dangling from their wings. Those bogies are obviously on their way to Tang Island to lend air support to the Cambodians."

Greene suffered through a high-G turn in pursuit of the planes. The bogies were painted in a jungle camo pattern: tobacco brown with wavy green mottling. As Greene got closer to the low-flying, relatively slow-moving enemy jets, he recognized their teardrop canopies, needle noses, dual jet intakes, and swept wings/swept tail configuration. Then he made out their insignia: yellow-outlined red stars and bars on their upper wings.

"Holy shit, fellas," Greene radioed to the rest of the flight. "Those are Chinese aircraft—"

"Bullshit!" Rodriguez exploded. "Now I *know* you're loco!"

"Listen up, lead!" Greene cut him off. "Before I came aboard the *Sea Bear*, I spent a year testing out flight simulators. I had to study up on just about every kind of non-friendly airplane there is, because I had to fly against computer-generated versions of them. I'm telling you that these three airplanes are Nanzhang Q-5 Qianjiji attack aircraft, the Commie Chinese answer to our own fighter bombers like the F-111."

"Lead, he sounds like he knows what he's talking about," Sweeny said.

"I guess," Rodriguez admitted grudgingly. "Damn, first the fall of Saigon, then the *Mayaguez*, and now this. Fucking Commies must all be working together. Stay out of their way, Wolf three. I'm radioing a warning to our guys over Tang. The Phantoms will take them out."

Greene was still closing on the Q-5 trio from behind, from six o'clock high. None of the gomer pilots had spotted him, or, if they had, they were ignoring him. Greene wondered why. Maybe the Q-5s were being distracted and reassured by the sight of Rodriguez and Sweeny's bomb-laden A-7s flying so unthreateningly low and slow out over the water . . . ? Or maybe the Q-5s *had* spotted Greene behind them, but they were thinking that he had expended all his ammo on the airfield?

Then the obvious answer occurred to Greene: These Q-5s intended to strafe the Marines landing on Tang Island's beach. That was their primary mission, and if they wanted to complete it successfully, they would have to continue to fly skimming the waves, because they were overloaded with heavy ordnance.

That might be your mission, but you're not going to complete it if I can help it, gomers, Greene thought, busily flipping switches on the armament panel of his A-7 to go from air-to-ground bombing mode to air-to-air gun mode.

"Wolf three, I know what you're up to!" Rodriguez transmitted. "Don't do it! Let the Phantoms have them! Do you read, Wolf three? Over!"

Greene's mind raced back to all those flight-simulator battles he'd fought and won on the ground at Wright-Patterson. Yeah, sure, he was an *electronic* ace, a master war gamester, but in real life he'd never shot down an enemy plane. His grandfather Herman Gold had been an ace in World War I. His uncle Steve had been an ace in World War II and in Korea, and had even scored a couple of MiG kills during his limited-combat tour in 'Nam, but not Robbie Greene, who'd flown well over a hundred combat missions in his Thud, but who'd never been in the right place at the right time to score an air kill—

Until now. Here they were, not computer-generated enemy planes but the real thing, looking sleek and sexy and ripe as peaches ready to be plucked from the branch. They were *his* peaches, and he was going to enjoy every juicy bite out of them that he could possibly take.

No way, Greene thought. *No way am I going to pass up this chance, even if I am stuck in a Mud Mover.*

The irony of it was just too delicious: the Q-5s were fighter bombers. Thanks to their dual 30MM cannons and AA-2 Atoll heat-seekers, their dual supersonic turbojets and their rugged, simple mechanical design, these Chinese aircraft were formidable dogfighters. But these particular Q-5s were presently flying a ground-support mission; they couldn't go into an ACM mode unless they jettisoned their ordnance. Greene, meanwhile, was flying a Mud Mover, but he had no ordnance, and at these low speeds and low altitudes his bird had something approaching fighter-plane capability.

"Wolf three, this is a direct order," Rodriguez thundered. "Do not bounce those Chinese whatzits!"

If a trick worked once, it might work again, Greene thought. He began clicking his mike on and off as he had with Colonel Dougan that fateful day he and Buzz Blaisdale had staged their mock dogfight over Dayton. "Something's wrong with my radio. . . . You're breaking up, Wolf lead. . . ."

"Goddammit, Wolf three! Don't do it! You stupid jerk!" Rodriguez alternately cursed and pleaded. "You're too stupid to realize it, but what you're attempting is impossible."

Difficult but not impossible, Greene thought to himself. *I've got an idea. . . .*

Actually, it was a modification of Sweeny's idea. It was the image of Sweeny taking out that fast-moving truck with a rocket salvo that had prodded Greene to formulate the tactic he was about to use against the trio of Q-5s.

Greene was grateful for his superior altitude as he put his A-7 into a dive to coax every ounce of speed out of her. About a mile ahead and below him, the Q-5s were flying three abreast, like great green-and-brown-mottled sea birds, skimming the waves.

Greene was now a half-mile away from the Q-5s, dropping down on them like a hawk toward a bevy of quail. The middle fighter bomber was entering into the red pipper gunsight that floated in the center of the A-7's ghostly green HUD display. Another few seconds and the show could begin.

"Wolf three, Wolf lead," Rodriguez said. "Phantoms are here! Back off and let them handle it."

Not on your life, pal, Greene thought savagely. *And not on mine*.

"Wolf three, this is Papa lead," Lieutenant Saunders radioed from his fast-approaching Phantom. "We're here! Now, get out of our missile-launch envelope so that we can use our air-to-airs."

Greene chuckled as he glanced up at the high-flying Phantoms, glinting specks wheeling like vultures in the sky. No way could the Double Uglies use their missiles as long as he was this close to the Q-5s. AAs did not distinguish between friend and foe. As long as Greene stayed tucked on the Q-5s' sixes, the Phantoms could only watch and wait.

The center Q-5 was now framed in Greene's cherry-red gunsight, but then Greene saw twin bursts of flame coming from the trio of Q-5s' dual engines. They were going to full throttle to try and get away.

Greene smiled as he watched great splashes rise up from out of the sea as the Q-5s jettisoned their ordnance. The Chinese pilots, like Greene's fellow Navy fliers, had finally come to the realization that Greene was going to go through with his audacious plan. Also, the Q-5s had likely spotted the Phantoms and realized that their surprise attack mission was scratched. There was no longer any point to the Chinese planes' hugging sea level.

Greene's HUD display told him that the range was a little over a thousand yards; Greene was not as close as he would have liked for what he had planned, but it would have to do. The Q-5s were supersonic aircraft capable of almost twice the speed of the A-7. If Greene allowed them to spool up their dual engines, he could kiss them good-bye.

The Q-5s began a three-way defensive split. Their problem was that they were still flying so low that their split was pretty much two-dimensional. They could only spread apart gradually as they climbed for altitude.

Greene kept the center Q-5 framed in his gunsight and mashed the trigger on his cannon. The M61 Vulcan gun mounted on the port side of the A-7's fuselage began snarling like a chain saw, its six revolving barrels spitting 20MM slugs at the rate of one hundred a second. The gun volley raised sparks off the center Q-5's mottled hide and raised plumes of water on either side of the airplane. Greene, laughing, kicked rudder: The A-7's nose yawed to left and to right, and the swinging cannon hosed down the Q-5s on either side of the center Commie bird, setting the ocean to boiling. At the same time, Greene triggered off a ripple salvo of all twelve of his 100MM rockets. His A-7 seemed to shudder in orgasm as the projectiles tore loose from their pods, and then the rockets' own engines lit, spitting fire and slashing smoking contrails as they streaked downward. Due to Greene's yawning maneuver, the rockets' trajectories spread wide to form individual, smokey talons, a claw meant to scratch the Q-5s into the sea.

The hundreds of rounds of ammo Greene had unleashed

upon the enemy planes tore into the Q-5s' wings and canopies, sending shards of metal and sparkling Plexiglass flying. Then the rockets struck. The port-side Q-5 was enveloped in flame and hammered straight into the ocean by a direct hit from a rocket. The center Q-5 was in the process of climbing when either cannon fire or a rocket sheared off its tail. The fighter bomber, trailing oily black smoke, seemed to hover motionless in the air for an instant before dropping ass first into the sea.

Fortunately for the gomer in the starboard Q-5, his banking airplane suffered only a few cannon hits and none of Greene's rockets had touched it. Unfortunately for the gomer in that bird, he banked his Q-5 too sharply in his attempt to get away. The Chinese fighter bomber's wing dipped into the water. It tore himself into fiery wreckage, cartwheeling across waves.

"I don't fucking believe what I just saw," Rodriguez murmured.

"Roger that," said Papa lead from his high-flying Phantom. "But then, I never saw *anything* like that before. . . ."

Greene thought fast, and then drawled, "Why, do you squids mean to tell me you don't know the old Fan Dance?"

(Three)

Captain's Stateroom
USS *Sea Bear*

"The Fan Dance? Is that what it's called, son?" Captain Chase muttered dubiously, scratching his chin.

"Yes, sir," Greene said. "It's called the Fan Dance, because when you yaw an airplane, the nose arcs from side to side, waving like a fan."

It was late Thursday night, several hours after all of the *Sea Bear*'s planes had returned home safely. The pilots and air crews had all been through their debriefings, and news had spread like wildfire throughout the carrier, to CINCPAC, and to the Oval Office itself concerning Greene's triple kill.

Now Greene, who was the hero of the hour, was lounging

in an armchair upholstered in black leather with brass studs, just like the one in which the skipper was seated. Greene was sipping a scotch on the rocks in a cut-crystal tumbler. Greene was thinking it was very good scotch, and he was feeling glad that there was a cabin boy in a white serving jacket standing attentively nearby, ready to pour Greene some more of it should he so desire.

The skipper's stateroom was extraordinary by ship's standards. For one thing, it was actually roomy and luxuriously furnished: there wasn't a piece of gray metal office furniture in sight. There was deep blue, wall-to-wall carpeting, plenty of comfy leather furniture, teak paneling, and lots of brass detailing and green glass lampshades. Wonder of wonders, the stateroom also had windows—well, they were portholes, actually—but they let in sunshine and fresh air untainted by the pungent odors of jet fuel and diesel oil.

Greene watched Captain Chase, amused by the skipper's obvious befuddlement at his "Fan Dance" bullshit. Captain Chase was a short, stocky, swarthy man in his fifties, who was never without an equally short, fat, usually unlit stogie clenched between his teeth. Thanks to his jowls, his bulbous nose, and that ever-present cigar, he looked a bit like Edward G. Robinson. Sounded like him, too.

"Fan Dance . . . eh?" the skipper repeated to himself.

"Yep. Air Force jet jockies cut their teeth on the maneuver," Greene said, managing to maintain a straight face.

"Commander?" The skipper turned to regard Gil Brody, who was sitting on the sofa nursing a bourbon. "You ever hear of any such thing?"

"I'm *sure* Commander Brody has heard of it?" Greene remarked expectantly.

"I believe I have, Skipper. . . ." Brody trailed off.

Captain Chase looked down at some papers on his lap. Brody shot Greene a dirty look. Greene winked back.

Captain Chase looked up, shrugging. "Well, whatever this Fan Dance business is, it sure as hell worked. I wish we could add those kills to the *Sea Bear*'s official talley stretching back to the Second World War, but, of course, under the circumstances, that won't be possible."

"Yes, Skipper, I understand," Greene said.

It seemed that according to all advance intelligence reports those Chinese planes simply should *not* have been there, and in true military intelligence tradition, the error was being dealt with by pretending that it did not exist, or rather, that the Q-5s had never existed. —

"I suppose it does make sense for the United States to turn a blind eye to what happened concerning those Chinese birds," Greene mused. "Especially in the wake of ex-President Nixon's visit to China . . ."

Captain Chase chewed philosophically on his stogie. "According to my understanding of the situation, the United States' diplomatic strategy is to respond with equal silence to the fact that the Chinese have made no mention of the loss of their airplanes. The State Department thinks that there was dissent in the highest levels of the Chinese government concerning the question of lending military support to the Cambodians during this crisis. The Chinese hard-liners evidently initially prevailed, but State thinks that due in part to those Chinese Air Force planes being lost, the more dovish faction in the Chinese government has now gained the upper hand." The skipper shrugged. "I guess the bottom line is that if the Chinese have chosen not to humiliate themselves by mentioning the clash, neither will the United States." He looked apologetically at Greene. "I'm afraid that means no mention of your victory over those three planes will ever be revealed to the public. As far as the world will ever know, there was no air clash concerning the rescue of the *Mayaguez.*"

"The world won't know about it, but I'll never forget it." Greene smiled. "Anyway, when I attacked them in the first place, I *did* kind of disobey orders."

"Kind of." Brody nodded, looking sour.

Greene hastened to change the subject. "The Chinese have long memories. Maybe this lesson we taught them will make them think twice about any future attempts on their part to confront the United States."

Gil Brody interjected, "And maybe in the future they'll return the favor we did them today of letting them save face in the international arena."

"The important thing is that the assault operation to rescue the *Mayaguez* and its crew was a success," Greene added sincerely.

"I'll drink to that," Gil Brody said.

"And to the marines who gave their lives for their country's honor," the skipper solemnly added.

The three men raised their glasses.

"Well!" Captain Chase briskly began as he set down his scotch, sticking his stogie back into his mouth. "It'd be nice if you could teach the *Sea Bear*'s pilots your Fan Dance maneuver."

"No problem, sir," Greene started to say.

The skipper overrode him. "But you won't be with us long enough for that."

"I won't?" Greene asked, blinking.

Captain Chase glanced at Brody. "Didn't you fill him in, Commander?"

Brody smirked at Greene. "Well, Air Force, I guess there's *something* you don't know." Brody explained to Chase: "I thought I'd let you give him his good news, Skipper."

"What good news?" Greene asked, mystified.

"You're going to Miramar," Captain Chase replied. "Top Gun School."

"I am?" Greene nodded slowly. "You mean as a student?"

Captain Chase laughed. "No, as a guest instructor! The Air Force has proudly agreed to the Navy's request that you teach the Fan Dance maneuver to our Top Gun fighter pilots. While you're there, you'll study the Navy style of ACM with *our* best jet-fighter jockies."

Greene looked at Brody. The air boss's bushy eyebrows arched mischievously. "You can't fight karma, Air Force."

"The *Sea Bear* is now headed for Australia," Captain Chase said. "We'll airlift you to the mainland when we get a bit closer; say, three days. From Australia, the Air Force will get you to the West Coast."

"Captain Greene," Brody began. "What do you think of the wisdom of the military and of Project Indian Giver now?"

"I don't know what to say," Greene murmured. "It's a dream come true."

"You don't have to *say* anything." The skipper chuckled. "It's what you've *done* that counts, Captain Greene." He paused, grinning. "Or perhaps I should say *Major* Greene."

"I'm being promoted?" Greene asked, astounded.

"Oh, Christ!" Brody pretended to complain, rolling his

eyes. "Now I *know* the Air Force is going to hell in a hand-basket!"

The skipper said: "The Navy and the Air Force can't very well decorate you for shooting down airplanes that don't officially exist, so the Air Force decided to promote you instead."

"Congratulations, Air Force," Brody said, grinning.

"Thanks, Boss," Greene said shyly. "And thank you, Skipper."

Captain Chase waved his gratitude aside. "Like I said, son, you earned it. I'm sorry I can't give you a set of USAF major's oak leaves to pin to your collar, but I don't have any. After all, this *is* the United States Navy."

Greene waited until he and Brody had been dismissed by Captain Chase and were in the corridor outside the skipper's stateroom to say, "You know, Boss. I'm, going to miss flying a Mud Mover."

"Oh, sure." Brody laughed sarcastically.

"No, really," Greene said. "Hell, I've got to admit that I'm looking forward to getting back into the driver's seat of a fighter, but I've learned something on board the *Sea Bear:* It really isn't the crate that makes the difference, but the guy in the cockpit, or rather, that *guy's* attitude." He paused, blushing. "I guess I learned that from you."

Brody looked thoughtful. "Hirato Soko, the great six-teenth-century Japanese samurai and zen poet, wrote, 'Life is not about learning, but remembering what was always inside us, long ago forgotten.' " He patted Greene on the shoulder. "Take care of yourself, Air Force."

BOOK II:
1975–1979

WIDESPREAD EUROPEAN ACCEPTANCE OF GAT
FIGHTER
  Belgium Joins With Its Neighbors in Purchasing Stiletto
                                  Aviation Weekly

VIKING ONE LANDS ON MARS
  Probe Spacecraft Sends Back Photos From Surface of Red
  Planet
                                  Philadelphia Post

DEMOCRATS CHOOSE CARTER AND MONDALE
  Pres Candidate Stresses the Upcoming Election Will Hinge
  on Honesty
                                  Norfolk Evening Bulletin

GAT POSTS RECORD EARNINGS
  Stock Soars as GAT/Aerospace Lands Space Shuttle Orbiter
  Contract
                                  California Business Weekly

CANARY ISLANDS AIRCRAFT DISASTER KILLS 574
  Worst Disaster in Aviation History as Two Jumbo Jets
  Collide
                                  New York Gazette

PRESIDENT TO TELEVISE SPECIAL ADDRESS TO
THE NATION
  Carter To Call Energy Crisis "Moral Equivalent of War"
                                  Los Angeles Tribune

GAT/SKYTRAIN ANNOUNCE WORLD BIRD PROJECT
  Internationally Built Stiletto Hybrid to Replace Current
  Crop of Fighters
                                  Washington Star Reporter

NICARAGUA REBELS SEIZE PALACE
  Somoza Struggles to Hold on Against Marxist
  Revolutionaries

  Boston Herald

GAT JETLINER CRASHES INTO CROWDS AT PARIS
AIR SHOW
  GC-600s' Airliner's Structural Innovations Faulted
    International Investigation into Possible Criminal Activity
    Promised

  PhotoWeekly Magazine

GAT STOCK PLUMMETS
  Investigators: What Did GAT Execs Know & When Did
  They Know It?

  California Business Weekly

CHAPTER 13

(One)

Gold Aviation and Transport
Burbank, California
18 October, 1977

Don Harrison swiveled around in his leather desk chair and stared out his office windows, pondering his own reflection trapped in the smoked glass. Harrison was wearing a gray silk suit of elegant European design, and his intricately patterned silk tie was a "Count somebody or other" original. He looked like a man in control. A tycoon. The image was bolstered by the accoutrements of power surrounding him. Reflected in the dark glass was Harrison's marble-topped oak desk. The office's moss-green wall-to-wall carpeting, paneled walls, and burgundy leather furniture groupings seemed to stretch into eternity behind him.

Harrison smiled wryly. Sure the overall image was that of a captain of industry, but if you looked a little more closely at the guy seated behind the desk, you noticed that his wispy, unruly hair was a little long around his ears, and that his gold-rimmed eyeglasses gave him the look of an aging but still boyish academic don. The smoked glass helped the youthful illusion along by smoothing out the creases that had formed around Harrison's eyes and mouth and shading out the silver in his hair.

Harrison rolled his desk chair closer to the windows to look into his own eyes. He purposely narrowed his gaze, trying for a look of grim determination.

It was no good. He could scowl and glower all he wanted, but his own inner nature underlined by the vague, abstract expression behind his soft hazel eyes betrayed him.

Harrison's eyes said that here was the archetype intellectual, a fifty-five-year-old man who even after the years spent in charge of this sprawling aviation company was still more comfortable in his old ivory tower than in the executive suite. His eyes proclaimed that here was a creative thinker, a man more in his element chairing an R & D think-tank brainstorming session than at a board of directors' meeting.

But that's what Steve will be all too ready to tell me, Harrison scolded himself. *No need for me to patronize myself! Anyway, people can change. A bold step like the one I want to take will tell the world that I'm a man of action just like my partner.*

But Harrison's determination wavered as he further studied his reflection. He brooded, *The problem with being a contemplative man was that you saw both sides of the question and thereby crippled yourself with indecision.*

The eyes, Harrison thought, sighing. The eyes never lied.

As Harrison stared out the windows, the light changed and his reflection vanished, to be replaced by the outside world. Harrison's top-floor corner office overlooked the GAT manufacturing complex's airfields, where the dozens of partially assembled F-66a Stiletto fighters were scattered like children's forgotten toys. These modified Stilettos were designated for European export. Their final assembly would take place at Skytrain's factories on the Continent and in England. The completed F-66a jet fighters would then travel to their final destinations: the various NATO European air forces.

Harrison felt supreme satisfaction as he looked down at the grounded armada of fighters. GAT had certainly come a long way since that dark period back in 1974 when it looked as if the company was about to sink under its own financial missteps and Tim Campbell's machinations to sabotage GAT's campaign to sell the Pont airliner in America.

Now the company still basked in the astounding success of the Stiletto fighter and the solid domestic sales record scored by the Skytrain-produced Pont. There were the royalties rolling in on the product patents GAT Aerospace had registered during its work on the Viking One spacecraft that had landed on Mars a year ago July, and there were the royalties to come from work GAT Aerospace was doing on the new space shuttle. Meanwhile, GAT had a new commercial jetliner in the works, and exciting improvements were in the cards for the Stiletto, including new controls meant to give the fighter previously unimagined air maneuverability, and a new wing designed to give the Stiletto greater range and increased weapons-load capability.

But of all the fledglings in GAT's nest, the most exciting and potentially lucrative on the drawing board was a proposed internationally built jet fighter, dubbed the World-Bird Project. World-Bird was conceived as a money machine that would do for GAT's military aviation division what Skytrain had done for GAT in the international jetliner business. As good as the Stiletto was, and despite the fighter's constant running improvements, the F-66 and its variants couldn't stay on top forever as the international warbird of choice. When the sun inevitably did set on the Stiletto, and it came time for the NATO countries to replace their F-66s along with the rest of their current mixed bag of fighters, GAT wanted to be in the position to claim a large slice of that lucrative pie. To that end, Harrison had put together under the GAT/World-Bird banner a delegation of international commerce experts and military strategists to stage an onslaught against Washington. The GAT/W-B lobbying team had met with the appropriate Cabinet-level administration, and congressional leaders to promote a two-pronged argument: that from a trade deficit viewpoint World-Bird would help to balance the United States' ledgers, and that should a war be fought on European soil, a standardized World-Bird fighter common to all of NATO's air forces would ensure against inventory problems concerning parts and weapons availability.

The lobbying effort had been a success. The United States had firmly endorsed the project as a unique international effort that would further the bounds of technology and strengthen NATO. The U.S. government was granting generous trade credits to the participating countries, and generous corporate tax breaks to the American companies involved, all of which were either GAT subsidiaries or independents buying into the deal under a GAT licensing arrangement.

In the international arena, GAT, thanks to its reputation in military aviation having been refurbished by the Stiletto, was leading the World-Bird Project through Skytrain Industrie. Harrison had initially feared that the consortium would give GAT some backtalk about the way the American company was commandeering the driver's seat for the World-Bird Project, but Steve Gold had said not to worry.

"Our British and French partners have learned their lesson after the way we came out on top last time," Steve had said. "Don't sweat it, Don. Skytrain will follow where GAT leads as long as we remain strong and prosperous. . . ."

And Steve had been right, Harrison now thought enviously, because Steve had the instinctive knack of reading people. Harrison supposed Steve had honed that gift in the military.

Harrison sighed. Or maybe some lucky individuals were just born with the ability to see into others, and know how to motivate, persuade, lead.

In any event, just as Steve had predicted, Skytrain had come along quietly concerning World-Bird. Since then, West Germany, Italy, and Spain had bought into World-Bird Phase One: a five-year timetable for research and development concerning the new fighter. Currently, negotiations were proceeding to bring in Israel, and in a real coup, Japan, although some of the European parties to the deal were complaining that if the Israelis came aboard, World-Bird could kiss the lucrative Arab arms market good-bye.

The intercom on Harrison's desk buzzed. Harrison pressed the talk button. "Yes?"

"Mr. Gold is here," the secretary said.

"Have him come in," Harrison began, but Steve was already barging in with a magazine clutched in his hand. Harrison batted down the surge of resentment he felt. Steve had always been the proverbial bull in the china shop, and always would be, but today was no day to let petty annoyances get in the way of things.

"Have you seen this?" Steve demanded, waving the magazine like it was a war pennant. It was the new issue of *Aviation Weekly* just out today.

"Yeah, I've seen it," Harrison replied.

It was fifty paces from the office's double doors to Harrison's desk. Harrison watched Steve approach, taking in his partner's casual style of dress: silk-weave sports jacket, linen trousers, knit polo shirt, and basket-weave leather moccasins. Hardly suitable office wear for a chief executive, but Harrison again reminded himself to ignore the petty annoyances.

He also studied Steve's face, thinking that the years hadn't softened the man the way they had Steve's father, Herman Gold. If anything, time—and baldness—had made Steve look more pugnacious. At fifty, Steve's hawk nose, strong jaw, and tanned scalp fringed with short, silvery blond hair gave him an accomplished, dangerous air—

Especially around those fighter pilot's hard brown eyes, Harrison thought. Steve still saw everything; his eyes were still as sharp as ever.

And the eyes don't lie.

(Two)

Steve Gold slapped the magazine down on Don's desk. He pulled a package of Pall Malls and his lighter out of his jacket pocket and then slumped into a nearby leather armchair.

"It's right there, the lead item in the 'New & Noteworthy' section," Gold muttered, lighting a smoke. He watched Don open the magazine and turn to the offending page. "I thought you'd said you'd read it?" he asked sharply.

"I did," Don replied, sounding weary as he settled into his chair behind his desk. Don read out loud, 'GAT to debut its new GC-600 jetliner at Paris Air Show.' "

"I think this high-powered office is going to your head," Gold remarked.

"What's that supposed to mean?" Don looked up from the magazine.

Gold looked around Harrison's office. His own digs just down the hall weren't anywhere near as elaborate, but then, he didn't need such trappings, despite his elevated status at GAT. Since the Skytrain/Pont/Tim Campbell furball of several years ago, Gold had expanded his role. Now, in addition to heading up GAT's military aviation division, Gold was GAT's commercial aviation marketing and sales honcho, and spent most of his time crisscrossing the country and the world putting out fires on the company's behalf. The job suited his restless nature. Gold had never been a desk man. He despised being stuck in one place in civilian life just as much as he'd despised it in the military.

"I asked you a question," Don said quietly. "What did you mean by your remark that this office has gone to my head?"

Gold said, "I meant that maybe you think that because you have my father's old office you're running the company all by your lonesome, like Pop did?"

"You know better than that," Don said, a hint of warning in his tone.

Better lay off, Gold thought. *You push Don too hard and he withdraws into his shell like a turtle, and then you can't touch him.*

"I *thought* I did," Gold replied earnestly. "I thought we were partners, but then something like this happens." He paused to gesture contemptuously with his cigarette toward the magazine on Harrison's desk. "And then I begin to have my doubts about you all over again. I can't believe you had the gall to go and make an announcement like that without consulting me! By sneaking behind my back to do it!"

"Now, that's not fair," Harrison protested. "We *did* talk about it."

"Sure we *talked* about it!" Gold angrily stubbed out his cigarette in the standing ashtray beside his chair. "You wanted to debut the jetliner this June in Paris, and I didn't. We left it unresolved. I *thought* we were going to talk about it some more, but you just went and decided things unilaterally, right? Let good old Steve be the last to know!"

"Come on, Steve."

"How do you think I felt this morning at home when my phone began ringing off the hook? I hadn't even *seen* the goddamn announcement yet, but there I was, fielding calls from newspaper business editors about the GC-600! Linda was looking at me like I was crazy!"

"You ought to have an unlisted number." Don smiled.

"I *do* have an unlisted number," Gold snapped. "For all the fucking good it did me today. Believe me, if the newshounds want you, they find a way. . . . And then I get to the office and I find a stack of messages on my desk from all the airlines' purchasing agents. All my contacts are pissed at me for not giving them advance notice on the announcement. So what am I supposed to tell them?" Gold made a moronic face. "Duhhhh—sorry fellas, but my partner neglected to tell me, heh-heh, duhhhh? . . ."

Don shook his head. "You know, it's funny that given our personalities and our usual points of view, this time *I'm* arguing for the bold step, while you're cautioning to go the safe and conservative way.

"It's not about personalities!" Gold said fiercely. "And don't try to change the subject!"

"Yes, *sir,* Colonel!"

Gold, staring at Don's faintly mocking expression, said: "For two cents I'd get up and punch you in the nose."

Don said what he always said at about this point in the argument: "You mean to say a war hero would hit a man wearing glasses?"

As usual, Gold struggled against the impulse to smile and lost. At the same time, he felt his anger melting away. "I'm gonna get me a phony pair of specs, and the next time you say that, boy, are *you* going to be in for a surprise."

"You still mad?" Don asked.

Gold shook his head. "Just listen, okay? I want to get this off my chest. We've been partners almost five years. I think we work together well, but I have to tell you that in my opinion you were out of line to have made that announcement without getting my okay."

Don hesitated. "You're right. I apologize."

"Apology accepted," Gold said.

"But what I did I did for the good of the company," Don quickly added.

"You should have stopped with the apology."

"Okay, now *you* listen," Don said. "The GC-600 is a two-engine fanjet, hundred-seat jetliner utilizing state-of-the-art noise-reduction and fuel-economy technology. It's destined to be a mainstay commercial aviation product for the future, especially as the hub-and-spoke system of air travel evolves in this country.''

Gold nodded. A lot of people at the airlines were talking about this hub-and-spoke system in which the airlines set up large centers, or hubs, to receive passengers from feeder routes or spokes.

Gold said, ''But there are a lot of airplanes that satisfy the needs of the hub-and-spoke system. The Pont, for one.''

''Sure,'' Don nodded. ''But the Pont and the rest of the liners in its class are all 150-seaters. I think a downsize bird will be just what the doctor ordered over the next few years, as the U.S. sees a rise in the secondary hubs—''

''Secondary hubs?'' Gold echoed faintly.

Don vigorously nodded. ''Sure! Wake up, partner! We've got a southerner in the White House, don't we? Carter's the first president from Dixie since old Zach Taylor in 1848.''

''How do you know shit like that?'' Gold shook his head.

''I tell you the South is rising again, and besides the burgeoning Sunbelt, you can bank on astounding population growth in the Southwest and the Rocky Mountain states. All that shifting population is going to bring about new urban centers.''

''Secondary hubs.'' Gold nodded.

''Right,'' Don enthused. ''And secondary hubs will require slenderized spokes to feed passengers into them. And that's when a quiet, fuel-efficient jetliner like the 600 will come into its own. I see the 600 as a small commuter airline's biggest plane, and the smallest plane a major airline will want in its fleet. The 600 is going to be a real winner, clearly overshadowing the competition.''

''You don't have to sell me on our own airplane,'' Gold said. ''You're the technical type, not me. I believe that the airplane is everything you say it is.''

''Then what's the problem?'' Don shrugged.

''The problem is that the GC-600 is everything you say it is, plus one thing more: it's not ready. Your own R and D people have told me that they feel uncomfortable about being pushed to have a prototype ready for the Paris Air Show this June.''

Don looked away. "Hey, like you said, the technical stuff is my department."

Gold picked up on Don's unease. "Are you saying your best people are wrong?" he challenged.

"I'm saying that I used to wear a white lab coat, and that I remember how it is when you hang out in the design studio as opposed to the executive suite. When you're indulging your creativity at a drafting board, *forever* isn't enough time to let go of your baby. You want to work and work on a project, constantly improving it, because there's *always* that final little tweak of fine tuning to be done."

"I'm not saying the 600 has to be perfect before we unveil her," Gold argued. "I'm just saying she has to be a safe, solid, airworthy machine. Your engineers tell me that—"

"My engineers talk too much!" Don snapped. "They ought to spend less time flapping their jaws and more time working!"

"Hey, I'm sorry," Gold backed off, realizing that he'd unintentionally hit a sore spot with Don. "I didn't mean anything by that remark."

Don leaned back in his chair. "I know." He shook his head. "It just burns me up that somebody in engineering—one of my *own*—would betray the company."

Gold nodded. In the business world as well as the military, there was nothing worse than a traitorous spy, but that was exactly what GAT had infecting its engineering department.

The first embarrassing leaks concerning the glitches and gremlins cropping up in the GC-600's development appeared in the trades about twenty months ago. Since then, the squibs airing GAT's dirty laundry concerning the GC-600 had regularly appeared in *Aviation Weekly* and the other industry publications, attributed to an anonymous source whom the various trades had in-house nicknamed "Icarus," much to GAT's displeasure. GAT did not favor having its new jetliner linked within the industry to that first great failure in manned flight: Icarus, who lost his wax wings when he flew too close to the sun.

From the start of the offending leaks, the trades had rigorously stonewalled GAT's attempts to find out the source of their information. Since Watergate, every publication liked to think of itself as heir to the tradition of protecting a "Deep

Throat'' source. The aviation trades were no exception concerning Icarus. It was Gold's wife, Linda Forrester, who was able to use her old journalism connections to find out from an industry reporter who owed her a favor that Icarus was one of GAT's engineers.

Trouble was, that didn't much narrow things down. GAT employed thousands of engineers. Sure, only several hundred were working on the GC-600, but it was the nature of R & D that all the engineers had computer access to the 600 project so that they could cross-reference the technical data to supplement their own ongoing work.

"I remember when your father was alive and I was his chief engineer," Don said, breaking into Gold's reveries. "Your father was a genius at inspiring the Engineering Department to meet deadlines. For one thing, Herman led by example. If he asked us to work eighteen hours a day, he made sure we saw him work twenty. But if inspiration didn't work, he didn't hesitate to use a judicious dollop of fear to drive his people to meet his goals." Don smiled. "We may have complained—we maybe even hated him now and again—but we never would have dreamed of betraying Herman the way one of our engineers is betraying us."

Gold asked, "Is Lane Associates getting anywhere discovering Icarus's identity?"

Don shook his head. "Otto Lane has his best security and anti-industrial espionage operatives on the case, but he says they've got to take it slow, and I agree with him." Don nodded seriously. You know, Steve, engineers can be a temperamental lot.''

"Tell me about it," Gold couldn't resist wisecracking.

Don, blushing, ducked his head. "Okay, myself included, engineers can be temperamental. They're—*we're*—creative artists as well as scientists. In any case, I've endorsed Otto's intention to run a very discreet counterespionage investigation, even if in this sort of work, discreet is synonymous with slow.''

Gold nodded. "I suppose that is best. The last thing we want to do is alienate more of our people by conducting a witch hunt in order to smoke out Icarus.''

"A mass exodus of engineering talent coming on top of the embarrassing leaks concerning the GC-600 would also shake investor confidence in GAT,'' Don added. "And that would lead to a sharp dip in the price of our stock."

"And leave management—namely us—open to a challenge," Gold said darkly. "It's no secret that industry opinion of our leadership of the company is on shaky ground as it is. It's a fact that World-Bird and the GC-600 are the first projects GAT has initiated without Herman Gold."

"Your father had a guiding hand in both the Stiletto fighter and the Skytrain Pont projects," Don admitted. "That's why the leaks are so punishing to us. Every new airplane project has it's share of glitches and gremlins, but the industry is watching GAT extra closely these days to see if we can persevere in our attempt to move the company out of Herman Gold's shadow. We got off to a mixed start with the Pont and managed to come out of it okay, but the sharks on Wall Street who remember the scent of our blood in the water are waiting and watching for our next misstep."

"And for GAT to have a spy in its midst just now further compromises our image," Gold said. "The industry has got to wonder what's wrong within our house if one of our own is telling tales." He paused. "And with all this going on, you still feel we should push to meet the external deadline of the Paris Air Show just eight months from now, as opposed to wheeling out our GC-600 prototype according to our own schedule?"

"I think we have no choice but to debut in Paris," Don replied. "We must move quickly to squelch the rumors circulating about the 600 and the company. Consider World-Bird's place in all this. World-Bird is costing us a mint. It will eventually prove to be a gold mine for us, but not for years, and World-Bird won't survive if GAT is not perceived as being on top of things."

"I agree with that," Gold said. "It's precisely why I'm questioning the wisdom of your announcement at this point in time. How will it look if June rolls around and the GC-600 is not ready?"

"It must be ready!" Don said forcefully. "It will be ready!"

"It's a gamble," Gold pointed out. "And I've never known Don Harrison to be a gambling man."

Don smiled. "Sometimes you have to go with a roll of the

dice. In this case, I feel that circumstances warrant it. For one thing, the Paris Air Show gives our engineers a finite deadline to shoot for; it will serve as a rallying point; it will represent the light at the end of the tunnel for them concerning the GC-600.''

"I hear you," Gold said, aware that many of the company's engineers were suffering the knowledge that a turncoat among them was questioning their abilities in public.

"For another thing," Don continued, "the announcement I made in today's issue of *Aviation Weekly* shows the industry that despite the leaks, GAT's management has confidence in the company's ability to produce the jetliner. I guarantee you that GAT's stock price will rise on the back of this announcement.''

"I hope you're right," Gold sighed.

"I hope so too," Don said. "Anyway, we had to do something to combat the leaks. Otherwise, the GC-600 will be the first airplane to be branded a lemon before the initial prototype is even built.''

"Well it was a balls-out move," Gold admitted. "I don't fault you for making it." He chuckled. "In a way, I'm proud of you. But next time, run it past me before you run up the colors, okay?''

"Yeah, I promise," Don said softly. "Christ, I hope everything turns out okay.''

"Me too," Gold said. "Because come June if the GC-600 prototype isn't ready for the Paris Air Show, we are going to look worse than ever.''

(Three)

In the sky above the California desert, east of Los Angeles
17 October, 1977

"We should be there in a few minutes, Mr. Layten," the pilot said.

"Yes, thanks," Turner Layten nodded, thinking that the annoying *whup! whup!* of the Bell Jetranger's rotors was only slightly muffled by the radio headset he wore in order to communicate with the chopper's pilot:

Layten studied the arid desert terrain through the helicopter's bubble canopy. The landscape baking under the blazing sun resembled nearby Death Valley. Everything was burnt brown, or the rusty color of a scabbed-over wound, or purple, like an old bruise. Here and there the ground was furred over with pale-green scrub and studded with leathery green cactus, but mostly everything was as dead-looking and dry as a bone left out to bleach in the sun.

"There's Chopper One!" said the pilot through the cockpit intercom.

Layten looked to where the pilot was pointing and saw the big, twin-rotor helicopter, which was painted green and yellow, just like this much smaller Jetranger. Amalgamated-Landis kept a fleet of several helicopters and private planes for executive use at the El Segundo facility, but the twin rotor bird named Chopper One was reserved exclusively for Tim Campbell. Chopper One had the interior room of a full-size trailer and had everything inside it: a fully equipped office, a media/communications center, a sleeping area/lounge, even kitchen facilities. Just now, Chopper One looked like some monstrous insect drying its wings in the sun. A tent or awning of some sort had gone up alongside the copter, and several jeeps, trucks, and other off-road vehicles were parked nearby.

"I'm setting her down, Mr. Layten."

"Yes, that's fine." Layten instinctively looked himself over, as he did whenever he was about to meet his superior. He was wearing tan chinos and a matching, short-sleeved safari jacket, an Aussie-style bush hat with one side of the brim pinned up, and wire-rimmed aviator sunglasses. His trouser bottoms were tucked into thick leather boots that covered his legs up to his knees.

Snakebite-proof boots, Layten thought, shuddering, and reached beneath the bush jacket to adjust the reassuring heft of the snub-nosed .38 riding on his hip. He'd been practicing with his gun—unloaded, of course—by drawing on himself in his bedroom mirror. Nobody, *especially* not Steve Gold, was going to take his gun away from him again.

The Jetranger set down about fifty yards from the bigger chopper. "You wait," Layten told the pilot. "I won't be long.'' He unbuckled his seat belt, pushed open the door, and hopped out.

The desert heat hit him like a sledgehammer after the air-conditioned cockpit. *Hell of a place to conduct a business meeting,* he thought as he bent low, holding on to to his hat, wincing against the storm of sand and grit churned up by the Jetranger's slowing rotor wash.

He hurried toward Tim Campbell's chopper, where deck chairs and a luncheon table had been laid out beneath the tent awning. Standing by the table was the serving staff, wearing crisp-looking white coats, and a tanned young woman in a black bikini and high-heeled sandals. She walked beneath the awning to one of the deck chairs, where she began oiling herself with suntan lotion.

The woman had her blond hair pulled back into a ponytail. She was beautiful, and as Layten got closer he tried not to stare at her, but it was hard. Her black thong bikini bottom only delineated and emphasized the heartstoppingly perfect curves of her flawless ass, while her bikini top barely covered her luscious breasts. Layten could see the suntan lotion sheening her cleavage. How slippery it would be to the touch . . .

She must have seen him approaching. She smiled at him, then lanquidly stretched her arms above her head. Her breasts rose, and her wonderful nipples so clearly outlined beneath the thin black fabric seemed to beckon to Layten.

Oh, God, Layten thought. *Oh, God.* His hard-on was raging. He had an instant, elaborate fantasy in which he regaled the blonde with stories concerning his mysterious past as a CIA operative, seducing her into making love right here in the desert. Hidden from prying eyes by the sand dunes, they would become naked, carnal animals basking like lizards in the sun as they rolled in each other's sweating, passionate embrace. . . .

Layten averted his gaze. Out of the corner of his eye he saw the blonde shrug, then turn away, to settle into a deck chair. Layten was hugely relieved, excepting his still throbbing erection. You couldn't be too careful; Tim Campbell could be highly possessive of his toys.

Layten gave the woman reclining beneath the awning a wide berth as he approached one of the chopper's crew members. The man, wearing a tan uniform with a green and yellow stripe down the sides of his trousers, and matching epaulettes on his shoulders, was standing beside the humming portable generators hooked up to supply power to the chopper's air-conditioning and refrigeration units.

"Hi, there, Mr. Layten," the crew member said, touching the visor of his baseball cap as Layten approached. "You looking for Mr. Campbell? The boss is still out hunting. You just follow that trail that starts over yonder."

Layten glanced distastefully at the winding trail that disappeared into the desert wilderness. "Maybe you'd better take me," he told the crewman.

"No can do, Mr. Layten. The boss told me to stay here and keep an eye on these generators. He's got some kind of fancy caviar to go with his champagne for lunch. Wants it icy cold, he said."

"Damn."

"Don't you worry, Mr. Layten," the crew member assured him. "You just follow the trail and listen for the shots. You can't miss him." He paused. "Just keep to the center of the trail. The boss and his boys have really stirred up the wildlife hereabouts."

"Wonderful." Layten walked away muttering curses to himself, desperately not wanting to leave behind the relative comfort of the Chopper One campsite as he picked his way around the rocks and clumps of scrub. The sun was beating down on him. His safari jacket was already soaked through with sweat. And he hadn't even reached the damn trail.

Gnats, or wasps, or some such nasty things were buzzing and whining in his ears. He hunched his shoulders and turned up his collar as he stalked along, trying to breathe in the blast-furnace heat as he started down the trail, which rose as it twisted its way into the hills. His heart was pounding like a jackhammer as he reached a switchback turnoff and kept going, steadfastly staring down at his boots, doing his best to ignore the rustlings and skittering movements in the rust-colored rocks and low, thorny bramble. He tried not to think about hairy, jumping tarantulas and glistening darting scorpions; but most of all, God help him, he tried not to think about *snakes*.

He huffed and puffed his way to the top of a low rise and saw Tim Campbell down at the bottom, standing in the center of a small clearing ringed with boulders. *When you're rich they call you eccentric,* Layten thought, studying Campbell. *And when you're poor, they just call you crazy.*

Well, in Tim Campbell's case, they'd call him very eccentric indeed. Campbell looked like an old desert rat, or maybe Howard Hughes or somebody like that, Layten thought as he took in his employer's leathery, tanned skin and Campbell's absurd dress. Campbell was wearing a white tee shirt, cut-off denim shorts, fingerless leather gloves, and a pair of the same kind of knee-high anti-snake bite boots that Layten had on. Campbell was also wearing a bright-pink baseball cap on his head, gold-rimmed, green-lensed, aviator sunglasses over his eyes, a red bandanna tied loosely around his neck, and a brace of elaborately tooled, light-tan leather cowboy holsters strapped around his waist. In each holster was a pearl-handled revolver.

Layten, remembering to stick to the middle of the trail, hurried down the sandy slope to where Campbell was standing with his hands resting lightly on the butts of his guns. About fifty feet beyond Campbell, some tough-looking men dressed in denim and protective leather were beating the brush. The men were looking for something; they hurriedly prodded into holes and beneath rocks with long, hooked sticks.

"Get a move on, you assholes!" Campbell yelled at the men. "Find me something, or else it'll be *your* asses I'll shoot!"

"Sir," Layten called out, coming up behind Campbell.

"Yeah, what?" Campbell gruffly began, turning. "Oh, it's you, Turner." He sounded more bored than surprised. "What brings you out here, son?"

"Mr. Campbell!" shouted one of the men out beating the brush. The guy sounded excited and a little scared. "I got you a big one here!"

"I'll be the judge of that, son!" Campbell growled. "Come on, then! Throw it over, and we'll see."

Layten watched as the man raised his hooked stick with something coiled around it and then hurled that something twisting and turning through the air toward the clearing. It hit the dirt about twenty feet from where Layten and Campbell were standing, and then coiled, ready to strike as it emitted a dry, rasping, rattling that sounded incredibly loud in the still desert.

"Oh, yeah, that's a big'un, all right," Campbell murmured.

Layten couldn't reply. He felt like throwing up, but he couldn't take his eyes off the rattlesnake. He'd always been afraid of snakes. Always. This one was at least five feet long and as thick around as a man's wrist. Its skin was a diamond variegation of brown the color of dead grass, and yellow the color of urine. As Layten stared at the snake it began to elegantly, silently slither toward him. Its flat, black eyes the color of onyx seemed to fix on Layten, making him weak in the knees. He began to shiver uncontrollably as the rattlesnake's tongue flicked out to taste the air.

Campbell drew his nickel-plated, elaborately engraved guns. They were custom-decorated, .22-caliber, six-inch-barrel Colt Peacemakers.

"Ain't that snake a beauty," Campbell breathed in admiration as he thumbed back the hammers on his single-action weapons and fired two shots at the rattler, which was now less than ten feet away.

The .22-caliber six-guns' reports sounded more like the snapping of twigs than, say, the loud crack of the .38 Smith & Wesson Layten wore. One of Campbell's shots missed, kicking up a spout of dirt, but the other hit the rattler square in the head, blowing its skull to bloody bits.

Layten sagged in relief as the decapitated reptile writhed in death, its tail rhythmically beating the blood-soaked sand.

"Yeah." Campbell nodded, sounding satisfied as he holstered his guns. "These .22 Magnums do the job. Find me another, boys!" he shouted to his beaters, who'd been watching the show. He then glanced at Layten. "That makes twenty I shot this afternoon," he confided.

"Yes, sir."

"Last time I was here, some environmentalist types got wind of what I was doing and complained 'bout how I was fucking with the ecology or some such cowpie by shooting up all these rattlers." Campbell shrugged. "So I paid off some of the local pols, and I ain't heard a peep from nobody about it since." He winked. "Take it from me, son. With enough money, you can kill *anything*."

Layten reached inside his safari jacket for the copy of *Aviation Weekly*. He turned to the page with the GAT announcement concerning the GC-600's debut at the Paris Air Show, and handed it to Campbell.

"This is just out today, Tim. As soon as the copy reached my office, I figured I'd better get out here to apprise you of the situation."

Campbell nodded. "Hold off on them snakes!" he yelled to his men as he quickly scanned the page. "Well, well, well . . ." He handed back the magazine to Layten. "Turner, you've done real well. I have to admit I didn't think you could do it when you suggested placing a spy inside GAT."

"I didn't place a spy, Tim," Layten respectfully corrected. "I *turned* one of their own people by bribing him to do our bidding."

"Cost us a pretty penny, too," Campbell said mildly.

"I'm sorry about that," Layten apologized. "But our expenditures concerning Icarus are about to end."

"How's that?"

Layten savored the moment: It happened so rarely that he was in a position to explain things to Tim Campbell. "Now that Icarus has been working for us long enough to establish a record of duplicity against GAT, we no longer have to pay him, but merely threaten to leak his identity, effectively destroying his career and his life, if he doesn't continue to cooperate."

"That's very good, Turner," Campbell complimented him. "But, in retrospect, I'm not surprised that an old ex-CIA spook like you could so easily switch over to *industrial* espionage."

Layten smiled thinly, clenching his teeth. "Spook" was what Steven Gold had always called him.

"Yep, you just keep running your little spy or informer or whatever," Campbell murmured. "And keep me posted."

"Tim, I still don't understand the point of this," Layten said. "I mean, where is it going?"

"Well, now, Turner," Campbell mused. "I don't rightly know. It's like when you throw a rock into the center of a still pond and the ripples start spreading. For now, it's enough that we've railroaded GAT into making that announcement. Once again, we're acting and they're reacting. GAT is on the defensive while we're on the offensive." He thumbed back his cap to wipe his brow with the bandanna around his neck. "There's times I think GAT has more lives than a cat, but that's all right with me, Turner, because I have patience. I'll just keep forcing GAT to use up its lives, and eventually they'll be down to scratch."

"Yes, Tim, it's just that . . ." Layten trailed off hesitantly.

"Speak up, Turner," Campbell ordered. "Say what's on your mind."

"Well, sir," Layten worried, "it's just that this is the first time since we've worked together going after GAT that we've actually crossed the line."

"What line?"

"Tim, we're breaking the law."

"Fuck the law!" Campbell said sharply, but he must have seen Layten flinch, because he immediately softened his tone. "Turner, you listen to me. Take them rattlers out there. Them snakes are fierce, implacable, cold as ice, and yet you give an old man like me the right assets—anti-snake bite boots and a gun—and that rattler is going to lose every time."

"You're implying that your wealth puts you above the law," Layten said slowly.

"I know it does, Turner. I ain't exactly been a choirboy my whole life."

Layten didn't say anything, but his thoughts reached back to Jack Horton, his old boss at the CIA. Horton had thought he was above the law, but thanks to Steven Gold, and a congressional investigation, Jack had found out otherwise. Trouble was, when Jack Horton fell, he took Turner Layten with him.

"Mr. Campbell!" eagerly shouted one of the men out beating the brush. "I got two of 'em, here, Mr. Campbell!"

Campbell chuckled to Layten. "I pay these boys fifty bucks a pop for every rattler worth shooting they find me." He shouted: "Throw 'em out!"

Layten watched as the pair of rattlers hit the dirt fifteen feet away. They were smaller than the first, but quicker. They began crazily slithering, tracing S patterns in the dust as they headed for the side of the trail and the sanctuary of the brush.

"Here, try your luck, son." Campbell handed Layten one of the six-shooters.

Layten gripped the Peacemaker with both hands, sighting down the barrel toward the nearer snake. He thumbed back the hammer and was about to squeeze off a round when Campbell, shooting from the hip, fanned off a flurry of shots from his remaining Peacemaker. The gun volley plowed up dirt without hitting either of the snakes. Then Layten fired, scoring a lucky shot that blew off a snake's rattle.

"Beautiful, Turner!" Campbell laughed as the snake disappeared into the scrub, trailing blood. "You just cut that fucker a new asshole!"

"Yes, Tim." Layten forgot his misgivings about the industrial-espionage laws that he was breaking on his superior's behalf in his own pleasure at having amused Campbell. "Let's hope I can perform the same service for Donald Harrison and Steven Gold."

CHAPTER 14

(One)

Axel Lyegate Memorial Auditorium
Tactical Air Combat Center
Ryder AFB, Nevada
29 May, 1978

Major Robert Blaize Greene peeked out through the curtains at the auditorium full of "visiting players," the Air Force personnel here at Ryder for the upcoming Red Sky air war exercise. Greene then looked back over his shoulder at the stage, which was dominated by a dramatic forty-foot-tall rendition of the shoulder patch of his squadron. The patch was round, and showed a winged Russian bear attacking head-on from out of a sky-blue background. The Russian bear had fiery red eyes, and golden lightning bolts clenched in its massive jaws. Around the top of the patch in blue against gold curved the letters ATTACKERS. Around the bottom of the patch, the same-colored lettering read: 37th ATTACKER SQUADRON.

Greene watched as the pilots in his squadron filed on the

stage to take their seats in front of the huge patch. His pilots were all dressed as Greene was: olive-drab flight suits emblazoned with their rank insignia, their "Attackers" patches on chest and right shoulder, black boots, and blood-red ascots.

"They all here, Buck?" Greene asked his administrative assistant, Captain Billy Buckmeyer.

"Yep, everyone's present and accounted for on both sides of the curtain," Buck said from offstage. "You ready to start hamming it up, Robbie?"

Greene started out shooting Buck a dirty look, but was unable to stifle his grin. "Well, maybe I do ham it up a little," he admitted. "On the other hand, it never hurts to instill a bit of awe and mystery about the Attackers into our guests."

"You just like to strut and bluster," Buck playfully admonished, wagging his finger like the schoolmaster he so resembled. Billy Buckmeyer was in his thirties, a balding, dark-haired, bookish man with black horn-rimmed glasses who favored wearing his full service uniform—tie, jacket, black-visored officer's cap—no matter how hot the weather. Buck wasn't a pilot, but he could handle paperwork the way Greene's hottest jet jockeys could handle their airplanes. Greene respected and desperately needed Buck for his abilities, but in addition to Buck being the chief cook and bottle washer around "Red Square," the Attackers' operations building, Buck was also Greene's best friend.

"You know, you missed your true calling," Buck was telling Greene. "You should have been a movie star."

"I *am* a movie star." Greene laughed. "I star in the action epic Red Sky, and my role is that of chief villain. That's what the Attackers are all about, right?"

Greene took one final look around the stage to make sure that all of his people had taken their seats, and one final peek through the curtain, to make sure the auditorium was settled. Then he nodded to Buck, who relayed the signal to start the proceedings.

This auditorium also served as the players' main briefing hall. (The Attackers had their own briefing hall back at Red Square.) The auditorium had plush Air Force–blue seats and carpeting, and sophisticated AV equipment. It was located in the below ground level of the Tactical Air Combat Command Center, a sprawling complex with a flat roof that was festooned with a nightmare forest of radio, microwave and radar transmitting gear. In addition to the auditorium, TACCC housed the Range Control Center, the Red Sky Operations and Intelligence offices, a series of smaller briefing rooms, and the visiting players' Personal Equipment Room. Across the street from the TACCC was the ramp where the visiting players' aircraft were parked and serviced.

"It's showtime," Buck called softly.

Greene, nodding, waited as the large silver screen was lowered. Visual aids would be projected on the screen during Green's presentation, and the screen would also serve to temporarily block the giant insignia patch and the seated Attackers squadron from the audience's view until the dramatically right moment.

The house lights dimmed slowly and then winked out, plunging the audience into movie-theater darkness. The curtains parted. Greene, guided by the glimmering stage footlights, took his place at the podium located stage right. He took several deep breaths to calm himself—he always suffered a twinge of stage fright at the start of these presentations—and then switched on the podium microphone.

"*You don't know him,*" Greene began. Like always, the amplified sound of his own voice booming from the auditorium speakers took him by surprise.

"*You call him bogie, bandit, gomer, Ivan, and countless other disparaging names, but all of your mockery does nothing to dispel your fear, because you don't know him.*"

Greene glanced at the screen, where slides of Soviet and Warsaw Pact MiG-21s and -23s—NATO code-named Fishback and Flogger—were being flashed.

"*You don't know how the enemy pilot thinks. How he fights . . .*"

Now the screen alternated between showing slides, newsreel, and gun-camera footage of USAF Sabres and Broad-Sword fighters mixing it up with MiG-15s, followed by Vietnam-era footage of Phantoms and Thuds dueling with MiG-17s and -21s. The light reflecting off the screen allowed Greene to study his audience. As tradition warranted, the first few rows were taken up with air-to-air fighter jocks. The rest of the seats were occupied with personnel belonging to Airborne Warning and REC, Defensive Suppression, Offensive Counter Air, Close Air Support, and transport/refueling sectors. Airborne Warning and REC included the reconnaissance people who crewed the unarmed F-4s, the AWAC aircraft crews, and the RESCAP specialists who flew spotter slow-movers and choppers; DeSup belonged to the Wild Weasle F-4 crews who ferreted out SAM and his AAA brethren; OCA were the close-air support fliers who piloted A-7 Corsair Mud Movers, while CAS was the province of the A-10 Thunderbolt Warthogs who killed tanks; and then there were the crews who drove the gargantuan C-130 Hercules transports and the crucial KC-10 aerial refueling tankers. Everybody who was anybody came to play war at Red Sky, because in the event of a real war, everybody here would be playing for keeps.

"In Korea we controlled the sky almost from the beginning," Greene now said as up on the screen the footage and photos unspooled, detailing the history to date of the United States' experience with jet-age air combat.

"Yeah, we had it our way in Korea, because we relied on seasoned World War Two fighter jocks to do the job. In Vietnam, it was a different story. Most of our pilots were not combat tested. What they knew about ACM they learned from books, and because of that, despite our superior warbirds, we got our ears pinned back by hard-as-nails Commie pilots, many of them flying MiGs that were not much more sophisticated than the ones that our fighter-pilot forefathers had so efficiently sent plunging into the Yalu."

Greene let the doleful freeze-frame image of a broken-winged F-4 Phantom plummeting to the ground trailing smoke and flames burn itself into his audience.

"In Vietnam, the Air Force and Navy Aviation played a game of catch-up ball, and we came out of it by the skin of our teeth, but we didn't win." Greene shook his head. *"I was there. Take it from me. We didn't win. But as the war wound down, we were getting better. Or at least the Navy was, thanks to an ACM training program called Top Gun."*

Greene paused to let the hostile murmurings rippling through the audience run their course at his mention of Top

Gun. The people in this auditorium were among the best front-line personnel the Air Force had; otherwise, they wouldn't have made the cut to be here in the first place. They were all proud blue suiters who didn't much cotton to being reminded that these days the Air Force had to share ownership of the sky with the United States Navy.

"Top Gun works so well for the Navy in part because it gives the squid fighter jocks a real-time taste of ACM flying against some of the best instructors the Navy has to offer. The Fighter Weapons School here at Ryder is a close equivalent to Top Gun. For three weeks the fighter jocks among you will be receiving a graduate course in advanced fighter tactics by FWS instructors, while the rest of you will receive similar advanced combat training in your particular specializations."

The screen, which had been showing candid photos of visiting players receiving their advanced instruction, now went to silver and began to rise. At the same time, the stage lights came on, revealing the the Attacker squadron seated in front of the huge rendition of their emblem.

"After three weeks, school will be over," Greene said. *"And war will begin. You will belong to us. The Attackers . . ."*

Narrow focus spotlights now illuminated the photographic murals lining the auditorium's walls. Greene watched as the audience swiveled to study the photos of the Attacker squadron's F-5E II jet fighters wearing Warsaw Pact paint locked onto the tails of various visiting-player aircraft.

"Three weeks from today, Red Sky will begin. You will be subjected to five days of air war conducted according to a specific scenario written by Red Sky intelligence people. The scenario will detail the outbreak of hostilities between a Communist nation on the western side of the Ryder combat ranges, and the United States, who will invade from the east."

Greene's outstretched arm encompassed the audience. *"As the Blue, United States team, your surveillance operations will attempt to send back intelligence about the Red team, your enemy. Your AWACS will attempt to locate his Combat Air Patrols and guide you to them. Your Wild Weasels will attempt to pinpoint and neutralize his AAA and SAM sites. Your Mud Movers and Warthogs will attempt to disrupt his front line and suppress his ground defenses and mechanized artillery. Your bombers will attempt to decimate his military-industrial complexes. Your transports and refueling tankers will attempt to run his gauntlet to resupply and refuel your air-strike forces.''*

Greene offered his audience an exaggerated, wolfish smile. *''And your fighters will attempt to wrest control of Redland's sky away from us, the Attackers, who have been trained and equipped to fly and fight like Russians. Five times a year, we declare war on those who would fly against us in Red Sky, the world's most realistic and complex aerial-combat exercise. We fly F-5E Tiger IIs equipped and painted to mimic Fishbeds and Floggers. You may think our little F-5 Scooters are inferior airplanes to your own, but we Attackers love them. We call our planes F-5 'MiGs.' We call them F-5 'Humiliators,' because we and our planes are honed razor sharp, and we enjoy making fools out of you green young men who think you're something special when you're strapped into your state-of-the-art hardware. Don't think of the Attackers as instructors, because we don't fly to teach you anything.''* Greene paused, staring down at the auditorium full of uplifted faces.

''We fly to kill you.''

The audience was crypt silent. Greene could feel hundreds of pairs of angry eyes upon him. He could sense the players' massed outrage at his taunts. They had become a lynch mob, out for his blood.

Good, Greene thought. He *wanted* to shake his audience's composure. To get them riled up and get their juices flowing; to get them to begin to approach a state of fevered mental pitch approximating what they might emotionally experience in the tense weeks, days, and hours leading up to a real war.

A lot of these pilots arrived at Ryder thinking that Red Sky was going to be just another cut-and-dried, fly-around-the-flagpole war game of the sort they might have experienced while training at their own bases, but nothing could be further from the truth. For one thing, Red Sky was big. The scenario took place over millions of acres of desert, with the various Ryder ranges tricked up to resemble different aspects of Redland, so that just knowing where the hell you were and how far it was to a place of safety was a challenge.

For another thing, Red Sky was edge of the envelope when it came to EBS. Sure, the Exterior Battlefield Simulations included the run-of-the-mill plywood and plastic tanks, and scrap-wood buildings for the players to bomb and shoot up, but Red Sky went far beyond the usual "Hogan's Alley" type knock-'em-down cardboard target setups in terms of combat realism, and in terms of keeping score. Thanks to a network of grid sensors spread around the desert ranges, transmitters placed on the airplanes, microwave relay stations, and powerful computers, every Red Sky mix-up could be displayed in real time to spectators back at Nellis, who viewed the computer-generated action as it occurred on the auditorium's multiscreens. Each evening, highlights of the day's battles were shown for the players in the auditorium, and then replayed, for the benefit of the specific players involved, in the smaller briefing rooms.

Most important for the players, Red Sky was complex. It might seem obvious to say that, but Red Sky's capacity to submerge participants in the sort of confusing electronic and sensory overload that had been experienced by combat fliers in Vietnam was in many ways the exercise's outstanding value. Once a pilot got a taste of his electronic gear and his radio screaming at him, mixed with the sensation of having a real, live bogie on his six o'clock, and maybe a simulated smoky SAM twisting up at him from the ground, that young man would begin to have an idea of what modern air war was like inside a cockpit, and how his own confusion might destroy him quicker than any MiG.

Best of all, Greene thought, in *this* war, despite all the simulated realism and electronic enhancements, the only wounds the visiting players might suffer would be to their pride. Sure, there was always the potential for tragic accidents when lots of overeager fighter jocks went streaking around a few hundred feet above the desert at six hundred plus miles an hour; being a fighter jock was not a low-risk occupation. By and large, however, these young men would live to learn from their mistakes, and, it was hoped, never make them again should they be confronted with a real war.

Greene moved to the conclusion of his presentation: "*This upcoming Red Flag exercise will be conducted during a tense international climate in the world. In Africa, there's war raging in Zaire between that ruling government and Cuban-backed rebels. In the Mideast, Iran endures bloody rioting between the Shah's backers and Moslem fundamentalists. In Central America, Nicaragua suffers as the Samoza government is rocked by Communist rebels. The Red Sky scenario being scripted for you might well have been torn from today's headlines.*

"On behalf of the Attackers squadron, I urge you to study hard these next three weeks." Greene's eyes swept the auditorium. *"Learn all you can, because when you confront us you're going to need it."*

"Nice performance, Robbie," Buck said, falling into step with Greene backstage. "Reckon there'll be a few extra pair of undies going to the laundry this evening."

"Like I said, scaring the shit out of 'em is my job," Greene said. He squinted as they left the cool darkness of the auditorium through the stage door, stepping out into the bright, hot, Nevada day.

"If that's your job, then you're overachieving," Buck chided good-naturedly.

"No way," Greene protested as he dug his gold-rimmed Ray-Bans out of his breast pocket. "It's the Attackers' role to play the villain, and we're method actors."

They cut across the sweltering parking lot toward Greene's car. It was a fire-engine-red (naturally) Porsche 911 Targa he'd bought with some of the money that Grandpa Herman had left him.

"You know, the bigger they come the harder they fall," Buck murmured under his breath.

"What's that supposed to mean?"

"It means you came on a lot stronger than usual back there with all that 'we fly to kill you' crap."

"Well, maybe I'm feeling *extra* frisky," Greene replied evasively. "Maybe I'm intending to run my squadron *extra* hard on this particular exercise. Make life *extra* miserable for this bunch of players."

"Why?" Buck eyed him speculatively. "I don't think I've ever heard you talk that way before. . . ."

"What's with these questions?" Greene countered. "Why shouldn't I put one hundred and one percent into my job?"

They'd reached the Porsche. Buck settled into the passenger's bucket seat as Greene swung himself behind the wheel, started her up, put her in gear, and began driving down the base's main drag, Thunder Alley. It was a half-mile to Red Square, the Attacker squadron's operations building.

"You know, Buck . . . I've been thinking," Greene mused. "I love what I do, and like every one of the pilots in my squadron I fought tooth and nail to get this assignment. I get to fly as much ACM as I can handle, and that's the best kind of flying there is." He nodded firmly. "I mean, it's a dream come true for me. . . ." He trailed off.

"But . . . ," Buck coaxed. He had his hat off and was holding it in his lap to keep it from blowing away. The few sparse hairs on his head were flapping like signal flags in the breeze.

Greene said, "But all that doesn't change the fact that, bottom line, the elite, ferocious Attackers are basically clay pigeons—hell, tackling dummies—for the visiting players." He glanced inquiringly at Buck. "Maybe we ought to be refining our tactics to give them even *more* of a run for their money? I mean, I hate the way some of these visiting players get off so easy."

"Is that *really* what's bothering you?" Buck coaxed. "Is it that some of the players get off easy, or is it one player *in particular* you're concerned about?

Greene saw that his friend was watching him closely. It was no secret that Buck was an extremely solicitous dude, kind of the father confessor for the squadron, but what accounted for that expression of concern mixed with accusation that was presently radiating from Buck's weak blue eyes magnified by his thick eyeglasses?

Then it came to Greene: Buck devoured paperwork the way other men took in food and drink. Obviously, Buck had scanned the visiting-player roster—all fifty-odd pages of it —and saw the name, which must have rung a bell. (Buck knew everything.) It would have been a snap for Buck to have run it through the computer. Then . . . bingo!

Buck asked, "You sure it's not the fact that this time around, as far as you're concerned, Red Sky is going to be a blood feud that's bugging you?"

"Goddammit, Buck," Greene cursed, staring straight

ahead as he tightly gripped the steering wheel. "You're about as subtle as a B-52! I mean, goddammit! I love you like a brother, but sometimes you just talk too fucking much for your own good!"

"Sorry," Buck murmured as they pulled up in front of Red Square, a cinder-block building painted white, with a blood-red hammer and sickle stenciled above the front door. "Forget I said anything," Buck finished, shrugging.

Greene thought, *"Love you like a brother . . ." Did I really say that? Talk about your Freudian slip!*

(Two)

Red Square
Attackers Squadron Operations Building

It was close to nine P.M. by the time Major Robbie Greene had caught up with the day's paperwork. His large office had white walls, an acoustical tile ceiling, tan metal furniture and file cabinets, and windows overlooking the OPS building's parking lot. The office was decorated with a framed, silk-woven, Soviet-style red star; configuration posters of Russian aircraft; and various plaques, notes of appreciation, and other thank-you mementos from the player squadron groups that had gone through Red Sky. It was a nice office. Lots nicer and roomier than a major warranted, but then, being the "head honcho Commie gomer" had its privileges.

Despite his comfortable surroundings, Greene prided himself on spending as little time as possible here. He was a flier, not a desk man. His usual MO was to let a week's worth of his paperwork mount to overflowing in one of the several In boxes he had scattered around the place and then settle in for a marathon session of skimming the bullshit and scrawling his name whenever required. He never could have gotten away with such behavior if he didn't have Buck to keep him abreast of the really important stuff, but then, he *did* have Buck, so, all in all, the burden of command wasn't much of a hassle for him, considering that he had a revolving roster of twenty-five pilots, twenty airplanes, at any one time five or ten Attacker pilot trainees, and three hundred ground and support personnel under his command. Greene's immediate superior was his wing CO, Colonel Larry Field, but the colonel was a good guy, content to leave Greene alone to run his squadron as he saw fit.

Now Greene leaned back in his swivel chair and swung his feet up onto his blessedly cleared desk. At this hour of the evening, everyone else had knocked off for the day, so Red Square was quiet. Greene was thinking about rewarding himself for going one-on-one with his In box and coming out on top by heading over to the O club for a cold one, when he heard a knock on his door.

"Come in," Greene called. The door opened. "Well," he said. "I was wondering when you'd get the balls to show up here."

"Thanks for the friendly greeting, brother dear," said Lieutenant Andrew Harrison. "Or let me amend that to half brother."

"You can amend it to no brother at all, as far as I'm concerned," Greene replied evenly. He looked Andrew over. The kid was a little under six feet tall, and built solidly. Andrew's thick blond hair was cut moderately short and worn casually brushed forward. He was just going on his twenty-second birthday, but already Andrew had the fighter jock's characteristic squint lines etched around his brown eyes that were the result of long hours spent scanning the sun-bright sky from various cockpits.

Greene noticed that Andrew was wearing his plastic photo ID badge identifying him as a visiting player pinned to the breast pocket of his service dress uniform. That was unusual. "You know," Greene began, "most of the visiting fighter jocks take pride in wearing their flight suits."

There was just the hint of a mocking smile on Andrew's face as he said, "I figured this would be more appropriate dress for a visit to a superior officer." He gestured toward a chair. "May I sit down, Major?"

Greene nodded, and when Andrew was seated, asked, "Well, what do you want?"

" 'What do I want,' " Andrew mimicked. "Yeah, you sure do know how to express familial warmth."

Little fucker is still a snotnose, Greene thought. "Listen to me," he said, cutting Andrew off. "I've had a long day, I'm tired, I'm in no mood to deal with that sarcastic, effete intellectual attitude you inherited from your father. I never could tolerate it when Don came on strong with it against me or Uncle Steve, so I'm sure as shit not going to put up with it from the likes of *you*."

"Yes, sir!" Andrew said, deadpan.

Greene studied him. "Lieutenant Harrison, I hope you don't intend to give me trouble during your stay?"

"It depends."

"On what?" Greene demanded sharply.

"On where we are," Andrew replied. "On the ground you're my superior officer and I intend to treat you as such." He grinned coldly. "But in the air, half brother of mine, all bets are off. I'm going to give you all the trouble you can handle when we fly one versus one during Red Sky."

Greene leaned back in his chair, smiling. "You think you're going to be a match for me one vee one?" Greene shook his head. "You don't have a prayer, kid."

"I'm good, Robbie."

"Sure you are." Greene nodded. "As far as you go," he qualified. "Your squadron had to be good, or else it wouldn't have gotten to Red Sky. Let's see, your squad is the 9th—the "Blue Wolves"—which is part of an F-66 Stiletto Tactical Fighter Wing based at Howard, right?"

"You've been reading up on me," Andrew remarked.

"I knew you'd show up at Red Sky sooner or later." Greene shrugged. "That thanks to our mother you had enough Gold family blood in your veins to make it this far."

"I'm going to make it all the way," Andrew said fervently. "I'm going to make it to the top! *Past* you."

"No, you won't," Greene calmly replied. "Your trouble, little Andrew, is that the dose of the right stuff you inherited from our mother isn't going to be enough to take you all the way." He shook his head in mock sympathy. "It's really too bad. Maybe if you'd had a fighter-pilot father, like I did, you'd have a chance of being *really* good, but your father is Don Harrison, a wishy-washy egghead with nothing between his legs but a slide rule."

"Don't talk that way about my father."

"And you're just *like* Don," Greene pressed on, gradually losing his icy cool. "That's why when it comes time to make that final cut between us in ACM, I'm going to come out on top, just like my father came out on top with our mother. Answer me this, little Andrew," Greene spat. "If my father had made it through the war that your father draft-dodged, do you think you ever would have been born?"

Greene had watched Andrew stoically take what he'd had to say the way an armored warbird endures .50-caliber blistering punishment. Now Greene tiredly prepared himself to absorb Andrew's answering volleys as hatred glowed like tracer fire from his half brother's brown eyes.

"Permission to speak frankly, Major?" Andrew asked harshly.

"Go ahead."

"Let me bring you up to speed on a few things," Andrew began, sitting rigidly in his chair. "I am *proud* to be Don Harrison's son. And he didn't draft-dodge the war. My father was given an exemption for reasons of national security, just like they gave to Grandpa Herman, because my father was such a talented aviation engineer. It was my father who led the design team that created the Amalgamated-Landis Cougar fighter, and the Bullwhip attack bomber, two combat airplanes that did more to win the Second World War then anything your fighter-pilot papa ever did!"

"You through?" Greene asked, angry all over again.

"No, I'm not! I want to tell you something else, Robbie. I think you're a son of a bitch. You always were a son of a bitch toward me, and now I'm convinced you always will be. Back when I was getting ready to come here, I entertained the notion that even if the two of us could never be friends, we could at least be cordial with one another, but now I know that's not possible, because you're too blinded with hatred."

"That's enough," Greene began fiercely, but Andrew ignored him.

"Because you need to blame me for your own neurotic hang-ups concerning the loss of your father—"

"Shut up!" Green thundered, finally silencing his half brother. A few seconds of silence ticked by in the charged office. When Greene next spoke, it was with a voice trembling with pent-up emotion. "Andrew, for as long as you're here at Ryder, I intend to treat you exactly as I would any other visiting player. No better and no worse."

"Oh, I think you'd better treat me *much* worse," Andrew warned. He leaned forward in his chair to plant his fists on Greene's desk, so that he could spit his words into Greene's face. "Because when we find ourselves one vee one, our fight is going to be *personal*, and after I'm through with you you're going to have to change that hot-shit Attackers shoulder patch you wear to show that bear's hind end, with its *asshole* shaved pink!"

Just then Greene could have easily wrapped his fingers around Andrew's throat and choked him to death. Instead, he took a deep breath and let it out, willing himself to regain his calm. "You're dismissed, Lieutenant."

Andrew stood up, came to attention, and sharply saluted. "Yes, sir! Major!" He turned on his heel and went to the door, where he paused. "Remember what I said, Robbie. I'm playing no-holds-barred." He strode out of the office.

Greene listened to Andrew's footsteps receding down the hall. He looked down at his hands and saw that they were shaking. His stomach was twisted up into knots, his heart was pounding, and his brow was bathed in sweat like he was in the cockpit and had just completed a six-G bat-turn.

How dare that fucking little punk talk to me that way! Greene endlessly repeated to himself. *How dare he!*

He waited until he was absolutely sure that Andrew was gone, and then made his way out of his office and down the corridor to the men's room, where the squadron had put up posters of Marx and Lenin, and a banner reading, "Gentlemen, we salute you . . ." over the urinals.

Greene went to the washbasins and ran a cold tap, splashing the water onto his face. He dried himself with paper towels and then leaned against the basin to study his reflection in the mirror. He was going to be thirty-six come December, but like most fighter jocks he looked older. His black hair and his mustache had become seeded with gray, and the creases around his eyes and at the corners of his mouth were becoming deeper.

It all happened so long ago, Greene thought, staring at his reflection. *So why do I still feel like that frightened little boy*

*on the day he found out that his mother was remarrying?
Why do I still feel bitter hate and fearful loneliness the way
I did on that first day I had to start living under the roof of
the man who expected me to call him "Dad" when I knew
he could never replace my father?*

(Three)

Lieutenant Andy Harrison went for a long walk after his confrontation with Robbie. Andy didn't know where he wanted to go, but he knew it wasn't back to his quarters, a trailer he was sharing with two other guys from his squadron, which had flown here all the way from Howard AFB in Panama.

It had been a hurting ten hours in the cockpit, all right. Andy considered the Stiletto a fine bird, but Grandpa Herman and Andy's father hadn't designed her to be a one-man jet-liner. Then again, how far a player had to fly in his own bird to Ryder was the luck of the draw. Some lucky-stiff players had only a hop of a few minutes' duration from their bases in California, for instance. The Red Sky philosophy was that the reality of modern warfare was one itty-bitty piece of combat, and a whole lot of getting to the fight. For that reason, all participants were expected to fly their airplanes from their home base to Ryder as if they were rushing to a hot spot somewhere on the globe, with stopovers allowed if tankers weren't available, but aerial refuelings being the rule. The Air Force wanted its pilots and air crews to be able to endure grueling stretches in the cockpit in order to get where they were going as quickly as possible. Sure, it wore a guy out, but as the saying went, "War is hell."

Andy's squadron had arrived late Friday, and they'd had the weekend to recoup. Now, on this Monday night, with a pleasant breeze blowing off the desert and the lights of Las Vegas brightening the horizon, Andy was feeling pretty chipper and ready for come what may.

He strolled about a half-mile down Thunder Alley, checking stuff out. The base was well-lit, and busy around the clock, with shuttle buses running twenty-four hours a day.

As Andy reached the TACCC complex, he thought about heading into the snack bar for a soda, but instead he went where he guessed he really wanted to be all along: He crossed the street to the players' aircraft parking ramp, near the maintenance complex.

Roy Rodgers talked to Trigger, and Gene Autry talked to Champ Andy thought. *So why I can't I talk to my warbird?*

Sure the F-66 Stiletto was just a machine, but it was Andy's machine: it had his name stenciled on the side of the cockpit. More important, his Ice Pick was going to be the means through which he was going to show Robbie Greene who was top dog between them once and for all.

The ramp was crammed with row upon row of airplanes parked six or seven abreast, interspersed with whining, orange painted electric carts belonging to the maintenance crews, who even at this late hour were still busy seeing to the visiting players' birds. The ramp held F-4 Phantoms, F-66 Stilettos, F-15 Eagles, A-7s, A-10s, choppers, and then there was the bigger stuff. In all, it was a massed air armada that stretched for over two miles.

The ramp was also lit to daylight intensity, and well patrolled by security details. Andy had hardly set foot on the ramp when he was intercepted by a four-wheel-drive vehicle wearing flashing blue lights. The guards toted M16s as they hopped out to check Andy's photo ID. Satisfied he belonged where he was, they looked up his squadron's location on their clipboard. It turned out Andy's Stiletto was parked with the rest of his squad's birds, a quarter-mile away, so the guards gave him a lift, remarking along the way that it wasn't unusual for a visiting player or two to become homesick for his bird the first couple of nights at Ryder.

As the security truck came to a halt, Andy hopped out, thanking the guards, but wearing a worried frown as he spotted his bird. Why was it his was the only Stiletto in his squadron being serviced? *Oh, no! What if there was something wrong? What if he was grounded?*

He hurried over to where a lone maintenance guy wearing baggy overalls and a duckbilled cap was standing on a metal scaffolding platform beside a box of ominous-looking tools. The maintenance guy had his back to Andy and his head stuck in the open bay just aft the Stiletto's nosewheel carriage.

"Hey, pal! What's wrong?" Andy anxiously demanded as he approached his plane.

The mechanic didn't turn around, but just but held up one work-gloved hand to silence Andy. "Hey, pal," Andy repeated. "I mean Sarge," he amended as he noticed the stripes on the guy's sleeve. "That's my bird you're working on."

"He's *your* bird in the air," the maintenance man said. "He's *mine* on the ground."

He? Andy thought. Who called an airplane 'he'? Andy shook his head. The mechanic's voice was somewhat muffled due to the fact that the guy had most of his head stuck into the open bay, but Andy still thought the guy's voice was pretty high-pitched. Like it hadn't changed yet. Just how young was the Air Force taking them into the Aircraft Generation squadron these days?

"Sergeant," Andy demanded, putting a little steel into his tone. "You're talking to a lieutenant who demands to know the status of his airplane!"

The maintenance guy pulled his head out of the open bay and turned around to face Andy.

"Holy cow, Sarge," Andy murmured. "You're a girl—"

"No, I'm a woman, Lieutenant," she corrected him, her tone amused. "Are you too young to know the difference?"

Girl or woman, Andy thought. *You're beautiful.*

She'd removed her cap, liberating her hair, which cascaded in shiny, auburn waves to her shoulders. Now, as Andy watched, she stood on her raised platform and performed an impromptu striptease. First she pulled off her work gloves, revealing long, slender fingers with pink enameled nails. Then she unzipped and shucked off her overalls. . . .

"Holy cow," Andy repeated, awestruck.

She was around five foot six and no older than twenty-two, a lean, green-eyed knockout just now sheened with sweat, wearing only a skimpy pair of thigh-length cutoff fatigue pants, knee socks, ankle-high black work boots, and a T-shirt chopped short to reveal her flat, tanned midriff. What was left of the T-shirt hid little. Andy was unable to take his eyes off her smallish breasts rising and falling beneath the T-shirt. Her nipples looked like BBs upholstered in sage-green cotton.

"I think you're out of uniform, Sarge. I know that these

days, Aircraft Generation squadrons are more than fifteen percent women, but that outfit cannot be regulation!''

She shook her head, chuckling. ''No, guess I am breaking regs to be dressed like this, but it gets *hot* wearing those overalls in this desert heat.''

''Hot, yes, very hot . . .'' Andy nodded slowly, starting to feel the heat himself as he noticed a bead of perspiration lazily glide out from beneath the ragged hem of her loose, high-cut shorts to travel the curve of her inner thigh.

''Anyway,'' she continued. ''Things always get a little loosey-ducey around here when you visiting players arrive all at once and we AGS personnel have got to get you all tweaked up for fun and games.''

Yes, I am feeling quite tweaked up for fun and games, Andy thought. His trousers were feeling awfully snug. He wondered if his throbbing erection was noticeable.

''Things will be a lot quieter for us grease monkeys from here on in.'' She yawned, turning to close the Stiletto's bay. ''I'm through for the night, and this will be my last stint on the graveyard shift until next month.''

Andy watched her sleek little butt flex and wiggle as she gracefully climbed down off the scaffolding platform. She was built curvy, but kind of narrow through the hips, so that Andy guessed he could probably very easily cup her nicely rounded ass in the palms of his hands.

''My plane!'' he exclaimed, abruptly remembering his earlier concern. ''What's wrong with—''

''Nothing's wrong with her, Lieutenant,'' she cut him off. ''Earlier, my crew's diagnostic checkout showed a glitch in your electrical system, but everything's okay. The fault was with our equipment.''

''That's a relief.'' He sighed. ''But thanks for checking it out. . . . I didn't mean to yell at you before.''

''No problem,'' she said, smiling, and then cocked her head to look at him. ''I guess you're feeling a little edgy about your training, and then Red Sky a few weeks from now?''

''Yeah.'' He nodded. ''How'd you know?''

''You're here,'' she said simply. ''You're not the first fighter jock to come around wanting to feed his mount a sugar cube the night before it all begins.''

"Yeah, the guards who gave me a lift over here said as much." Andy nodded, then smiled. "You know, it's sort of funny that you should use a rider and horse analogy, because that's what I was thinking when I decided to come over."

"Great minds think alike," she said brightly.

Andy laughed. "There's Roy Rogers and Trigger, and Gene Autry and Champ—"

"Champion," she corrected him. "Gene Autry's horse was named Champion."

"Oh . . ." His mind went blank. They stood quietly for a moment. She was watching him like she was expecting him to say something else, so of course his mind had to go triple blank. He'd always been awkward with girls, goddammit!

"Well . . . ," she said.

Shit! Quick! Think of something, Andy frantically thought. *Don't let her leave.*

"My name's Andy Harrison," he said, holding out his hand.

"Gail Saunders." She smiled, shaking hands. "Listen, Andy, don't freak out. You're going to do fine."

"You think so?" he asked, feeling shy.

"Sure! Listen. Take this from someone who's seen it all before. Major Greene comes on real strong in his opening speech, and when you first see those Attackers coming at you led by Greene in that flat-black F-5 of his, you're going to think: *Sweet Jesus! Here I am up against the Angels of Death!*"

"Something like that," Andy agreed wryly.

"Oh-ho!" Gail said, her big, beautiful eyes opening wide. "I get it now. You want to be the Warlord, don't you?"

Andy colored. "The thought had crossed my mind." It wasn't much of an impressive-looking award, really, just a small rectangle of walnut with a silver silhouette of a delta-winged fighter, engraved with a pilot's name, his unit, and the date of the Red Sky exercise in which he was proclaimed "Warlord": the fighter jock with the highest kill score during Red Sky. . . . No, the Red Sky Warlord award wasn't much to look at, but looks weren't everything. To a fighter pilot being Warlord was like winning the Academy Award, the Super Bowl trophy, and the heavyweight boxing championship of the world, all rolled into one.

Gail said: "Let me tip you off to a not very well kept secret, but one you greenhorns usually don't immediately glom onto. It might help you to get a leg up on your dragon quest."

"I'm listening," Andy said.

"Okay. The Attackers have got to fly ACM according to Soviet tactics," Gail began. "That's their whole reason for existence, and Soviet tactics suck, if you'll pardon my French. Once you and the rest of the visiting players get used to the rules of the game, you'll eat the Attackers for lunch." She paused, shrugging. "You always do!"

"I hope you're right." Andy sighed.

"I am," she promised. "And anyway, even if Red Sky can get pretty heavy at times, bottom line is that the war between you players and the Attackers is only a game."

Andy threw back his head and laughed.

"What's so funny?" Gail demanded.

"Nothing. Everything," Andy managed, shaking his head. He took a deep breath. "Listen, it's only a little after ten. Can I pay back all your kindnesses by buying you a drink?"

Gail hesitated." I don't drink."

"Neither do I!" Andy said quickly.

"Come on, don't hand me that!" She eyed him skeptically. "I've never met the fighter jock who didn't consider beer to be as crucial to him as jet fuel was for his warbird!"

"Well, you've met one now," Andy told her. "Actually, what I've been dying for—it's the only thing that relaxes me—is a black-and-white ice-cream soda."

"Well, there is the ice-cream parlor over by the commissary."

"Would it be open this late?"

She nodded. "Most stuff here is open twenty-four hours to accommodate personnel coming off duty."

"How about it, then?" Andy asked. "Have an ice-cream soda with me?"

He could see her thinking it over. Her wide-set green eyes were evaluating him. The tip of her pink tongue was just peeking out from between her pearly teeth. *She's going to shoot me down,* he mourned.

She said, "I prefer banana splits."

"It's a deal!" he said eagerly.

She smiled. "Come on, then, we'll just swing by my quarters. You can wait in the car while I get cleaned up and changed into something a little more appropriate."

"You've got wheels?" Andy asked, surprised.

"Check it out, right over there." She pointed proudly to a battered, pine-green MG convertible parked alongside the ramp. "He's a 'fifty-nine 'twinkie'; a twin cam based on the BMC B-series engine—"

"There you go again with that 'he' stuff," Andy interrupted. "Most people call planes and cars and stuff 'she'."

"Do they?" Gail shrugged. "Funny, I never noticed. Anyway, I bought him for a song about a year back. I haven't worked much on his body, but he runs fine. I rebuilt his engine in my spare time."

"Really?" Andy shook his head. "I'm impressed. A friend of mine once had one of those old sports cars. I remember him saying he could never find parts."

"Well, we've got a pretty good machine shop here, so I was able to jerry-rig a lot of what I couldn't buy off the shelf," Gail said.

"Anything you can't do, Sarge?" Andy teased her.

"Probably, but I haven't run across it yet," Gail countered, smiling hugely. "Now, come along, Lieutenant. You owe me a treat."

(Four)

He's just what the doctor ordered, Gail thought as she walked with Andy toward the MG. For one thing, he was incredibly good looking, but more important, he was funny. Of the two qualities in a man, it was a sense of humor that always served to hold her interest over the long haul.

Not that there was going to be any long haul with this one, Gail reminded herself. He wasn't the first visiting player to hit on her in the two years that she'd been stationed here at Ryder, and she had a rule about not getting involved with these guys, because what was the point? Five weeks later, they would be back at their home bases in South Korea or West Germany or New Jersey, or wherever. . . .

No, she wouldn't have accepted Andy's invitation, cute and funny as he was, if she hadn't been feeling down in the dumps. She was coming off the tail end of a seven-month relationship with her boyfriend, one of the fighter jocks permanently stationed here at Ryder. *It was really too bad,* Gail thought. When she'd first started dating the guy, she'd entertained the notion that he was going to be "the one"

"What are you looking so sad about?" Andy startled her by asking as they got into the MG.

"Oh, nothing. Just thinking," Gail said, hiding her discomposure by starting up the car and then peeling out.

God, but the fire had burned hot at the start of the relationship, Gail thought, thinking back seven months ago to that first time her boyfriend had kissed her. When their lips had met that first time, she'd seen sparks the equal of the fireworks display visible for miles here at Ryder when the visiting players executing their nocturnal bombing runs on the live ordnance ranges. Sadly, however, the passion between them hadn't lasted. This past month or so, they'd done more bickering than lovemaking, so they'd decided to stay apart for a couple of weeks in order to cool down and see how they felt about one another.

Gail executed a racing change at the corner of Thunder Alley, and pushed the MG hard down Tiger Boulevard, past the motor-vehicle pool and the big water tower. She purposely took the old sports car to its performance edge, coaxing the speedometer to nudge seventy, and then glanced at Andy's handsome profile to see how he was taking her daredevil driving: He was slumped in the worn leather bucket seat. His hair the color of wheat was blowing in the windstream, his soulful brown eyes were slit-closed, and he was wearing that shit-eating grin the fighter jocks wore whenever they were riding in something mechanical that was pushing the edge of its envelope.

Yes, indeedy-do, Lieutenant Andy Harrison, Gail thought. *You are just what the doctor ordered to take my mind off the past and help me sort out my feelings.*

She grinned to herself as it occurred to her that her being seen around the base in the company of this dreamboat just might get back to her boyfriend and make him jealous. Well, so much the better in terms of bargaining chips for her own game plan. She was no longer sure of her feelings toward her boyfriend, but who knew? Maybe if he became a little more romantically attentive, she might thaw toward him?

In any event, having Andy flying escort on her wing gave her the tactical edge, and that's what counted. Her boyfriend might be the acknowledged master of ACM, but this was a different sort of one-vee-one combat, an eternal duel in which a man and a woman sent heat-seekers streaking toward one another's heart.

"Yes indeedy, Major Robert Blaize Greene," Gail vowed. *"You're going to find out that if you break up with this girl, she isn't the type to sit home at night washing her hair and crying her eyes out over you."*

CHAPTER 15

(One)

Paris Air Show
Le Mouret Airfield, on the northern outskirts of
Paris
12 June, 1978

Harrison sipped a glass of Roederer Cristal champagne. He was standing within the air-conditioned comfort of the GAT hospitality suite's glassed-in terrace, watching as the GC-600 jetliner prototype taxied along the runway in preparation for a short demonstration flight over Le Mouret.

Everything's going terrifically, Harrison thought. It was the third day of the Paris Air Show, the ten-day annual extravaganza that was international aviation's premier trade event, attracting more than a hundred thousand industry executives and involving more than a thousand aerospace companies. Happily, the show had so far been dominated by GAT and its newest addition to its jetliner family: the GC-600.

This afternoon, for example, attention had been focused on the GC-600's scheduled demonstration flight. The large, luxuriously appointed hospitality suite overlooking Le Mouret's tangle of runways was packed with aviation-industry representatives and members of the media. Earlier, Harrison had taken advantage of the reporters and cameras to hold an impromptu news conference announcing that at the show GAT had received orders for the first twenty production models of the GC-600. Harrison was now hosting the reception indoors, while Steve Gold worked the industry crowd that had chosen to view the demonstration flight from the outdoor viewing area beyond the hospitality-suite complex.

Harrison was wearing a dove-gray, tropical wool, double-breasted suit and a black silk turtleneck. He had initially thought the outfit was a little too flashy for him—he felt naked without a tie—but his wife, Susan, had insisted he wear it, telling him it made him look like Robert Redford. Harrison was glad he'd listened. Steve Gold had complimented him on the look, and Steve was certainly up to the minute when it came to fashion.

Now Harrison felt dapper and Parisian, comfortable and uniquely in control of things. Susan, looking chic in a cream-colored suit and dark, textured nylons, was hobnobbing with a cluster of guests near the ten-foot cutaway scale model of the GC-600 that was the room's centerpiece. GAT's best sales and marketing people were sidestepping the cruising waiters bearing trays of hors d'oeuvres and champagne as they handled inquiries concerning advance GC-600 sales and interest in the World-Bird fighter-plane project.

Harrison was on his second glass of champagne. He'd been too nervous to eat this morning, so now he was feeling just the slightest bit pleasurably woozy as the commotion whirled around him. There were the reporters busy jotting on their pads, likely racking their brains to come up with new superlatives to describe GAT's triumph; the airline purchasing agents clamoring to get the attention of the GAT sales team; the camera crew hired by GAT to film the proceedings for the next stockholders' meeting. . . . It seemed to Harrison that the next big problem facing GAT would be what to do with all the money the company was going to make.

There was a scattering of applause from the spectators on the terrace as the GC-600 lifted off. The trim little one-hundred-seat fanjet airliner was painted GAT's signature colors of turquoise and scarlet. The 600 climbed quickly due to its light weight. On this first demo flight it was flying without passengers, and the plane required only a two-man cockpit crew thanks to its computer-augmented controls. Harrison glanced towards the outdoor viewing area in the distance several stories below and saw that an array of tripod cameras were pointing their long, black telescopic lenses like antiaircraft weapons to capture on film the striking image of the gaudy GAT bird rising against the white overcast Parisian sky.

This may not be airplane heaven, but it'll do for now, Harrison thought as he flagged a passing waiter carrying a champagne-laden tray and exchanged his empty glass for a full one.

Perhaps the sweetest bonus coming out of all this was that Harrison fully expected the GC-600's successful debut to at last erase from the industry trade publications the embarrassing headlines built upon the continued, anonymous leaks that had come from the traitor inside the company. The private investigators who Harrison had put on the case had yet to come up with the so-called Icarus's identity, but after today who the bastard was and what he said would no longer matter.

Icarus had done some serious damage to GAT's image through his leaks reporting the internal dissension between the engineering, marketing, and management areas of the company concerning the new jetliner's readiness. Of course, it was just like the press to blow the situation out of proportion. Sure there'd been some internal tension at GAT these past eight months, and sure there had been some honest differences of opinion about the advisability of accelerating the construction of the GC-600 prototypes, but Harrison had stuck to his guns—he'd *led*—and he'd turned out right. The jetliner just now soaring in triumph above Paris was his vindication.

Harrison was distracted by a colleague coming over to offer his congratulations. As Harrison was shaking hands with the man, he heard somebody blurt: ''Something's wrong! That airplane's not flying right!''

Harrison turned quickly, peering fearfully into the sky, and saw that the GC-600 had banked too sharply during its approach back to the airfield. It was knifing toward the airstrip with its wings perpendicular to the ground.

"The jetliner's out of control!" somebody shouted.

Behind Harrison, the reception's genteel tumult dwindled quickly as people roughly shouldered past Harrison to get to the windows for a view. Harrison kept his eyes on the jetliner, which was now fluttering like a butterfly as its pilots struggled to regain control.

Jesus Christ, it's going to crash, Harrison realized. *This can't be happening. . . .*

There was a brittle cracking sound. Harrison looked down to see that his hand was wet with wine and blood: he had crushed his champagne glass.

He looked back up at the pastel creation that carried upon its swept wings his company's future. The jetliner had flipped over onto its back and was now hurtling toward the earth upside down. The overwrought scream of the 600's tortured turbofans was growing louder, rattling the terrace windows.

She might overshoot the runway, Harrison realized as around him spectators began flitting away off the terrace. *She might hit the—*

"Everybody get out!" Harrison turned and shouted. "She's going to hit the hospitality suite!"

Pandemonium erupted. The terrace was quickly deserted. Within the hospitality suite proper chairs and tables were overturned by the mad crush of shouting people who were battling their way to the exits. The place was emptying out fast.

But's there's no way, Harrison thought. *No way we're all going to get out in time.* "Everybody down!" he yelled. "Find cover! Get behind those tables! As far from the windows as possible!"

Miraculously the people clustered towards the rear of the logjams at the doors did as they were told. Harrison, looking wildly around for Susan, saw her standing near the bar, looking distraught: She'd been searching for him.

"Susan!" He ran to her across the food-littered, champagne-sodden carpet, past the tumbled tables and chairs and the toppled cutaway model of the GC-600. Susan tried to hug him when he reached her but he shook her roughly, commanding, "Quick! Get over the bar!"

"What?" Susan shook her head, dazed and confused.

"I said—" He stopped abruptly, realizing that she couldn't

hear him. The engine wail of the fast-approaching jetliner was now deafening.

Harrison picked Susan up, set her on the bar countertop, and pushed. She went over sprawling on all fours. Harrison glanced toward the terrace, caught a glimpse of the GC-600 filling the windows as it cartwheeled toward the tarmac, and hurled himself over the bar.

He landed hard on his hip but ignored the pain as he moved quickly to crouch protectively over Susan. He heard the crash: the initial, ear-shattering ring of the plane's impact, and then the prolonged screech of tormented metal scraping against airfield pavement, sounding like the world's biggest automobile accident. He braced for the secondary blasts as the fuel touched off, and they came, a thunderous series of explosions that grew abruptly louder as the terrace windows imploded in a wall of flying glass that tinkled like wind chimes against the draperies and carpet. The explosions faded, replaced by the sound of crackling, wind-blown flames, shouting, and the rising, mournful two-note song of the European sirens on the emergency vehicles racing toward the scene.

"You all right?" Harrison asked Susan, still huddled beneath him. She nodded, whimpering. Inside the hospitality suite, now filled with the acrid stench of burning kerojet fuel, there began to rise scattered moans and cries.

"Got to help. See who's been hurt," Harrison muttered, rising up. "What?" he demanded of Susan as he helped her to her feet. "What was that?" She'd said something, but his ears were still ringing from the explosions.

"I said Steve and Linda were down there!" Linda repeated.

"Oh, Christ," Harrison felt sick. In his own fear, he'd momentarily forgotten they'd been outside. *Steve and Linda.*

(Two)

Steve Gold and Linda Forrest had been outdoors at the flight-viewing area for the hour leading up to the GC-600's demo flight. The large, level, concrete space extended like an apron in front of the set-back hospitality-suite complex. The viewing area was landscaped with shrubs and flowers in concrete planters. It had wooden benches, and was fronted by a steel balustrade that kept spectators a safe distance from the runway aircraft access ramps. The area's rear portion was graced by a large fountain with a ten-foot-diameter concrete basin and a geyserlike spray that shot up twenty feet, creating a dramatic curtain of water. Walkways flanking the fountain led to the hospitality suite complex and the pavilions housing the show's trade displays.

There were shouts and applause, and a burst of activity over where the press people had their cameras set up as the GC-600 raced down the runway and into the sky. Linda was standing near the railing. Gold caught his wife's eye and waved to her. Linda smiled back, raising her clasped fists above her head to signal her congratulations. *Rightly so,* Gold thought. It had been a long haul to get to this point. He hadn't believed that Don Harrison could get his engineering people to pull it off, but Don had, and Gold was ready to give him full credit for the achievement.

Linda was dressed in slacks and a cotton sweater, a light raincoat over her shoulders against the threat of rain. She'd come along on this trip at Gold's request strictly as a tourist, to keep him company. She'd been a good sport keeping herself busy nosing around Paris while Gold was occupied with business, so tomorrow he'd promised to steal the day to spend with her taking a drive to Versailles.

But that was tomorrow. Today Gold was working hard, pressing flesh as he maneuvered through the crowd in his suit and regimental-striped turquoise and scarlet tie, the same GAT colors that decorated the GC-600 just now soaring overhead. Don Harrison had been apologetic about asking Gold to hang around out here, but Gold had been quite willing to skip the hospitality-suite news conference concerning the advance GC-600 sales. Don Harrison loved doing that kind of shit, and Gold was content to leave it to his partner. He himself had received his share of the limelight back during the Korean War, when the Air Force had paraded him around the country as an ace hero in order to drum up support for the war effort.

And anyway, Gold felt that somebody from the top level of the company should be out here. There were GAT sales people around, but what if some of the airline reps who'd chosen to witness the demo flight outdoors in order to prove to themselves how quiet the 600 was wanted to talk major business?

Gold was chatting with some Arab airline purchasing agents looking to spend their oil money on new equipment when he glanced up at the GC-600. It was bat-turning its way back over the airfield. He thought, *That plane can't do that. What the hell is Ken up to?*

Ken Cole was captain of the two-man crew on board the the GC-600. Gold had known him in the Air Force, and considered him one of the best test pilots in the business. Gold also knew from personal experience that the guys in the cockpit counted for a lot, but every airplane had performance parameters, its envelope within which it had to stay for safety's sake. For some damn reason, it appeared to Gold that Ken Cole was just now straying way beyond the envelope of the GC-600.

Maybe I'm just being paranoid, Gold thought. *After all, I've been uptight about this whole idea of rushing the 600's debut since last year*. Gold looked around at the other guests in the crowded flight viewing area. Nobody else seemed perturbed, and a lot of these people were knowledgeable aviation experts. *Yeah, I guess I'm just being paranoid,* Gold decided. But then he saw Linda approaching, her expression troubled. He excused himself, stepping away from the Arabs, to meet her.

"I think there's something wrong with that plane," she whispered to Gold.

He looked back at the plane and saw it flip over on its back and begin a swan dive toward the ground. *But just because you're paranoid doesn't mean somebody isn't chasing you.*

"You're right," Gold whispered, his heart beginning to pound. "It's going to crash."

"That's not funny," Linda scolded.

"I know."

Around them, others who had come to the same conclusion as Gold were already hurrying toward the viewing area's exits. Knots of people were crowded around the narrow entrances to the twisting walkways flanking the fountain. Others had vaulted over the steel baulustrade to put as much distance as possible between themselves and where they thought the stricken bird was coming down.

"Come on!" Gold said, grabbing Linda's arm and joining the frenzied exodus.

"Which way?" Linda cried out above the growing banshee wail of the dying jetliner darkening the sky above them.

Damn good question, Gold thought distractedly, looking around. They were close to the balustrade, but it was too late to try to escape by going over the railing and onto the airfield, *toward* the likely crash point. And the walkways flanking the fountain were packed.

The fountain.

Gold looked at it, and then up at the falling jetliner. He guessed about thirty seconds to impact. He'd seen plenty of emergency landings and crashes in his Air Force career; he'd been in the driver's seat during a few of them. He now used that experience to judge the falling 600's angle of approach, calculating that the bird would hit the runway about a hundred yards from the viewing area.

"The fountain's our only chance!" he yelled to Linda over the engines' growing racket, pulling her along as they began the hundred-foot dash to the concrete basin. Halfway there Gold, looked over his shoulder and saw the GC-600 hit.

The 120-foot-long jetliner impacted approximately where he'd guessed it would. It hit with its nose angled toward the viewing area, its wings perpendicular to the ground. There was a horrific sound like pealing thunder as the plane hit and bounced, and then there was the sound of fingernails clawing at a blackboard amplified thousands of times over as the jetliner cartwheeled, shedding debris in a cloud of smoke and fire. Both wings sheared off, to glide like scythes along the now oil-fire-splattered tarmac. Gold saw the 600's fuselage crumple like a beer can. *Ken,* he thought, *and Dave Wentworth, the copilot. . . .* But there was no way anybody or anything could have lived through that crash.

They'd reached the fountain. Without a word Gold flipped Linda into the eighteen-inch-deep water. She submerged and came up sputtering, glaring at him, her drenched hair a tight helmet around her skull.

"Are you c-crazy?" she demanded, shivering, her skin constricted to goose bumps from the frigid water. "I'm f-freezing! W-why'd you d-do that. The c-crash is over!"

"Like hell it is!" He fearfully glanced upward at the dark cloud of debris from the wrecked aircraft that would soon be falling upon them.

Linda tried to say something more, but her words were lost in the fountain's curtain of falling spray.

Then Gold heard the first earthshaking *crump!* as one of the jetliner's fuel tanks caught, the blast billowing upward in an orange ball of flame and oily black smoke. There was another fuel tank explosion. Then another. The rapid concussions rocked Gold. He threw himself into the frigid fountain beneath the curtain of spray one step ahead of the heat blasts. The cold water shocked him; his balls constricted tight against his groin. *Let's hope it's cold enough.*

"Deep breath and hold it!" he ordered Linda, shoving her head down into the water and submerging himself at the same time. He had his eyes open underwater, and saw the oil-and-fuel-soaked fragments of debris pelting the fountain's surface like shrapnel, hissing and trailing bubbles through the clear water. A couple of pieces of something or other stung his back through his clothing, but thankfully the debris was small and had been sufficiently slowed and cooled by its trip through the air, through the curtain of spray, and then the basin water to do too much damage. Gold put his arm around Linda, tucking her in beneath him as best he could in the buoyant water to try and spare her being hit. Meanwhile, he prayed that no large pieces were at the moment falling toward them.

Within seconds the rain of debris hitting the fountain slowed, then vanished. Gold warily lifted his head from the water. The wailing of sirens instantly accosted him. There were a few isolated puddles of fire floating in the fountain, but otherwise it was clear. He hauled Linda to the surface and heard her exhale noisily, gasping for air. They quickly climbed out of the fountain, streaming water from their drenched clothing.

One of the paramedics now on the scene came over to ask if they were all right. Linda and Gold nodded, and the paramedic offered the blanket from his stretcher. Gold wrapped the blanket around Linda, who was shivering. He then looked around.

The concrete ramp was littered with smallish, smoldering debris, some of it still sadly wearing a singed, blistered coat of scarlet and turquoise paint. There had been some injuries to those who had been last into the walkways flanking the fountain, but nobody looked seriously hurt. Gold turned toward the hospitality suite complex and saw that every window facing the airfield had been cracked or broken by the shock waves or the debris generated by the fuel blasts.

Gold looked at the fountain. He had no doubt that it had saved himself and Linda from serious injury, maybe even saved their lives. He hoped the architect who'd designed the fountain was a woman, because he fully intended to kiss that individual should they ever meet up.

Out on the tarmac, the charred remains of the GC-600 sat enveloped in wafting black smoke. The emergency fire vehicles had soaked down the wreck with foam, extinguishing the fires.

Linda came over to Gold. Her hair was still soaked, and she was wrapped like an Indian in her blanket. Gold put his arm around her, brushing her wet hair out of her eyes. "You look like a drowned rat," he said tenderly.

"Oh, thank you." She fingered his sodden jacket lapel. "And didn't I tell you you couldn't wash linen?"

"Come on," he said. "Let's go find Don and Linda. They'll be worried about us."

(Three)

**Duvalle Hotel
Paris
16 June, 1978**

In Paris, Don Harrison always preferred to stay at the Duvalle. It was smaller and more personal than either the Ritz or the Crillon, but every bit as luxurious.

Harrison always reserved the same suite. It had two bedrooms, one of which he used as an office, two baths, and an adjoining parlor furnished with comfortable armchairs and sofas upholstered in striped satin. This hotel suite with its ornate mirrors, Boilly portraits and luminous still lifes decorating its walls had always served as Harrison's sanctuary from the rigors of travel and conducting international business.

Until now, Harrison thought, sighing. On this trip the lovely suite had become less a restful oasis and more a beleaguered bunker from which GAT was conducting what amounted to a desperate defense to rescue its reputation and future.

Harrison was seated in the parlor, sipping cognac. His tie was loosened and his shoes were off. Surrounding his chair were thick folders and scattered papers, the results so far of the preliminary investigation into the cause of the GC-600's crash. It was Friday night, a little before six, four days after the awful accident. Since the GC-600 had fallen out of the sky last Monday, Harrison and Steve Gold had endured a gauntlet of official inquiries and news conferences during which they'd been grilled by an increasingly hostile French press about what GAT might have done to prevent the crash.

From the start of this fiasco, Harrison had been pretty much out of his depth public relations—wise. It was one thing to appear at a news conference in order to pat oneself on the back over some achievement and then pose for pictures. It was quite something else to face a public inquisition—especially when the public was too ignorant to understand the answers to their shouted questions. Harrison was first and foremost an engineer who was more comfortable talking the specific technical language of his profession. At the press conferences and at the preliminary hearings called by the French authorities (who were more interested in grandstanding than getting to the facts), Harrison had suffered a hard time keeping himself from lapsing into jargon concerning his confidence in the overall design of the GC-600 and its fly-by-wire control technology, which it shared with the Stiletto fighter and which allowed the jetliner to be safely piloted by just a two-man crew. Harrison's long-winded technical explanations had been miscomprehended by the French press as attempts at obfuscation. Meanwhile, the press kept hammering away, demanding to know GAT's position on the leaks now that they had been proved right?

Of course, the fact that the GC-600 had crashed didn't necessarily mean that the jetliner's design or technology was flawed. Trouble was, the emotions of the moment were running hot. Harrison had concluded that some of the French overreaction toward GAT concerning the crash was due to the residue of bad feeling in some of the French aviation industry over the fact that Aérosens and Skytrain Industry had come out second best to GAT in that contretemps surrounding the Pont airliner back in 1974.

Harrison looked bleakly at Susan who was sitting on a sofa, pretending to be leafing through a magazine. His wife was wearing a silk robe. She had on no makeup, and her silver-blond hair was pulled back into a tight bun. But there was no point in her getting dolled up, Harrison thought. It was an ordeal to leave the hotel. As soon as they stepped out of the lobby, the reporters were on them like a pack of beggars.

"You know," Harrison told her softly. "If I haven't said it before, I'm awfully sorry I'm dragging you through this."

She looked up from her magazine to smile at him. "My mother went through much worse with my father. It comes with the territory."

"I love you very much," Harrison said.

Susan blushed. "Don't look at me! I look awful."

"You look beautiful."

Susan said, "Keep talking like that and I'll follow you anywhere."

Harrison was contemplating asking her to follow him into the bedroom when the telephone rang. "Would you answer that?" he pleaded. "I can't bear to talk to any more reporters today."

Susan reached for the telephone on the end table. She listened a moment and then hung up. "It was Steve. He and Linda are coming down."

Harrison nodded. Steve and Linda had a suite on another floor of the hotel. *Thank God for Steve*, Harrison thought. Steve had turned out to be as good at this public-relations damage-control stuff as Harrison was bad. For one thing, the cameras seemed to like Steve. He came across well over the airwaves. And Steve had the knack of being able to communicate with the reporters and officials on their own level, and through them, directly to the public. Harrison supposed that Steve's war-hero background helped somewhat in all that. And then, of course, there was the fact that Steve was not very well formally educated and didn't care a rat's ass who knew it.

Right from the start of this mess, Steve had cleverly stressed his credibility as an experienced veteran in the cockpit in order to claim that it had been pilot's error that had caused the crash. That opinion had initially seemed to prevail among the experts after they'd weighed the testimony of those who had witnessed the aircraft's severe maneuvering just before the crash. On Wednesday the French Minister of Transportation had issued a statement saying that while the investigation was still only in its beginning stages, there was so far no evidence allowing the authorities to call into question the proper functioning of the aircraft. Things had looked good, or at least as good as possible, but then yesterday the European Pilots Association had issued a statement alleging that the accident had been caused by technical problems arising from the fact that the GC-600 was designed to be flown by only two crew members while most jetliners called for a three-man crew.

Harrison had been shocked by the blatantly obvious partisan nature of the pilots union claim and had fully expected it to be ridiculed, but then, he always had overestimated the intelligence of the public. On Thursday a couple of newspapers had trumpeted the allegation, and a few labor unions had put the bite on the French government, which caused the Transportation Minister to back away from his statement, explaining that it was premature to absolve GAT. And so the witch-hunt would continue.

There was a knock on the door. Susan got up to let in Steve and Linda.

Linda was dressed in one of those slacks-and-sweater outfits she tended to favor. Steve was wearing chinos and a plaid sports shirt: *comfortable clothes for a long night's work planning our defensive strategy for tomorrow*, Harrison thought.

"Want a drink?" Harrison asked.

"Love one," Steve said. He winked at his sister as he added to Harrison, "That's okay, Don, don't get up."

Harrison laughed. "Thanks, because I happen to be too exhausted to get up." He kicked the folders lying about his stockinged feet, sending them skidding a short distance across the carpet. "I've got to reread all this crap before the hearing at the Ministry tomorrow."

"You lucky duck," Steve muttered from the bar, where he was pouring himself a scotch on the rocks. "I'd rather talk aeronautics with a bunch of eggheads any day than try and stop the hemorrhaging concerning the 600's advance orders."

"It's going that badly, huh?" Susan asked. She glanced at Linda. "Want some white wine?"

"Love some." Linda nodded gratefully.

"It's chilling in the fridge behind the bar. I'll get it," Susan replied.

Steve was saying, "It looked as if I had not only been holding the line, but also regaining some lost ground with our customers, especially after the Minister's first announcement, and when I'd made it clear to our prospective buyers that we were willing to share all the data results from our flight tests on the remaining two GC-600 protos."

Harrison nodded. "But then came that damned pilots union assertion."

"Right," Steve said, taking his drink with him over to the couch, where he lit a cigarette. "The airlines were already a little queasy about the idea of opening up negotiations with their pilots unions concerning reducing the cockpit crews by one man. Now they're scared that if they buy the 600, this crash will give the pilots the ammo they need to take their argument against the plane to the public."

"What a damned mess," Harrison said mournfully.

"I suppose we're going to have another room-service dinner," Linda complained mildly. She and Susan were seated at the bar with their glasses of wine.

"Do you really mind?" Harrison apologized. "Steve and I have got a lot of work to do for tomorrow, and frankly, I don't think I'm much in the mood to be gawked at in a restaurant." He sighed. "Thank God it's mostly property damage and questions about the reliability of the airplane we have to contend with.''

"What you're saying is, thank God no one was killed," Steve added.

"Except the pilot and the copilot," Linda said somewhat sharply, frowning at Steve.

Steve nodded. "Of course, except for them," he said. "I didn't mean anything by leaving them out, honey." He smiled sadly. "I guess maybe because I was a pilot I said it the way I did. You see, I know personally that sometimes a pilot ends up like a sea captain. Sometimes he—*we*—have got to go down with our ship.''

"No, I'm the one who should be sorry for snapping at you," Linda insisted. "I guess I'm feeling just a little edgy being cooped up here, feeling ostracized and in a state of siege.''

The telephone rang. Steve reached for the receiver. "Yes?" He listened a moment and then told Harrison, "It's long distance. The switchboard is putting it through now. Our corporate counsel in L.A.''

"Sam Wilcox?" Harrison frowned, glancing at his watch. "It's early morning, West Coast time.''

"Yeah, Sam," Gold was saying into the telephone. "I can hear you fine. What's up? Huh? You're shitting me!''

"What is it?" Harrison demanded. Steve put his hand up to silence him.

"Yeah, Sam," Steve said wearily, rolling his eyes at Harrison. "Yeah, absolutely it's a phony. We would never do such a thing— That's right. That's right. Yeah, I agree. I think— Huh? *What?* That serious? Really? Okay. Yeah, sure. We'll take your advice, pal. Right now. Yep! Bye. And Sam? Thanks. This one was above and beyond the call of duty.'' He hung up.

"Well?" Harrison demanded.

"Sam Wilcox was calling us from home. He says that this morning's *Los Angeles Gazette* is running a front-page article that claims GAT knew all along that there were safety glitches in the GC-600's fly-by-wire control system.''

"That's absurd!" Harrison cried out.

"The *Gazette* bases its allegations on anonymous sources.''

"Our old friend, Icarus," Linda said dolefully.

Steve nodded. "The paper claims that it's been supplied with a copy of a memo signed by Don Harrison advising Steve Gold to fudge over any safety questions from potential customers by offering advantageous financial incentives."

"I never wrote any such memo!" Harrison blurted. "It's so blatantly, obviously a setup! As if the airlines would purchase an unsafe airplane just because we knocked a few bucks off the price . . ." He shook his head. "Surely nobody would swallow such malarkey."

"Like they wouldn't swallow the European Pilots Association's allegations?" Susan asked dryly.

"Oh, my God," Harrison murmured sadly, covering his face with his hands.

Susan said, "It's perfectly obvious that Icarus has moved from revealing embarrassing leaks to creating them by forging that memo."

"We all know that," Linda offered. "But the rest of the world doesn't."

Steve nodded. "Which leads me to what *else* Sam said. He strongly advised that we should take the first flight home."

"Sure." Harrison nodded vigorously. "We've got to get home to refute those damned scurrilous lies."

"It's worse than that," Steve said. "Sam says that before he called us he contacted a French law firm with which he's done business. It seems that there's a real possibility in light of this latest allegation that if we delay, the French authorities might move to hold us on criminal charges."

"Are you kidding?" Susan squeaked, her eyes huge with disbelief.

"You hear me laughing?" Steve scowled. "Two men died in that crash. If a case could be made that we strongly suspected their lives were in danger and still sent them up in that airplane . . ."

"Let's get packing," Harrison said. "Steve, would you call the front desk and let them know we're checking out? See if the concierge can get us booked on a flight—"

"To anywhere," Steve finished for him, picking up the telephone.

CHAPTER 16

(One)

In the sky over the ACM ranges
Ryder AFB, Nevada
14 June, 1978

Lieutenant Andy Harrison's Stiletto cut through the sky at 25,000 feet over Pablo Mesa, a stretch of mocha desert broken by ridges the color of burnt toast. Andy was flying with his squadron section and his section instructor when he saw Major Robbie Greene's flat-black F-5E coming at him like Darth Vader in pursuit of Luke Skywalker.

You son of a bitch, here you come like a bad penny, Andy thought as he eyeballed Robbie's little black Scooter, a speck at seven o'clock high on Andy's port wing. As Andy watched, he saw Robbie roll his ship sideways into a descending attack approach meant to put him smack on Andy's tail.

Goddamn you, Robbie! Andy knew from hard experience gained growing up in the same house with his half brother that Robbie intended to humiliate Andy in front of his squadron buddies and the instructor, Captain Tom Bartlett, whose Stilletto was painted a brilliant bumblebee-striped yellow and black so that the students could easily locate him here in the classroom of the sky.

These past couple of weeks in Fighter Weapons School had been spent living in the classroom and the cockpit. Andy and his squadron had studied the physics of air combat until their dreams at night were filled with equations concerning energy, attack angles, and lift vectors. When they weren't busting numbers, they were cramming themselves full of facts concerning the Soviet Union's methods of training pilots, how the Reds organized their air force, the Commies' air formations and tactics, their radar command and forward air-control capabilities, and so on.

Mornings at school were devoted to books and blackboards, but in the afternoon the students got to put what they'd learned to practical use in the air. Andy and his squad section had spent their first few hops showing their instructors what they could do in basic one-vee-one visual-contact dogfights, and then moved on to gradually more complicated radar intercept and ground-control-guided mix-ups involving multiple birds.

Andy and his fellow squadron members found themselves learning about each other as well as their airplanes. The instructors encouraged the squadron to form alliances and partnerships of pilots within itself so that two guys could be flying, say, a MiG sweep, and both would know what the other would do in a given situation without a word needing to be said on the radio. The instructors emphasized that while this "pilot's telepathy" had always been important in the lightning-fast pace of a dogfight, these days it was especially crucial given both sides' modern technological ability to jam communications.

Since Stilettos were single-seat jets, a large part of the training was also devoted to scanning procedures in which a flight divvied up responsibility for watching the sky. Right now, a squadron member named Johnson flying on Andy's port side in the four-ship line-abreast formation was supposed to be responsible for the section of sky just now occupied by Robbie's black-package F-5E, but Johnson hadn't yet called the bogie.

Robbie pressed the radio transmit button on his throttle and said, "Mustang three to lead. We've got company about seven o'clock high."

"Roger, three," Captain Bartlett replied. "I was wondering how long it would take you Mister Magoos to spot him. Mustang Two, wake up, son! That should have been your call."

"Roger, sorry, lead," Johnson replied. "I did see it, but that little guy has got to be an F-5E."

"That's *the* F-5E," Bartlett corrected. "That's Major Greene's black beauty."

"Roger," Johnson said. "That's why I didn't call it. I didn't figure we'd be playing with the Attackers until Red Sky began."

Bartlett said, "You guys call *everything* from now on, because it's almost 'Anything Can Happen Day' here at the Mickey Mouse Club."

Andy smiled. Next week would be their last week of training. They would be given "check rides" to receive their mission ready status, which would mean, among other things, that they were fully conversant with the rules of engagement during Red Sky, and that they could handle their birds down as low as a hundred feet above the desert floor.

Bartlett continued. "Your last week of training you can expect us to throw any number of wild cards your way, and that includes guest appearances by the Attackers."

But that's *next* week, Andy thought, perturbed. So why was Robbie loitering around the schoolyard today?

"Mustang lead, this is Knight seven," Robbie said, dialing into the flight's frequency. "I saw your little duckies flying all in a row and couldn't resist coming on down to have me a snack. Tell me, Mustang lead. When are you going to let them remove their training wheels?"

"Not today, Knight seven," Bartlett said easily. "You go pick on somebody your own size."

Andy heard Robbie laugh coldly: "Yeah, I guess you're right. Your whole flight put together isn't *my* size. Especially not this little fellow flying number 34."

Andy gritted his teeth. Number 34 was his bird.

Robbie drawled, "Mustang lead, let's see what what your fledglings are made of."

Andy gasped, hunching his shoulders as Robbie put on a burst of speed in order to rise up over his Stiletto, and then drop down so that his black F-5E's belly was almost grazing the top of Andy's canopy. Andy couldn't help himself from dropping his bird out of formation in order to put some breathing room between himself and Robbie.

"Dammit, Major Greene!" Bartlett exploded. "Are you crazy?"

"Sorry, Captain, but I just couldn't resist," Robbie chuckled. "And sorry, 34. Didn't mean to make you flinch."

The black F-5 lifted off lightly, insolently banking across the flight's path. Andy, seething with embarrassment over the way he'd let Robbie bluff him out of formation, stared at Robbie's bird, its foot-tall "1" designation done in Soviet-style red with yellow piping on its black nose and tail.

"Bye-bye, 34," Robbie taunted. "Remember, come Red Sky, you can run, but you can't hide." The black 5-FE's dual tail pipes glowed orange as Robbie climbed swiftly away.

Andy felt furious, impotent, and foolish. He hadn't seen his half brother since their confrontation in Robbie's office over two weeks ago. Since then Andy had once again come round to the notion that he and Robbie might be able to bury the hatchet, especially in light of GAT's hour of need. The newspapers and TV news broadcasts had been full of nasty insinuations against GAT management concerning the GC-600 jetliner crash in Europe a couple of days ago. Andy was considering going to Robbie and telling him that it was time to put their own differences aside in order to help the elders in the family put the wagons in a circle against outside enemies.

But I guess nothing matters to Robbie but his hatred, like an all-consuming fire, Andy now thought grimly as he watched the black F-5E shrink in his cockpit HUD display. Suddenly he grinned, seized with a delicious idea: Everybody knew you had to fight fire with fire.

He pressed his helmet back against his headrest and cobbed his throttle to full military power. The Stiletto leapt forward out of the line-abreast formation, and once Andy was safely distanced from the rest of his flight, he went to full afterburn, in order to swiftly close what had become a several-mile gap between himself and Robbie.

"Mustang three, what do you think you're doing?" Bartlett demanded.

"I intend to teach a black crow to eat crow," Andy replied, thinking, *Maybe, just maybe, I can take Robbie right now.*

Normally he knew that he wouldn't have a chance in hell against Robbie this early on in his training, but at present they were a good twenty minutes' flying time from Ryder, and Robbie had used up quite a lot of fuel showing off in order to humiliate Andy. The F-5E didn't carry much juice in the first place, so Robbie had to be getting low. That would mean he'd be reluctant to go full military throttle, never mind use his afterburner, which would give Andy the advantage in a dogfight.

"Mustang flight, where you all going?" Bartlett suddenly complained. "Goddammit! Has the *whole world* gone crazy?"

Andy glanced back over his shoulder to see that the rest of the flight was eagerly following him to see the outcome of this contest. He felt better knowing his friends were around. It was like they were a good omen.

It's going to be okay, Andy thought as he checked his sheet of radio call frequencies, and then tuned in to talk to Robbie on the Attackers channel. "Knight seven," Andy began transmitting. "Fight's on, Seven. I'm gonna turn you into deep-fried chicken Kiev!"

The black F-5E banked sharply in reply. Andy gritted his teeth against the G's he was pulling as he put the Stiletto into its own tight bat-turn in order to stay with Robbie. The horizon tilted and Andy's stomach corkscrewed. The sweat popped out on his brow as his G-suit inflated around his legs and gut to keep his blood from pooling around his ankles. But then the discomfort he was experiencing was rewarded as he watched the black F-5E that was looming in his HUD display begin to slide toward the ghostly green circle of his gunsight.

Robbie must have sensed Andy's gunsight closing in on him. The F-5E's tail pipes glowed orange as Robbie accelerated. Andy, watching the little black bird strain to get away, smiled to himself: *You can't win the game that way, Robbie.*

Andy carefully inched forward his own throttle—the Stiletto's speed superiority was such that if he wasn't careful he'd overshoot—and settled in for a cross-sky, turning pursuit. As the gap closed between the Stiletto and the F-5E, Andy wondered how it could be so easy. Hell, he could call a Sidewinder kill right now. . . .

He decided against it. Make-pretend missile kills without third-party electronic confirmation calls were at best inconclusive, forcing the combatants to play the "I got you/you missed me" game. Another few seconds and Andy would be close enough to call a guns kill. That way his win would be definite, and Robbie's humiliation would be that much more intense.

Andy smiled as he saw Robbie drop his black bird's nose toward the tan and brown desert, now 20,000 feet below. He guessed that Robbie was diving in the hopes that the F-5E could trade some of its altitude for extra speed. The move was a desperate one, and convinced Andy that the supposedly hot-shit Major Robert Blaize Greene was clearly out of ideas and anxious to put some distance between himself and the Stiletto in order to buy a little time to think.

Andy increased his own speed as he dropped the Stiletto's nose in order to follow Robbie down. He wanted to end this dogfight in record time. After all, people were watching.

Andy's dive drew him to within 1,500 feet of the F-5E. His gunsight was about to lasso Robbie's bird, a black cross trailing a fiery glow outlined against the lighter, sand-colored desert floor that was now hurtling upward. Andy centered the pipper on the F-5E's tail pipes and thumbed his radio switch.

Bye-Bye, Robbie, he thought. "Guns, guns," he began gaily.

And then the incredible happened. One moment Robbie's bird was still diving toward the ground, and the next the black bird's nose was up and it was slithering away out of Andy's gunsight the way a wiggling trout will slip from an unwary fisherman's net. Before Andy quite knew what had happened, his ultrapowerful jet had overshot Robbie's nimble little bird.

"Mustang three, no kill. I repeat, no kill on Knight seven," Andy heard Captain Bartlett announce.

Who made him referee? Andy thought distractedly. The Stiletto's altimeter was unwinding fast. Andy struggled to level out, and then began wildly searching behind his three-nine line—the area of sky between three o'clock and nine o'clock behind his wings—for a glimpse of Robbie.

"Hey, Harrison!" Johnson radioed. "Don't look now, but Knight seven is on *your* tail."

(Two)

Major Robbie Greene watched through the F-5E's canopy as Andrew streaked past in his Stiletto at nine o'clock low, overshooting. Green then skidded his little Scooter around, dropping sideways through the sky in order to save gas as he gave pursuit.

Andrew's F-66 was a beautiful-looking bird, Greene thought. The Stiletto was painted ghost gray, with a blue wolf's head against a white circular background on its vertical tail, and number 34 painted in large black numbers on its nose. Earlier, Greene had been on a routine flight through this sector when he'd spotted the Stiletto flight being led by its bumblebee-striped instructor. Curious, Greene had made one quick pass, which was when he'd identified Andrew's airplane by its number, and then used his afterburners to come around behind in order to bounce his half brother.

It had been totally out of line for Greene to have hassled Andrew, of course, but Greene was feeling especially mean toward his half brother for a couple of reasons. There was Gail Saunders, of course. Initially, Greene had been somewhat relieved when he'd heard that Gail had been seeing another guy because it got him off the hook with her, but Greene's attitude about that had done a nosedive when he'd found out that it was Andrew who was poaching on his territory. Gail was her own person and could see who she wanted, Greene knew, but that didn't mean he'd cotton to her putting out the welcome mat for his half brother.

But Gail wasn't even the half of it. What was really pissing Greene off was that he felt Andrew's father Don Harrison was currently to blame for this mess GAT was currently facing concerning the GC-600 crash in Paris. Greene had telephoned his mother and grandmother concerning the incident, and from what they had implied he concluded that if Don hadn't been so all-fired anxious to debut the jetliner, the accident never would have happened. No doubt Uncle Steve was doing his best to keep the company flying straight and narrow, but Don Harrison was fucking things up.

Like father, like son, Greene now thought as he locked onto Andrew's six. As soon as Andrew had called "Fight's on," Greene had known he'd had the kid licked from the way Andrew had come rocketing after him. The Stiletto he was flying was a fabulously powerful, easy-to-fly bird, thanks to its computer-augmented fly-by-wire controls. Maybe the Stiletto was too easy to fly, because the F-66 could run away with the overconfident and underexperienced fighter jock, in much the same way a powerful car can creep over the speed limit on a highway if the driver becomes lax. That's what had happened when Andrew had overshot Greene. Greene had simply waited for the Stiletto to build up speed on its downward straightaway plunge, and for Andrew to become distracted by his anticipation of his kill. At the right moment Greene had more or less stood on his Scooter's brakes. Poor Andrew was streaking past before he quite knew what was happening. Maybe next time the kid would pay more attention. The Stiletto was capable of outmaneuvering the F-5E, but then, a crate was only as good as the man inside it.

Just now, Andrew's Stiletto had leveled out at 9,000 feet and was gradually climbing as it hightailed it across the sky. Greene allowed the gap between himself and Andrew to widen. For one thing, his F-5E couldn't catch a Stiletto, and for another, Greene didn't have the gas to try. The F-5E's little fuel tanks gave it notoriously "short legs," and Greene was coming close to bingo fuel: just enough juice to get home on. It meant he couldn't afford to engage in any fancy maneuvers to bag Andrew, but then, there was more than one way to skin a cat.

The Stiletto was now about a mile away. Greene watched as Andrew hit his afterburner, stood his Stiletto on her tail, and pretended she was a rocket ship going to the moon.

Greene smiled. That was what all the new kids on the block did: count on their hardware to get them out of hot water. Andrew was figuring to go where Greene couldn't and in that way get the altitude advantage to bounce the F-5E. Greene expended a little more of his increasingly precious fuel to accelerate, closing the gap between himself and Andrew, and then used his little Scooter's leading edge slats and automatic maneuvering flaps to point his bird's nose up toward the Stiletto—as if he were *planning* to climb, or to send a Sidewinder right up the Stiletto's white-hot tail pipe.

Yes! Greene thought in supreme satisfaction as Andrew was suckered into his ploy. Quick as a wink, the Stiletto had slid over the top of its climb to point its nose directly at Greene in order to counter his bluff. Greene watched the Stilleto come toward him like a roller-coaster car rambling down the track. As Andrew disappeared beneath the F-5E's long, flat nose, Greene bat-turned to follow him down, grunting against the Gs as he exchanged a canopy full of blue sky for a panoramic view of the desert.

Greene was careful to keep his throttle well back. He would let gravity provide his afterburn. Meanwhile, he knew that Andrew would have to lose energy leveling out of his own power dive. It would be in that instant, while the Stiletto was leveling and slowing, and the F-5E was still diving and accelerating, that Greene would gain momentary advantage.

But the Stiletto was still spiraling down toward the desert floor. *Pull out, kid*, Greene thought nervously. He didn't want the kid splattered across the sagebrush. How would Greene explain it to their mother? And after all, you couldn't humiliate a dead man. . . .

Greene was vastly relieved to see the Stiletto finally flatten out of its dive. Andrew was down around 3,000 feet now; he had nowhere to go but up. Greene watched as Andrew raised his bird's nose in order to climb. The Stiletto, flat out of energy, slowed noticeably. Greene could catch her now.

He held his dive. At 5,000 feet, about a quarter-mile behind and above the Stiletto, Greene put his circular gunsight on the F-66's spine and radioed "Fox two", the call sign for a Sidewinder missile launch.

Greene then realized that Andrew might later claim that, if this fight had been for real, the hot desert floor might have decoyed the heat-seeker. He dropped the F-5E a couple of thousand feet in order to level off behind Andrew, locking his pipper on the Stiletto's glowing tail pipe, and again called "Fox two," indicating that he'd just launched a second imaginary missile to go chasing after the Stiletto on a beeline straight up its ass. Then, just for the hell of it, Greene called, "Guns, guns," meaning that if this had been for real, Greene would just now be mopping up Andrew's remains with his F5-E's twin, 20MM cannons.

"*Mustang three, you are a mort,*" Greene heard Captain Bartlett radioing to Andrew.

"Captain, you should have counted the little squirt out when I launched my first fox," Greene chided mildly.

"I wanted to give the kid a little advantage over you," Bartlett explained. "Not that it made any difference."

"Roger." Greene checked his fuel. Another few seconds dawdling around here and he'd have to get out and push, but as it was, he was pretty confident that he'd make it back to Ryder with at least enough gas left in the tanks to soak the cotton wad in a Zippo.

And as Greene pointed his F-5E toward home, he had the pleasure of listening to Captain Bartlett lecturing his class;

"*Mustang three, you have just been deep-fried by one of the best. Mustang flight, what have we learned from watching the way Major Greene waxed Lieutenant Harrison?*"

(Three)

Ryder AFB

"I can't begin to tell you how stupid I felt," Andy was complaining. "Major Greene made me look like an idiot!"

Gail smiled sadly in commiseration. *Join the club,* she thought. *Robbie's good at making people feel like idiots.*

It was a little after seven P.M. She and Andy were at the ice-cream parlor near the commissary. It was a boldly colored, brightly lit, bustling place, popular with families on the base. The parlor had a black and white tiled floor, round marble tables, and bent wire chairs with pink seating cushions. The walls were decorated with childlike depictions of airplanes buzzing sundaes and banana splits the size of aircraft carriers. Gail had brought Andy here in the hopes that she could cheer him up after the awful waxing he'd taken earlier that day. She herself had just worked a double shift and was bone-weary, but when Andy had called with the doleful news she'd roused herself to shower, and then put on her best white sundress, the one that showed off her tan and her auburn hair. She was determined to bring Andy out of his funk, because a fighter jock's self-confidence was his primary asset, and Andy was seriously lacking in that department thanks to Robbie Greene.

And thanks to me, Gail thought guiltily. She blamed herself for the drubbing Andy had suffered. In all her scheming to make Robbie jealous, it had never occurred to her that he would go so far as to persecute Andy in retaliation. What had happened today was all the more mind-boggling because it had come so unexpectedly. She'd been seeing Andy just about every night for the past couple weeks, and she hadn't heard a word from Robbie about it. As a matter of fact, their mutual friends had told her that Robbie seemed not the least bit perturbed that she was seeing someone else. She'd not seen fit to tell Andy about her previous relationship, reasoning that any sensible Red Sky player would be scared off by the knowledge that he was dating the girlfriend (make that ex-girlfriend) of the leader of the Attackers squadron. Now she couldn't bring herself to tell, because if she did, what would Andy think of her for having gotten him into this humiliating mess?

"Listen, Andy," she murmured, trying to comfort him. "There was no way you could have beat Major Greene."

"She's right, man."

Gail looked up. A dark-haired, gangly, hawk-nosed young man in a flight suit with lieutenant's bars on his shoulders was standing over their table.

"Oh, hi, Stan," Andy said. "Sergeant Gail Saunders, allow me to introduce Lieutenant Stan Johnson."

"Hi," Gail said, shaking hands with Johnson.

"Sit down and join us, Stan," Andy invited and as Johnson pulled out a chair. Andy told Gail, "Stan's one of my squadron mates who was there today, a witness to the rout."

Johnson shook his head. "He's kicking himself like he actually had a chance," he told Gail. "Face it, Andy. You were waxed from the word go."

"You're not exactly cheering Andy up." Gail glowered

at Johnson, feeling impelled to rise to Andy's protection. He was a funny kind of fighter jock, she'd come to learn. Andy was confident, sure; there was an underlying steeliness to him very much like the quality of strength she'd come to know in Robbie, but Robbie had a blustering side to him as well. Gail guessed it stemmed from some sort of insecurity. She didn't know what exactly. In all the time they'd known one another—slept together—Robbie had never seen fit to confide in her.

Andy wasn't like that. He didn't seem to feel the need to bluster, to ruffle his mane to seem larger than he was. Take the way Andy dressed when off duty, in a summerweight service uniform of silver-tan trousers and short-sleeved shirt with his rank insignia pinned to his collar. She liked it that Andy was secure enough in his identity that he didn't feel the need to strut around in a flight suit like the rest of his breed.

"Stan's right," Andy said, desultorily fiddling with the straw in his black-and-white ice-cream soda. "I never had a chance, I was just too dumb to know it. It was only later, when Captain Bartlett reconstructed what happened for the squadron's benefit, that I realized just how badly I'd been outclassed."

"It was like watching a matador handle a bull," Johnson marveled. "Greene just kind of hung in the sky like a chopper, popping his flaps, causing Andy to overshoot so that he could put himself on Andy's tail."

"But I still wasn't all that worried," Andy ruefully added to Gail. "What did I have to worry about, even if Greene was on my six? I had the superior, more powerful bird."

"And that's when Major Greene used your own superior strength against you, like in judo or something," Johnson chattered.

"Thanks, Stan, but you don't have to quote Captain Bartlett's words back to me," Andy sulked. "I remember them quite well."

"I was explaining things for the sergeant's benefit," Johnson said, sounding miffed. "It was eye-opening to watch the way Andy was zipping back and forth, powering through the sky"—Johnson's left hand was drawing swoopes in the air

—"while Greene's little black bird was just sort of making these minimal, *ultracool* moves." He fluttered his right hand in tight turns, keeping his fingers pointed toward his left.

Gail glanced inquiringly at Andy.

"The major had to keep his maneuvering to a minimum because he was so low on fuel," Andy explained, pausing to cast a scowling glance toward Johnson. "Greene moved around just enough to keep me where he wanted me." He smiled thinly. "The way a cat just kind of now and then sticks out a paw to swipe at a wounded mouse."

"You've got to be making it sound worse than it was," Gail insisted.

"Actually, I'm making myself sound better." Andy smiled sadly.

"It was like the major was doing mind control on you or something." Johnson shook his head. "It was like he knew what you were thinking before you did—"

"Of course Major Greene knew what Andy was thinking!" Gail said impatiently.

Both men looked at her blankly. "What's that supposed to mean?" Andy asked.

Gail rolled her eyes. "Smarten up, you two! I've seen it so many times, I'm sick of it! You guys always show up at Red Sky thinking you're something special, and then you're dumbfounded when the instructors and Attackers are able to wax you. When will you guys get it through your thick heads that you're here to *learn*, not to show off! The staff here flies ACM day in and day out. There's no way any regular-duty Air Force squadron is going to be able to compete with them off the bat. The thing to concentrate on—assuming you lugheads *can* concentrate on anything besides your own egos— is how much better the squadron will be doing toward the end of the training program."

Johnson was nodding. "That's what Captain Bartlett told us today."

"Well, he's right!" Gail said adamantly.

"You think so?" Andy asked softly. He was looking into her eyes like Johnson wasn't there. He took her hand.

Gail felt a pleasant shock at his touch. She resisted her impulse to pull away. Poor Andy had already taken enough hits to his self-confidence on her behalf.

And anyway, it wasn't as if she didn't like him touching her. She liked it fine. They'd been holding hands and necking a little since last weekend, with Andy was proving to be extremely adept at getting her over Robbie. So much so that now Gail was worried about how she was going to get over Andy once he was gone, if she allowed herself to fall for him.

Now, studying Andy, the way he was looking at her with his dark eyes so intent, she felt her heart surrendering despite the consequences. *He really cares what I think*, she realized. *What I have to say matters to him.*

In all the time she'd been with Robbie, she couldn't recall one time he'd actually listened to her. It was weird. The two men—Robbie and Andy—often struck her as being two peas in a pod, but at other times the difference between them was like night and day.

"Listen up, Lieutenant Harrison," she began. "Haven't you learned quite a lot today?"

"Yeah, I did." Andy nodded.

"Okay. Then you must realize that the tricks Major Greene pulled on you today he'll never be able to pull on you again, and he doesn't have an unlimited bag of tricks."

Take it from me, I ought to know, she added to herself as she watched Andy expectantly to see if she was getting through to him.

He squeezed her hand. "I am going to beat him, Gail," he vowed softly. "You'll see I will—"

"That's fine," she murmured, feeling moved. "I think you can beat him." She swallowed hard. Her heart was pounding. "In a way, you already have."

She wasn't sure what she would have said next, if they hadn't been so rudely interrupted.

"Well, well, isn't this a scene right out of Norman Rockwell," Major Robbie Greene sneered, standing with his hands on his hips, looking down at the table.

"What do you want?" Andy demanded.

"It's a hot night."

What a bastard he can be! Gail thought as she watched Robbie shrug, feigning innocence. As if he didn't know they'd taken to hanging out here!

"I just came in for an ice-cream cone," Robbie continued.

"I didn't expect to find you children. I would have thought it was past your bedtime."

He stared accusingly at Gail, or maybe she was just reading too much into his expression, but in any event, she had trouble meeting his gaze. Here Robbie was, the same guy as always with his good looks and dreamy eyes, but tonight, looking at him standing there in his flight suit with that red ascot wrapped around his throat and that ugly expression on his face, Gail felt like she was gazing at a stranger.

She noticed Andy looking at her, then Robbie, and back again, trying to figure out what was passing between them. Then Andy curtly addressed Robbie: "Haven't you caused enough trouble? Why don't you just get the hell out of here?"

"Easy, pal," Johnson cautioned. "You're talking to a superior officer."

Robbie said, "I see the little man is having an ice-cream soda to console himself over his whipping. Are you sitting on a pillow, little man?" He winked at Gail.

Andy warned quietly, "You're not in an airplane now. Beat it, before I knock you flat on your ass."

"Jesus, Andy!" Johnson gasped.

You can say that again, Gail thought. A lowly lieutenant just didn't speak to a major that way. She watched anxiously for Robbie's reaction.

Robbie's eyes met hers. "And you!" he snapped. "Tell me, what's it like being with brand X after you've had the real thing?"

Andy jumped up to shove Robbie away from the table. Gail sat frozen, her hand to her mouth: Robbie looked ready to belt Andy. But then Robbie looked around, noticing how the people at the surrounding tables were watching.

"This is not the place," Robbie quietly told Andy. "Would you care to step outside, little man?"

"After you, Major." Andy nodded grimly.

"Stop it! Both of you!" Gail commanded. "I won't have this." She realized that she would have to tell him about her previous relationship with Robbie. It would be humiliating for her, but at least it might defuse the tension. "Andy, there's something you need to know—"

"Stay out of this Gail," Andy cut her off.

Robbie's eyes had widened as he stared at Gail. "You mean he doesn't?"

She shook her head, realizing that Andy was so angry that he'd been totally oblivious to the admittedly cryptic exchange just now between herself and Robbie.

"Well, are you coming, or have you chickened out, Major?" Andy demanded.

Gail felt a momentary surge of hope as Robbie shook his head. Robbie seemed to have cooled down now that he realized that Andy was in the dark concerning the history between himself and Gail.

"I'm not going to fight you, Lieutenant," Robbie said, turning away. "You wouldn't stand a chance. I'm a black belt in karate."

Thank you, God, Gail was thinking, but then Andy had to go and say to Robbie, "What you are is a black belt in being an *asshole*."

Robbie whirled, hissing. "You just never know when to quit! Outside then! This won't take long!"

"Will you two please stop behaving like spoiled children!" Gail began.

"Stan!" Andy interrupted. "Stay here with Gail. See that she doesn't follow us."

"You can't keep me here against my will!" Gail said indignantly.

"Lieutenant," Robbie addressed Johnson. "You will keep the sergeant here. That is an order."

"Yes, sir, Major," Johnson said reflexively. He turned beseeching eyes toward Gail. "I'm sorry. Please, just sit."

"After you, Major," Andy said evenly.

Gail watched helplessly as the two men threaded their way past the tables out of the ice-cream parlor.

(Four)

Greene lead Andrew out the ice-cream parlor's front door. They stalked silently to the alley behind the building, where the streetlights barely penetrated the shadows cast by the dumpsters and garbage cans arrayed against the building's wall.

"I believe this is private enough for what we have in mind," Greene said calmly.

"Fight's on!" Andrew growled, hunching his shoulders and clenching his fists.

Greene brought up his own hands to defend himself as the two of them began circling. Greene was sorry things had come to this, and sorry in the first place that he'd come to the ice-cream parlor where he'd known he could find Andrew and Gail. Greene had come wanting to rub Gail's nose in the fact that she'd chosen the lesser of the two men, but it had taken the wind right out of his sails when he'd realized that Andrew knew nothing of Greene's past relationship with Gail, and that Gail obviously didn't know that he and Andrew were related.

Thinking about it now, it all made sense, Greene decided. Gail was not the kind of girl to talk freely about her past, and why would Andrew have brought the matter up? Early on in their shared history, the two half brothers had agreed on one thing: to deny their filial existence to each other and to as much of the outside world as was possible. Greene never talked about Andrew in terms of the kid being family, and suspected it was vice versa on Andrew's part.

And now here the two of them were, shuffling around, eyeing each other like nervous bantam roosters newly deposited into the cockfighting ring. *Neither one of us really wants to fight,* Greene realized.

Greene was about to suggest they knock it off when Andrew made his move. Greene had been expecting the kid to clumsily swing at his jaw, or else try to punch him in the stomach: that's what your average person did in a fistfight. What Greene was not expecting was Andrew's surprisingly adept roundhouse kick. Andrew's torso bent sideways and his leg came around straight and true to catch Greene square in the chest. Greene staggered back but managed to remain on his feet.

"Say, kid, you've had some martial-arts training, haven't you?" Greene remarked, brushing the dirt from Andrew's shoe from his red ascot.

"Some," Andrew nodded. He was back in his guarded,

semicrouch position. "What do you say? Want to quit before you get hurt?"

Greene laughed. He moved toward Andrew with his own hands slightly lowered in order to lure in the younger man. Andrew took the bait, dancing in to throw a punch at Greene. Greene easily deflected the punch with a sweeping, outside-middle-area block, and then countered with a punch that caught Andrew's shoulder, followed by a side foot thrust to the side of Andrew's knee.

Andrew's leg folded and he fell hard against the garbage cans, sending them clattering as he sprawled to the pavement in a pool of sticky, empty, cardboard ice-cream tubs and banana peels.

"That's always been your problem, Andrew," Greene taunted. "You start out okay, but then you get cocky. . . ." He trailed off abruptly, feeling shaken, remembering how others had used to criticize *him* the very same way.

Andew was up on his feet, wiping as best he could the sticky, melted ice-cream residue from his uniform. He was shaking his head, looking groggy, but he gamely advanced on Greene while executing a flurry of front snap kicks and karate punches.

Greene backpedaled, bouncing lightly on the soles of his feet with his hands on his hips, merely swaying his body from side to side in order to avoid being struck. Andrew was totally overmatched, Greene realized as he dispassionately observed Andrew's karate form: the kid's technique was perfectly good. It was just that Greene had enjoyed the benefit of many more years of training and sparring experience. Andrew could no more touch Greene on the ground than the kid had been able to touch him in the air.

Andrew was slowing down a bit. He was breathing heavily, his kicks were losing their snap, and his punches were growing limp.

It was no fucking wonder, Greene thought. *The kid had been windmilling around like the guys in those kung-fu flicks when they speeded up the cameras.*

Greene saw an opening and executed a lunge, driving the point of his elbow into Andrew's solar plexus that left the kid gasping. Greene snapped out a karate thust to Andrew's stomach, doubling the kid over, and then moved in, feinting a left toward Andrew's chin. When Andrew brought up his hands to block the phony punch, Greene danced around him, turning sideways and stepping in close in order to drive his elbow into Andrew's kidney. As Andrew grunted, arching his back, Greene spun around to slash his open hand against the side of Andrew's neck.

Andrew's eyes rolled up and he crumpled, semiconscious. Greene moved quickly to catch him so that he didn't strike his head against the pavement.

"You'll be okay in a few minutes." Green laid him down on his side in a relatively clean spot in the alleyway and then straightened up, backing away. "Fight's over."

"No," Andrew called weakly, forcing himself up on his elbows.

"Stay down!" Greene said sharply.

"I won't lose to you," Andrew managed, his speech slurred and his eyes still rolling. "I won't lose! Not twice in one day!"

Greene stood transfixed, staring down at his defiant half brother. The sense of personal déjà vu, of looking in a mirror, was awesome and overwhelming.

"Stay down," Brody said.

"I don't lose," Greene replied . . .

This had all happened before, Green realized, thinking back some three years to the *Mayaguez* incident, when the *Sea Bear*'s air boss had wiped the mats with him in the aircraft carrier's gym.

Now, as Greene stared at Andrew, who was struggling to continue the fight, he remembered how he himself had been pitted against a seemingly insurmountable foe. But there the similarities ended, Greene brooded, for Brody had shown mercy toward him, while he'd been acting hard as nails toward Andrew. Greene recalled the valuable lesson that Brody had taught him: Life is not about learning, but remembering. Well, wasn't remembering what he was doing now?

"Andy," Greene murmured.

"What?" He sounded amazed. "You know, Robbie? I don't think you've *ever* called me anything but dirty names and Andrew."

"Andy, I . . ." Greene was having trouble finding the

right words, and then, before he could summon up what he wanted to say, he heard noise coming from behind. He turned to see Gail Saunders come running into the alley.

"What have you done to him, you bullying bastard!" Gail cursed at Greene as she ran to where Andrew was lying.

"I'm okay," Andrew muttered, sitting up.

"You sure?" Gail's tanned legs flashed beneath her white dress as she knelt to put her arm around him.

Andrew nodded. "The worst damage is to my pride." He glanced at Gail. "How'd you get away from Johnson?"

"I dumped your ice-cream soda in his lap." She shrugged. "It kind of distracted him." She glared at Greene. "But *you!* You *son of a bitch!* If there was anything still between us, it's gone now. You can be sure of that!"

"I've been sure of that for a while." Greene realized he felt sorry about it, but it was so.

"It's your loss!" Gail snapped.

"I know that too," Greene acknowledged softly.

"What's going on here?" Andrew demanded. "Is there something I should know?"

As Greene walked away, he heard her explanation.

"I'm so sorry, Andy! This is all my fault! Major Greene and I used to go out. Yes, it's true, he's been picking on you because he was jealous of me seeing you, and—Andy? What is it? Why are you laughing?"

"Gail, honey, this isn't about you."

"Huh?"

"Robbie and I have been tussling like this since I was born."

"Huh? Are you telling me that you two guys know each other?"

"Gail, Robbie's my brother. . . . Gail? Now, why are you laughing?"

(Five)

The trailer Andy shared with three other members of his squadron had fold-out furniture, a galley kitchenette, a small bath, a cramped seating area, and light-blue walls with woodgrain vinyl trim. In the way of entertainment there were a few paperbacks, some tattered skin magazines, and a radio just now turned low to a rock station that was playing the Eagles' "Hotel California."

The trailer's lights were off. Several lit candles stuck onto jar lids were scattered about, casting their lambent glow. A soft breeze rattled the rattan shades over the trailer's screened jalousie windows, and every now and then a strong gust would cause the candles' flames to waver, casting long shadows and creating a strobe effect over the narrow bed where Andy lay cradling Gail in his arms.

"I want you to know I usually don't sleep with guys this early in the relationship," Gail murmured dreamily.

"I feel like we've known each other a long time," Andy said.

"I guess we have," she agreed, ". . . in some ways."

Andy buried his face in her hair, inhaling the entwined scents of herbal shampoo and the salty tang of her lathered body. Her musk was all over the twisted, sweaty sheets.

"Penny for your thoughts?" Gail asked.

Andy smiled. "I was thinking that I'd better remember to change these sheets or else my roomates will go crazy."

"Oh, God! You're terrible." she trilled, nudging him in the ribs.

"Ouch!" Andy winced. The spot she'd caught was still sore from Robbie's elbow strike.

"Oh, I'm sorry!" Gail said quickly. "You poor baby." She gently stroked his side. "It still hurts, huh?"

Andy nodded. "Of course, I only lost that fight in order to garner your sympathy and thus lure you to my bed."

"Yeah, right," she scoffed. "And I'm sure that if you could have only kept the fight going a little longer, Robbie would have worn himself out using you like a punching bag." She flipped over on her side on the narrow bed in order to nestle like a spoon against him. "By the way, where *are* your roommates?"

"Well, Johnson is probably at a dry cleaners. . . ."

She giggled. "You should have seen his face when I dumped that soda in his lap. It's funny now, but at the time I was really pissed off when you and Robbie ordered me to stay inside. When I was a little girl growing up in Motion,

South Carolina, I never could cotton to folks telling me what I could or couldn't do. That I couldn't help out my daddy at his garage in town, for instance. That it was unseemly"— she spat the next word—"*unfeminine* for me to want to fiddle around with engines. Everybody kept telling me about how I was *meant* to become a schoolteacher, or a nurse, or a *ballerina* or some such shit."

Andy laughed. "I love it when you talk dirty."

"Ugh, men!" she fumed. "Andy Harrison, you're better than most, but that still leaves you an insufferably smug dolt."

"Yes, *Miz* Sergeant, ma'am."

"Shit up and kiss me, you sex object, you."

Andy kissed her, pleased to have been able to get her off the subject. Just like Grandma Erica, Gail was a real women's libber, a bra burner, not that Gail's delicious tits needed one. Andy did respect her for her accomplishments, but sometimes she got a little too strident. However, he'd learned that if he was careful about it he could kid her out of it.

"I gave my other roommates a quarter," Andy said. "And sent them to the movies."

"Huh?"

"Remember back at the ice-cream parlor when you were worried about how badly I'd been hurt in the fight, and insisted on driving me home? Well, from the way you were babying me, I kind of had a hunch we'd end up here, so when I excused myself in order to clean up in the men's room I took the opportunity to make a phone call to tell my roommates to clear out."

"Oh? And they listened to you?"

Andy nodded whimsically. "It's like an unwritten social contract that whenever single guys room together, all the rest have to clear out if one guy gets lucky."

"Hmm, and do you often get lucky?" Gail demanded teasingly.

Andy lifted her hair to kiss the nape of her neck. "Never *this* lucky."

"You've got an answer for everything, haven't you?" She didn't particularly sound like she was complaining. "Oh! What are you *doing* to me? And whatever it is, don't stop!"

Andy was gently rolling her nipple between his thumb and

forefinger while he stroked her long, supple thigh, tarrying his palm at the sleek curve of her hip. She had a marvelously toned body thanks to her strenuous work climbing around on scaffolding hefting heavy jet-engine parts. She was firm with muscle where other girls were soft, and that had initially been disconcerting to Andrew. Making love their first time tonight, Andy had felt like he was in a wrestling match. Gail had not been shy about making clear what she wanted, at times literally manhandling him into the desired position. . . . But then it had been challenging fun at last pinning her down, and she had surrendered deliciously. Together the two of them had really set this old trailer rocking and creaking on its springs, and when they'd orgasmed together, Gail had howled so loudly that her cry had been answered by a far-off coyote. That had reduced the both of them to an endless bout of helpless laughter.

On the radio, "My Girl," by the Temptations, was seguing into "Silly Love Songs," by Paul McCartney and Wings. They listened quietly to the music for a few moments and then Andy gently turned Gail around in order to kiss her. He saw the sad look in her eyes.

"What is it?" he asked, concerned. "Are you having second thoughts about coming here?"

She shook her head. "No, I wanted this as much as you." She sighed. "I was thinking about the story you told me concerning you and your brother."

"Half brother."

"Oh, Andy! How sad it all is! I wish I could do something."

"I appreciate that, but you can't," Andy replied. "When it comes to Robbie and me, it's the Hatfields and the McCoys all over again."

"There's only one way there's ever going to be peace between you two," Gail said. "You're going to have to beat him at his own game. You're going to have to come out on top during Red Sky."

"I agree with you, but I'm not sure I can beat him," Andy replied. "I had no conception of how good he was until I tangled with him in the air today."

"It doesn't matter," Gail insisted. "You just have to recognize your own abilities and stop letting him psych you out." She paused. "That may not be as difficult as you think. I think you've begun to psyche him out."

Andy shook his head, puzzled. "What do you mean?"

Gail shrugged. "It's hard to explain, but back in that alley, just before he turned away from us, I caught a glimpse of something in Robbie's eyes. It was . . . ." She paused, shaking her head. "I'm not sure what it was, but somehow I got the impression that a part of him wants you to beat him."

"You think he's going to make it easy for me?" Andy asked doubtfully.

"No, he'd never do *that*. You'll still have to try your best, and it won't be easy, but . . . ." She trailed off. "I can't explain what I picked up from Robbie earlier tonight. You'll just have to trust me. After all, I know him pretty well."

"That's for sure." Andy cursed himself for letting it slip out, but he just couldn't help himself. He knew he had no right to be jealous or upset or anything at all concerning Gail's prior relationship with Robbie, but knowing and feeling were too very different things.

"Andy, is this going to be a problem for us?"

He'd been braced for a justifiably angry retort, but instead, when Gail spoke, her hesitant tones had betrayed her own vulnerability.

"Andy, you didn't ask me back here . . . to . . . to try and get even with Robbie?"

"Oh, no, babe," Andy said, shocked. *How ironic it all was,* he thought to himself as he hugged her tightly. She'd volunteered no particulars concerning her relationship with Robbie beyond what she'd confessed in the alley, and earlier, just after their lovemaking, it had been on the tip of his tongue to ask her how he'd compared. But, of course, he couldn't bring himself to be so crass, and anyway, he was a little bit afraid to hear the truth. He'd already lost twice to Robbie today. A third loss in this particular arena would have been truly unbearable.

And for the last few hours he'd imagined that Gail considered herself in the catbird's seat, when all along she'd been just as paranoid.

On the radio, Rod Stewart was crooning "Tonight's the

Night'' as Andy asked Gail, ''What did you mean before, at the ice-cream parlor, when you said that in a way I'd already beat Robbie?''

''What did you think I meant?'' she challenged.

''That maybe I . . .'' Andy was finding it hard to speak. He didn't want to make a fool out of himself, and yet he had to take the chance of revealing his own feelings. ''I guess I'm hoping that you meant that you'd kind of forgotten about Robbie because of me, and that—''

She pressed her fingers to his lips. ''Yes, that's what I meant.''

He kissed her.

She asked, ''When are your roommates going to be back?''

He said, ''About a half hour.''

''Then we have time to do it once more?''

''If we start now.''

CHAPTER 17

(One)

**Gold Residence
Malibu, California
25 June, 1978**

"Yeah, Don, I understand, and I agree with you," Steve Gold said into the telephone.

It was a Sunday morning. Gold was in his study in his home, wearing nothing but bathing trunks and a canvas billed cap to protect his scalp from sunburn. The telephone call from Don Harrison had summoned him from his deck overlooking the sand and surf of Malibu, where he'd been spending a little quiet time with his wife and the Sunday papers.

"Okay," Gold said. "I'll meet you at the office this afternoon. Yeah. No problem. On the contrary, I'm looking forward to this. Talk to you later."

Gold hung up and then left the study, moving through the rambling three-bedroom beach house into the living room, which was casually furnished in glass and bronze, natural rattan, woven leather, and white wicker. The house had more furniture in it than when it had been Gold's bachelor digs, but not much more. Neither he nor Linda liked clutter, and you didn't need much in the way of decoration when your living room had a glass wall looking out onto a wide swatch of beach leading down to the ocean. A sliding door set into the glass led out onto the deck, which stretched the length of the ocean side of the house. Gold could see Linda out on the deck. She was wearing a black two-piece bathing suit, and was lying on her back on a chaise longue, the newspapers and a mug of coffee within easy reach.

Gold gazed fondly at his wife. He was lucky to have her, and he knew it. Linda had stood by him like a friend, helping him keep his perspective throughout the hellish days since the GC-600 had crashed at the Paris Air Show.

In the two weeks since the crash, GAT had fought for its survival on two fronts. In France, where it was announced that no criminal charges would be filed against GAT or its officers until all the facts were in, GAT had pushed hard for a speedy and thorough conclusion to the on-site crash investigation. In America, Don Harrison had combated the media firestorm that had resulted over the *L.A. Gazette*'s publication of the incriminating memo suggesting that GAT management knew the GC-600 was unsafe by publicly branding the document a forgery and then threatening legal action against the *Gazette* for publishing it. The *Gazette*, unable to substantiate the forged memo, quickly backed off, publishing a front-page apology to GAT. Meanwhile, in Burbank, GAT used its outrage over the forged memo to justify to the company's employees a no-holds-barred, hard-hitting housecleaning to ferret out Icarus.

A GAT engineering team was sent to France armed with data that made a strong argument that pilot error had been the cause of the accident. GAT's rigorous test flights of the two remaining GC-600 prototypes, and computer simulations run in the lab, indicated that the pilots of the ill-fated 600 had turned off certain safety controls built into the fly-by-wire system to allow them to perform the severe air maneuvers that led to the crash.

As soon as Gold had heard the explanation, he knew in his gut it was true. He'd been a jet pilot. He knew that the men who flew the fast movers could often exhibit a foolhardy side. Most important, he'd known the crashed airplane's pilot, Ken Cole. Ken was a natural daredevil. Why else would he have chosen to become a test pilot? Gold knew that it was Ken's impulse decision to shut down the safety controls built into the GC-600 and to execute those fancy maneuvers for the crowds watching that had led to this tragedy.

The French anti-GAT hysteria finally began to abate four days ago, with the conclusion of the examination of the GC-600's wreckage and the recovery of the intact black boxes that re-created for the investigators the events in the cockpit in the seconds before the crash. The Air Ministry released a statement supporting GAT's assertion that the pilots had shut off the safety controls. The investigation was closed with the GC-600's reputation cleared, and orders for the jetliner again began to filter into GAT, but only a trickle where initially there had been a flood.

Yeah, GAT was alive and well, Gold now thought, but that didn't mean the company hadn't taken some hits.

For one thing, its stock price had dropped dramatically in response to the controversy surrounding its new jetliner and its fly-by-wire control system. That same control system ran the Stiletto, and a refined version of it was meant for the World-Bird Project. Many nations that already flew the Stiletto grounded their aircraft and put their spare-parts orders on hold during the investigation. Other countries outright canceled their orders for the fighter craft. What was even worse, some participants in World-Bird where now evidencing doubt about whether they wished to continue their involvement. . . .

GAT would eventually get back some of its Stiletto and GC-600 lost business, Gold knew, but no way would the company get back all of it. What would happen with World-Bird it was still too soon to say. The worst thing of all, however, was that no matter what GAT now did, there was no way it could erase the last glimmerings of doubt about the company from the minds of the world. Like a man acquitted after a lengthy murder trial, GAT had come out of its ordeal vindicated, but with its reputation forever tarnished. The bottom line was that GAT had been wounded. The wounds would heal, but slowly. GAT would walk with a limp for some time to come.

Or maybe forever, Gold brooded as he stepped out through the sliding door onto the deck.

"Was that the boys calling?" Linda asked.

"No," Gold replied. His stepsons called home every Sunday from their prep school in New England. They would be home for the summer at the end of the month, or, at least, home for the month of July. In August, they'd be off to sleep-away camp. "It was Don," Gold said.

"What did he want?" Linda asked sleepily. "God, you'd think he could get along without you for one Sunday morning."

"He called to tell me Otto Lane's detectives have got Icarus," Gold said.

"What?" Linda sat up. "When? Who is he? How did it happen?"

"Once a journalist, always a journalist," Gold laughed as he sat down beside her in a deck chair. "You left out 'where?' and 'why?' "

Linda pretended to glower. "*Where* will be your behind connecting with my foot, and *why* will be because you're not answering my questions."

"Okay! I surrender! Interrogate me."

"That's better." Linda nodded, sitting up. "First of all, how did they catch Icarus?"

"They didn't. He turned himself in yesterday afternoon. It seems the guy—"

"His name?" Linda interrupted.

"Oh, sorry. His name is Virgil Holloway, and no, neither I nor Don has ever heard of him," Gold elaborated. "He's an associate engineer—one out of a thousand—in our commercial aviation department. He told Otto Lane that he started this whole business of leaking stuff about GAT over two years ago when he became angry at the company because his section manager gave him a negative job rating on his yearly evaluation sheet."

"And *that*'s what caused all this trouble?" Linda remarked in disbelief.

"Poor old Halloway didn't get his seven-percent raise," Gold explained. "He could have appealed his supervisor's evaluation, but he was too timid, too afraid to make waves and maybe lose his job, so he brooded in private, swearing his revenge upon the scarlet and turquoise colors that had betrayed him.'' Gold frowned. ''It was all so stupid. So needless . . .''

''Talk about the mouse stampeding the elephant.'' Linda shook her head. ''But why'd he turn himself in?''

''Halloway was becoming increasingly distraught concerning the forged memo. His connection at the *L.A. Gazette* was threatening to leak on the leaker, if you'll pardon the expression.''

''You mean the reporter who ran the story concerning the forged memo was threatening to reveal Halloway's identity in retaliation for Halloway having gotten his newspaper into hot water?''

Gold nodded. ''I've heard that heads are going to roll at the *Gazette* over this.''

''No great loss to journalism,'' Linda sniffed. ''The *Gazette* never should have run that story without bothering to get second-source confirmation concerning the memo.''

''Meanwhile, Otto Lane's in-house GAT investigation was proceeding along,'' Gold continued. ''Halloway figured it was only a matter of time until he was discovered, and that maybe things would go easier on him if he turned himself in to take his punishment.''

''So what happens now? I suppose Otto Lane has turned Halloway over to the police?''

''No . . .'' Gold hesitated. ''Otto waited to get our okay on that, and Don and I have agreed that there's no point.''

''I don't understand,'' Linda said, frowning. ''This man had been a thorn in your side for over two years. Why wouldn't you want to turn Halloway over to the law?''

''What would it accomplish?'' Gold asked. ''I mean, a trial would just stir up a lot of old news that GAT would just as soon leave buried.''

''What about Halloway's punishment?'' Linda cocked her head, examining Gold with those big, beautiful X-ray eyes of hers. ''You feel sorry for him, don't you?''

''Who? Halloway?'' Gold hesitated, and then nodded. ''I guess I do, a little. According to Otto Lane, Halloway's a broken man who wasn't all that emotionally stable to begin with. Sure, at first Halloway thought he was great shakes socking it to us, but as the months wore on, turning to years, his anger vanished and he found himself trapped in a web of his own making. He's suffered a nightmare of guilt, always looking over his shoulder, waiting for retribution.''

''Have you fired him?''

''We're going to let him stay on at GAT,'' Gold replied. ''We'll just steer him away from any security-sensitive projects. From here on in, Virgil 'Icarus' Halloway will likely be one of our most loyal employees.''

Linda looked at Gold with great seriousness. ''You know, there was a time in your life when you would not have been so merciful.''

Gold blushed. ''Ah, your mother wears Air Force boots.''

She nodded slowly. ''Yes. I think I shall take credit for working this change upon you. I've been a good influence.''

''Maybe you've softened me up in my old age,'' Gold smiled.

''I take credit for softening up a *part* of you in old age,'' Linda replied. ''However, I take even greater credit for keeping another part of you *hard* in your old age.''

''Talk is cheap, lady,'' Gold growled.

''Well, then''—Linda smiled languidly—''shall we retire to the boudoir, where I might work some magic upon you?''

''So soon?'' Gold pretended to complain. ''We just had a magic show this morning.''

''Time flies when you're having fun.''

As they were walking into the house, Linda mused, ''So the Icarus case ends with the culprit going scot-free.''

Gold shook his head. ''I never said that.''

(Two)

Sunset Boulevard, Los Angeles
27 June 1978

It was ten-thirty on a sunny Tuesday morning when Turner Layten drove along Sunset Boulevard, past Hollywood High, eventually slowing to nose his Jaguar XKE convertible into the Sunset Burger Barn parking lot. The eatery was built back in the forties as a giant replica of a triple-decker cheeseburger, with windows cut into the bottom half of the bun where the bubble-gum-chewing carhops in their cheerleading skirts and roller skates had once placed and received their customers' orders.

Of course, the carhops were long gone, so that now you had to get out of your car and go up to the windows to fetch your own greasy garbage, Layten thought as he prowled the parking lot in his growling Jaguar, looking for Virgil Halloway's beat-up, orange Volkswagen Karmen Ghia.

But Halloway wasn't here yet. *How irksome for the man to keep me waiting,* Layten thought. Especially since it had been Halloway who had called him, to plead for this meeting, claiming he had something urgent to discuss.

Breakfast was over at the Burger Barn, and the lunch rush had yet to begin, so the lot was fairly empty. Over near the rest rooms there was a dark-blue Ford Econoline van, its side lettered ACE DELIVERY. The van's drivers were drinking coffee and smoking cigarettes; goofing off on their employer's time, Layten thought. The man behind the van's wheel stared at Layten as he drove by. Layten gave the slackard a scowl of disapproval, just to show the fellow that Layten knew what was what.

Other than the van, there were just a couple of nondescript cars: a white Chevy Impala hardtop and a green Ford something or other. Each had a single, youngish man in a tie and jacket inside. Layten guessed they were salesmen, killing time until their next appointments with a cup of coffee and the sports pages.

After Layten had cruised the lot looking for Halloway, he parked in the rear corner of the lot, as far from the other vehicles and the restaurant as he could get. His meeting with Halloway called for privacy, and besides, the grill smells wafting from the Burger Barn's ventilators were disgusting. He shut off his engine and waited. The sun was beating down, and, of course, his white Jag's black leather upholstry just soaked up the heat. *Should have gotten the cream-colored leather,* Layten chided himself.

He was wearing a blue-and-white-striped seersucker suit, pink cotton button-down shirt, and blue paisley bow tie: all from Brooks Brothers, of course. It was just about the coolest outfit a man could wear and still be dressed in a businesslike manner, but in heat like this even if Layten were stripped down to his boxers, he'd still be sweating like a pig. He wished that he could remove his jacket, but a man had to make sacrifices when he carried a gun.

Where the blazes was Halloway? Layten shucked his tan and green houndstooth-check cap to mop his brow. An underling had ought to know better than to keep his superior waiting in this heat. Layten would speak to Halloway about it. Yes, he would lay down the law. That imbecile Halloway could do with a little less of Layten's velvet glove and a dash more of his iron fist.

Ensnaring Halloway a little over two years ago had been pathetically easy, Layten remembered. When Tim Campbell had presented Layten with the task of infiltrating GAT, Layten had asked around among the engineers at the El Segundo Amalgamated-Landis plant if they knew of any GAT engineering people dissatisfied with their careers. He'd told them that A-L was looking to hire some engineering talent, so that if they knew of anybody at GAT who was looking to make a switch, that person should call Layten's office.

Every profession has a grapevine, an informal professional network where job information is exchanged, and so it wasn't long before the calls started coming in. Layten was forced to sit through an interminable number of phony job interviews before a certain individual by the name of Virgil Halloway showed up. Within a few moments of meeting Halloway, Layten knew that he had found his man.

Poor Halloway had come to the El Segundo office thinking he might be offered a job, and so he was, but not one like he'd expected. During the interview, it had been child's play to draw the fellow out. Layten lent a sympathetic ear and soon Halloway was spilling his tawdry little tale of woe concerning how his talents were not being sufficiently appreciated at GAT. Halloway wanted revenge upon GAT for slighting him, and Layten offered to pay the lowly engineer for exacting that revenge, cloaking the endeavor in intrigue to inject a little excitement into Halloway's miserable existence. At first Halloway leapt eagerly to the task, but as the months wore on his anger cooled, as did the draw of the money Layten was paying him. After all, Halloway could not actually spend his ill-gotten gains without drawing attention to himself. GAT, by that point, was trying to sniff out Icarus's identity. Eventually, Halloway came to Layten seeking to end their relationship. Halloway explained that he was no longer angry at GAT, that all he now wanted was to remain working there in peace, that he would no longer spy on the company.

Layten couldn't have that, of course; Tim Campbell would have been *tres* disappointed. Accordingly, Layten had been forced to discipline Halloway, threatening to expose him as Icarus if he didn't continue to do Layten's bidding. Halloway didn't like it much, but he did as he was told. He had no choice if he wanted to save his own hide.

Things came to a head several Mondays ago when the GC-600 jetliner crashed at the Paris Air Show. As soon as Layten had heard about the crash he'd summoned Halloway to this parking lot, where he'd played his trump card. He'd offered Halloway a managerial position at Amalgamated-Landis— fat chance of that ever happening—if the man could come up with some incriminating dirt on GAT in light of the crash. A day later, the ever-gullible Halloway produced his dynamite: a memo from Don Harrison to Steve Gold admitting the GC-600 had dangerous structural flaws.

Tim Campbell was overjoyed when Layten presented him with a copy of the memo. Tim used his influence to pressure the *L. A. Gazette* into immediately running the story, but then it turned out that the memo was a forgery. Tim Campbell was livid over the news, but nobody had been more flabbergasted than Layten himself. He never would have thought a little worm like Halloway could have possessed the audacity to fake the thing.

In retrospect, however, the phony memo had more or less served its purpose, Layten now thought smugly. It had been more salt poured into GAT's wounds.

Layten glanced at his Rolex as Halloway's orange Karmen Ghia clattered its godawful ugly way into the parking lot. Halloway was exactly four and a half minutes late. Yes indeed, the man was going to suffer a severe dressing-down on account of his tardiness.

Layten waited impatiently for Halloway to spot him and drive over, parking next to the Jag. He got out of the Karmen

Ghia, a short, pudgy man in his early forties, poorly dressed in a dark-blue plaid madras sports jacket, ink-stained white shirt and dark tie, and baggy chinos. Halloway had a bulbous nose, thinning gray curly hair, and a wispy beard that did nothing for his appearance and was often littered with stray crumbs of food.

"Thank you for meeting me on such short notice," Halloway said, getting into the passenger side of the Jag.

"You're lucky I didn't leave," Layten said curtly. "You're late."

"I know!" Halloway nodded quickly. "I'm sorry, Mr. Layten! I—I had to make sure I wasn't being followed on my way here."

"Very well," Layten said, mollified by Halloway's meek behavior. "Just don't let it happen again."

Layten turned slightly in the driver's seat, letting his seersucker jacket gap to allow Halloway a peek at the gun on his right hip. Halloway's eyes widened suitably and Layten considered his point well made. Every so often, a dog had to be reminded of who was its master.

"Now, then"—Layten nodded—"what was so urgent?"

"They know about me," Halloway began, clearly overwrought.

"Who?" Layten demanded sharply. "GAT?"

"Yes, sir," Halloway replied. "I went to them, sir—"

"You *went* to them?" Layten exploded. "You pathetic fool!"

"I *had* to, sir," Halloway whined. "They were on to me. It was that damned forged memo!" Halloway's eyes grew wet. "God, I never should have done it! I never should have given it to you!"

"Spilt milk," Layten said coldly. He was disgusted by Halloway's emotional display. Weren't they making men with backbone anymore? "If they've nabbed you, then what are you doing out of jail?"

"They don't want to involve the police," Halloway said, sounding hugely relieved. "The way they see it, the damage I did them is over and done with. They feel a trial would only reopen old wounds."

"I see. . . ." Layten thought about it. Yes, he supposed he would do the same if he were in Steve Gold's and Don

Harrison's place. But now for important matters; Layten forced nonchalance into his tone as he asked, "I suppose you told them about me?"

Halloway seemed surprised by the question. "No!" he declared. "I'd never do that, sir!"

"They didn't ask why you did what you did?" Layten skeptically challenged. "Who put you up to spying on their company?"

"They accepted that I had my own motives for wanting to hurt GAT," Halloway said simply.

Oh, perfect! Layten thought, elated. "Well, then, that's very good, Halloway. I must say, considering the circumstances, you showed great presence of mind to make sure that you weren't being followed here to this meeting with me."

"Thank you, sir!" Halloway gushed. "But now I need your help, Mr. Layten," Halloway blurted. "I protected you! I kept you out of it." He paused, eyeing Layten nervously as he said, "At least I've kept you out of it *so far*."

Layten was vastly amused. "Why, Halloway! Are you trying to blackmail me?"

"No, sir," he said quickly. "It's not anything like that! It's just that they're not done with me. Not by a long shot! They said they've got lots more questions to ask. They're poking around in my life. It's only a matter of time before they find out about my bank account, the one I established to stash the money you paid me. When they find that money they're going to ask me where it came from. What am I going to tell them?"

"I haven't the slightest idea," Layten muttered, disgusted. It looked as if he were going to have to have this fool eliminated. He would speak to Tim Campbell about it. Tim knew the right people for this nasty sort of job.

"I've got every penny of the money you've already paid me to betray GAT," Halloway was saying. "But I need more—say, another fifty thousand—if I'm to go far away where they can't ever find me. If they can't ask me any more questions, then your part in this will never be revealed."

Layten thought about it. He had no intention of paying Halloway the money, but if he *pretended* to agree to pay, and then set up a rendezvous in some deserted spot where

Halloway thought he was going to receive the money, it would make the job of eliminating him much easier. The more Layten considered the idea, the better it seemed. The whole thing could be orchestrated to look like a suicide. Yes, it would be perfectly understandable why a ruined man like Halloway might decide to end his misery by taking his own life.

Layten smiled. He loved things nice and neat.

"Very well, Halloway," Layten said. "I'll give you the money."

"Oh, thank you, sir!"

"There, now," Layten said benevolently. "No need to carry on. Why shouldn't I help you out in your hour of need? You've done good work on mine and Tim's behalf—"

Layten stopped abruptly, angry at himself for letting that last bit about Tim slip out, but then, he'd been preoccupied with his plan to eliminate Halloway. Up until now, he'd kept Tim Campbell's name out of this business; Halloway had no idea Campbell was involved. Layten now watched Halloway closely. Then he relaxed: poor Halloway seemed so emotionally distraught that he'd missed the reference.

"Anyway, Halloway," Layten smoothly continued. "It will be my great pleasure to hasten your exit from the scene."

"Thank you, sir."

"Thank *you*, Halloway. You did the right thing by coming to me. You run along, now."

As Halloway got out of the Jag, Layten distastefully noticed that the chubby engineer had left a sweat imprint on the black leather upholstery. Layten started up the Jag's engine, put the XKE in gear, and rolled out of the parking space. He was heading past the white Chevy, gliding toward the lot exit, when the Impala coughed to life, swung quickly around, and darted forward to lengthwise block Layten's path.

Layten hit the brakes and then pounded his horn, thinking, *Damned L.A. drivers!*

The Chevy's driver got out of the car. Layten stopped honking his horn. The man was in his twenties, and looked pretty brawny beneath his suit jacket. "Shut off your engine, Mr. Layten."

What in blazes? Layten put the Jag into reverse and twisted around in the driver's seat in order to see to back up—

He kept his foot on the Jag's brake. The green Ford had pulled in behind him, blocking his escape.

"Turn off the engine, sir, and give me the keys." The young man from the white Chevy was now standing beside Layten's door, looking down at him. Layten caught a whiff of the young man's after-shave—Canoe, it smelled like—as he leaned in past Layten to turn off the Jag's ignition, then extract and pocket the keys.

"What's going on?" Layten protested, but not all that strongly, because he knew exactly what was going on and felt like kicking himself for not realizing it earlier. He thought about going for his gun, but there were too many of them: The dark-blue Ford Econoline van that had been rolling toward Layten now parked alongside his Jag. The van's two drivers stayed in the cab, but the van's rear doors opened and out of the back popped Steve Gold, followed by two more men whom Layten didn't recognize.

"Hi, Turner," Gold said, coming around the van. "Guess what, your goose is cooked."

Layten gestured toward Holloway, who was walking over to the scene. "He was wired, I suppose?" he asked tiredly.

"Yep," Gold said cheerfully, and pointed to one of the men who'd gotten out of the van with him, a fiftyish, tall fellow, with a steel-gray crew cut and the hard look of an ex-cop. "Turner Layten, meet Otto Lane," Gold said. "Otto's people worked out the technical stuff." Gold winked at Layten. "However, Turner, I *do* want you to know that the setup itself was *my* idea . . ."

"And I was *glad* to do it, you bastard!" Halloway spat at Layten. Halloway tore open his ink-stained shirt to display the tiny mike and the wires taped to his flabby chest. "You pulled the rug out from under my life, and now I'm glad I could return the favor!"

"Would you get out of the car, Mr. Layten?" The young man who had taken the Jag's keys now opened the car's door.

Layten did not want to step out of the car, but he did as he was told. He heard Halloway exclaim, "Be careful, he's carrying a gun!"

"Ah, Turner, still up to your old tricks?" Gold sighed. "Would one of you guys take care of it? I've already had my turn disarming Mr. Layten."

"Otto Lane runs a private security agency," Layten blustered as the young man standing beside him deftly lifted his seersucker coattails in order to pluck the revolver from his hip. "His operatives have no right to deprive me of my personal property or detain me!" He broke into a cold sweat as he looked around at the circle of impassively staring faces. "I—I demand you call the authorities."

"I will if you force me to," Otto Lane threatened.

"I intend to file kidnapping charges against all of you!" Layten thundered.

"And GAT will file industrial-espionage charges against you, Turner," Gold countered. "Think about that. Thanks to this tape, we've got enough on you to convict. It would mean jail, and you wouldn't like jail, old man. For one thing, they'd take away that jaunty little cap you're wearing. Of course, the guys in jail would just *love* you."

Jail, Layten thought. He'd almost gone to jail last time, when they'd tarred and feathered his old CIA boss, Jack Horton. Layten had warned Tim Campbell that it might come to this, but Campbell had refused to listen. Yes, it was Tim's fault this had happened!

Oh, God, jail. Layten could feel himself caving in inside. He knew the kind of men who were in jail. He knew what they would do to him. He'd never survive it. He couldn't abide jail.

Layten's stomach was so severely churning that he was afraid he might vomit. He had to go to the bathroom. He couldn't see: everything was going dark. . . .

"I—I need to sit down," Layten muttered. "I'm feeling faint."

"Yeah, you are looking a little peaked, Turner," Gold remarked. "Go on, sit down right there on the ground."

Layten sagged to his knees, hanging his head. He'd broken out into a cold sweat and his teeth were chattering. He glimpsed Halloway snickering at him, and saw that Gold and Otto Lane were exchanging knowing glances. It didn't matter. Nothing mattered anymore, especially not his hatred of Steve Gold. All that mattered was saving himself.

"Listen, Steve," Layten whispered hopefully. "It's not me you want. Maybe we can make a deal?"

(Three)

**Campbell Residence
Beverly Hills, Los Angeles
28 June, 1978**

"Steve Gold to see Mr. Campbell."

"Yes, sir." The armed, uniformed guard manning the entrance to Campbell's sixteen-acre estate worked the controls that opened the electrically operated wrought-iron gates. "Mr. Campbell is expecting you. He asks that you join him in the greenhouse. When you reach the main house, just continue on to your left along the drive. The greenhouse will be brightly lit. You can't miss it."

Gold flicked on the Corvette's high beams as the guard waved him through the gates. It was almost eleven P.M. on a cloudy night, and black as pitch. *Almost as black as my mood*, Gold thought. He steeled himself; he had to go through with this. He let the 'Vette creep forward, carrying him into the lion's den.

The crushed-gravel drive curled like some immense serpent through the lushly landscaped grounds, but finally Gold rounded the final bend and caught his first view of the flood lit house, a vast jumble of gray limestone studded with turrets and terraces. When Campbell had built this monstrosity back in the forties, he'd probably intended something majestic, but what he'd ended up with was Dracula's castle hemmed in by palm trees.

"*Sixty rooms*," a mutual acquaintance had once told Steve Gold in describing Campbell's house. "*Yes, sixty, and just him there, alone with his servants. There are entire wings that haven't seen a living soul for years. He won't let the servants dust. Says he likes the cobwebs, that the spiders are his kindred souls. Corridors filled with crates of antiques, paintings, furniture that he purchased who knows when and then never bothered to unpack.*"

Gold drove slowly around the mansion, until he spotted the long, low, glass greenhouse, a brightly lit oasis of jungle that resembled an immense, glowing emerald surrounded by the black velvet of the night. Gold parked by the greenhouse door and got out of his car.

He was almost bowled over by the heat and humidity as he entered the greenhouse. Within seconds his jeans and cotton polo shirt were soaked through with sweat and clinging to his skin. The greenhouse was lit by long, fluorescent tubes casting that pinkish sort of light plants were supposed to favor. The floor was damp gravel, with lots of drains. There was a small cleared area right by the door furnished with a glass patio table and two canvas deck chairs. The rest of the space leading into the greenhouse was filled with rows of long tables packed with an unending assortment of plants. More plants overflowed the shelving built against the greenhouse's glass walls and hung from the roof rafters, and tall palms in huge wooden troughs weaved their canopy over everything, so that like in a real jungle, you couldn't see more than a few feet into the mass of foliage.

"Tim?" he called, peering around. "Hello?"

"Hello, Steven," Tim Campbell said, stepping out from behind a bushy potted something or other just a few feet away.

Gold had to smile. He hadn't seen Campbell for years, not since the two had crossed swords over that Pont jetliner situation. Now Gold thought that for a man approaching eighty, Campbell looked good. Tim was barefoot, clad in a white-and-blue-striped, short-sleeved boatneck pullover and white duck trousers. His thick gray hair was poking our from under a straw sombrero. Campbell looked like one of those old codgers you see beachcombing in Malibu, the ones who looked like they've been carved from driftwood, and are just as ancient and just as indestructible.

Campbell was looking spry, chipper; like a kindly old granddad, Gold mused, feeling guilty over the purpose of this visit. This was, after all, good old Uncle Tim.

Like hell.

Gold reminded himself that it was the prettiest mushroom in the forest that would kill you quickest if you took a bite. *Get your mind right,* he ordered himself. *Or this kindly old granddad will eat you alive and pick his teeth with your bones.*

"Thank you for seeing me on such short notice," Gold began. "I know it's late."

"Nah, no problem." Campbell shrugged. "I don't sleep much anymore. Here"—he gestured toward the table and chairs—"let's sit down."

"Thank you." As Gold sat, he thought he glimpsed movement in the foliage at eye level behind Campbell, but he dismissed it as his imagination.

"I had this furniture moved in special for you when you called earlier this evening asking to see me," Campbell said. "I usually hang out back there." He gestured over his shoulder toward the greenhouse's interior. "But it can get a little close. Most people don't like it."

"Yeah, I can imagine." Gold took a seat. He was dying for a cigarette, but didn't think it was appropriate to jeopardize the well-being of all these exotic plants with cigarette smoke. "The reason I called you . . ."

He stopped, his attention again distracted by a twitching leaf, and then his eyes widened as he saw a smallish, bright-blue snake with coral markings slither out of the wall of green flora to drape itself over a branch.

"Tim?" Gold was pointing a wavering finger at the snake when he heard more rustling and saw a brown tortoise the size of a basketball waddling along between two large clay pots. Above his head something flapped on leathery wings between the palm fronds, too fast for him to discern.

"They like you," Campbell remarked. "Usually, they hide when strangers are near."

Gold was about to bolt when he was frozen in his chair by a close-by, prolonged, hissing sound, like steam being vented. He looked wildly around, and then he saw it coming toward him out of the foliage: an emerald-green lizard the size of a basset hound was spitting at him as it sent the gravel flying with its thrashing, yard-long whip of a tail.

"What the fuck is that?" Gold's voice wavered. His eyes were glued to the lizard as it imperiously stalked into the cleared area in order to settle beneath Campbell's chair.

"This here's my attack dragon," Campbell said.

"Goddammit, Tim!" Gold started to rise out of his chair.

"Nah. Calm down." Campbell chuckled. "I'm just busting your chops. Don't be afraid of Bayou."

" 'Bayou' as in swamps?" Gold asked, relaxing a little. The lizard seemed not to be paying him much attention.

"Nah. Bayou as in 'Iguana-be-loved-*by-you*.' "

"It's an iguana?"

"Yep, and while he looks mean as hell, iceberg lettuce is Bayou's favorite dish. He's an even-tempered lizard." Campbell paused, glancing at Gold's feet. "However, some things do tick Bayou off. Those aren't alligator shoes, by any chance?"

"Any more creepy-crawlies around?" Gold demanded.

"Oh, sure." Campbell nodded. "Lots of them. Lots and lots. I love reptiles. They're my favorite animals. I don't give a shit about plants. Only keep all this crapola around to keep my little babies happy."

"Jesus, Tim." Gold scowled, his eyes searching the greenhouse. "Can't we have this conversation somewhere else?"

"Hey, like I told you: not to worry. I put away all my *dangerous* pets when I knew you were coming." Campbell paused, scratching his jaw. "At least, I think I did. . . ."

Gold finally had to laugh. "You're still one crazy son of a bitch."

"The craziest," Campbell agreed. "Now, what do you think you have to tell me?"

Gold began with the story of how Icarus had turned himself in on Saturday, and then continued by telling Campbell about yesterday's sting operation that had nabbed Turner Layten. "Otto Lane has been holding Layten incommunicado," Gold finished, feeling a bit flustered by the way Campbell had so impassively taken the news of his chief henchman's downfall. "We're still interviewing Layten," Gold added meaningfully, looking for some reaction—any reaction—from Campbell. "That's why you haven't heard from Layten."

"And I guess I *won't* be hearing from him," Campbell said "Not now that Layten's going to be prom queen in some federal prison. Let me know his mailing address. I'll send him some Vaseline, he's going to need it."

"He's not going to prison," Gold said.

"Oh?" Campbell nodded. "How kind of you to let him off the hook. Your father is likely smiling in heaven over your good deed." He paused. "Well? Is that it, now? Are we done? 'Cause if we are, I got some white rats waiting to walk the last mile to becoming the blue plate special for a twenty-foot boa constrictor I caged up in your honor."

"No, we're *not* done," Gold said, growing angry. "Layten isn't going to jail because he's cooperating in our investigation. He implicated you, Tim. We've got you on industrial espionage."

"You've got nothing," Campbell said flatly. "Layten can spill his guts all he wants. No doubt he already has. I'm denying I had anything to do with this industrial-espionage shit. Okay?" He grinned. "I'll even repeat it louder, in case *you're* wired, Stevarino."

"I'm not," Gold said. "You want to frisk me?"

"Nah, I believe you, son," Campbell said. "Anyway, the way you're sweating like a pig, there, if you was wired, the do-hickey would have shorted out by now. But getting back to what I was saying, Layten can sing all he wants. He's got no proof to back up his allegations, 'cause I'm real careful about never leaving around any proof of my less savory dealings. Sure I set up this Icarus scheme against you, and I enjoyed every moment of it while it lasted, but you're out of your mind if you think you can convict me in court pitting Layten's word against mine."

"Actually, I never really thought I could pin industrial-espionage charges on you," Gold admitted. "I've always known you put lots of buffers between yourself and your illegal activities."

"You bet your ass I got buffers," Campbell declared. "I put so much distance between myself and my dirty work, my cock's got to call me long-distance to tell me to take a piss."

Gold smiled. "I can't get you on industrial espionage. But how about insider trading?"

"What?" Campbell eyed Gold the way Gold had earlier eyed the iguana. "You sure the heat in here ain't getting to you, Stevie? You're starting to babble."

"You bought shares of GAT when the price went down due to the GC-600 crash, right?"

"Yeah, sure I did, but so what?" Campbell asked. "That just proves I'm an astute investor."

"Here's how it's going down," Gold said, leaning forward to tick off the points to Campbell. "GAT's legal representatives have contacted the Security and Exchange Commission to make the case that we have witnesses—Halloway and Layten—who will testify that you orchestrated the campagn of industrial espionage against us, including the forged memo that depressed the price of GAT stock, and then you bought GAT on the cheap, confident the price would soon rise, because you had insider knowledge that the memo would prove phony.''

"It's your *case* that's phony!" Campbell laughed. "It's fucking ironic that out of everything I've ever done, you try to hang me on the one thing I *didn't* do! I had no idea that memo was forged!"

"I know that, Tim, but then, that's only the truth, so who gives a flying fuck about it? Halloway and Layten will testify that it was *you* who fabricated the memo. They'll do this for GAT in exchange for us not pressing charges against them.''

"Steve, you're not listening," Campbell admonished. "I bought heavy into GAT when the price was low, because I thought that maybe I could orchestrate a proxy battle against you at the next stockholders' meeting. I didn't want to profit from the purchases. What the hell do I need with more money?''

"It doesn't matter Tim." Gold shrugged. "We've made a credible allegation against you on insider trading, and because of that the SEC will be all over your business dealings.''

"It'll never happen." Campbell scowled. "All you got is circumstantial evidence backed up by the testimony of a couple of lightweights.''

"It's already happening. It started today.''

"Bullshit!" Campbell looked contemptuous, but worried. "I'll call in every favor owed me to block this.''

Gold smiling apologetically. "Well, I've *already* called in a few favors owed GAT. That's how I managed to get a green light on at least a preliminary investigation into your financial dealings, but then, that's all it'll take, won't it, Tim? I mean, in this sort of matter one thing leads to another, right? An SEC investigator poking around here discovering this, and another one there uncovering that, and pretty soon your entire, nasty house of cards built over a lifetime of double-dealing will come crashing down on you. I don't think they'll put you in jail. Not a man your age, but they'll take it all away from you, Tim. You won't have your wealth and power anymore. You'll just be a harmless old man.''

I've done it, Gold thought as he watched Campbell's response to his harangue. At first Campbell had looked disdainful. Then angry. Then appalled. Finally, much to Gold's satisfaction, Tim Campbell looked scared.

"Steve, listen. You don't have to do this. You know why? Because we're already even! Okay, maybe I put a little dent into GAT, but I can make it up to you. Name your price."

"My price is your head on an SEC platter," Gold said calmly.

"I meant money!" Campbell snarled. "Name your price in money, goddamn you."

"What you took from GAT money can't buy back," Gold told him. "You're responsible for Icarus. If Icarus hadn't muddied the waters with that memo, GAT might have relatively easily put behind it the GC-600 crash. As it is, thanks to Icarus—thanks to *you*, Tim—all the old speculation has been revived about the solidity of the company and the stability of its management, namely, Don Harrison and myself." Gold paused. "But it's more than just this one incident, Tim. Whenever something bad happens to GAT, you turn out to be behind it. That has got to end, and it's going to end. Now."

"No more bullshit, Steve." Campbell pointed his gnarled finger at Gold. "The bottom line is that this insider-trading thing you've cooked up could ruin me. You're right, son. There's shady business dealings I'm involved in that have nothing to do with GAT. Because of that, I can't afford to have them SEC sons of bitches crawling up my asshole with flashlights."

Gold stood up. "Sorry, Tim."

"Wait!" Campbell was frantic. "There must be something I can do? Steve?" He forced a hideous, crocodile smile. This is your ole uncle Tim talking! What can I do to make you change your mind about pursuing this?"

"Nothing, Tim." Gold smiled. "There's finally nothing you can do. Isn't that a pisser?" He watched the iguana crawl slowly out from beneath Campbell's chair.

Campbell said, "Your father wouldn't do this. You know that, son? Herman Gold wouldn't take it this far."

"I do know that." Gold took a few tentative steps toward the big iguana, which stood its ground, watching his approach with beady, expressionless eyes.

"I was wrong about you, Steve," Campbell murmured, almost to himself. "I thought you were weaker than your father, but I was wrong."

Gold reached out to gently tilt up Campbell's chin in order to look him in the eyes. "Yes, Uncle Tim, you were wrong."

Gold then bent to stroke the iguana's head. At his light touch the lizard closed its eyes, tilting its broad snout up into his palm. Gold had expected the thing to feel slimy. He was surprised to find the creature's textured green hide was pleasantly dry.

Gold left the greenhouse thinking that the creepy-crawlies weren't scary if you knew how to handle them.

(Four)

After Steve left, Tim Campbell spent the rest of the night in the greenhouse, tending to his pets. At four in the morning, he went to the telephone mounted on the wall near the sinks and dialed the estate's garage, where the telephone rang quite a few times before the sleepy-voiced attendant picked up.

"Whozit?"

"This is Mr. Campbell."

On the other end of the line, there was a shocked intake of breath. "Yes, sir! Mr. Campbell! This is Pablo, sir!"

Campbell didn't have the slightest idea who Pablo was. The estate's majordomo handled all the personnel bullshit. "Yeah, listen here, pal. I want a car."

"Yes, sir! I'll wake the chauffeur, sir."

"I don't want any of the limos. I want a car *I* can drive. Tell me what I've got lying around these days, pal."

"Well, sir, there's the pair of Rolls', the Bentley . . ."

"Something sportier," Campbell decreed.

"Yes, sir. Well, the Jag is having some electrical problems. But there's the Ferrari, the Lamborghini—"

"Oh, yeah!" Campbell exclaimed. "The Lamborghini. I forgot about that one. Let's see, that'd be a 'sixty-four, 350 GT. Red, I seem to remember. It can do 150 miles per hour thanks to its 270-horsepower V-12 engine."

"Gee, Mr. Campbell, you know your cars," the attendant said, sounding surprised and impressed.

"Nah. I don't know shit about cars, but I know value, pal. That there little Italian cherry of mine is worth plenty because it's in original, mint condition, and Lamborghini only built thirteen of 'em, in the first place. It's one of a kind." Campbell snickered. "Just like me."

"Yes, sir . . ."

"You gas her up, or whatever needs to be done. I'll be around to collect her in ten minutes."

The red Lamborghini two-seater sports coupe had a light-tan leather interior, a five-speed transmission, and enough dials, gauges, rocker switches, and toggles to outfit a fighter-plane cockpit. Campbell had the garage attendant show him how to work the important stuff, and then he got in the car and drove off amidst much gear-gnashing, leaving his estate and heading toward the coast.

The Lamborghini's shifter remained balky, and Campbell was a little rusty because he hadn't driven a car in years, but there wasn't much traffic to contend with at this ungodly hour of the morning. Once Campbell reached the Pacific coast highway heading south, he was able to put the Lamborghini in fifth gear and leave her there, averaging a hundred miles an hour.

It was fun driving through the night with the windows rolled down and the wind carrying the salty tang of the sea whipping around inside the little hardtop's cabin. The wind's roar melded with the V-12's steady tiger's purr, filling Campbell's ears, lulling him, so that he was able to silence the turmoil in his mind as he concentrated on his high-speed driving.

About the time the sky had started to lighten, Campbell had slowed down, flipping on his high beams as he looked for the turnoff he remembered that led to the breathtaking view of the ocean. A lifetime ago, a bank junior loan officer named Tim Campbell and his new bride, an ex-waitress named Agatha, would often pile into their beat-up old Plymouth coupe to make this drive and spend a lovely few hours staring out at the Pacific with their arms around one another, dreaming about the future.

Campbell spotted the little sign that read "Scenic Overlook," and turned onto the steeply inclined road, dropping the Lamborghini into low gear as the GT fishtailed on the loosely packed graveled surface. Campbell took it slow, not wanting to end up in a ditch as he followed the twisting, climbing, two-lane road. An early-morning fog had set in, creating swirling wraiths around the dark tree trunks that lined both sides of the high-banked trail.

Ghosts, Campbell thought, smiling to himself, wondering if Aggie was out there tonight, or maybe Herman Gold's ghost was flitting among the trees, keeping a spirit's pace with the red GT, laughing.

The road ended at a large, fan-shaped parking area with white wooden guardrails. It was still too dark to see the pounding ocean, but Campbell remembered that hundreds of feet below those rails the thunderous sea was enternally breaking itself apart against glistening rocks.

Campbell eased the Lamborghini into the parking area and stopped with the GT's nose up against the rails. He took the car out of gear but left the engine running: for one thing, he was afraid he might not be able to restart it if he shut it off; for another, he enjoyed the powerful sound of its guttural warbling playing counterpoint to the cymbal crash of the sea.

As Campbell waited for the sun to rise above the cliffs behind him, he finally let himself think about his earlier confrontation with Steve Gold. The kid had him by the balls, there was no doubt about it. Sure, Campbell could fight the SEC investigation that Steve had hung over his head like the sword of Damocles. Hell, with the kind of legal clout he wielded, Campbell could likely tie up any power on earth in years of costly litigation if he had a mind to, but what the fuck kind of golden years was that for him to look forward to? There would be endless court appearances to endure, and hundreds of government accountants infesting his offices like parasitic vermin. His business associates would treat him like a leper, and rightly so. Campbell would be unable to wheel and deal with an SEC cloud hanging over him, and negotiating a deal was the only real pleasure left in his life. Steve had been right: he would end up a pitiful old man.

The oddest thing about it all, however, was that Campbell was not all that pissed with Steve for what the kid had done to him. No, in a funny way, Campbell was proud of Steve Gold.

"Herman," Campbell told the tall, fog-shrouded figure he saw leaning against the guardrails. "Your kid did good. Your company will prosper, and just like always, you've got your old partner Tim Campbell to thank for that. I taught your boy what you never could: how to be ruthless. Steve was your son, but he's my protégé."

Below Campbell, the black sea applauded against the rocks. Above him in the leaden sky the first seabirds of the day were laughing joyously in celebration of the coming dawn. The Lamborghini was trembling impatiently, like some great beast waiting to be freed.

"Herman, the feud is over," Campbell said. "It turned out we've been partners all this time despite our own worst intentions. Together we made your boy. Together we've launched GAT toward its future."

Campbell thought the figure glimmering in the fog raised a hand in salutation, but perhaps it was just a tendril of mist swirling in the rising sea breeze.

Anyway, the fog was dissipating with the arrival of the new day. The blood-red sun was peeking above the high cliffs behind Campbell, brightening the interior of the little red sports car. Campbell watched the sea come alive in luminous shades of green and blue that stretched endlessly to a pink and orange horizon.

"Time to go," Campbell said.

He struggled to put the Lamborghini into reverse, and then backed away from the guardrails about one hundred feet, until the GT's rear tires were on the roadway.

Time to go.

Campbell threw the Lamborghini into first gear and stomped the accelerator. The GT's rear tires spun, then bit into the gravel, and the powerful sports car rocketed forward, pressing Campbell back against his seat as it splintered the guardrails. Campbell cried out as the car leapt into empty space, hanging in the sun for an instant before plunging toward the sea. His head slammed the windshield and he blacked out.

Campbell's last thoughts were that he'd lived to be older than Herman Gold.

Ha-ha.

And that he who dies with the most toys wins.

(Five)

**GAT
Burbank
29 June, 1978**

It was around noon on Thursday. Steve Gold was in Don Harrison's office, filling Don in on his meeting with Tim Campbell late last night, when Don's telephone rang

"Yes?" Don said, picking up the receiver. He listened a moment and then told Gold, "It's Susan. I won't be a minute. Yes, honey. What's up?"

Gold watched Don's face turn white as Harrison listened to whatever it was that his wife had to tell him. "Yeah, thanks for calling, honey. Yeah, your brother's with me now. I'll tell him. Bye."

"What's happened now?" Gold asked as Don hung up.

"Susan had been watching the midday television news. They announced that Tim Campbell's dead. It seems his car went off a cliff."

Viking funeral, Gold thought. *Good for you, Uncle Tim, you old bastard.* "I guess it won't be necessary for you to make those calls. That investigation I threatened him with won't have to proceed after all."

Don nodded. "That's if I could have pulled the strings to get it going in the first place. That was quite a bluff you pulled. I'm surprised you didn't talk it over with me before you took it upon yourself to go see Campbell."

"I wanted to spare you, partner," Gold said lightly. "It wasn't your fight. It's *me* who Campbell's stooge Turner Layten hates, and it was *my* father who Campbell thought had wronged him."

"Excuse me," Don said, sounding peeved. "But this was GAT's fight, not your own."

"I stand corrected," Gold said dryly. "I promise that next time I get my hands bloody I'll make sure you're right there beside me so you can get equally splattered. Satisfied?"

"Your hands *are* bloody, you know," Don said softly. "I think we need to talk about this a little. Is that okay?"

Gold took a deep breath and let it out slowly. "Okay. We can talk about this a little bit."

"You weren't the least bit surprised to hear that Campbell had killed himself?" Don began.

"I knew that Campbell would never stand for the indignity of a government investigation." Gold nodded. "I knew that just the possibility of the SEC poking around in his doings would scare the shit out of him. I'm not saying that I knew for a fact that Campbell would kill himself. He had other alternatives once he'd bought my bluff. He might have taken as much of his dough as he could and gone to ground in some foreign country where U.S. law couldn't touch him. . . ." Gold trailed off. "But then, keeping a low profile was never Tim Campbell's style."

"So you drove him to suicide."

"I prefer to think of it as having protected GAT by removing the only enemy we had who could possibly have brought us down."

Don hesitated. "Do you think your father would have approved your actions?"

Gold sighed. "Tim asked me the same thing last night when I managed to convince him that I'd set the SEC hounds on his heels." He shook his head. "No, Pop wouldn't have approved of any of this. But Pop was a fighter pilot. He understood that war is about survival. I think that he would have wanted GAT to survive, whatever the cost." He smiled wryly. "And in a funny way, I think *Tim* would have approved of my actions against him. He lived by the law of the jungle."

"Last question," Don said. "Does Linda know about any of this?"

"No," Gold said quickly. "And I'd rather she never knew. I'm not proud of what I've done, you understand? I mean, I did it for us. All of us. The family, but—"

Don cut him off, saying, "I know why you did it. It's

one of the reasons that I have come to love you like a brother.''

Gold smiled, pleased to see that Don's mood had lightened. He would do his own mourning—for Tim Campbell, for himself—in private. "A guy can always use a brother.''

CHAPTER 18

(One)

Ryder AFB, Nevada
30 June, 1978

Lieutenant Andy Harrison had trouble sleeping the night before the last day of Red Sky. During the previous four days of the war-game exercise, Andy had accumulated seven air-combat kills, making him a leading contender for winning the Warlord trophy. Trouble was, there were a number of fighter jocks with comparable tallies, so the ultimate winner would be decided during today's ACM. Whoever was going to come away with the Warlord trophy was both figuratively and literally still up in the air.

At 0400 hours, Andy gave up on sleep. He rolled out of bed and quietly made his way to the trailer's bathroom to get first dibs on the shower. His unease about this last day of Red Sky activity was compounded by the fact that throughout the war games he had yet to run into his half brother.

For the past four days Andy had been searching the sky with a mix of anticipation and dread for Robbie Greene's flat-black F-5E, but the lead Attacker simply had not appeared. As a matter of fact, Andy hadn't seen Robbie since they'd had it out behind the ice-cream parlor a couple of weeks ago.

At first Andy had found Robbie's phantom-like disappearance during Red Sky to be both aggravating and unnerving. It was just like his condescendingly superior older half brother to be still calling the shots and controlling the situation. What was Robbie waiting for? Why couldn't they get the fight on and get it over with?

It was Gail Saunders who'd straightened Andy out, telling him that he was nuts to be psyching himself out like this. Gail had pointed out to Andy that the Ryder combat ranges covered a vast area, and that there was a lot going on simultaneously. Meanwhile, the Attackers' F-5Es had minimal fuel capacity, which meant they could hang out above the designated targets looking for a fight for only about twenty minutes or so at a time before needing to return to base for refueling. (The Air Force's F-5E's were not equipped for aerial fill-ups from the orbiting tankers.) Gail had gone on to make the point that if Andy took all this into account, he would see that it was merely due to chance that he and Robbie had not run into each other.

Or maybe it's been my good fortune, Andy now mused as he stepped into the shower, letting the spray wash away the night's cobwebs, if not the night's lingering fears. Andy couldn't forget how slick Robbie had been during their first dogfight. *No way am I going to win the Warlord trophy today if I end up being shot down by Ryder's resident gunslinger.*

By 0600 hours, Andy's roomies were up and the radio was on, the trailer rocking to Mick Jagger and the Rolling Stones singing "Under My Thumb." Everyone was dressed in their flight suits and sipping coffee as they waited for the shuttle bus to come around to haul them over to the mess. Once there, Andy forced himself to choke down some breakfast. It was going to be one hell of a long Friday.

From the mess the hundreds of Red Sky participants walked over to the Tactical Air Combat Center for the mass briefing. By 0700 hours, the auditorium was filled and the mass briefing for today's war scenario was set to begin.

The operations commander appeared on stage, and the big AV screen came down to show news footage documenting the ferment in Nicaragua, where Somoza was trying to hang on against the Commie rebels. It was just a little background color to set the tone for today's fictional scenario meant to stimulate a possible situation at some hot spot somewhere on the globe.

"Good morning, gentlemen," began the operations commander from behind his lectern. "The newly installed Marxist government of the Central American nation of Palahorra has defied our Blue government's warnings, allowing the Red Empire to supply it with MiGs and Russian ground-attack helicopters. Clearly, Palahorra means to export its ideological revolution to its neighbors, and just as clearly, Blue Land will not stand for that. The President has ordered a preemptive strike."

The newsreel footage ended. Now the giant screen displayed a series of maps of the various Ryder ranges marked to show the areas of enemy-force concentrations.

"Intelligence reports that Palahorra has been anticipating today's military action," the operations commander continued. "Red defenses will be on full alert, with greatest concentrations of enemy ground forces as depicted on these maps. Red air will enjoy superiority over Fox Range sector 3, the location of Fidel Airfield and Nikita Helipad. Blue Air will stage several air strikes at major Red targets simultaneously with our main strike against the airfield and helipad facility in order to divert enemy defenses. For further info on secondary likely active SAM and AAA sites and specific mission responsibilities, refer to the intelligence summaries you'll receive during your individual flight briefings, but here's the general rundown for the day's strikes: Mission Package 5-A: Eagle Range sector 2, SAM site and truck convoy. Mission Package 5-B: Lion Range sector 4, AAA site and Karl Marx Railroad Yard. Mission Package 5-C: Miami Range sector 1, SAM site and Lenin Fuel Depot. Mission Package 5-D: Conway Range sector 9, SAM/AAA sites and Tolstoy Industrial Complex. Mission Package 5-E: Dragon Range sector 3, tank convoy. Mission Package 5-F . . ."

Andy tensed. 5-F included his squadron flight.

". . . Mission Package 5-F: Fox Range sector 3, SAM/AAA

sites, tank defenses, Fidel Airfield and Nikita Helipad Complex. Mission Package F-G . . .''

Yes! Andy exulted. His Stiletto flight would be flying MiGCap straight into the heart of the enemy, which meant that he'd have ample opportunity to raise his kill score.

And maybe have his long-awaited run-in with a certain flat-black F-5E, for one final chance to prove who was the fiercest tiger in the sky.

Up on the stage, the operations commander was reading off the mission packages for the Airborn Warning, RESCAP and aerial refueling personnel. Andy tried to concentrate, but he couldn't keep himself from daydreaming about the possible coming battle between himself and Robbie Greene. Finally, the ops commander turned the lectern over to a succession of support staff—weather, intelligence and weapons officers—who lectured on their specific areas of expertise. The first couple of rows of fighter jocks in the auditorium perked up when it was the weapons officer's turn to speak.

''Supply still reports negative supply of Sparrow air-to-air missiles,'' the weapons officer announced. ''Accordingly, we will again be flying without them.''

There were assorted groans from some of the fighter pilots, but Andy just grinned. A lot of the high kill scores racked up during the beginning part of the week had resulted from overuse of the Sparrow. A Blue pilot flying an advanced F-15 Eagle, F-4 Phantom, or F-66 Stiletto could get a radar lock on an Attacker and call a ''Fox One'' simulated Sparrow shot to score an easy kill before he'd even seen the enemy, but the pilot who depended on long-range Sparrows to score wasn't getting much practice in ACM, which was the whole point of Red Sky. On Wednesday, Operations had countered certain pilots' over-reliance on Sparrows by decreeing that Blue Airfield ordnance supply had run out of the long-range hummers. Now it appeared that the shortage would persist through this last day. Andy was glad of that because it increased his chances of winning the Warlord trophy. Throughout this exercise, he'd prided himself on not calling Sparrow shots. He'd *wanted* the Attackers to get into the fight, to give him a real run for his money, so that he could learn as much as he could. All seven of his kills had been made at relatively close range with Sidewinder heat-seekers, or eyeball-to-eyeball with guns.

On the downside, Andy's decision to pick knife fights with the Attackers had caused him to be shot down a number of times, which had handicapped him in his pursuit of the Warlord trophy. When the radio call came that you'd been shot down, you had to take yourself out of the battle by flying to a specified regeneration point before you could resume participation in the exercise. This made being shot down a real bummer, one you wanted to avoid almost as much as you would in a real war, because in addition to the heckling you had to take during each evening's debriefing, the flight to and from the regeneration point cost you time that might have been spent in combat, which lessened your own opportunity to score more kills, further lengthening the odds against you winning the Warlord trophy.

On the other hand, the repeated dogfights into which Andy had thrust himself had made him a lot better pilot then he'd been two weeks ago, when Robbie had waxed him. That was why Andy was so eager to get another shot at his half brother. He was reasonably confident that this time, if luck was with him, he could take the bastard.

The mass briefing broke up at 0800 hours, and the personnel filed out of the auditorium and down the corridor to the classrooms used for the individual flight briefings. During the next hour Andy found out that his flight of four Stilettos had been assigned the call sign "Pinto" and would be commanded by Captain Marty Beckman. Beckman was a compact, swarthy man who talked fast and flew faster. On the ground he was a bundle of nerves, but in the air during ACM he was as cold-bloodedly patient as a spider waiting for a fly to hit its web. Beckman went over the specifics of Pinto flight's mission, which was to fly MiGCAP for the A-7 Corsair Mud Movers and A-10 Warthogs that would be attacking the enemy's airfield and helipad.

At 0900 hours, Andy and his fellow pilots moved on to the visiting players' personal equipment room, where he stowed his personal belongings in a locker and shrugged on his flight gear. It was when he was grabbing his helmet that he noticed the folded sheet of paper taped to the visor. He removed the handwritten note and read:

Andrew

Here it is, last day. Final-exam time. I hear you think you've learned a thing or two, but blood will tell, half brother. I'll be waiting for you above Nikita Helipad. I know you've been assigned that sector to patrol today. Have you got the balls to confront me? Or has the best man already won? I still say you're only half the pilot I am, and you know why.

R.

"Damn you, Robbie," Andy murmured as he crumpled the note.

"Problem, Harrison?" Beckman asked, turning around.

"No, sir." Andy said evenly, stuffing the note into his pocket. "No problem at all."

It was 0930 hours when the shuttle bus deposited Andy and his flight mates at their parked aircraft glittering in the desert sun. The concrete ramp was bustling with maintenance carts and planes taxiing into takeoff position, but Andy knew it would be a few minutes at least before his flight would be going anywhere. A whole lot of planes had to get into the air at the start of each morning's Red Sky exercise, which made for one hell of a traffic jam out on Ryder's spaghetti tangle of runways.

Andy looked around for Gail, and saw her directing her crew over on the ramp sidelines. She was dressed in baggy overalls and had her hair tucked up beneath a cap, but Andy, looking at her, saw in his mind's eye her nude, supple form tucked beneath him while making love.

They'd spent their every spare moment together these past four weeks, and now Andy couldn't remember what his life had been like before he'd met Gail. He sure didn't want to think about what his life was going to be like without her, but that time was fast approaching. The Red Sky closing ceremonies, including the awarding of the Warlord trophy, were scheduled for Sunday. On Monday, Andy's squadron would be starting back to Howard AFB in Panama.

"Hi, there." Gail grinned as Andy came over to her. "You all psyched for the big day?"

"I was." He took the note out of his pocket and handed it to her.

Gail read it quickly. "You know this is just bluster."

"I doubt it." Andy tried to tamp down the despair he was feeling. "Robbie won't lose today. He'll *never* lose, because he's always going to hold all of the cards."

"You're wrong!" Gail argued. "You can't let yourself think that way!"

"Don't you see?" Andy muttered. "I was right. Robbie has purposely stayed away from me all this week. He *wanted* to let me build myself up, all the better so he could knock me down!"

"So what?" Gail demanded. "Assuming all that's true, what difference does it make?"

"Come on!" Andy said impatiently. "Don't you see he's been playing a game of cat and mouse with me just the way he did in the air that first time? It says right there in his note that he knew all along I was going to be assigned to this mission package today."

Gail put her hands on her hips and stepped in close to Andy, jutting up her chin to stick her face into his, like a drill sergeant instead of an AGS sarge. "Of course he knew your assignment. As CO of the Attackers, Robbie participates in personnel scenario assignments. But I still want to know what damn difference it makes. You can't let Robbie Greene playing his mind-fuck games rob you of your confidence. If you let that happen, then Robbie won't have beaten you in the sky today. You'll have beaten *yourself!*"

Andy studied her. "You really think I can do it? That I can beat Robbie?"

"It's not going to happen just because I believe in you," Gail told him, smiling now. "You need to believe in yourself, and the way to start is to forget that he's your half brother Robbie. Just see him as Major Greene, just another Attacker pilot."

Andy looked toward the ramp where the other pilots had climbed into their fighters and lowered their canopies. Only Andy's jet remained empty, its canopy upraised as if summoning him.

"Get going." Gail smiled. "I'll be here when you get back."

Andy blurted, "I love you! I mean, I realize we've only known each other a short time, but—"

Gail, her green eyes shining, put her fingers to his lips, reiterating, "Get going. And know that wherever you go, however long it takes, I'll be here when you get back."

A half hour later, the 5-F mission-package strike force was at twenty-five thousand feet, two minutes from their target. Andy Harrison's ghost-gray Stiletto was part of the four-ship, MiGCAP Pinto flight cruising at high altitude on the lookout for enemy fighters.

Andy could see the entire mission-package armada of airplanes spread out around him. Up ahead were the F-4 Phantom Wild Weasels flying advance guard to pinpoint SAM sites with their radar. Directly beneath Pinto flight, outlined against the dark-brown desert terrain, were three chevrons of silver A-7 Corsairs loaded down with live ordnance. Flying closest to the ground, at about 15,000 feet, were a layer of six olive-drab, A-10 Thunderbolt Warthogs, the tank killers.

The brief flight from Ryder to Fox Range had passed quickly. Now Andy's helmet came alive with radio transmissions as the strike force crossed into the target sector.

"Pinto flight, Pinto lead!" flight leader Captain Beckman radioed. "Heads up! We've got SAM activity!"

Up ahead, Andy saw the smoky white trails of the simulated SAMs scratching their way into the azure sky, and then the lit-up, bright-orange tail pipes of the F-4 Wild Weasel SAM killers as they dipped toward their burrowed prey in order to make sure that SAM's first shot became his last. Andy anxiously looked around for more SAMs that might have been playing possum when the F-4s flew by in order to get a shot at the main strike force. Smoky SAM was more than just a Red Sky visual effect. If the Air Force crews manning the phony SAM sites could lock their video camera's cross hairs on your bird for ten seconds, Operations back at Ryder would override all radio transmissions in order to call you out. Then, just as if you'd been shot down in a dogfight, you'd have to leave the exercise in order to tag the regeneration point.

"Pinto flight, Pinto lead," Beckman radioed. "Strike force is splitting."

Andy nodded to himself. The plan was for the entire strike

to split right down the middle, with half going after the airfield and half attacking the heliopad complex. Pinto flight was assigned to fly MiGCAP for the strike aimed at taking out the Red chopper base.

"Pinto flight, be prepared for heavy adversary air," Beckman called. "AWAC has picked up multiple bogies traveling high at our head-on intercept. It looks like the Attackers want to protect their choppers at all cost."

"Looks like we lucked out." Andy's wingman, Lieutenant Stan Johnson, chuckled.

"Roger that," Andy said. "If the Attackers concentrate their forces here, one of us is bound to come away with a fat tally for the Warlord prize."

"Or get our asses whipped," Beckman added meaningfully. "Stay alert, and don't get cocky! We may think we've learned all of the Attackers' tricks, but there's always one more thing to learn."

"There go the Warthogs to get the tanks defending the chopper pads!" radioed Beckman's wingman, Lieutenant Calvin.

Andy had always thought the turbine-fan-powered A-10 Thunderbolt looked like an airplane that belonged back in World War II. The dark-green, close-support attack craft had an attack bomber's ungainly silhouette thanks to its straight wings and its engines, like two fat barrels attached to its rear fuselage just forward of its tail section. The A-10 was designed to fight low. Its considerable ability to carry wing-mounted ordnance aside, its main reason for existence was its massive, nose-mounted, 30MM GAU-8/a cannon, the weapon it used to kill tanks. The GAU-A Gatling gun was twenty-one feet long *without* its huge ammo drum, which carried 1,100 rounds, each the size of a quart bottle and tipped with armor-piercing uranium.

Now Andy watched as the three A-10s that had come along to the heliopad target dove to turn their awesome firepower against their targets, which were obsolete, retired Army tanks scattered about the desert floor to simulate enemy mechanized armor. The old tanks were arranged to suggest that they were here to provide defense to the heliopad about a quarter-mile beyond. Andy saw the Warthogs begin to fire, the smoke and flame spewing from their chin-mounted cannons. Immediately the desert floor was set to boiling by the 30MM fusillade, and the targets were pulverized. The old tanks, their rusting cannons poking up toward the sky like the upraised trunks of angry elephants, were chain-sawed into twisted, flaming chunks of metal set rolling across the sand beneath the impact of the 30MM rounds like tin cans being plunked by rapid, accurate fire from a .22 rifle.

Their work done, the A-10s climbed back into the sky to give the A-7 Corsairs their chance to go to work. The enemy helipad was a one-hundred-foot-square outline scratched into the desert floor, protected by a larger circle of flashing strobe-light setups meant to simulate AAA fire. The A-7s were all carrying live ordnance: bombs, rockets, and loaded cannon. It would be the Corsairs' task to first accurately target and take out the AAA emplacements and then bomb the helipad.

Andy and the rest of Pinto flight were cartwheeling high in the sky, on the lookout for MiGs, when the A-7s began their attack. Andy saw the first rocket salvo being fired, the 100MM Matra rockets sizzling downward like streaks of fire to demolish the helipad's defensive batteries. It was one hell of a light show: The ground strobes were flashing madly like crazed, monstrous fireflies as the rockets erupted in white smoke and cherry-red flame, sending debris flying. Above it all, the glittering silver A-7s were crisscrossing the sky in tight bat-turns, like enraged hornets darting over their torn open nest.

Andy was looking forward to seeing the A-7s drop the really big stuff they were carrying beneath their wings when his constantly scanning gaze caught distant movement in the crystal-clear sky. He looked hard and counted five specks arranged in the classic Soviet step formation: three were flying line abreast, while higher up and about a quarter-mile back, two more were bringing up the rear. Andy radioed his alert: "Pinto lead, three. Five bogies approaching at four o'clock!"

There was a moment's silence crackling over the airwaves, and then Beckman calmly answered, "Roger, three, I've got them."

"Yahoo!" Johnson cheered. "Nice call, three! How about it, boss?" he now addressed Beckman. "Since our element spotted them, we get first crack, right?"

"Roger," Beckman replied. "Happy hunting, Andy. Your

two-ship gets dibs. My element will remain here to shepard the lambs.''

''Roger,'' Andy replied, appreciating Beckman's strategy as he and Johnson peeled off to do battle with the enemy, now about five miles away. It wouldn't do for all of Pinto flight to be decoyed away from the strike force, leaving the Mud Movers and Warthogs vulnerable to possible attack from another formation of enemy fighters that might be waiting in the wings.

Meanwhile, the enemy planes were holding their step formation as the Stiletto two-ship dead-on approached; merge point was now about three miles. Andy was still too far away to make out the Attackers' individual camo paint schemes, too far away to see if there was a flat-black one mixed in the formation. *Oh well, what the hell*, Andy thought. *A kill was a kill*.

''Man, look at them out there arranged like bowling pins,'' Johnson muttered. ''Don't I wish we still had Sparrows now. The two of us could take out all five from here.''

Andy laughed. ''Hey, it isn't fun if you do it the easy way.'' He dialed his radio to the Operations frequency and transmitted: Ops, Pinto element three/four, do you copy?''

''Roger, Pinto three,'' replied one of the controllers who refereed the war games from hundreds of miles away, thanks to his high-tech radar and microwave equipment.

''Ops,'' Andy continued. ''Pinto three/four engaging five bogies, Fox Range, sector 5-D, do you copy?''

''Roger, Pinto three,'' Ops said. ''Fight's on. Out.''

''Out, Ops,'' Andy said, dialing back to Pinto flight frequency. Now, thanks to the sensors mounted in the participating aircrafts' wings, Ops would follow the action, recording it for replaying later during the mass debriefing if events warranted.

''Pinto three, what say I take the two flying high?'' Johnson radioed. ''You take the trio flying low.''

''Why so generous?'' Andy kidded his wingman as he ran a quick check on his weapons systems. Everything was in order. His HUD air-to-air combat display was framing in luminous green the five aircraft now rapidly looming in his windscreen.

''Hey, man, I've only got three kills to my credit so far

this week," Johnson explained. "I've been hurting since they took away my Sparrows. I know I haven't got a chance at winning the Warlord trophy, but *you* do. If I can't have it, I'd at least like to see somebody from my squadron nab the prize."

"Thanks, pal," Andy said as the Attackers formation broke apart in a five-way defensive split. "Let's get 'em!"

Range was now one mile. Andy could easily make out the various paint jobs on the five F-5E's busy carving up the sky. Robbie's black bird wasn't among them, and once again, Andy wasn't sure how he felt about that: was he more disappointed or relieved?

But there was no time to think about that now. It was time to go to work.

Andy saw Johnson's Stiletto leap forward on a cone of flame as his wingman went to afterburn to make a tight circle through the sky. Johnson put himself behind the rear pair of Attackers that were painted a mottled tan and chocolate to blend into the desert floor when viewed from above. The two stub-winged F-5E's banked steeply to get away in a classic Attackers gambit that had proved highly effective a few days ago, thanks to the little F-5E's maneuverability and the visiting players' inexperience. This time, however, Johnson was ready for the trick. He pulled his Stiletto up and climbed steeply, then rolled inverted, dropping down right smack on the banking Attackers' tails.

Andy heard Johnson call, "Fox two," indicating to Ops that he'd fired a Sidewinder. A few seconds later, Ops overrode all frequencies to announce, "Ivan four, you've been burned," and one of the Attackers Johnson was pursuing dropped away to fly off to the enemy regeneration point.

Johnson stayed on his remaining bogie's six, again calling, "Fox two."

"Ivan 14," Ops called. "You've been burned."

Good for you, Stan, Andy thought. *You've just added two kills to your tally.* But now it was time for Andy to bag his own pigeons.

The trio of F-5E's he was after were spread out to try and cage in his Stiletto, but before they could tighten the noose around Andy he used his bird's superior speed and agility and his own ability to sustain G-punishment to fly out of their trap. The desert horizon in front of his Stiletto tilted madly, and Andy grimaced against the physical stress he was suffering as he skidded into a severely tight bat-turn that put him into position to attack the nearest enemy plane. The Attacker craft was painted green and tan, with a large 67 stenciled on its nose and vertical tail. As Andy came around into position on his target's six, he executed a low-speed yoyo, popping his speed brakes and going into a shallow dive in order to drop beneath the Attacker craft, taking advantage of the fact that the F-5E pilot had a large blind spot beneath his bird's long, broad snout.

Lose sight, lose the fight, Andy thought. Once he was safely tucked beneath the Attacker with a clear shot at the guy's underbelly, he pulled up, using the Stiletto's zoom ability to close to point-blank range.

"Guns, guns!" Andy called over the radio, squeezing the trigger mounted on his control stick, which activated his bird's cameras. He kept his eye on the small video monitor mounted beneath his HUD display as he kept his target framed in the cross hairs of his camera for the stipulated three seconds, waiting while the equipment installed in his bird for the Red Sky exercise relayed the picture to Operations.

Ops decreed, "Ivan 67. You've been shot down."

"Pinto three!" Johnson called. "Twin bogies on your tail. I'm on my way!"

Andy immediately banked away, jinking his bird to make himself a difficult target. He glanced behind him and saw the two blue and yellow F-5E's on his six-o'clock dive out of sight. *They're trying to pull their own low-speed yoyo move,* Andy realized.

Andy waited a beat, calculating when the Attacker duo would be beginning their pull-up toward his belly, and then lifted his Stiletto's nose, going to afterburn in a short climb that culminated in a rolling maneuver that put him on a course head-on at his pursuers.

The F-5E's, taken by surprise, executed a two-way defensive split. Andy locked onto the tail of the closest and called, "Fox two!"

Ops was awarding him the kill as he closed on the last bogie from five o'clock. The Attacker must have noticed Johnson coming in fast from eleven o'clock, because the

F-5E went to afterburn, banking starboard, intending to skid out of the way and leave Andy and Johnson staring at each other across empty space.

As the Attacker turned, Andy cut across the F-5E's twin glowing tail pipes, executing a bat-turn of his own that kept him locked onto the enemy's six. He called a Fox two, and knew he had his target dead to rights. Ops agreed, raising his score to ten.

"Beautiful flying, Andy!" Johnson congratulated him.

"Thanks," Andy replied.

"Roger that," Captain Beckman cut in.

"Thanks, sir!" Andy chuckled, glancing toward the strike force, which was now a distant, orbiting cartwheel of glinting specks against the blue: a guy ate up a lot of sky in a dogfight. "I just hope ten kills is enough to win the Warlord trophy."

"I think you've got bigger worries than *that*, Andrew."

What? Where? Andy thought as Robbie's voice filled his helmet. Andy stood his bird on its tail and went into a frantic, vertical roll to search the clock for his tormentor.

Robbie's laughter echoed in Andy's ears. "What a lovely pirouette," Robbie sneered.

Andy saw the flat-black Attacker craft emblazoned with the red 1 on its nose and tail dropping down to fly alongside him. Andy thought, *How does the fucker do that? One instant he's not there, and then he is. Does he have the power of invisibility?*

"Sorry I'm late for our appointment, Andrew, but I had pressing business elsewhere ridding the sky of you visiting players. Then I thought it would be prudent to return to base for a refueling."

"That's okay, Robbie," Andy managed, trying hard to put the grit back into his voice, even though he was feeling anything but confident about the coming, inevitable confrontation. "In case you haven't noticed, I was sort of busy myself, clearing the sky of unwanted Attackers."

"Yeah, I've been watching you mop the floor with my guys," Robbie replied. "It was a very impressive performance, but now are you ready for some *real* dogfighting? I've got a full twenty minutes' worth of gas to spend here, although I hardly think it's going to take anywhere near that long to settle this little rematch."

Andy checked his own fuel. Yeah, he had plenty of gas left. *Lucky me*, he thought. *I've got enough gas, but what about nerve?*

Andy's spine had turned to jelly. He'd hardly gotten over his last humiliation at Robbie's hands, and now here it was time to suffer another ass-whipping. *I can't do it*, Andy thought. *He's too good. I can't beat him.*

"Well?" Robbie taunted. "You want to try? Or you just want to give up? It'll be just be you and me, Andrew." Robbie paused to ask sharply, "Isn't that right, Beckman? You and the rest of Pinto flight will stay out of this?"

"If that's what Lieutenant Harrison wants?" Beckman hesitated.

Andy's finger hesitated before pushing his radio's transmit button. *No way in hell I can beat him.*

"That's what I want, Pinto lead," Andy said. "Okay, Robbie. It's just you and me. Fight's on!"

(Two)

"Fight's on!" Major Robbie Greene heard Andrew say.

Greene popped his speed brakes, dropping back behind the Stiletto, which immediately went to afterburn. Fire licked out from the Stiletto's tail pipe as it shot away. Greene cobbed his own throttles. He was pressed back against his seatback as the dark F-5E hurled forward.

Let's make this short and sweet, Greene decided, preparing to call a Sidewinder shot. Greene had been hoping for a better showing from Andrew. He'd been hoping that the kid might at least put up a valiant struggle before losing. He'd been hoping . . .

Greene paused, pondering it, concluding that he wasn't sure *what* he'd been hoping concerning Andrew. He'd had mixed emotions toward his half brother since their run-in behind the ice-cream parlor a couple of weeks ago. Take that dream he'd had, for instance. In the dream Greene had been involved in an air duel with Andrew just like this one, except with live ammo. In the dream Greene had won the shoot-out, blasting Andrew's Stiletto out of the sky, but just before the ruined Stiletto fell away Greene had pulled up alongside it to peer into its cockpit. He'd seen himself sitting wounded where Andrew was supposed to be.

The dream had so unsettled Greene that he'd decided to stay away from Andrew for the rest of the time the kid was at Ryder. Greene wasn't clear in his own mind why he'd changed his mind early this morning, scribbling that note of challenge and having an aide affix it to Andrew's helmet.

Now, as Greene prepared to call his Sidewinder kill on Andrew, he told himself that he'd done the right thing by challenging his half brother to this rematch. Maybe someday they could bury the hatchet. Maybe not. Regardless, it was important that today Greene proved to the kid who was the better fighter jock.

Andrew's Stiletto was just a quarter-mile ahead now. It was time to end the rivalry between them once and for all.

"This is good-bye, Andrew," Greene radioed. He fixed the fleeing Stiletto in his gunsight and radioed, "Fox two . . ."

At that instant the Stiletto went into a steep climb, directly into the sun! *Nice move,* Greene thought, smiling. Leading a heat-seeker into the sun could blind its infrared tracking system. Now Ops would not award Greene the kill, because Andrew had managed to wrest for himself the benefit of the doubt.

"Ivan one," Ops radioed as expected. "Negative Sidewinder shot on Pinto three."

"Nice move," Green radioed to Andrew as the Stiletto executed a vertical reverse, falling over out of its climb. "Nice, but not nice enough. Here I come after you, kid."

As Green pulled back on the stick to chase after the Stiletto, he was kind of surprised by Andrew's lack of aggression. Andrew seemed content to play a defensive game. *Where were the kid's balls?* Greene wondered as he once again closed on Andrew's six. He was about to call another Sidewinder shot when the Stiletto in his gunsight abruptly slipped away. Andrew's bird had dropped its nose and cut its thrust, so that now it hung in the sky like a sea gull balanced in the wind!

How did he do that? Greene wondered. Meanwhile, he couldn't do a thing about it; he *had* to overshoot. As Greene swiped past, giving up the offensive edge, he saw the Stiletto's nose came around to point at his tail, and then Andrew's bird leapt forward in pursuit.

Greene wondered, *Where did Andrew learn that trick? I've never seen anything like it.* But Greene had a more important puzzle to ponder, like how to get one extremely angry Stiletto off his ass.

(Three)

"This is good-bye, Andrew." Robbie called only a few seconds into the dogfight.

When Andy heard that, he was ready to throw in the towel. Robbie had managed to instantly lock onto Andy's tail, and now he was about to once again humiliate Andy. Andy was resigning himself to submitting to the defeat, but then he remembered what Gail had told him about self-confidence.

Son of a bitch, Andy thought. *Gail's right. If I give in this easily, Robbie won't have beaten me. I'll have beaten myself.*

As Gail had urged him to do, Andy forced himself to blank from his mind all he knew about his opponent, telling himself that this bastard on his tail was just another Attacker. No more, no less.

"Fox two," Robbie called.

And Andy zoomed upward, into the blinding sun. Sure, it was a long shot, but Ops just might give him the benefit of the doubt if he could make the ref think that there was a possibility the heat-seeker heading for his tail pipe might have lost its way nosing through the sunshine.

"Ivan one, negative Sidewinder shot on Pinto three," Ops called.

Yes! Andy thought gleefully, and then it hit him. His fear of Robbie had magically left him. He was no longer afraid. He was having fun.

Time for Lieutenant Harrison to show Ivan one what the lieutenant had been practicing this past week.

Andy dropped away from the sun by executing a vertical reverse, and then leveled off, flying as straight and true as a jetliner in order to sucker Robbie in. It was now a waiting game. Andy had to restrain himself from making his move too soon, even though it seemed to him that the black F-5E already looked close enough to crawl up his tail pipe.

Steady now. Remember what Gail told you. You can beat him.

Andy tried to clear his mind so that he could better anticipate when Robbie might decide to call his shot. He'd been doing some experimenting with his bird during his stint here at Ryder, perfecting a move that wasn't in the books, but he knew his opponent, and realized that when you were flying against a veteran like Major Greene, you could only use a trick once.

When Andy felt he could wait no longer—that his opponent was about to call another Sidewinder shot—he almost simultaneously did a number of things: Andy dropped his fighter's nose and slammed forward his throttle to idle; he popped his speed brakes and lowered his landing flaps. Then he kicked rudder, enduring the pain of a 6-G rotation as the Stiletto hung in the air spinning on its nose like a top. It sure was sweet to see Robbie's black bird go shooting past.

Now it's my turn, Andy thought, pulling in his boards to slim down his bird. He cobbed the throttle and sprinted forward after his kill. The black F-5E bounced around the sky like a cue ball on a pool table, running through an extended repertoire of aerobatics designed to throw off its pursuer. Andy stuck to his opponent's six like glue. He was itching to call a Sidewinder shot, but Major Greene kept jinking, denying Andy the positive shot he needed if the Ops ref was to award him the kill.

"Hey, Andrew," Robbie taunted. "You want me bad enough to run with the jackrabbits to get me?"

The black bird steeply dived. Andy followed his adversary down, perhaps an eighth of a mile behind. The desert's tobacco-brown terrain was rising up at them now. Andy checked his altimeter as Robbie continued to plummet, wondering what Robbie thought he was doing, but he continued to call his opponent's bluff by staying locked on the F-5E's tail. They were down to about 200 feet when Robbie finally leveled off, the black bird rising and falling as it followed the hills and dips of the desert landscape. Andy poured on the juice, closing to within a few hundred feet of Robbie's tail pipes, experiencing the gut-wrenching, deck-level roller-coaster ride for himself. Andy realized now that he wasn't going to call a Sidewinder shot; that only a gun kill would do to settle the score.

Andy inched forward his throttle, thinking it wouldn't do to overshoot. He was trying to catch the dust-streaked black bird in his gunsight, but Robbie was jinking like mad to deny him the opportunity. Meanwhile, the chase had taken them farther east, back toward Ryder. Andy recognized his whereabouts from the landmarks: a tall rock spire and a deep arroyo that ran through this section of the desert.

"Okay, Andrew," Robbie suddenly called out with what sounded like a hint of desperation in his tone. "You can hug the deck, but can you dig a tunnel?"

What is he talking about? Andy wondered. What did the guy have in mind? Then the black bird veered toward the arroyo, and Andy realized what his crazy half brother meant to do.

Robbie's F-5E vanished from sight as it dropped down below ground level, dipping to fly *between* the banks of the dried-up river bed.

"You're one good pilot, Robbie," Andy radioed grimly. "But if you can do it, so can I."

Andy plunged his Stiletto into the arroyo behind Robbie. The sensation of flying *below* ground level was as exhilarating as it was horrifying. The high brown walls of the arroyo were a blur whipping past just a few feet on either side beyond the Stiletto's wing tips, and then there was the river bed *itself* to contend with, maybe thirty feet below the Stiletto's belly.

Now it was a question of who was going to lose his nerve first, Andy thought as he gritted his teeth, concentrating on not smashing himself to pieces flying in this trench. Robbie was now about five hundred feet ahead of Andy, who'd dropped back to avoid having the turbulence of the F-5E's jet wash funneling back along the arroyo pitch him into the clay banks. Andy was sweating like a pig. He didn't think he could keep up this level of concentration for much longer. He felt like the arroyo was closing in on him, but who knew? Maybe it *was* growing more narrow.

Time to try a little mind-fucking of my own, Andy decided, mashing his radio transmit button. "Hey, Robbie! I've been watching you. You came pretty close to the port edge, that time, pal! You prepared to play in this sandbox forever? 'Cause *I* am."

Evidently, Robbie had had enough of playing in this sandbox. He climbed to starboard, leaving the arroyo behind as he clawed his way into the sky. As Andy followed Robbie up on the straight climb, he had no trouble framing the black F-5E in his gunsight and pulling the trigger.

"Guns, guns!" Andy roared into his radio as his camera rolled, freezing for posterity's sake the image of the black bird pinioned squarely in his cross hairs. Andy counted to three, imagining the video signal wending its way to Operations, so that everyone could see him waxing the great Major Robert Blaize Greene.

"Ivan one. You are a mort." Operations called. "Congratulations, Pinto three! That was superb flying!"

"I've waxed you, Robbie!" Andy crowed. "How does it feel, sucker?"

(Four)

"How does it feel, sucker?" Andrew's triumphant taunt echoed in Greene's helmet. Greene was exhausted. From the moment that Andrew had pulled his incredible stunt of somehow getting his Stiletto to hang spinning in the air, Greene had been on the defensive.

How does it feel, sucker? Greene had tried every trick in the book to shake Andrew, and he hadn't been able to do it. Then he'd tried a few tricks that weren't in the book, like hugging the deck to give the jackrabbits a haircut, and finally, turning his jet fighter into an earthworm, literally trying to fly below the deck to try to shake the godawful avenging fury on his tail.

How does it feel, sucker? Greene had steeled himself, screwing up every ounce of courage to dip into that arroyo, only to witness Andrew following him in like it was nothing more than a cakewalk. He'd known then that he was at the end of his rope; that Andrew had waxed him; that it was only a question of how long Greene could keep Andrew from administering the inevitable coup de grace.

I'm beaten, Greene had thought as he'd climbed into the sky. The hairs had risen on the back of his neck as he'd sensed Andrew zeroing in. Then he'd heard Andrew call out, *"Guns, guns!"* and Greene had waited stoically for the Ops call that would seal his fate.

"Attacker one, you are a mort."

"How does it feel, sucker?"

Robert Blaize Greene realized that he was smiling as he banked his black bird around to head back to base.

How did it feel? Greene felt relief.

(Five)

Ryder AFB

It was late Friday night. Andy and Gail were at the ice-cream parlor. Red Sky was over, except for its closing ceremony on Sunday, of course.

"I can't believe I won," Andy murmured.

"You mean you can't believe you won the Warlord trophy?" Gail smiled, squeezing his arm.

"That, and I can't believe I beat Robbie." Andy shook his head. "It's like it's a dream."

"What makes it even better," Gail said, giggling, "was that bagging him was the kill that put you over the top to win the award."

"Congratulations, Lieutenant!"

Andy looked up, not recognizing the gaggle of pilots who'd surrounded the table, but then, so many people he didn't know had been coming up to him, wanting to pat him on the back and shake his hand. Most of the final mass debriefing held in the auditorium earlier that day had been devoted to his dogfight with Robbie. The audience had watched the electronic playback of the air battle, coupled with the video footage from Andy's gun camera. Both Andy and Robbie had been called up together to the lectern to give running commentary on the footage. When it was over, the assembled personnel of Red Sky had given Andy a standing ovation. During it, Andy had looked at his half brother, trying to see how Robbie was taking the indignity of it all. It had been no good. Andy couldn't tell. Robbie had kept a master's poker face throughout the proceedings.

Finally, the debriefing was over. Now there'd be no more fuss made over the dogfight until Sunday, when Andy was to receive the Warlord trophy. That was fine with him. He'd come to find being in the center of a dogfight was a hell of a lot easier to take than being the center of attention.

"I wish people would drop it," he now confided to Gail as the well-wishers went away. "I feel weird being hailed as some kind of hero when all I really wanted to do was settle a personal feud."

"Doesn't matter," Gail replied. "As of today, you're Jack the Giant Killer around here, and you might as well get used to it."

"I suppose," Andy said. "But I still wish I knew how Robbie was taking all this." He sighed. "He was totally deadpan during the debriefing. Like it hadn't mattered to him in the least."

"How come you're suddenly so concerned about Robbie's well-being?" Gail asked knowingly. "I thought you two didn't get along?" she teased.

"It was never *my* decision that we didn't get along," Andy muttered. "He's been calling the shots concerning our relationship, or lack of it, ever since I was born. Damn, I wish I knew what he was thinking now."

"It looks like you're going to get your wish," Gail murmured. "Here he comes now."

Andy looked up. "Oh, Christ." He scowled as he watched Robbie approach. "Who was it who said be careful what you wish for, you might get it?"

Beneath the table, Gail was squeezing his knee. "Have courage, lover. You won the battle, now don't lose the war."

"Hi," Robbie said, looked uneasy as he reached the table. "Can I sit down?"

"Sure." Andy waited as Robbie settled himself. He wondered what to expect. He had the craziest desire to *apologize* to his half brother for beating him.

"I wanted to congratulate you on winning the Warlord

trophy," Robbie began. "And on beating me. I . . ." He hesitated, looking like he was having trouble getting the words out.

"Maybe I'd better go," Gail suggested quietly. "This is family business."

"No." Robbie shook his head. "You heard me insult him, you should be here to hear me take back what I said." He smiled wryly. "Anyway, I've got a hunch that one of these days *you're* going to be family."

"I have a hunch you're right," Andy said, putting his arm around Gail.

Robbie nodded. "I was wrong about you, Andrew. I'm sorry I insulted you . . . and your father."

"Your stepfather," Andy interjected.

"You're as good a pilot as I am," Robbie pushed on, sounding like he was having a hard time doing it. "No! You're a *better* pilot than I am! You proved that today. I—" He shrugged, looking close to tears. "Ah . . . there's a lot more things I want to say—*need* to say—but I don't know how to even begin. . . ." He trailed off, hanging his head.

"You can start by calling me Andy."

Robbie looked up at him. Andy smiled. "That's what my *friends* call me: Andy."

"You're making this a lot easier on me than I deserve," Robbie said slowly.

"Maybe." Andy shrugged. "But after all the tough times we've been through together, I figure it's about time we had it easy."

"Amen to that." Robbie nodded. He grinned.

Andy wondered what gesture should next be made. It was too soon for a filial embrace. Maybe someday. He extended his hand. Robbie shook it.

"One small step for mankind," Gail joked, watching them. "One giant leap for brotherhood."

"There's a couple more things, Andy," Robbie said, sounding a little more relaxed. "Number one, there's a tradition here at Red Sky that the guy who wins the Warlord trophy gets a shot at the next available slot for the Attackers Squadron. At the moment you're at the top of that list, and one of my guys is leaving. . . ."

"He'll take it!" Gail said quickly.

Robbie laughed. "It's *his* decision, Gail." He looked at Andy. "It's a tough job always playing the bad guy, but then, you do get to spend your days flying ACM."

Andy nodded. "I'd take the slot even if I weren't involved with Gail. I think there's a lot you can teach me Robbie. I'm anxious to learn."

"And vice versa, kid," Robbie murmured. "And vice versa."

"You said there were a couple of things?" Andy prodded.

"Yeah, right," Robbie said. "Well, just before coming here, I called home to invite the family to Sunday's closing ceremonies. I mean, I know Steve will get a big kick out of seeing you get the Warlord trophy. Steve is going to fly everyone, Grandma included, here to Ryder in the company Lear jet. . . ."

"You're going to like Grandma Erica," Andy was confiding to Gail. "You're just like her."

"Mom and Don will be coming too," Robbie elaborated. "As a matter of fact, it was Don I called to invite everyone."

"Really?" Andy remarked, pleasantly surprised.

"I've got a lot to make up to Don, as well as you, Andy," Robbie explained. "I told him as much when I called."

"How did Don react?"

Robbie said, "He was . . . surprised. To say the least."

"I would imagine." Andy chuckled, and explained to Gail, "Robbie and I got along *well*, compared to how Robbie and *Don* get along."

"Oh, boy. . . ." Gail rolled her eyes.

"I know I've got to turn over a new leaf with my stepfather," Robbie said quickly. "I want to. I'm ready to. It's just that I'm not sure I know how." He looked away. "Andy, I could use your help."

Andy smiled. "Sure. What are brothers for?"

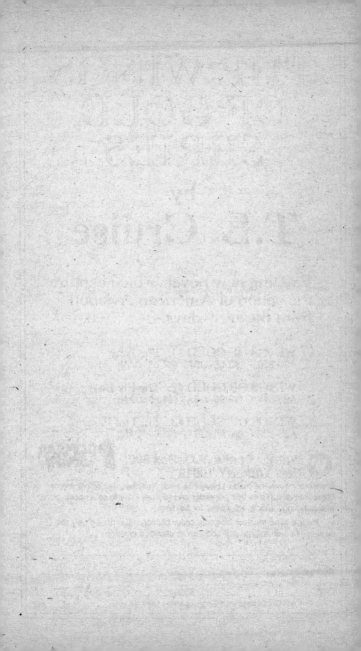